COUNCIL
OF
CALIPHS

Aidan de Vries

COUNCIL
OF
CALIPHS

Erser & Pond

Cover design by Doug Porter

Published in Canada by Erser & Pond Publishers, Ltd.
1083 Queen St., Suite 225, Halifax, N.S., Canada B3H 0B2

Library and Archives Canada Cataloguing in Publication

de Vries, Aidan
    Council of Caliphs / Aidan de Vries

ISBN 978-0-9781761-0-5

    1. Title

PS8607.E975C68 2006   C813'.6   C2006-905925-X

*This book is dedicated to
my wife and children,
with my love.*

*Things fall apart, the centre cannot hold
Mere anarchy is loosed upon the world...
The best lack all conviction, while the worst
are full of passionate intensity.*

William Butler Yeats

MAIN CHARACTERS

Marina Kortikuova, Adjunct Professor of Russian History at Chechen State University

Ivan Welland, Counselor of the Department of State, Washington, D.C.

Imam Mansur in Grozny, Chechnya

Akhmad, PhD student in Marina's class at C.S.U.

Kahnsultan Akhmatov, confidant of Montcalf's

Wilson Bagwell, Chairman of Alpha Group Energy

©iStockphoto/duncan1890

Simeon Montcalf, Under Secretary of State for Political Affairs

©iStockphoto/absolut_100

Julia Boudreau, Secretary of State

©iStockphoto/jhorrocks

The President of the U.S.A. (POTUS)

©iStockphoto/Fotosmurf03

Tim Morrison, Director of the CIA

Mitch Richmond, Deputy
Director of the CIA

"Brooklyn" Brocklyn,
Ivan's assistant

Lieutenant Robert Mercer,
United States Navy Seal

Sawdah Dudaev, mother of
Akhmad, Marina's student

Acknowledgments

A disturbing but minor result of the world conflict between fanatical jihadist terrorists and the rest of us has been the unavoidable development of a paranoid malaise that has settled over the entire population of the planet. Little old ladies traveling to see their grandchildren are looking over their shoulders to see if the passenger seated across from them is behaving suspiciously. All the travelers in every airport are being admonished to report to the security police any luggage, package, or parcel that has been abandoned, orphaned, or discarded. At enormous cost to the taxpayer we are all being searched, scanned, prodded, questioned, probed, photographed, scrutinized, and inspected on the mere chance that we might pose a danger to our fellow travelers. We submit to this treatment because the risk is real, no matter how statistically unlikely it is that we are in mortal danger at any given minute.

A personal sadness deriving from this new *weltschmerz* is that this author, indebted to many, can acknowledge none by name, lest they be put in harm's way. I'm sure that no friend, relative, or co-worker of my acquaintance would wish me to put his or her life on the line just to achieve mention in the folio of a fictional book by a pseudonymous writer striving not to be a posthumous one. Therefore I am leaving your names out, though I silently recognize my indebtedness.

It is a source of particular sorrow to me that I am obliged to make the crucial and invaluable contributions of Mrs. de Vries anonymous. Her literary, linguistic, creative, artistic, and intellectual abilities were used with excellent results. Her keen eye and organizing talents were also brought to bear on the manuscript with transforming effect, but I dare not speak her name. Unfortunately, even such a basic thing as my gratitude has become hijacked by terrorists.

PART ONE

Chechnya

CHAPTER ONE

Imam Mansur, surrounded by his three bodyguards, was attending the opening dedication ceremony of Grozny's brand new Olympic-style athletic facility. His right hand was in the pocket of his aba, his finger on the button of a radio-controlled signaling device. He was standing at the opposite end of the large stadium, far from the podium where the President, in the name of the Chechen State Council, would very soon declare the stadium to be officially open. Dinamo Stadium was the gift of the Russian people to the Chechens. It was meant to symbolize the peace and good will that Vladimir Putin and his government were offering to their wayward Caucasian cousins.

A large number of dignitaries had assembled earlier and were seated behind the speaker's platform. The President mounted the wooden stairs leading to the dais, accompanied by enthusiastic applause and loud band music. After waving and gesticulating to the crowd for an appropriate amount of time, he signaled that he wanted silence so he could begin his speech. The crowd and the dignitaries on the platform with him sat down and became silent as they waited for his ceremonial dedication speech to begin.

Imam Mansur witnessed the proceedings with a twisted, surreptitious smile. He had been waiting for this special moment for three full months, ever since his henchmen had advised him that they had, according to his instructions, successfully incorporated a live 155-millimeter artillery shell into the reinforced concrete under the platform, along with the attached detonator connection that he had invented and assembled.

Mansur was pleased with himself for having had the foresight to plan this event so far in advance. His decision to be the one who actually pushed the detonator button was based on pride in his own achievement and the desire to see with his own eyes the death of the hated infidel dignitaries. He could not know exactly what the President was going to say, but the imam was prepared to wait for the point in the speech that would provide the most dramatic effect for his counter statement.

"Citizens of our fine Republic and honored guests," the President intoned, "I am very proud to be a Chechen at this particular time in our history. Dinamo Stadium is a symbol of the close friendship we have with our brothers in Russia. The building of this magnificent edifice for the use of our citizens is only the first of many future cooperative efforts between our two peoples. I am sure we will find many fine uses for this glorious stadium, and I know you will all wish to express your gratitude to the Russians for their thoughtful gift, which will help to bring peace among us as we enjoy many fine athletic activities in brotherly competition. I am sure you will all make Dinamo Stadium a symbol of this. "

There was some hesitant applause, but the crowd was nervous that day. Brave talk about defeating terrorism in Chechnya was almost an invitation for immediate reprisals. The increased paranoia in the stadium was partly due to the recent terrorist attack on the school in Beslan, which had hit the Russian security establishment hard. Imam Mansur smiled as he remembered the successful attack that he had masterminded. Three hundred and thirty had died, most of them children. Another five hundred and fifty people had been injured.

In order to avoid any repeat performances, Chechnya had been flooded with Russian government employees trained by the ex KGB to be observers and reporters. They performed routine clerical tasks, but along with these duties they kept the information flowing into the headquarters of the secret police. It was hoped that this intelligence source would make it possible for them to apprehend fanatic, extremist Muslims and political separatists before they could complete their terrorist missions.

In this climate everyone was suspicious of everyone else. Eventually any and all such suspicions came to the attention of the newly-appointed chief of terror analysis, a man by the name of Igor Leshenko, who lived undercover in Grozny as a lowly police inspector. He was a thick-set man with a shaved head and a flat nose which had been crushed in his days as a heavy-weight boxer in Moscow. Leshenko hated his nose. It reminded him of his frequent failures in the ring where, according to him, men with half his strength and expertise were always getting away with dirty tricks when the referee wasn't looking. But now he had come into his own. He was earning twice the salary he used to make in Moscow, and had ten times the power. It galled him that nobody else knew it so far.

Kahnsultan Akhmatov, an elderly gentleman dressed in a white jubba and turban, was sitting behind Imam Mansur, about two seats to his left. From this angle he was able to see the imam's profile as he listened to the speech being given by the President of the Chechen Republic. It was hard not to notice the imam's scornful expression as he listened to the President's words. Every so often he would lean toward one of his companions and make some sort of a comment that would elicit an appreciative snicker. It seemed inappropriate to Kahnsultan that an imam would talk while the President was speaking, but the men reacted with obsequious nods and smiles, apparently unaware of the imam's breech of good manners.

"They must be bodyguards," Kahnsultan said to himself, turning his attention back to the dais.

"We've been allies with our Russian friends through many, many wars," the President was saying. "Together we defeated the supposedly invincible Napoleon, together we decimated Hitler's troops, and together we will also defeat terrorism."

While the applause for these sentiments was ascending from the audience, Imam Mansur's finger was descending onto the button in his pocket.

Instantly the deafening explosion, the smoke, and the blood and body parts of the President and twenty-three of his now dead supporters burst forth with the same violence as a direct artillery hit.

Panic spread everywhere at once. People were pushing, screaming, stumbling, falling, and trampling others in their attempt to flee. A number of officials were going against the crowd, pushing toward the dais in an effort to see if there were any survivors.

Imam Mansur's three bodyguards suddenly produced truncheons which they used to cut a path through the crowd so the imam could proceed toward the exit. He did not speak, but his calm demeanor prevented a stampede among those close enough to see him. He had not felt this deeply satisfied since he had masterminded the simultaneous explosions that forced two Russian planes to crash earlier in the year.

The Imam's serene expression in the midst of all the surrounding chaos and terror went unnoticed by everyone except Kahnsultan Akhmatov, the Muslim gentleman who had been seated behind him and who was now following in the wide swath created by the bodyguards.

At that moment Leshenko had taken it upon himself to practice a little crowd control in the Dinamo Stadium. He was hoping that the screaming, stampeding multitude might give him a good excuse to bring his billy club down on a few non-Russian heads.

Leshenko was not one to worry about profiling or making fine distinctions. He didn't care if a Chechen skull belonged to a Muslim terrorist or to a good, law-abiding Muslim. They were all exactly the same, as far as he was concerned. If the ungrateful bastards were going to blow up elementary schools and Olympic stadiums to express their dissatisfaction with the barrels of rubles that the Russians were spending on them, then he would give them something to *really* complain about.

"Move it! Move along," he roared to the panic-stricken crowd. "Go that way. What's the matter, you need one of your sheepdogs to herd you over there?"

Imam Mansur suddenly emerged next to Leshenko as he barked his commands. He eyed the inspector for a fleeting moment with an expression of condescending disdain, then he motioned to his bodyguards to follow him in the opposite direction to the one Leshenko had indicated.

"Who the devil does that idiotic cleric think he is?" the inspector muttered under his breath, wishing the man would do something to break the law so he could have him brought up on charges. "The dumb bastard preaches at a local mosque, and he acts like he's Allah Almighty."

Leshenko turned and spat with contempt. The spittle landed on the polished shoe of Kahnsultan, the gentleman who had been seated behind Imam Mansur.

"And what do *you* want?" Leshenko said, in a combative tone.

"Nothing, sir. Nothing at all," said Kahnsultan hastily. "I was only trying to find my way out of here. I don't wish to cause any trouble."

"Well, keep moving," Leshenko barked.

Kahnsultan walked as quickly as possible toward the exit, disappointed that this short and unnecessary interlude with the self-important policeman had caused him to lose sight of the imam and his three companions.

"Strange," Kahnsultan thought. "Those four men were the only people in this whole stadium who were completely composed at the time of the explosion. I must try to find out who that imam really is."

Cambridge, Massachusetts

CHAPTER TWO

In the pantheon of science gods, Ivan Welland was content to be a foot soldier. He was a modest young man from Dallas, Texas, and had no great ambitions for his future other than to pursue excellence for its own sake. He never pushed himself to the fore. Even in the classroom he would back away from arguments as much as possible. He would do his best to maintain neutrality until all the inaccuracies simply forced him to react.

Ivan's reactions, however rare, were famous when they did occur. The fact that he was 6'7" tall, had powerful shoulders, and could muster a fearsome scowl beneath his thick shock of untamed brown hair, all tended to abbreviate the collegial mental fencing matches when they arose. He was always surprised when he was told that he was imposing. He had bumped his head a sufficient number of times to know that he was tall, but in personality he felt himself to be more Ferdinand than Bull.

Training as a mathematician and physicist at Harvard, he expected to pursue his career in the normal way—dissertation, teaching, research, and publications leading to tenure and eventually a full professorship. He was perfectly cast as an academic, and Harvard, as far as he was concerned, was the ideal place for him. He felt at home among his peers, and Widener Library easily provided him with all the reading material he could ever want.

He was a voracious reader, but more than just a reader, he was a retainer. His years in the Widener stacks had introduced him to many exciting ideas that lay outside the purview of math and physics. After attaining his MSc, the young Texan began to ask himself what field of study might better include his growing interest in his ever-expanding intellectual world.

After much thought he eventually decided to switch his focus to Russian Language and Literature. To his ears, *Ivan Welland, the famous linguist* had a nice ring. His grand-mother, born in Nizhniy Novgorod, had spoken Russian to him since the day he was born. He had always been interested in languages, particularly in how they evolved, changed, and differed from one another. Perhaps he could translate ancient tongues, or maybe even solve the problem of the origin of the Basque language. Challenges would no doubt abound in this field. Or would they? Might he not get lost in academic minutiae? He was well aware that God is thought to be in the details, but he also knew that the devil makes his appearance there as well. In and of themselves, the details interested him only as part of a much larger picture.

He began to see literature as a field that would allow him to explore the broader questions. But would the academic system permit him to do this, or would he be forced to become too much of a specialist? He didn't want to be broad and shallow in the affairs of the mind—he preferred to be broad and deep, but he knew of no departments of in-depth Dilettantology.

Ivan was worried that the leap from math to Russian would be viewed askance by the decision-makers at Harvard, but his excellent academic record and his interviews with the Chairman of the Russian Department and the Dean of Arts and Science convinced them that he was worth the risk. He was not only accepted into the PhD program in Russian Studies, but he was also offered a teaching assistantship which made it financially possible for him to continue in his new career.

Within two years Ivan had completed all the course requirements leading to a PhD in Russian Studies. He had received straight A's in the program, thereby proving to his professors that they had made the right decision in taking a chance on him. All that remained for him to do was to take his final oral examination and write his dissertation. He was looking forward to settling down to a full-time position in a New England college, where he would launch his career as a writer and teacher.

But his plans were about to change, although at that point Ivan had no way of knowing just how radical the change would be. He had spent another long day in Widener Library studying for his orals, when it suddenly occurred to him that he hadn't checked his snail mail for three days. He yawned, stretched, stacked his books neatly in his carrel, and walked out into the blinding light of yet another warm day in May.

He found only one letter in his mailbox. It was from a man called Simeon Montcalf, an employee of the State Department, who asked him to make an appointment to see him about an important matter. Ivan had no idea what this was about, but he dutifully called the number as requested in the letter. Mr. Montcalf told him to meet him in an office in the Arts and Administration building at nine o'clock the following Tuesday. This left Ivan with several days to ponder what the State Department could possibly want.

Tuesday rolled around and Ivan, after thinking about what to wear, decided to go casual. He arrived at the office where Montcalf awaited him and knocked on the door.

"Come in," said a deep voice.

Ivan found Mr. Montcalf seated behind an ordinary-looking desk suitable for a government clerk. He was a man of about fifty, with soft, pudgy hands, thinning hair, and rimless glasses.

"Close the door," said Montcalf, in a peremptory tone.

Ivan sat down on the only other chair in the room, and Montcalf began speaking to him in Russian. His accent sounded educated. Ivan was quite sure that Montcalf was testing him to see how competent he was in spoken Russian. Eventually the topic of Russian literature was casually introduced, and not by accident, it seemed to Ivan. Montcalf asked him what he thought of Count Vronski's character. Had he read Pasternak, Solzhenitsyn, Turgenev?

Ivan shifted his weight impatiently, wondering when he was going to get to the point.

"How would you like to work for the U.S. government for a little while?" Montcalf asked, as though reading his mind.

Ivan blinked. "Well, what would it involve, exactly?"

"The State Department needs intelligent scholars to give us policy advice from time to time," Montcalf said. "We need people who are familiar with cultures and customs of foreign countries with which the U.S. has relations."

"I don't know," Ivan said hesitantly. "I'll be taking my orals soon, and then I have to write a book-length thesis. I don't think I'll have time to get too involved in other things."

"Do you have a plan for financing this project?"

"Well, I was going to get a loan from my parents. I haven't asked them about it yet, but I'm sure they'd be willing to work something out."

"The State Department is willing to pay your expenses while you write your dissertation over the next year," Montcalf said, leaning back in his chair.

"Really?" Ivan tried not to look too surprised. "What would I have to do?"

"Nothing too complicated. You might occasionally be asked to translate something into English, or give us an opinion about current events."

"That's all?" Ivan said after a moment. "And for this you'll pay my living expenses for a year? You mean food and rent and utilities, all that kind of thing? Maybe I'm not getting it…"

"Don't worry about the strings. Trust me. It's a good deal. You might have to go to Washington once in a while for various briefings, and you'll need to be prepared to do some foreign traveling once in a while, if necessary. But you can write your thesis in between things. If you accept this proposal, you'll get a contract to serve as a consultant to the State Department."

"So I can stay in my apartment, then? I can keep my carrel?"

"Of course. You'll be close to your thesis advisor, too. You won't find us interfering too much with your life."

Ivan continued to look hesitant.

"Let me tell you something, young man," Montcalf said, looking slightly irritated. "I'm making you an excellent offer. It's an honor that isn't extended to just anyone. We've done our homework. We know your abilities and your talents, and we would like to help you excel in everything you do. We think you're worth it. I'd also like to think you have the perspicacity to understand the value of the offer."

"Perspicacity," Ivan mused. "What a strange word for him to use. It almost sounds rehearsed. I wonder if he says that to all the students he interviews."

"You have three days to make up your mind," Montcalf said, interrupting Ivan's thoughts. "I'm on an annual recruitment trip to Harvard, and I'll be returning to D.C. as soon as possible."

"Is it all right with you if I discuss this agreement with other people?"

"Of course you can. You're not being hired by the CIA. Besides, you're obviously too large to be a good spy. We couldn't possibly hide you behind a potted palm."

After thinking hard about the ramifications of accepting the government's offer, Ivan decided to go for it. Not having to take any more money from his parents would punctuate his having become an adult. Since he had made a career decision that was unpopular with his father, it didn't seem right to make his dad pay for it, too.

Ivan continued studying for his orals. He intensified his reading program, concentrating on great Russian authors of the past, but also including the secret writers of the Soviet period, and the modern ones as well. Although the body of Russian literature was large, his speed-reading skills allowed him to make excellent progress. At three books a day, he finished reviewing all the reading material in record time.

He was expecting a call from Montcalf soon. Maybe he would have something exciting for him to do. He had mentioned that he should be prepared to travel to some foreign countries. Ivan scanned the map of Russia that hung on a wall in his apartment, trying to imagine where Montcalf might send him.

The phone rang right on schedule.

"Hello Welland," said Montcalf, in his hearty voice. "I received your contract."

"Good to hear from you, Mr. Montcalf."

"I have your first assignment for you. How would you like to go to Chechnya?"

"Chechnya? Wow," Ivan said, drawing in his breath.

"Wow is right," Montcalf agreed. "It's a plum of a job."

Ivan, of course, had many questions, and one by one they were answered. It seemed the U.S. State Department wanted to get a personalized view of the situation. They wanted to know how the man in the street in Chechnya felt about Russia. Ivan was to find out about attitudes, not artillery. Yes, it was an intelligence-gathering mission, but the information collected was to be social, cultural, religious, and political, not military in nature. He was to tell people that he was a free-lance writer and reporter. He would be given identity papers to substantiate this.

"Get out there and talk to the people," Montcalf said. "Go to the pubs, buy some folks a few vodkas, and get them to talk their heads off. Just be sure to remember everything."

Ivan didn't know much about Chechnya except that there was an independence movement in progress that was creating a lot of trouble. Ethnic Chechens wanted separation from Russia, and the mother country was taking a dim view of it. There was unrest, dissatisfaction, and occasional outbursts of violence. Why, then, would they want to send an academic to this dangerous place? As far as he could see, he didn't have much to offer. He wasn't a Muslim. He didn't speak any Caucasian languages, and he wasn't sure he would understand their dialect of Russian. He had never been to Chechnya, and had no family ties there, either.

"So why send *me*?" he kept asking himself. He wondered if he really should be going to Chechnya. But what would become of his stipend if he refused to go? Who was pulling the strings to get him into that part of the world? Hadn't there been some dangerous terrorist activities in Chechnya?

"Don't worry about a thing," Montcalf said. "They know what they're doing over at headquarters, believe me. They have their reasons for choosing you."

"But there must be other people…" Ivan began.

"No, it's *you* they want," Montcalf interrupted him. "Look, you want reasons? I'll give you reasons. First, they want you to go because they need an intelligent, Russian-speaking American. And second, they don't want you to have any previously formed opinions about Chechnya. They want your unprejudiced view of the present situation, so that anything useful that comes out of your visit can be used in forming government policy."

"It sounds to me as though they need a diplomat, not a scholar."

"No, that's where you're wrong. They don't need any more of those guys. All they ever do is waste government money entertaining other diplomats like themselves. What we need is someone who can talk to ordinary people and assess their hopes and aspirations."

Ivan thought about it for a minute or two, and then he finally decided to take Montcalf up on his proposal. He felt it was his duty to keep abreast of events in Russia, and perhaps this visit would provide material for an article.

"Good decision," Montcalf said. "Do a good job. Uncle Sam is footing the bill. I'll see you when you get back."

Click. Dial tone.

Grozny, Chechnya

CHAPTER THREE

Ivan sat in the Boeing jet, looking out the window.

"March break in Grozny," he mused.

He never would have guessed that he would be going to Chechnya. It was a long way from Dallas and Cambridge. His flight would land in Moscow, and he would change there to take the train to Grozny.

His tickets and travel documents had been delivered to him by messenger at the Russian Department at Harvard, just two days before his departure. He had worried about the delay, but he had dealt with enough Russians in his life to know that nothing was accidental. Obviously someone did not want him to bandy those documents around any longer than necessary.

His itinerary called for him to change to the train that left from Kursky Railway Station, and to continue on from there. He looked around at the airport and found it to be similar to most others he had seen in his travels. After passing through customs and retrieving his suitcase, he located the exit so he could catch a cab to the train station for the long ride to Grozny.

He arrived at the station quite early. He was surprised by the number of people sitting around, some of whom looked as if they had been camped there for days. Others looked like extras from a movie about Mata Hari. Dark men in dark, untailored suits glanced surreptitiously at him. He had the distinct impression that not many American tourists had passed that way recently.

In the waiting room a swarthy man leaned toward Ivan and offered him a cigarette. He seemed to want to talk just to pass the time, but Ivan guessed there would be a full report on his boss's desk in the morning.

Ivan told the man that he didn't smoke, but thanked him for his offer. The man was surprised and rather relieved that Ivan spoke Russian. The conversation progressed from *"Where are you from?"* and *"How is it you speak Russian?"* to Ivan's counter questions of *"Where do you live?"* and *"What do you do in Chechnya?"* After all, Ivan thought to himself, Montcalf wanted him to speak to the locals.

It turned out that the man was not from Chechnya. He was a bureaucrat who worked for the Russian government in Grozny. He had been home for a family visit in Moscow, and was not too thrilled to be going back to Grozny. He gave Ivan a totally one-sided description of the political situation in Chechnya. The Russians were right, he explained, and the separatists were wrong. It was as simple as that. The foolishness would end just as soon as the terrorists and insurgents were caught and imprisoned. He lamented the ingratitude of the Chechens toward the wonderful bene-volence of Mother Russia, who had showered them with special treatment in order to placate them and make them happy. But instead of showing their appreciation, they had bombed everything in sight, including their own city.

Ivan frowned to himself. There was nothing new to report to Montcalf from this conversation. He could have read the stranger's diatribe in any issue of *Pravda.* He was glad when they were separated during the boarding process.

After the one-sided conversation in the waiting area, Ivan was relieved to be sitting in the aisle seat next to an attractive young woman. His companion for the thousand-mile train ride was in her thirties—too old, he thought, for mutual attraction. Ivan was glad of this because any conversation would be unhampered by latent or overt sexual innuendos. He always hated situations in which gender issues were threaded through ordinary human communications in subtle, and sometimes not so subtle, ways.

The woman in question couldn't help noticing the lanky stranger sitting next to her. His knees poked into the back of the seat in front of him as he attempted to keep his legs out of the aisle while the conductor moved about the car. She let out the tiniest of giggles.

Ivan detected the not unfamiliar sound. People often laughed at him as he dealt with the problems of a world that was far too small for his comfort.

"How do you do?" he said to her in Russian. "I am Ivan the Terrible traveler, at your service."

His seat companion smiled. She noticed his accent, but said nothing.

Ivan continued looking in her direction, and told her that he was a doctoral student in the Russian Studies Department at Harvard University, and an American free-lance journalist trying to write an in-depth story of the events that were taking place in Chechnya. He said he hoped to be able to present all sides of the story fairly, and in a way Americans could understand.

"I've no preconceived notions and no political agenda," he added. "And I have only two weeks to write my story."

The young woman laughed out loud this time. She felt it was just like an American to think he could absorb centuries of history in only two weeks. In the tactless style of Russians she told Ivan he was foolish to think he could do any kind of justice to the Chechnya/Russian problem on his two-week vacation.

"I agree," Ivan said. "But I don't have to write the story in Grozny. I'll do most of it when I get home. So I don't have to go into the history too deeply while I'm here. I just want to get a feel for the situation in Chechnya by getting to know the local people and finding out what they think."

His companion nodded, but remained quiet.

"So what do *you* do, anyway?" Ivan asked, after a pause.

"I am professor of modern history at university. I am called Marina Kortikuova."

It was Ivan's turn to smile. He looked at her warmly. They had already found common ground in the first few minutes of their acquaintance.

"Well, I'm pleased to meet you, Professor Kortikuova," he said, extending his hand. "My name is Ivan Welland."

"How do you do, Mr. Terrible Welland?"

"Ivan. Please call me Ivan." She had a firm handshake.

"Tell me, Ivan, what do you know of Chechnya so far?"

"Well… do you want the short version or the long one?"

"I prefer short version," Marina said, hoping she could soon start reading the book she had brought for the trip.

Ivan immediately launched into what sounded like an *Encyclopedia Britannica* rendition of the origins of the people of the Caucasus. Then he quickly outlined the history of the area ever since it became a separate entity in the seventeenth century. He spoke of the larger historical figures, such as Imam Shamyl, Sheikh Mansur, and the late President Dudayev, killed by a Russian rocket. He related the high points from the time of the dissolution of the Soviet Union, the foundation of the Republic of Ichkeria, the separatist movement, the installation of Islamic law, the Russian invasion, the election of pro-Russians to control Chechnya, and the present situation where Al Qaeda-supported rebels in the mountains were resorting to terrorism against the Russian-occupied and militarily-controlled nation as a method of reestablishing an independent Islamic nation under Sharia law.

"Have I got it right?" he asked finally.

Marina sat up a bit in her seat as she realized how small she must have seemed to the tall student sitting next to her. She wondered if all Americans knew the history of the Caucasus as well as this young man. No, it was not possible. His knowledge of history was better than that of her students.

He spoke with an educated, old-fashioned sort of speech, but his Russian was excellent.

"You are correct in what you say," Marina told him, "but explanation not complete. You do not say why things happened as they did, and it does not mention huge cost in lives."

"I realize this," Ivan said. "That's why I've come here. I hope that by being with the people and learning something of their hopes and fears, I can do justice to their story. If there's something I can say or do to improve it, or if I can help to make the situation clearer, then I will have succeeded."

Marina was studying his face as he spoke. There had been so many instances of false witnessing and double-dealing in Chechnya that she was hesitant to take anyone at face value. But she could detect no sign of deception in this young American. She had lived through the period when everyone who spoke in public had to assume there was a KGB agent standing nearby. She herself had once been taken in for questioning about something she had said about Bolshevism in one of her history classes. In the new "democratic" Russia, the policies were different. Or were they? If she had ever publicly espoused the liberation of Chechnya, would she have been allowed to continue in her position? No. The young man beside her could get away with it, though, at least in his own country.

"I am from Moscow," Marina said at last. "But I teach in Grozny, in university that is paid for and supported by Russian government."

"I understand."

Ivan supposed that she was trying to tell him that she was only allowed to justify the Russian position that Chechnya could not be allowed to secede from the Russian federation. To support the guerillas would have ended her career.

"You see, Russian Czar Nicholas prevented Ottoman Empire from seizing Caucasus, so this area is still part of Russian nation."

Ivan already had some idea of the complexities of politics in Chechnya, but so far he had only heard one side of the story. He wondered if Marina Kortikuova could be open-minded about independence in Chechnya. He also wondered if he could be neutral himself, as sympathy for secession meant supporting Islamist terrorists. He had two weeks to make up his mind.

"I enjoy to hear your opinions after you are in Chechnya for some time," Marina smiled, when they finally came to the end of their journey.

"I'd be delighted to share them with you," Ivan said, helping her off the train. "We must keep in touch."

"Yes, this is so," Marina smiled. She wondered if she would ever see this tall American boy again. Then she shrugged and walked toward the bus stop. What was she thinking? He was much too young for her, anyway.

Ivan's hotel in Grozny was an old one, in the center of the city. It was either a miracle of good fortune or a testament to Russian precision-bombing techniques, because it was the only building in sight that hadn't been severely damaged by bombs or shells. It was a run-down hotel, however, even before the conflict in Chechnya began. Still, it had a certain Mediterranean cum Arabic architectural style that was not unpleasing. The courtyard, with its multi-arched arcade on three sides, looked like a simulated palace interior in Granada. Marble staircases in three corners led to the dark wooden doors of the rooms.

A swarthy young bellhop, who seemed to resent having to speak to him in Russian, showed Ivan to his room. After putting his suitcase down, opening the drapes, and telling him where the restaurant could be found, he moved closer to Ivan to receive his tip. This young man's world-weary attitude summed up the first impression Ivan had of Grozny. Since he was to be in this room for two weeks, he unpacked his clothes into the drawers of the dark, heavy dresser. Ivan didn't know if this was the only hotel in Grozny, or if Montcalf's people were saving money by having him stay in these bare-bones quarters. He didn't mind, however. He didn't need any distractions. His one addiction was reading, and he enjoyed doing it in plain surroundings.

He opened the night table to see if anything was inside. He recoiled slightly when he discovered a copy of the Koran in Russian. Actually he was happy to have this volume at hand. He had always meant to read the Koran, but it was hard going, especially in translation. Learning Arabic was one of the things on Ivan's *to do* list, but he hadn't gotten around to it yet.

"Too many years with Mendel, too little time with Muhammad," he mused as he held the Koran under the light. He made a mental note to see if he could obtain an English translation so he could compare it to the Russian version. He was aware that no matter how well one knew a foreign language, one never quite mastered it as well as one's native language. It was possible that in the hotel somewhere there might be a copy of the Koran in English. He would ask at the desk as soon as he went for dinner.

As he went into the bathroom to clean up, he thought about what an anachronism it was that so many places in the world still use the old English term, *water closet*. When he looked at the bathroom he understood better why many cultures preferred to call it a closet, because a bathroom requires that there be a tub and room enough to use it. There was neither. When he looked more closely, he found the shower fixtures in the deepest corner of the closet, just beyond the toilet. There was a drain situated at the lowest point of a depression in the floor. Since there were no shower curtains, one was apparently expected to let the splashing water land where it might. A plain glass mirror above the sink was the only adornment in the completely white-tiled room.

He reviewed the protocol that would have to be followed to avoid entering the water closet with his shoes on after he showered, and before the maids cleaned up, as any water that remained on the floor would be tracked everywhere in the room on his shoes. Was all this just to avoid the cost of buying shower curtains? It was not the only detail that would puzzle him. Many other Western inventions that improved ordinary devices were totally ignored by the Chechens.

He picked up the room key, opened the heavy door, and went out, closing and locking the door behind him. The door seemed to him like a very substantial deterrent to anyone trying to get in by breaking it down. A potential thief would be much more likely to use a passkey or pick the lock than resort to a battering ram. He wondered if he could turn in his door for a thinner one, in exchange for a shower curtain.

Ivan's naturally long stride took him across the lobby in seconds. He approached the restaurant door, which was decked out as though it were the entrance to a seraglio. Before opening the door he wondered if the interior would also be decorated in the style of the Sultan's harem. He felt disappointed when he entered the very ordinary restaurant interior. The square tables with white cloths and straight-backed wooden chairs had been made of the same dark wood used for the door to his room, and the maroon drapery fabric was the same used for the seats. He was also disappointed to see that there were no waitresses dressed in harem pants—only waiters in white shirts and black trousers. They did have colorful cummerbunds, however.

The maître d' seated him at a small table and handed him a menu in a leather folder. Soon he was approached by a slender young waiter, who asked if he wanted a cocktail. Ivan never really liked alcoholic drinks, although he would take an occasional beer or glass of wine with dinner. He decided to ask for a glass of the house wine, mostly because he wished to see if there was a cheap one that was good.

He returned his attention to the menu and selected borscht and the goulash. If they couldn't make those two items well, he would be surprised. He gave his dinner order to the waiter, and told him that he was going to the lobby for a moment, and would be back soon. Somehow Ivan knew this waiter wouldn't care, unless he didn't receive a tip.

At the front desk, Ivan asked a dour middle-aged female clerk if he could have a copy of the Koran in English. Although she might have found the request unusual, she didn't show the slightest hint of emotion.

"I do not know if I have copy in English," she said. "But I find out and tell you later."

Ivan guessed she would consult her boss, as she probably did about everything, before she told him that they did not have a copy of the Koran written in English.

"Thank you. I'll be in the restaurant, and I'd be grateful if you could bring the book to me there."

He felt that by phrasing his parting sentence in a way that made it seem that there could be no doubt about there being an English translation in such a fine hotel, the clerk would have to uncover a copy or the hotel would lose face.

The waiter soon arrived with the borscht. The beet soup was steaming hot in the bowl, and some onions were visible under the island of sour cream that floated in the middle of the large portion. It looked traditional and homemade. It turned out to be just as good as it looked, and Ivan spooned it down hungrily.

A minute or two later the waiter removed his bowl and replaced it with a heaping portion of hot goulash. This looked promising, too. It had quite a few pieces of meat floating in reddish brown gravy which covered a small mountain of noodles, but the paprika dominated everything. The combination of the flavors was very good indeed.

Ivan liked bread, but not just any bread; it must be whole grain or seed bread with a tough crust. He used to tell people that he liked bread that fought back. The bread that had been in the basket on the table was just the right kind, but alas, it was cold. Other than that, everything about the meal had been perfect. He guessed that his friends back at Harvard would have rated the meal as good peasant cooking, heavy on the nutrition, but light on subtlety.

Just as he had made the decision to skip dessert and have coffee, the desk clerk came through the harem doors, looked around, spotted Ivan, and headed in his direction. He noticed she had a book in her hand. When she arrived at his table she held out the book, with a tiny crack of a smile. Ivan took the Koran in his large left hand and simultaneously reached in his right-hand pocket for a tip. The woman, who was about the same age as his mother, politely refused to accept the tip. Like his mother, she was probably proud to have been able to help, although he doubted his Southern Baptist mother would have approved of his choice of reading.

Ivan opened the book and began to look at it while he drank his coffee. He would do his best to synthesize the English and Russian versions. Where substantive differences occurred, he'd consult an Arabic speaker to determine the best understanding of the passages. Perhaps an imam at a mosque could help with this. He also felt that a greater knowledge of the history of the Arabs and Ottomans was needed, and that Marina Kortikuova might be able to help with this aspect of his strategy.

He began setting things up in his room so he could begin his study of the two Korans. Since there wasn't a table large enough to accommodate both books and a notepad, he decided to put the three items along the edge of the bed. He sat on the chair with his knees spread apart as far as possible to allow himself to get as close as he could to the books. He was amazed that he was not tired, even though he had only fitfully slept on the train the night before. Whenever he was excited by a project, he could go without sleep for hours on end.

By dawn Ivan had read the entire Koran in English, and had compared it to the Russian translation. Whenever he thought a passage could be clearer or have a different interpretation, he highlighted it in the Russian version. He had already read the Bible through several times and was thoroughly familiar with it. Where there were discrepancies between the Bible stories and the same stories as recorded in the Koran, he noted them on his pad. When the light of dawn came through the maroon drapes, he stripped off his shirt and pants, laid them over the back of the chair, and tumbled into bed.

Ivan had always been a light sleeper. Perhaps it was because he felt that life presented so many interesting things for him to think about. He never liked being unconscious in case he missed something. He was one of those no-alarm-clock people who could simply make up his mind what time to wake up, and he would awaken at that time.

That morning he set his mental alarm for two hours later and went off to sleep at once. At seven o'clock he opened his eyes, looked at his watch, and rolled into a sitting position with his size thirteen feet flat on the floor. He washed, shaved, and dressed. His intention was to eat breakfast, obtain a city map, and walk to whichever large mosque was nearest. Then he would try to catch the imam between the first two of the five daily prayer sessions. He would attempt to get his questions answered at once, but most likely he would have to make an appointment to see the imam at a time that was convenient. His alternate plan was to call Marina Kortikuova to see if she could meet with him, or failing that, get him permission to use the university library so that he could do the historical and cultural research necessary to improve his reading of the Koran.

Once again he crossed the lobby and entered the hotel restaurant. He was surprised to encounter the same waiter who had served him the previous night. This time the waiter was happy to see him. Ivan surmised that the tip he'd left the night before had been adequate. He asked the young man his name.

"You can call me Ali."

Ali soon brought him coffee. He assumed that everyone took their coffee black, for no cream was served, although there was sugar on the table. Ivan used neither. He sipped the coffee and received the usual bitter hit.

"Are you Muslim?" Ali asked, eyeing his copy of the Koran.

"No, I'm just a student," Ivan said.

Ali seemed content with the answer.

"Can you tell me the way to the nearest mosque?" Ivan asked.

"You are fortunate in your request, because the principal mosque is nearby. When you leave the hotel you turn left, go two blocks, turn left again, and you will see the mosque there."

CHAPTER FOUR

After breakfast Ivan settled the bill, said goodbye to Ali, and headed out to the street. In the bright light of day Grozny looked very dull. There was rubble everywhere, but people were heedlessly detouring around the wreckage as if it didn't exist. Following Ali's directions, Ivan turned the second corner and found himself standing right in front of the Central Mosque.

It was huge, and it was intact. Ivan thought, correctly, that the believers of Islam must have given credit to Allah for the fact that the mosque had survived the rockets and bombs that had scarred the nearby buildings. It was, in fact, amazing that the minarets and the domed building remained untouched by the war that had raged around it. Particularly significant to the Muslims would be the fact that the Orthodox Cathedral of Saint Michael had been totally destroyed.

Ivan went inside and knocked at the door of the imam's quarters. A voice invited him to go in. His first impression of the room was that it was surprisingly well appointed, and quite Arabic in the feeling it evoked. The imam, who was a man of about forty, had a full black beard with grey tinges, and was wearing a round hat with white clerical garb.

"Good morning, sir," Ivan said, extending his hand to the imam, who made no move to take it. "My name is Ivan Welland. I'd like to study the Koran, and I'm hoping you can recommend a Koranic scholar who might help me."

The imam scrutinized Ivan for a while, piercing him with a dark and thoughtful gaze. He took his time about it, obviously feeling no compunction to answer right away.

"Sit down, please," he said at last, indicating an ornate guest chair across from his hand-carved, throne-like seat.

"My name is Mansur Shamil al Fatihoun, but you may call me Imam Mansur."

Ivan realized that he was in the presence of someone of considerable importance. He seemed in complete control of his surroundings, as if he had been born to rule. For a mostly sedentary religious leader, Imam Mansur seemed to be in excellent physical condition. Something about this tall, dark man reminded Ivan of a panther, capable of pouncing with incredible speed and athleticism, but one who spent most of his time observing his prey until just the right moment to attack. He wondered if he was just a large mouse in the eyes of this Chechen cleric.

"Sir," Ivan began, "I should let you know right away that I don't speak Arabic, but I do speak English and Russian, so I felt I might get more out of my reading if I compared both translations to each other to see if the meaning of the verses was substantially different in any important ways. I've noted here in the Russian version some places where the meaning was either unclear or different from the English version."

Ivan showed the imam the highlighted areas.

"If you have time," he continued, "I'd be most grateful if you could help me clarify these questions. I also promise to study Arabic myself just as soon as I finish my PhD thesis."

"Where are you studying, Mr. Welland?"

"Harvard University, the Department of Russian Studies."

"Ah, Cambridge, Massachusetts. I remember it well. I did an MSc in electrical engineering at MIT. That was before I became a clergyman. What is your thesis topic?"

"It will be about Chechnya, sir, but I'm not exactly sure of much else. That's why I'm here, to get acquainted with the country, the people, the culture, and the religion, which I hope will help crystallize my thoughts about a thesis topic."

"What do you know already about Chechnya?"

"So far the only thing I know about Chechnya is what I've read in the American newspapers. I only arrived here yesterday, so I have a lot to learn. I have the feeling there's a great lack of understanding concerning Chechnya among the American people, and our government policy reflects that."

"Yes, well we can certainly use more understanding on the part of America. You said you arrived only yesterday. Judging from the number of notations in your copy of the Koran, you must have worked on it for a long time before you arrived."

"No, I did this last night in my room at the hotel. Have you any suggestions about how I can resolve my problems with the various translations?"

Some time passed before the imam answered. He was obviously thinking about whether he personally should take on this brash American student, but he must first ascertain the degree of Welland's current knowledge of the Koran. He decided to see how much this man had managed to absorb.

"Let me ask you a few questions to see how deep your understanding of Islam is at this moment. What do you think is the most central idea of the Koran?"

"There is no God but Allah," said Ivan.

"And the second most important point?"

"Muhammad the Messenger gives us the word as he received it from God, and therefore he is the last Prophet, completing the work of all earlier ones, and so the Koran is the infallible final word from God," Ivan answered.

"Good," said the imam. "Are you familiar with the Old and New Testaments of the Bible, Mr. Welland?"

"Yes, I am. I've read the Bible through several times, and I've studied the New Testament thoroughly."

"You are a Christian, then?"

"Yes. Will that prevent us from discussing the Koran?"

"No, not at all. It is better that you are religious. If you were an atheist, we would have no common ground. Now, what is the difference in the style of writing between the Bible and the Koran?"

"The Koran is written in the first person. That is, it's supposed to be God speaking directly to man. In this way it's unlike the Bible, which is history, stories, and men relating God's words to other men."

"Excellent, the Koran is God speaking to man."

Ivan noticed the imam's choice of words. He supposed there was no "supposing" in anything Mansur said. This was an excellent opportunity to have his questions about the Koran and Muhammad answered by an expert who knew English, Russian, Chechen, and Arabic. He also thought the imam would try to convert him to Islam, and he didn't know how he felt about that. He didn't want the imam either to think he was weak and easily swayed, or to be suspicious of ulterior motives. He decided to play it straight with Mansur.

"Would you consider taking me as a student, just for the two weeks that I'm in Grozny?" Ivan asked him. "I'll be going to the university to see if they'll allow me access to the library. If they do, I'll study the writings of Muhammad, and when you have time we could discuss what I've read."

The imam was intrigued by this young scholar who seemed to have no doubt about his ability to learn so much about Islam so quickly. He handed him an envelope.

"Read this, and come back tomorrow at ten o'clock."

He stood, said *Salaam aleichem,* and walked out of the room. Ivan, having been dismissed, left by the same door.

Ivan opened the envelope as soon as he left the mosque. To his great disappointment it turned out to be nothing more than a simple tract listing the five pillars of Islam. He had hoped to have a deep conversation with the imam, but it looked as though he was going to have to earn that right by first memorizing the basics of Islam. He sighed, and shoved the tract into his pocket. As he went to the university, he noticed the signs of the ferocious battle that must have been fought on those streets. Rubble was the dominating feature of the city of Grozny.

When he reached the university, he asked a student the way to the library. Fortunately the library building had only sustained partial damage, so that inside things looked nearly normal. He approached the desk and introduced himself as a scholar from Harvard, there for a short time to do some research. The librarian didn't seem terribly excited to receive that information, but when he mentioned that Imam Mansur had suggested that he speak to her about obtaining a temporary pass to enable him to use the library facilities, she adopted an accommodating manner. She dug into her desk drawer and handed him a special library card.

"Thanks," Ivan said. "I'll tell Imam Mansur how helpful you've been."

A bright, pleased expression passed over the librarian's previously impassive features.

Ivan felt safe and secure, as he always felt when he was in a library. He didn't know it, but he was not safe in this library, or anywhere else in Chechnya. The eyes of the students seated at the study tables all seemed to be watching him as he picked books off the shelf and leafed through them in typical Welland fashion. He could tell at once that most of the books were written from the Russian point of view.

Ivan was the king of libraries. He had spent so many hours in them that he felt instantly at home. He cruised around for a while and studied the organizational system in use. He noted the location of the classifications that he was interested in—theology and Chechen history. He put his copy of the Koran on a table and headed for the book-shelves. When he returned to the table, he had accumulated three volumes on Chechen history. He opened the first one, which dealt mostly with the early peoples of the area, and began reading. He went about twenty percent slower in Russian than in English. Even at this reduced reading rate, he read about five times more rapidly than the average reader.

His summary of Chechen history boiled down to a few facts that he scribbled in his notebook. The ethnic people were called Nakhs. These tribal people were polytheistic, but over the centuries Christian influences from Russia and

Armenia replaced their religious beliefs. One thing that stood out in his mind was how fiercely the Nakh people had fought the outsiders to remain independent. He made a mental note to explore the reasons why Sunni Islam had succeeded in laying down roots in the region, while every other outside ideology had been repulsed. The Chechens didn't always win, and there were times when they had to regroup, but they always rose up again to oppose outsiders such as Persians, Ottomans, Russians, Cossacks, Czarists, Ingushis, assorted Communists, and most recently, those who wanted to make Chechnya one of the twenty-one Russian Republics.

During the recent failed attempts to separate from Russia, 100,000 Chechens died. This is a huge number of deaths, as the population of Chechnya itself is only between 700,000 and 1.5 million, depending on the source consulted. At the present time it is estimated that 375,000 people live in Grozny. The Russians had found it impossible to take a census due to the casualties of war and the vast number of refugees that move away to avoid the fighting. No Chechen would tell the truth or even give accurate details to the census-takers anyway, lest there be reprisals.

Ivan had been so absorbed by his reading that he hadn't noticed the attention he was receiving from a nearby student. There had been a considerable number of passers-by that had taken note of the rapid rate of Ivan's page turning, but this young man had decided to seat himself right next to Ivan. Montcalf was right when he told Ivan back in Cambridge that he could never be a spy because he was too big to be inconspicuous. He had nearly finished the second volume when he saw that the student was now studying at his table. Subconsciously he knew that someone else was there too, but he continued to work. He thought he'd look around as soon as he finished his book.

When he did look up, he was surprised to see the two at his table, plus several more students standing behind them, just staring at him. Did they have no business of their own?

The sight of this young American reading machine had captivated all the students. At first they were incredulous, then interested, and then committed to finding out about this behemoth that had landed in their university.

Ivan had just stacked book number two on top of the first volume and was preparing to read the third, when the student asked him in Russian if he was American.

Ivan was faced with the inevitability of being interrupted in his studies. He looked at his watch. It was one o'clock, and time for lunch.

"Tell you what," he answered in Russian, "if there's a cheap restaurant where we could go to eat, I'll answer your questions one by one if you agree to answer mine. Okay? My name is Ivan Welland, by the way. What's yours?"

"I am called Akhmad Dudaev."

It was very natural, considering the recent conflicts and political turmoil, for the students to be curious about who this stranger was and what he was doing in Chechnya, a place seldom visited by American tourists or students.

It was agreed that the two students seated at the table would go with Welland for lunch. They could then spread the word about him to any others who asked. So Ivan and his new companions walked to a small café that served chureks, a variety of cornbread that was traditional in Chechnya.

During lunch Ivan fielded the student's questions to the best of his ability. They were conventional questions for the most part. Akhmad Dudaev wanted to know where Ivan was from, how it was he spoke Russian, and why he was in Chechnya. Ivan felt he had to reciprocate by asking him, in turn, where he was from.

"Most university students are from the countryside," he replied. "Most study petroleum engineering, and some study architecture. Russia tries to buy back Chechen loyalty with large infrastructure projects, and most students seek to find such work. Three bridges are under construction, and they repair roads and rail lines. Most jobs are in these fields."

When political topics arose, there was both an elevation in conversational intensity and an unspoken skepticism.

"Why America not help Chechnya when we wanted to leave group of Russian Republics?" the student asked him. "With United States of America on our side, we could be independent nation now."

That seemed a very large and improbable leap to Ivan, but he realized that this young separatist was desperate for any help he could get for his beleaguered little country. They had faced down the Russian bear for years, only to be frustrated yet again. That part was very understandable, but assuming that America should or could come to their aid was naïve in the extreme.

"Everybody wants America to intervene when problems arise," Ivan said, looking a bit helplessly at his expectant face. "But we don't have the manpower to be everywhere at once."

"Americans are wealthy," the student persisted. "We see how you live. We go to films. You should help the world."

"And we do. We have huge foreign aid programs."

"Yet we sit here and eat chureks. Let them eat chureks!" exclaimed the student, which got a laugh from Ivan.

Akhmad noticed Ivan's marked-up copy of the Koran and wanted to know if he was a Muslim. Ivan answered that he was a Christian, but he was studying the Koran with Imam Mansur.

All at once the conversation came to a complete halt. Akhmad and the other student suddenly remembered that they had a class to go to and a paper that needed to be written. They tried not to make it obvious, but they left so quickly it was clear that the name of Imam Mansur hit hard when it was dropped.

CHAPTER FIVE

The following morning Imam Mansur, with his best air of implacability, greeted Ivan promptly at ten o'clock, but once again without extending his hand. Was this an unspoken unfriendliness? Was it a conscious effort to avoid touching an infidel? Ivan felt that he was functioning secretly on many levels, and would probably never reveal his true thoughts or let his proud demeanor slip. Ivan couldn't shake the idea that he was in the presence of someone very special. He had met men of great reputation and position before in the course of his studies, but he had never met one that emitted such a strong aura of confidence and danger.

"Mr. Welland, did you read the material I gave you?"

"I did, Imam Mansur." Ivan threw in the title as a sop.

"Good, then we'll begin. What are the Five Pillars of Islam?" he asked, in a tone one would use on a child.

Ivan was annoyed by the rote teaching method. Did the imam expect him not to know the simple material he had given him? Or was he just testing the waters of his authority over him to see if he would submit? Islam was all about submission. Ivan decided to go along with this method of teaching, even though it stuck in his Ivy League craw. He resolved, however, to take this fellow into deeper waters as soon as he got the chance. Meanwhile, Ivan dutifully recited from memory the five pillars of Islam.

"Do you believe the Koran is Allah speaking to us?"

"No, I don't believe it, at least not entirely. Forgive me, but I would not have come here to talk to you personally about the Koran if I had not had some questions."

"There are no questions that the Koran does not answer for those who believe," Mansur said loftily.

"Well, I'm concerned about the verbal transmission of the Koran. Christians use this method too, but we have a linear connection to the original source documents through the ancient Hebrew, Greek and Latin texts that existed long before Muhammad. The written word travels better through the centuries than verbal rendition. So I wonder about the authenticity of the Koran's sources."

"The Koran could not have come about without the will of Allah," the imam replied. "Muslims know the word *Qu'ran* means recitation, and they regard it as the Standing Miracle. The Koran is the ground plan of all knowledge. It is perfect and is without parallel. It was memorized and then transcribed from memory over a period of twenty-three years. A man cannot create such a work without the help of Allah. Not to believe in the authenticity of the Koran is the ultimate suspension of reason."

"If what you say is true," Ivan replied, "it is indeed a supreme miracle. More important, though, is what the book says, and why it says it."

Mansur stood up. "Mr. Welland, you are an interesting young man, and you will make a good Muslim some day. But for the time being I must discontinue our talk, as I have pressing business. I'll see you tomorrow at ten o'clock."

"All right, sir. I'll be here. It was nice speaking with you."

Imam Mansur didn't deign to answer. He gave Ivan one of his piercing, intimidating looks, then turned on his heels and abruptly left the room, leaving Ivan to see himself out.

It was almost noon. Ivan decided to see if Professor Marina Kortikuova was available to have lunch with him. He wanted to tell her he had read her book, and that he was eager to discuss it with her. He planned to complete phase two of his research in the library that afternoon anyway, and it would be nice to have lunch with one of the two people he was acquainted with in Grozny. He walked to the University, asked a student for the History Department, and was directed to the second floor of a nondescript cement building.

"Professor Kortikuova?" he said to the receptionist.

"Third door on the right, just up the hall."

He knocked on the door. After a few moments he heard someone invite him to go in.

"Ah, Mr. Terrible Welland!" Marina said when he poked his head through the doorway. "How are you? I wonder how you get along here in Grozny all by yourself."

He liked Marina. She seemed to be a typical female Russian professor—asexual and brusque. She probably wouldn't spare his feelings by any unnecessary tactfulness. The impression he had from reading her book was that she was not particularly original, and this was perhaps why she was teaching in Chechnya instead of Moscow. On the other hand, she might have been writing whatever she had to say in order to get it published.

"I found your book in the library," he said.

"Really? You will read it soon?"

"I've already finished it," said Ivan, smiling when he saw how her face lit up at the mention of her book. He knew that authors are a lonely bunch, and they rarely get any feedback about the books that take them so many years to research and write. Not like actors on the stage, who get instant reactions from the audience.

"Well? You like it?"

"Why don't you let me invite you to lunch, then we can talk about it as long as we like. What do you say?"

"I say yes," said Marina, with a bright smile.

Ivan didn't actually care very much if they discussed her book or not. Authors so often are too sensitive about their work, and he didn't want to say something that she might construe as a criticism. What he really wanted to do was memorize all the details of her interesting face and learn everything he could about her life. He also wanted to find out what she knew about Imam Mansur.

"Good," he said, standing up. "You pick the place."

They walked to a small restaurant that Marina liked. They were greeted warmly by the owner, who showed them to a table near the window with a view of Isayev Avenue, the address of most of the Russian government buildings. Their window seats provided a view that made Grozny look reasonably intact. The Russians had been careful not to bomb their own buildings.

Marina ticked off all the good things that had been accomplished in Chechnya because of its being a part of Russia. To Ivan it was like reading her book a second time.

"Is good for this economy when oil will begin to flow again," she said. "But Chechens do not make it easy. They prefer to be poor and independent and not to accept help from Russians."

Just then a waiter appeared at their table with the food. There was no need for a menu, as everyone was served the same meal. It was mutton again. Ivan supposed the Chechens knew it was more economical to allow lambs to grow into full-grown sheep.

"I want to know the Chechens better," he said, chewing on a tough piece of mutton. "I've read the Koran in two languages and I've compared the translations. Now I have some questions, and I need help from someone who knows the original language of the Koran. I don't suppose *you* know Arabic, do you?"

"No. I speak no Arabic. How important is this, anyway? You read Bible in English or in Russian, and you do not believe is necessary to learn classical languages, ya?"

"But it's not just the language. I'd like to know a whole lot more about how the Koran is being applied in today's political world. Anyhow, I think I've found someone who fits the bill. Do you know Imam Mansur?"

Marina shifted uncomfortably in her chair.

"I do not know him personally, but I have heard much. Russians say he is connected to terrorists, but no one can prove this. I think you must be careful of what you say to him. How do *you* know him?"

"I went to the mosque and asked to speak to the imam, that's all. You Russians always suspect plots and intrigues.

Anyway, the guy was reasonably pleasant, but I think he wants to convert me."

"Convert you, or *use* you, perhaps? You Americans think Russians are too suspicious, but we believe you Americans are too innocent. American press says that what happens in Chechnya is because people want freedom, so they rebel against Russian imperialists. Americans think Chechen cause is pure and Russian purpose is subjugation. But is not true. This idea comes from cold war attitudes when Russians and Americans created balance of power by opposing each other. But now America is only superpower in world. So your politicians think they can throw blanket of democracy over rest of world and everything is fine, but you must look under blanket. That is where you find biggest sins."

Ivan could see that Marina was heating up.

"Tell me about the hidden agenda that we Americans are naively failing to see," he said gently.

"Is Islamist extremism," she replied in an excited but hushed voice. "Do you think all terrorism is caused by political differences? Do you think you give people right to vote and all problems go away? We had elections here in Chechnya and people voted for Islamist leaders, who then led country to separation. They had already autonomous republic, one of twenty-one in Russia, but was not enough. They were not happy. Why? Because these men want to spread Islam everywhere, taking power either by sword or by votes. You understand what I say you? You will see. Ask Imam Mansur questions, and you will see that I am right."

"Are you trying to tell me that Islam is an international conspiracy that aspires to take over the whole world?"

"Not just Islam in general. I talk about *radical* Islam. Please consider following. Chechnya has population of one and half million people of many ethnic backgrounds, and it dares to make war with Russia. How do they get finances? Where do they get weapons to fight? Who pays?"

"Those are all good questions. There's lots of corruption going on with arms deals on all sides."

"Is true, but you do not see whole picture. Think about Iraq. America overthrows Hussein, holds elections, and people elect leaders recommended by Muslim clerics. So who wins war? Not Americans. Before war in Iraq, streets were full of Saddam supporters, and now they are filled with Al Sistani supporters. Victor in war is radical Islam. You Americans think that you see separation of mosque and state, but is not true. You see elected officials, ya? But behind scenes Muslim clerics they pull strings. They have people kneeling before them every day in mosques. They tell them for what to vote and for whom to vote."

As they walked back to the university, Ivan suddenly remembered he hadn't spoken to Marina about her book.

"I understand now why you took such a strong position against the Chechen separatists in your book," he said. "At first I thought you were just trying to adopt a pro-Russian stance to please your Russian publishers. But now I can see that what you're really concerned about is how Islamist terrorists are winning the separatists over by promising to help them in their cause."

"Is true, ya? For long time now Islamist extremists help disaffected people everywhere. In America, too. Many Americans have become Muslims, and you do not mind. You think is good, because in America you have freedom from religion. This is why terrorists make progress. Is like parasite that lives on host, and host smiles and says parasites have rights just like every citizen. Now you see small picture of world situation right here in Chechnya. Chechens want independence, so they sell souls to Islamist terrorists, but they will not be independent under Sharia law. When they will realize this, is too late. If America does not wake up, is too late for whole world."

CHAPTER SIX

Ivan returned to the university library and headed back to the history collection. He wanted to understand as much as he could about Chechnya's hostility to Russia and the history of the country's ties with Islam. If Marina was right about Chechnya's being a microcosm of the worldwide march of Islamist terrorism, Ivan wanted to learn more about it, and as quickly as possible.

The volume on Chechen history that he chose as his introduction was organized in encyclopedic fashion, with the history in chronological order. He didn't mind that format, but he hoped that he would learn more about the inner motivations of the people involved in making Chechen history. Unfortunately the book didn't prove edifying from that perspective. He always wondered why, when historians had all the advantages of hindsight, they seldom made clear the motives of the individual participants. He thought it would be better to invent motives than to ignore them. After all, history as written after the fact is usually very different from the way the events actually took place.

The passage he was reading described the cowardly, premeditated murder of President Akhmad Kadyrov in the Dinamo Stadium at the Victory Day parade. The bomb, a 155 mm artillery shell, had been encased in cement at least three months prior to the explosion so as to avoid the metal detectors that had been built into the reviewing stand at the time of its construction. Twenty-three others, including the chairman of the State Council, had died in the assassination. The perpetrators had never been caught.

There was no question in Ivan's mind about its being a premeditated murder. The plotters had planned their moves well in advance, so they must have been sure their problems with the Russian puppet government were not going to go away any time soon. Even the most liberal western view of history would have decried these methods to achieve… what? The separatists would hype freedom, liberation, and self-government. Their method of attaining their objective, however, belied the lofty goals of the movement. The fact that their plan involved the deaths of innocent bystanders was not likely to score points for the cause behind the plan. Ivan was pondering the arguments of the perpetrators when he realized that Akhmad was sitting next to him again.

"I am noticing how fast you read," Akhmad said. "Are you able to retain what you read at that speed, I wonder?"

Ivan was used to being asked that question, which, along with some basketball reference because of his height, was the conversational opener that most people used.

"Excuse me, I ask stupid question," Akhmad continued. "Of course, if you do not retain information, it is waste of time to read quickly. Forgive me for interrupting."

Ivan liked Akhmad. He had thick reading glasses, non-descript clothing, an aquiline nose, full lips, soft hands, and a pleasant manner.

"It's okay," he said. He felt annoyed at having to put his book down, but he was there to talk to people. In fact, Montcalf would say it was his job. "What area of history interests you most?"

"Modern European, especially Caucasian history. It is most interesting here, as you can see from poor condition of city. No need to go anywhere else for excitement. This is one of hot spots in world right now. We will need good historian to write it down so it can make sense to others, and that is my job. Ha, ha."

"Who is your professor?" Ivan was hoping to hear a colleague's name that he could drop on Marina.

"Professor Marina Kortikuova," Akhmad replied.

Ivan laughed. "It's a small world. I sat next to her on the train from Moscow. We became acquainted. I like her very much."

"I like Professor Kortikuova, too. I write my doctoral thesis for her. She tries to be fair, but she is Russophile."

"I know what you mean. I read her book. Listen, it's getting late. Would you like to join me for dinner?"

"Yes, sure," said Akhmad. "I like very much."

They left the library and walked to the hotel, making small talk and joking as they went.

They were an unlikely pair. Akhmad was about average Chechen height, five feet seven or so, and the oversized Welland was a foot taller.

"How did Professor Kortikuova like your thesis?" Ivan asked.

"She likes it," Akhmad said, "but is hard to do research here because the internet is heavily policed. The Russians monitor all sites that might have political implications. The search for terrorists was as strong in Russia as it was in America after 9/11. But paranoia factor is always in red alert stage in Chechnya."

"I'm not surprised. Putin was the head of the KGB."

"Yes, and he has not forgotten how it works. He has nose of bloodhound, and his dogs are always on trail of terrorists."

They went inside the hotel and walked across the lobby to the restaurant. Ali greeted them, looked a bit dubiously at Akhmad, and sat them at Ivan's usual table.

"Ali, this is my friend Akhmad, and we need some beer."

Ali gave them both menus, and left to get their order.

"Why do you think Chechens hate the Russians so much that they would die to be free of them?" Ivan asked.

"What you need is for me to give you recounting of entire history of Chechnya, but if you have patience I will try to tell you," Akhmad smiled. "Chechens are different ethnic people from Russians. We descend from early people of Caucasus."

Ivan nodded.

"Russians provoked Chechens many times in past," Akhmad continued. "In modern era it started with invasion of Caucasus by armies of Czar Nicholas first one in 1830s.

And they did this after Chechens *helped* the Czar to repel Napoleon! For almost thirty years brave Chechens resisted Czar's superior forces, but eventually we were incorporated into Russian Empire. During this war Russian and Cossack troops made criminal outrages against our people. Up until 1917 we were obligated to endure imposition of Russian language, customs, politics, and business methods. But as you have seen, this scheme did not work. We still speak our language and we do things our way."

Ivan looked thoughtfully at Akhmad as he continued to relate the painful struggle of the Chechen people.

"Then came 1917 and overthrow of Czars. Chechnya declared independence, but Bolsheviks, like Czars, refused to let go of Caucasus. In 1923 we were forced once more to give up our dream of independence. But we were good Chechens. When Germany invaded Caucasus and Russia, we fought common enemy together."

Ivan nodded, listening carefully to everything his new friend was telling him.

"In spite of our strong fight against Nazi invaders," Akhmad continued, "that paranoid Stalin accused us with *collaborating* to Germans! And so between 1944 and 1957 he exiled 400,000 people from Caucasus and sent them to Kazakhstan and Siberia. Those people had to leave home and go to hellish existence in poverty and disgrace. Do you believe they were welcomed in new land? I think no. You can see now that there are reasons for hatred and distrust that Chechens feel for Russia."

Ivan nodded, saddened by these stories of treachery.

"After Great Patriotic War, Akhmad continued, "those of us who were not exiled were forgotten. Squabbling and agitating always for independence resulted in restoration of Chechen-Ingush Republic in 1957, but not independence. Many exiled people returned to Chechnya, bringing with them hatred for those who had sent them to Siberia. Desire to separate from Russia became big dream in Chechnya. When

Soviet Union collapsed in year 1991, then Dudaev declared independence."

"Dudaev," said Ivan. "Isn't that *your* name?"

"Yes. Dzhokhar Dudaev was our President and my father."

"Was?"

Akhmad held up his hand. "I tell you soon."

Ivan nodded.

"When Chechnya tried to secede again, Boris Yeltsin sent in army, but Supreme Soviet would not allow him to engage in war against separatists. So many compromise solutions were discussed, but true independence was not possible. In 1994, Yeltsin attacked separatists to preserve integrity of Russian Federation. Chechen independence fighters were providing bad example to other republics. That was start of what we call *The First War*."

Akhmad drained his glass and wiped his mouth with the back of his hand. Ivan motioned to Ali for another round.

"Big numbers of Russian troops came to Chechnya," Akhmad explained. "Bombing and shelling went on night and day. But Chechens did not give up, even though many, many people died. Separatist fighters conquered maternity hospital in Russia to force Russians to peace table, but it was no good. In 1996, my father was killed by Russian missile that homed in on his communications equipment. That is how he died."

"I'm so sorry," Ivan murmured.

"He was brave man," Akhmad said. "His death helped to bring peace talks that ended war. But sorry, peace did not last. Negotiations fell down, and there was new war."

Akhmad drained his glass.

"President Yeltsin named Vladimir Putin to be Prime Minister," he continued. "Then Russia began Second War against Chechnya. But Yeltsin's failure to resolve Chechen situation made him to resign at end of 1999. Putin became President and doubled Russian military effort, and finally forced Chechen fighters to withdraw from Grozny to the safety of nearby mountains."

Ali appeared with two cold bottles of beer on a tray, and placed them on the table. The two young men poured their glasses and toasted each other soberly.

"But wars in Chechnya and Afghanistan were not so comfortable to the Russians," Akhmad went on. "It made it difficult for them to hold on to their status as superpower. When 9/11 happened in America, Putin saw opportunity to link himself to Bush by saying that Chechen independence fighters were *terrorists*. This changed international opinion. At first people said Russians were unfairly holding down freedom fighters in Chechnya, and then they said we were all murderous terrorists. Unfortunately, desperation had driven the separatists to actions that were of a terrorist character, such as bringing down two Russian planes on same day, and school hostage situation. Because of these incidents America was very happy to have Russians to help against terrorists."

Welland was staring intently at Akhmad as he listened. He realized that if he were a journalist, he would face a daunting task to report all this in an unprejudiced fashion. He was expected to give his impressions to Montcalf when he got back home, but he would be in a much more difficult position here in Chechnya if he were to voice almost any opinion that could alienate him from one group or another. Ivan had felt for quite a long time that it was becoming increasingly difficult for someone watching the news on television to differentiate between the commentary and the reportage. He didn't envy the statesmen who were trying to handle this hot potato.

When Akhmad stopped for a sip of beer, Ivan suggested they order dinner. "You seem to be relating all this in chronological order," he smiled, "so if we stop to eat now you can finish the most recent history of your country after dinner."

Ali came over and took their dinner orders. He had been standing nearby and had probably been trying to listen to them all along.

"I wouldn't want to be a politician in this country," Ivan said, after Ali had withdrawn. "It's far too dangerous."

"We are accustomed to this now," said Akhmad, smiling bitterly. "Anyway, that is why I decide to be historian and not politician. Many of our Chechen heroes did not live even to my age. Have you not noticed how we are always having free elections in this country? They occur after separatists blow up something, or assassinate someone. In this case it was my namesake Akhmad Kadyrov, the Russian-supported President who was blown up by bomb planted three months earlier in the Dinamo stadium's reviewing stand, which is example of long range militant Islamist tactical planning. So we had new election in 2003. We do not have peace or independence, you understand, but we do have elections. In Russian-sponsored elections, pro-Moscow candidates win with big numbers."

"It looks as though it'll be that way for us in Iraq, too," said Ivan. "If they don't end up having a civil war."

"Yes. But either way, everybody dies in vain," said Akhmad. "As you see, it is easy to be cynical in Chechnya. Anyhow, I am like most Chechen people. We are sick of war, and we feel tempted to make the best deal we can get from Russians and keep walking. But war continues, and people are confused and angry. We make history here nearly every day. So what do you think of all this, soon-to-be Professor Welland?"

Ivan wasn't sure exactly whose side Akhmad was on, but he could see he wanted to get on with his own life, even if it meant that his country would, at least for the time being, be a puppet state in the Union of Russian Republics. Ivan made up his mind to stall, rather than state a position. He didn't want to disappoint his new friend, but he still had lots of questions about the recent history of Chechnya.

"Do you think we could get together again soon, perhaps tomorrow afternoon, so I can ask you some questions that are bothering me?" Ivan asked him.

Akhmad agreed to meet him again the next day. The two men shook hands, and Akhmad went on his way. As Ivan turned to go to his room, he noticed that Akhmad had left an envelope containing the draft of his thesis on the table. He thought that if he hurried he could catch up with him and give him back the manuscript. He knew he might worry if he thought it was lost. He put a tip on the table and took off walking at flank speed in the direction that Akhmad would have taken.

After a few minutes he thought he saw the outline of Akhmad up ahead. He decided not to call out to him, as it was getting late and he didn't want to create a disturbance. Besides, in a couple of minutes he would catch up with him anyway. Akhmad's shadowy figure reached the corner of the next block and turned left. Ivan strode along, sure that he was gaining on him.

When he reached the corner he also turned left, straining his eyes to catch sight of Akhmad in the semi-darkness. Just as he turned the corner he tripped over a large object on the sidewalk. Both his arms flailed about as he tried to find something to hold on to, but he was unable to stop himself from falling. The obstruction on the sidewalk was large and heavy, like potatoes in a sack, but softer and not lumpy. He moved his hands over it, exploring its contours, then recoiled quickly when he realized the object was wet and sticky.

Then suddenly he drew in his breath. He had tripped over the motionless form of a fellow human being. A drunk, or a street person, maybe. What was the sticky substance he had touched? He hoped it wasn't vomit. It couldn't be. There was no odor.

He scrambled to his feet, electrified, not wanting to have such intimate contact with a stranger in the dark. Then he leaned over and peered more closely at the body. He already knew who it was before his brain could catch up with him.

Akhmad's throat had been slit open, and crimson blood was pumping out of the wound in arterial spurts.

"Akhmad!" Ivan cried, bending over to look at him more closely. "Oh God! Akhmad!"

He was still alive. Ivan could hear a gurgling sound.

"Help!" Ivan shouted. "I need help here!"

As he looked around he could see dark figures slipping quickly away. Lights were turned off in windows. He ran out into the street and tried to stop the cars, but the drivers moved quickly out of sight. He had no cell phone. He banged on the door of the nearest building, but there was no answer.

He ran back to Akhmad, tearing off his shirt along the way, and tried to press it into the wound to stem the flow of blood. In the shadowy darkness he could see his white shirt developing a dark stain where he was holding it against Akhmad's neck. He felt desperate. How can you make a tourniquet and apply it to someone's neck without killing him? What would a physician do in a case like this?

He straightened up and began running back the way he had come, hoping to find someone to help, to call an ambulance, or to call the police. He was nearly all the way back to the hotel when a police patrol car came up the street towards him. He flagged it down, and when the police saw him covered in blood they drew their pistols. Hands in the air, Ivan begged them to call an ambulance. They responded by placing his hands behind his back and handcuffing them. After searching him for weapons, they forced him into the back seat of the cruiser and slowly drove to the scene that Ivan had described. Then they radioed their headquarters for medical assistance.

Akhmad was silently still. Ivan strained to see him clearly from the window of the police car. Dark blood seemed to be everywhere. The amount of blood he had lost looked so profuse that Ivan had to assume there was no hope. The officers waited for the ambulance, and when it came the medic pronounced the victim dead. The police officers got back into the cruiser and drove Ivan straight to police head-quarters.

CHAPTER SEVEN

Ivan was taken to an interrogation room to wait for the arrival of Inspector Leshenko. The room was small, dingy, and furnished only with an old table and two chairs. To Ivan it appeared that the police in Chechnya had reclaimed this room from the set of an old black-and-white movie, so he expected his inquisitor to look something like Humphrey Bogart, or perhaps Edward G. Robinson.

Ivan was sitting on the edge of one of the rickety chairs, his hands still cuffed behind his back. From Akhmad's description of life in Chechnya, he knew he was in one of the world's great cesspools of suspicion. He was not looking forward to the arrival of the Inspector.

His mind was preoccupied as he sat waiting for the vaunted inspector to show up. He wondered if in any way his friendship with Akhmad had been responsible for getting him killed. He also was very upset with himself for letting go of the envelope that contained Akhmad's thesis. He had dropped the thesis at the scene when he had fallen over his friend's body. No doubt the police were reading it at that very moment.

Then suddenly he realized that even if he hadn't left Akhmad's work at the scene, the police would have taken it from him when they arrested him. Would the subject matter of Akhmad's thesis cause trouble for his friends and family? And what about his professor, Marina Kortikuova? Would she be implicated?

Inspector Igor Leshenko had been called at home and informed of the details of the case. When he was told that the victim's last name was Dudaev, he knew he had no choice but to take charge of the case personally.

"Why the hell do they have to murder people at bedtime?" Leshenko groaned, hating the thought of having to put on his uniform again and go back to the station at that hour.

He looked at himself in the bathroom mirror. At least he didn't have to comb any hair on his shiny pate. He snorted, then put his finger up his flattened nose. The broken bridge wouldn't allow the finger to achieve its desired goal, so he held one nostril and blew the contents of the other one into the sink, leaving it for his wife to clean up.

Leshenko was a master of the old Soviet police system of dossier collection. He had a file on virtually everyone, and the one belonging to the Dudaev clan was long and deep. Akhmad's father was a former leader of the separatist movement, and another son had been killed in a skirmish between Russian soldiers and Chechen rebels.

Anyone related to the revered Islamic patriot was of special interest to Inspector Leshenko. He'd been entrusted, after all, to gather intelligence that would help maintain Russia's control in the oil-rich Caucasus.

"One less Dudaev troublemaker for me to have to deal with," Leshenko muttered as he strode through the main entrance to the police headquarters.

He was both personally aggravated and professionally curious about the American suspected of killing a member of the Dudaev family. He sat down in his office, called for coffee, and read the statement that his officers had prepared. Then he slowly went over the scant information he had on file about the American from Harvard. He was already fairly sure that Ivan Welland, whose passport had been taken from him at the time of his arrest, was not the murderer. Americans didn't slit throats. The ritualized killing was typical of the *modus operandi* of Islamist fanatics. He had seen this kind of murder altogether too frequently to be deceived into thinking that an American scholar had done it.

But why would Islamist terrorists kill one of their own, and a Dudaev, to boot? More than likely the killer was one of *his* own—a cop getting rid of a rabble-rouser—and what was needed now was a scapegoat and a cover-up story.

Professor Ivan Welland would do very nicely. Meanwhile the question of what this American was doing in his territory was likely to be of much larger political and economic significance. He'd hold the murder charge over the suspect's head, and then use the threat of criminal prosecution as the incentive to make him divulge his real reasons for showing up in Chechnya.

He drained his second cup of coffee and sauntered over to the interrogation room, pleased with himself for having kept the American waiting so long.

"Hello, Mr. Welland," he greeted him affably. "My name is Inspector Leshenko. Sorry I couldn't get here sooner. Too much work, too little time."

Ivan was suspicious of the self-assured friendliness that Leshenko was trying to project. Underneath the phony exterior he had a studied, overworked, impatient manner, like someone afraid to be caught doing nothing.

"Mr. Welland, we can get this interview over with very quickly if you admit that you murdered Akhmad Dudaev. Did you?"

"Certainly not."

"You were discovered running from scene of murder, covered in blood. How do you explain that, Mr. Welland?"

"I wasn't discovered. *I* discovered *your* police car and asked for their help."

"Their help? Why would police help murderer?"

"I needed their help to radio for an ambulance so I could save the life of my friend."

"I believe you called to policemen for help only to help yourself. You were caught red-handed with blood of victim over you, and you wanted to make police officers believe you were innocent by pretending that you needed their help."

Ivan knew that Leshenko was toying with him. But the inspector commanded all the power in the situation, so Ivan decided to play along, admitting nothing, and depriving the officer of the pleasure he would obviously get from making him angry, or even worse, getting him to break down.

"Detective Leshenko, I'm totally innocent of this crime, and I have no need to convince an investigator of your level of competency of the fact that I had no weapon to slit the throat of my only friend in Grozny. Furthermore, why would I leave my shirt on the wound of a dying man if I had just killed him?"

Leshenko stared at Ivan with distaste. He seldom had the opportunity to humble an arrogant American, especially one who was younger and better educated than he was. He looked forward to extending the interrogation.

"Why are you *really* here in our country?" he demanded, suddenly dropping his pseudo-friendly attitude.

"I'm a graduate student, looking for a topic for my thesis. That's all. I'm only here for a short time."

"Perhaps long enough to kill a few more Chechens, ya? I think maybe you are agent of American CIA? Even if you are who you say, how can you dare to write about Chechnya when your experience of country is so short?"

"I have come to learn, not to teach anything, Detective Leshenko," said Ivan, subtly demoting the official while at the same time trying to sound as pleasant as possible.

Leshenko noticed the effrontery. "Inspector!" he barked. "I am *Inspector* Leshenko, and I am in charge here."

Just then one of Leshenko's men came in and whispered something in his ear.

"Bring her in," said Leshenko.

The man bowed slightly and left the room. A moment later he returned, accompanied by a woman dressed in a long coat, her head covered with a scarf.

Ivan felt the blood rise to his face when he saw that she was Marina.

Leshenko quickly rose to his feet to greet her.

"Please, sit in this chair, Professor Kortikuova," he said, guiding her to a hard wooden seat.

Marina glanced at Ivan, but decided not to acknowledge him. She knew that the Chechen police were not necessarily on her side, even though she was a Russian. They had been trained to be suspicious of everybody, without exception. In Chechnya one was always guilty until proven innocent. But what was Ivan doing here? And why had they called her in for questioning?

"Brace yourself, professor," Leshenko said, obviously relishing his position of power over Marina. "I have bad news for you."

Marina's eyes darted over to Ivan in spite of herself. Was he in trouble? Was it something serious? What did it have to do with her? She hoped there was something she could do to help. But would this man believe anything she said?"

"Do you have student called Akhmad Dudaev?"

Akhmad? Is this what the questioning was all about? What could Akhmad have done to run afoul of the law? He was a sweet boy. Harmless. A number one scholar. How could he possibly be in trouble with the police?

"Professor Kortikuova, please answer question," said Inspector Leshenko.

"Yes… Yes, Akhmad Dudaev is my student. Has he done something wrong?" she asked, looking worried.

"Well, that depends how you look at it," said Leshenko. He would enjoy playing cat with this attractive little mouse.

"How I look at what?"

"How you look at circumstances."

Marina just sat there, feeling confused. Ivan could have strangled the man.

"Dudaev has done something unacceptable. Something unethical," Leshenko continued.

"What on earth could that be?" she asked, wondering what her mild, peaceful, respectful student could have done to get himself into trouble with this unsavory detective, or whatever he was.

"Do you not think it is unethical, Professor, to allow yourself to be killed? Does not Dudaev have mother? Did he have no concern for her feelings?"

Marina stared at him, unable to understand what he was saying or where he was trying to lead her with his questions.

"Have you nothing to say about this matter, Professor? Are you implicated in some way? What are you trying to hide from me? Has cat run away with your tongue?"

Ivan could stand it no longer.

"Marina, the inspector is trying to tell you that Akhmad was murdered earlier this evening."

"I'm conducting this investigation, thank you very much Mr. Welland," Leshenko snapped.

"What? Murdered?" Marina exclaimed. "Akhmad was *murdered?*"

"That is correct," Leshenko said, furious that Ivan had had the temerity to interfere with his little game.

Tears of grief began brimming in Marina's eyes, but she was shaking with outrage at the same time.

"Are you trying to blame Akhmad's murder on Akhmad himself? What do you mean, *he let himself* be killed? Why you are saying he is responsible for sorrow of mother?"

"A real man knows to defend himself," Leshenko said lamely, but he wasn't enjoying himself any more. He felt like someone who had been interrupted while telling a joke by a listener who delivered the punch line ahead of time.

Marina would have liked to do a little punching, too, but she was overwhelmed with grief at that moment.

"My God, oh my God," she wailed. "Why Akhmad? He would not hurt fly. Why Akhmad?"

She began to weep, with tears streaming down her face. Leshenko seemed to be sitting impassively by, but he was actually studying her closely, conducting a sexual appraisal to decide if this bereaved woman was suitable to satisfy his lewd desires. His eyes lingered on every part of her body, imagining them being revealed to him in a time of mutual lust. He was convinced that mature, unmarried intellectual women had a torrent of seldom-used sexuality, held back by a dam of fear and false modesty. He had only to begin to open the gate and an emotional flood would burst forth. He thought it would be a nice touch for him to offer her his handkerchief to dry her tears. He checked it surreptitiously, to make sure it was clean.

"I must ask you to identify the body of your friend, Professor Kortikuova," he said considerately, handing her the handkerchief and making an effort to sound soothing and sympathetic. "We must be sure it is done correctly. My men will take you to see it. Come with me."

Ivan watched Leshenko as he led Marina down the hall. He knew on every level what was going on in the inspector's mind. He would bet anything that he would ask Marina for a date. Not that day, of course, but very soon.

Leshenko came back into the room and sat down. Now that he had developed an interest in Marina, he was less attracted by the idea of playing games with Ivan.

"You Americans!" Leshenko snorted, eager to bring the interview to a close. "If you were more righteous and less self-righteous, nations of world would like you better. You can go, now. I have to investigate murder."

"When I was arrested I had a copy of Akhmad's thesis," Ivan said. "I dropped it when I stumbled over his body. May I have it back, please?"

"Certainly not. It is evidence. Don't think for a minute, Mr. Ivan Welland from Harvard University, that you are no longer a suspect. You are not to leave Grozny without my permission."

Ivan stood up to go. Leshenko, like Imam Mansur, was not used to being looked down upon by a taller man, and he didn't like the experience.

"You are too tall," he remarked accusingly. "Be careful someone does not cut you off at knees."

Leshenko opened the door to his office as an indication to Ivan that he was now free to leave. As he stepped out of the office he came face to face with Marina in the hall.

"Oh Ivan, Akhmad is dead," she sobbed, while Leshenko leered at her. "I identified body. It was terrible. His throat was cut same way Muslims do to traitor of Islamist cause."

"I know," Ivan said. "But they seem to think *I* did it."

"That's ridiculous," Marina said. "You could not possibly do so terrible thing."

At that moment, with tears in her eyes for her lost student, she still managed to come to Ivan's defense. Later he would always remember this instant in time. It was at that moment when he first realized that he cared deeply for Marina.

Leshenko was impressed by the woman's little outburst. He took it as another indication of her pent-up passion, so he was not angry with her for daring to speak to him that way. He was delighted, in fact. He would have this woman, he told himself, and she would enter realms of physical ecstasy that she hadn't even imagined before.

"You seem to be acquainted with suspect," he remarked to Marina.

"I know him well enough to be certain that he did not kill anyone," she replied angrily.

As Marina and Ivan turned to leave, Leshenko gave her an appraising look.

"And you, Russian lady, are you enjoying your *glasnost* with this man?"

Marina didn't dignify his insinuation with a response. As she left the police station with Ivan, she heard the inspector's laughter echoing down the hall.

"How did he know I was from Harvard?" Ivan asked Marina when they were outside. "Did you tell him?"

"No. I have never before seen or talked with this man," she said firmly. "And he did not know that we knew each other, either, until we met in hallway after I went with him to room where I identified Akhmad's body. Do you remember this?"

Ivan remembered. Marina was right. He was exhausted and ready for sleep, and no doubt she was too, yet she was on top of every detail of the evening's events. He was moved by her kind heart and impressed by her excellent brain. He looked forward to getting to know her better.

Back in his office Inspector Leshenko was also looking forward to learning more about this young woman and her American friend. He would slowly uncover their plots and their motivations, and he would uncover Marina herself, if everything went according to plan.

When Ivan got back to his hotel that night, the clerk at the registration desk gave his bloody shirt the once over and passed him a message that had come for him while he was out of his room. It was written in ornate, old-fashioned handwriting.

Dear Mr. Welland, the note began. *Mr. Montcalf of the U.S. State Department has asked me to look in on you. I shall meet you in the restaurant of your hotel at 8 a.m. I will recognize you. Sincerely, Khansultan Akhmatov.*

Simeon Montcalf was going to be shocked to hear about everything that had happened to him in Chechnya, Ivan thought. His mind was still swimming with memories of his ugly encounter with the inspector. But in just four days he had met a beautiful Russian history professor, conversed with a mysterious imam, shared chureks with the son of a famous Chechen leader and all but witnessed his murder, of which he was now being accused.

He had been looking forward to his conversation with Akhmad the next day, but now he would never see him again. The world was surely not a better place without the presence of that gentle, intelligent young man. What gave anyone the right to think they should be free to slit the throat of an innocent human being? Akhmad's story would have to be told by Marina now, through the thesis that might be published posthumously if it could be pried from Leshenko's grubby hands.

CHAPTER EIGHT

The next morning Ivan crossed the hotel lobby and ducked into the dining room, just in time for his appointment with Montcalf's contact, the man who had left him a note the previous day. The ever-present Ali was on duty as usual.

At exactly eight o'clock a distinguished-looking man went into the restaurant and approached Ivan's table. He stood up as the gentleman drew near.

"Hello, Mr. Welland. I am Kahnsultan Akhmatov. I trust you received my message. May I join you?"

"Of course. Will you have breakfast?" Ivan asked him.

"Yes, thank you very much."

Ivan gestured to Ali to take their orders. When this was done and Ali had poured their coffee, Ivan asked his visitor about the reason for their meeting.

"Simeon Montcalf, for whom I perform the occasional favor, has asked me to look after you and to make sure you get home safely."

"I didn't know there was any question about my safe return," said Ivan. "But I thank you both for your concern."

"Keep my telephone number handy," said Kahnsultan, surreptitiously handing Ivan what looked like a business card. "Even better, commit it to memory. You may use it at any time, and for any reason, but please be prudent about what you say when you are on the telephone. We are in a police state, and you never know who might be listening."

"I'll be sure to call you from a public phone."

"Good. And if you ever wish to talk to Mr. Montcalf directly, you must come to my home and call him. I have a secure line."

"I see. I wondered why I wasn't provided with a cell phone, but obviously cell phones are not as safe as secure land lines. And of course, I didn't really expect to be in any kind of danger."

As Ali approached with the food, Kahnsultan broke off the conversation and remained silent until the waiter had removed himself.

"Are you in danger, Mr. Welland?"

"I think so," Ivan said. "Well, I know so," he added.

As the two men ate their breakfast, Ivan told Kahnsultan all about Akhmad and Marina and how Akhmad had been killed the night before. He also related how he had been questioned by Inspector Leshenko, who had accused him of murdering Akhmad in spite of the fact that he had no weapon. What's more, he had tried to save the victim, and had asked the police for help. Then Marina Kortikuova, the young man's professor, had showed up at the police station to identify the body, and now Ivan was worried that he had put her in jeopardy through guilt by association.

"You know his professor, then?"

"Yes, we met on the train to Grozny from Moscow."

Kahnsultan had listened carefully to everything Ivan told him. Now he put down his knife and fork and addressed him in a very serious tone of voice.

"I don't like the sound of this at all," he said, as he wiped his lips with his napkin. "I believe you should come to my house at your earliest convenience and tell Mr. Montcalf exactly what has happened. The murder of a member of the Dudaev family is a serious matter, and your closeness to the situation could be life-threatening. The perpetrators might find it convenient to make you the scape-goat."

"Who do you think is behind it?"

"It's difficult to say. It could be the Russians, of course, who think they're getting rid of one more terrorist separatist, or it could even be the terrorists themselves, who see him as being in collusion with the Russians for some reason."

"But a Muslim killing a fellow Muslim? Isn't that a bit of a stretch?"

"The Islamist extremists would not hesitate to murder a fellow Muslim or anyone else, for that matter, whom they thought was getting in the way of their ultimate plan to spread Sharia law throughout the world. Ten, fifteen years ago I would not have said such a thing, but the Islamist jihadists have been testing the waters for quite some time now, and they have found they can get away with almost anything. The United States did nothing about the attacks on their embassies and their warship, so the jihadists went even farther and gave you 9/11. Although Bush has taken a strong stand with his invasions of Afghanistan and Iraq, the international response has been critical. Even the Americans themselves are divided on the issue of how to respond to these reprehensible acts of terrorism. I can only say that I am deeply saddened by the loss of innocent lives at the hands of these madmen, and I am also sad that they have decided to appoint themselves the sole interpreters of our holy Koran."

Their talk went silent as Ali cleared the plates away.

"You can never tell in this police state who is listening when you talk," he said in a low voice. "We should be more careful not to express any strong opinions while we are here. But please come to my house as soon as you can, so I can put you in direct touch with Mr. Montcalf."

Just then Ali appeared again with coffee. Khansultan stopped talking until he withdrew.

"I have another question I'd like to ask you," said Ivan when Ali was out of earshot.

"Please," said Kahnsultan, with a little bow of the head.

"I was just wondering... why do I have the feeling that Imam Mansur is something more than the pastor of a church, for example, in the American context? Whenever I mention his name I get this unspoken but strong reaction, sort of like the after-shock of an earthquake. Do you think he's behind some of the extremist activities?"

"I do not know, but you could be right. The imam is a Saudi Wahabist. I understand that he is a strong supporter of the Madrasa fundamentalist Islamic schools throughout the Middle East. I don't know what hold he has on these people you speak of, but I am sure that Montcalf will be interested in anything you find out about him. His influence is great, yet he seldom leaves his mosque. Here in Chechnya we are Sunni Muslims. We are influenced by the Sufi version of Islam, but our religious traditions are Muslim, not Arabic. Yet there are some other influences that are penetrating our country. Some 1,800 people are said to have disappeared without a trace in the last two years, and right now it is my duty to make sure that you don't join them."

Kahnsultan's job description meshed with Welland's. They agreed that Imam Mansur possessed great power, and shouldn't be trusted under any circumstances. Nevertheless, they thought it best for Ivan to keep his appointment with him, and continue to pursue his study of the Koran. If he gave up too quickly, the imam might get suspicious. Ivan and Khansultan shook hands and went their separate ways.

Ali hurried over to clean the table and collect his tip.

Imam Mansur invited Ivan into his office at exactly ten o'clock. Ivan was once again conscious of the whiteness of his clerical garment. He couldn't imagine how it could be so clean. Did he wear a new one every day, or did he send it out to a superb laundry? There were no laundromats in Grozny, so how did he do it? He guessed it would be improper to ask.

"Mr. Welland," the imam said. "Please take a seat."

Ivan did as he requested.

"How are you doing with your study of the Qu'ran?"

"I find it very interesting, sir."

"Interesting? Is that all? Do you not find it truthful?

"Not completely," said Ivan, aware that he was entering dangerous waters now.

"What specifically do you not believe?" the imam said, with some annoyance.

"Well, for instance, Muslims claim that the Bible is swarming with errors and contradictions. Yet the Koran is derivative, depending on the Bible stories of the earlier prophets for part of its content, yet claiming that it comes directly from Allah. How can this be?"

"Parts of the Bible are correct, and others are corrupted," Mansur said. "The ones in the Qu'ran are correct."

"To my mind it's more likely that a verbal tradition that has come down over thirteen centuries is corrupted. The Bible, after all, is written in documents that can be examined by scholars. How can you argue with the Dead Sea Scrolls?"

"Ah yes, the Dead Sea Scrolls. Found by an Arab, then taken by the Israelis before anyone else could see them. Are we to believe anything the Jews say?"

"The Koran is a political handbook as well as a behavior manual. Jesus was a carpenter, after all, but the Gospels do not teach us how to be carpenters. And in the same way, Muhammad was a businessman, but he does teach business classes in his holy book. Jesus was a total pacifist, while Muhammad was Commander-in-Chief of his army. I believe in the separation of Church and State. In its ethical teachings the Bible preaches love and forgiveness, but I find the Koran often teaches hatred and revenge. When we read about fatwas and jihads, and the way the infidels should be treated, I just can't believe it comes from a loving Creator."

The emotions that Ivan had subdued when reading the Koran were now beginning to surface, but he told himself he must not let them distort the points under discussion.

"You have read the Qu'ran," Mansur said, regarding him coldly. "But you have not understood it. To truly understand it you must first understand Arabs. I believe you have had a good education, but you still lack sufficient knowledge of the history and soul of the people for whom the Qu'ran was created. I pray that Allah will see fit to send you to live with us for a few years so that you may clearly see the light of Islam. Until that time I fear we two can only bandy words about. In order to achieve communication we must first of all share many experiences of life. Souls must suffer as they make their way up the holy hill to approach the perfect life described in the Qu'ran, as conveyed to us by our most holy Prophet Muhammad, may peace be unto him. Now tell me something, Mr. Welland," he continued, leaning forward and scrutinizing Ivan closely. "Why did you really come here?"

"I came to write an article about Chechnya. In the U.S. there's a lack of understanding about the country. From their standpoint the Caucasus region is in Russia, so I thought my article might also form the basis for a thesis."

"I see," said Mansur. "And what will your position be?"

"I'm not sure yet, but one of the topics that interests me deals with the effects that Islam has had in the Chechen search for independence. I felt very ignorant about Islam. That led me to study the Koran, which brought me to you. I intend to be fair in my treatment of all sides, but I need to hear what the sides are saying. So my question to you is, does Islam have a part to play in the independence struggle in Chechnya? And if so, what is it?"

The imam paused for a moment before he spoke. He did not wish to be identified as a leader in the fight for independence. He could not afford to be branded as a terrorist, or his work in Grozny would be over.

"I am a cleric, Mr. Welland, not a soldier. The people of Chechnya are a separate people. The language isn't Russian. The customs aren't Russian, and their religion is not Russian Orthodox. I believe Allah wishes Chechnya to be liberated and take its place among the Islamic nations of the world."

The cleric had lied about not being a soldier. Actually he was a warrior for the Prophet, and had fought well with mind and body in many places for the glory of Islam, but of course Ivan could not know this. What he did know was that the imam's description of his beliefs probably summarized the position of most of the Muslims in his congregation.

"Do you believe there is some right on both sides of your struggle? That is a question that Abraham Lincoln wrestled with during the Civil War. Is there no hope of a compromise that would bring peace in this war?"

"I think your President Lincoln was tired of fighting," said Mansur. "A great leader can never be seen to be tired. Fighting for Allah is a joy. The truth is, I am disappointed in Lincoln. His generals must have won the war for him. He was assassinated too, but a really great leader should never allow himself to be assassinated. Muhammad, peace be unto him, was truly a great leader, and though many men tried to kill him, he was too clever, with Allah's help."

Ivan took this comment to be a cheap shot at Jesus for allowing himself to be killed, but he didn't dignify it with a protest. It also struck him as odd that Leshenko had said that Akhmad should not have allowed himself to be murdered.

"Is there hope for a resolution to the Chechen war?"

"There is not only hope, there is certainty," Imam Mansur replied. When Islam rules, Allah will give us peace."

Peace through victory. It occurred to Ivan that he had read somewhere that *Mansu*r means *victor*.

Imam Mansur rose to his feet.

"Salaam, Mr. Welland. I have enjoyed our talks. I hope that we will meet again someday."

He bowed slightly, then turned abruptly and strode into his antechamber. Ivan was left alone to show himself out.

Neither man realized how soon they would meet again, and what dangerous circumstances would surround their next encounter.

Ivan trudged along the street toward the University, thinking sadly about what a mess Chechnya was in. He was glad to find Marina in her office. He was longing to talk to her about the events of the night before, and he was also concerned about how she was feeling after finding out about Akhmad's death. Marina was equally glad that Ivan had decided to drop in. She invited him to share her lunch with her.

"I have question for you," Marina said as they ate.

"Shoot," Ivan said, with his mouth full.

"What?" Marina looked startled.

"No, I mean, just tell me your question."

"I go to Akhmad's funeral tomorrow. But I hate to go alone, so far away. It is in Tolstoi-Yurt. I borrow car."

"Say no more. I'd love to go with you."

"You do?" she said, looking pleased. "I am so glad."

"How long does it take to drive to Tolstoi-Yurt?"

"I think half hour. Maybe little more. I come to your hotel in car after breakfast. What about eight o'clock? Is good?"

"That'll be fine," Ivan smiled. "I look forward to it."

"I still cannot understand why Akhmad was murdered. What did you two discuss at dinner last night?"

"We talked about the modern history of Chechnya... It was mostly facts and chronology, and not much opinion or criticism. I can't imagine how our conversation could have been connected with his death in any way at all. He was proud of Chechnya, of course, and how bravely the people had fought for independence from the big Russian bear..."

"Did anyone overhear you?"

"No. Well, the waiter might have caught a few snatches."

"The waiter? He is obviously Muslim." Marina began to grow agitated. "I know what is Akhmad's attitude to situation in Chechnya. I have read his thesis. He advocates peace with Russia. The violent Muslims, the jihadist separatist Chechens, they would see this as unpatriotic cowardice. They would see him as traitor to his country, to be punished with death." Her voice began to rise. "They have killed him! They have killed my student because he wanted peace!"

CHAPTER NINE

A closeness was beginning to develop between Ivan and Marina. As far as Ivan was concerned, he was glad to have the mutuality of a friend who spent her days in the ivory tower. And Marina, for her part, was pleased to have the company of a young scholar from America whose opinions would be considerably different from the ones she usually heard.

They meandered slowly through the park, discussing Akhmad's murder from every possible angle. Neither of them believed that the repulsive Leshenko was really going to try very hard to solve the case. They feared that because of the man's prejudices towards Islam and Americans, he would not be very motivated to hunt for Akhmad's killer. They felt saddened by the fact that the Chechen student's friendship with them might interfere with the justice due to him. They eventually agreed to do what they could to solve this case themselves, and bring the culprits to justice in the spirit of *perestroika*.

"Marina, do you think there's any chance that Akhmad was actually killed because of us?"

It wasn't the first time the thought had occurred to Ivan, but he had held off questioning Marina about it until he felt she was ready to delve into some of the more unpleasant possibilities surrounding the murder.

Marina stopped walking and looked at Ivan, searching his face to see if there was anything he was attempting to hide from her. She wondered if she could trust this huge American boy. Had he been planted in the seat next to her on the train? Was he going to betray her, and if so, to whom? Her mind was racing through the unmentionable scenarios

that naturally occur to those who have grown up in the days
of the KGB. They had changed the name to the FSS, but
everyone, including the Russian Mafia, still called it the
KGB. The Russian President, Vladimir Putin, was the former
head of the KGB, after all. Things couldn't be too different
now.

"How can you ask to me this question?" Marina said. "I
do not know about you, but I had nothing to do with death of
Akhmad."

Ivan realized he should have approached this topic a bit
differently, but the idea had overtaken him suddenly. He
should have respected the Russian propensity for creating
plots and recognizing the scheming of others. He was quite
familiar with this paranoid fear of the KGB from his
discussions with Russian émigrés in the U.S. He was
acquainted with many expatriates, so he knew something of
the Russian predilection for subterfuge. He didn't want his
relationship with Marina to devolve into one of mistrust. If
they were to work together they would have to have full
confidence in each other or they wouldn't get anywhere. He
took Marina by the shoulders and held her still.

"Marina Kortikuova, I swear to you that I am not an agent
or representative of any government, religion, or group.
Everything I have told you about myself is true, and anything
I tell you in the future will be true to the best of my
knowledge."

He took his right hand off her shoulder and held it up,
saying, "I swear this to you. Do you believe me, Marina?"

She looked up into Ivan's clear, unblinking eyes and
thought she saw there a truthfulness that gave her complete
confidence in him.

"I believe you, Ivan."

"Okay, then let me explain what I meant when I asked
you if you thought we could be in some way responsible for
what happened to Akhmad. You're a Muscovite who is
teaching Chechen students. There are separatist elements

here that might not like that very much. Although you're trying to learn to speak Chechen, you'll probably never be accepted as a Chechen. And you're not a Muslim, either. There may be people here who don't appreciate it that a Christian, and a woman, is teaching their young people."

Marina listened to him thoughtfully, but said nothing.

"In my case, I'm an American Christian, which to some Muslims is a double curse. I'm only going to be here for a short time, and in this short time I'll presume to know enough about Chechnya to write an article about it. Some people here might not like what I have to say. It could be the Russians, or it could be Islamists who hate me, and they might just possibly hate me enough to send me a warning by killing my friend. We might have been seen as having tainted one of their own. You, by making a Russophile of him, and me, because I was talking to him about freedom and Christianity and democracy. So, in the sense that we may be regarded as a dangerous twosome, we may have been sent a message to cease and desist."

"I don't know, Ivan. They must have had other reasons, too. What you say might be true, but you must remember that politics are complicated here in this part of world. People have secret agendas."

Just before they entered Marina's office, Ivan suggested that they search it to see if there were any electronic bugs. In his mind it was unthinkable that anyone would bother to bug the office of a lowly history professor, but they had to be sure from now on that they were not being monitored. Ivan opened the window drapes to allow as much light in as possible. Just as he was about to turn back into the room he noticed a tiny little microphone pinned to the top left corner of one of the maroon drapes. It was hidden behind the folds of the drapery, and could not be easily seen whether the drapes were closed or open.

The discovery, though shocking in itself, was doubly so when Ivan realized that the drapes in his hotel room were made of the same dark red fabric. It was not a big jump in logic to think that his room in the hotel was also bugged. He silently pointed the bug out to Marina. They tacitly agreed to leave it where it was. Ivan wrote a note and passed it across the desk to Marina. In it he told her that they should go to his room and to her apartment, to see if there was any place where they could talk without being overheard. She nodded in agreement.

He said out loud that he wanted to go to the library and continue his reading projects. Marina mentioned that she had to prepare a class, so she'd stay in her office. Ivan made a twiddling motion with his fingers to signal that she should walk with him. They left together without saying another word.

Once out on the sidewalk they headed for Ivan's hotel.

"We need to find out who our enemies are," Ivan said. "We have at least two things on our side. First, we're on to them, and they may not know it. Second, we're trained to use our brains, so we have a good chance of reaching the right conclusions."

"Be careful what you say, Ivan. These people are not so brainless. That is what makes them dangerous. They may seem like thugs and bureaucrats, but they are connivers."

"I suppose that's a form of braininess, but it has nothing to do with real intelligence."

"Well, I think you are breaking hairs. Right now I am interested to see if they have at least the brains of a bug. I believe that we will find that my apartment is bugged too. People who resort to this activity are of certain kind. They are suspicious, yes. But why? I think is because they are insecure. They are afraid to lose what they have, and at same time they fear change. In our context here in Grozny, who are these people? We have Russians. They do not want to lose Caucasus because they have already made big investment in wars to keep area and oil in Russian control. They do not want other republics to see that independence from Russia is good option, so they do not allow Chechnya to separate."

"As I see it," Ivan replied thoughtfully, "the Chechen people are locked into the middle ground of the struggle. They're torn between two great opposing forces. They'd dearly love to be independent from Russia, but if they were, they'd have to submit to fundamentalist Islam. They're just prizes in the game, and it's taking a terrible toll on them, as well as on the players from both sides. The contestants on either flank refuse to give up, so the Chechens are the pawns that will inevitably be sacrificed."

"What will happen to them, then?" Marina asked.

"Well, whenever a pawn, or a group of pawns, moves closer to the position of one side or the other, they become dangerous to the other side. You pointed out that Akhmad was tired of the fighting and was willing to consider the idea of Chechnya staying in the Russian Federation, as long as they were given a modicum of self-determination and some hope for economic improvement. I believe, from reading your book, that's the course of action you'd recommend, too. I suspect it's the American position as well."

"You are right. This is true."

Ivan moved on to the third force, the Islamist jihadists. "The jihadists want to spread their tentacles all over the world," he commented, "and they've done a very good job of it so far. About one billion people are reported to be Muslims, something like 20% of the world's population, and they're growing much faster than any of the other religions. The trouble with Islam is that you can't separate the religious from the political ideas. They have incredible hidden support from other Muslims who funnel oil money and weapons into the hands of their brothers in Chechnya. Although they certainly can't rival the sheer brute power of the Russian army, they hope to wear the Russians down with their freedom fighters, and with their dramatic bloody acts of terrorism. The Islamic idea is that the people with the most commitment will eventually win, and nobody is more committed than a suicide bomber."

"But there is more to it. Is very complex," said Marina.

"I know, I know. To the casual observer it looks as if desperation is the terrorists' main motivation. If you look a bit deeper, though, there are other things at work. When you consider what the relative costs of the 9/11 attacks were to Al Qaeda and the radical Muslim movement, we must admit it was the biggest bang for a buck in the history of warfare. They used our own American planes as their weapons. All they needed were sixteen men willing to die for Allah."

As they approached his hotel, he suggested that Marina wait outside. He explained that the hotel staff was no doubt watching him, and much as they would love to report to their leaders that he had taken a woman to his room, he didn't want to make trouble for Marina.

He searched his room for a bug, but found nothing, not even on the drapes. He went to the bathroom, washed his hands, looked around, and satisfied himself that both his room and bathroom were bug-free.

On his way back to the street he passed the desk and asked for his messages. He had one from Kahnsultan. He put it in his pocket, intending to read it later.

"No bugs," said Ivan, when he rejoined Marina. "They must have figured it was pointless to put one in my room. I live alone, and I don't talk to myself, so why bug it?"

"Maybe they think same thing about me," Marina said.

"Come along, we'll go there and check it out."

Marina's apartment was typically Russian communist in design and function. It was long on basics, very short on imagination, and bereft of luxury. The building was made of stone, but the creature comforts were from the Stone Age. Ivan had hoped that the post Soviet era architects would be more creative than their recent forebears had been. Marina's apartment, however, was an anachronism of design that traced its origins to the end of the 19th century tenements built to house immigrants in New York City. He guessed that the pendulum had swung to its maximum arc when architecture moved from the extreme extravagance of czarist St. Petersburg to the absolutely bare essentials of the Communist revolution.

As he looked around he realized how spoiled he had been all his life. He had always lived in comfortable accommodations; even his student rooms were more livable than Marina's little one-bedroom apartment. Ivan liked simplicity, but quarters like these reminded him of San Quentin. Shared showers without curtains and toilets without pull down seats were not high on his "A" list of interior decoration.

They carefully searched her apartment for electronic bugging devices. When they found none in the obvious places, they turned their attention to the ceiling light. Ivan was tall enough to reach the fixture, and there it was – a tiny receiver. Marina was glad it was not a camera as well. She had a momentary vision of some greasy slobs sitting around a TV screen looking her over as she dressed, and commenting on her body parts.

Ivan's thoughts were more practical. He wondered if the other professors who lived in the building were also bugged. It struck him as strange that the building lacked so many modern features, yet it was equipped with the latest in spy electronics.

"Kafka, cum Stalin," he thought. At least now they knew somebody cared.

They hadn't spoken to each other while they were inside the apartment. Neither of them wanted their mysterious audience to connect them to each other too closely, as it might hamper their investigations. So five minutes later they left the apartment and began a long walk around the city of Grozny. Occasionally Marina would point out some civic point of interest to Ivan, as though she were a guide providing tourist information to a visitor, but their actual conversation dealt with finding out who was spying on them. They had developed a companionable style of thinking out loud that seemed to work for them.

Ivan led off by listing some questions to consider. Of the three possibilities – the Russians, the Chechens, and the Islamist jihadists – which group was most likely to be interested in a relatively inconsequential and unthreatening person like Marina?

"It could be Russians," Marina said, "because they are familiar with KGB, so they have experience with bugs. But I think they are more interested in Chechen professors, not Russian professors. So why would they put bug in *my* office?"

"Maybe they bugged all the offices. That way when professors move around, they have all the bases covered. The same could apply to your apartment, too, where there are many professors living in the same building."

"Maybe," said Marina, somewhat dubiously.

"The Chechens are too disorganized to accomplish an electronic surveillance. If they had sufficient interest – a big *if* – they probably wouldn't be able to keep it from the Russians, anyway. After all, many of the people in power in the Chechen government are either Russian or Russian sympathizers."

Independence was in the heart of many Chechens, and the most zealous among them would look at Marina as just another advocate of the Russian position. As Ivan saw it, the Chechens had achieved as much independence as they could possibly get at this point. They had elections, representation among the other Russian Republics, a great deal of autonomy, and the Russians were guiltily pouring money into reconstruction and the upgrading of Chechnya. The squeaky wheel of separatism had gotten all the oil it could expect at this time. Total independence could wait until a more propitious moment, and in the meantime people could get on with their lives. Many Chechens felt this way about their situation, and more and more seemed to be coming around to this position.

"Recent elections have shown that majority of Chechens are tired of war," Marina said. "Chechens know Americans sympathize with cause of independence, but they also know that Americans will not help with troops, or weapons, or money. American policy is more concerned about America and Russia being on same side against terrorism than it is about Chechnya gaining independence. So Chechens not interested in bugs."

"That leaves the third group, the Islamist jihadists," Ivan said. "For them, the issues of governance and religion are intertwined. Islam and separatism are one entity as far as they're concerned. Extremists from this camp would certainly be interested in keeping an eye on everyone."

"I believe is so," Marina nodded.

"I had a meeting with Mansur this morning and…"

"What?" Marina interrupted him. "You talked with Imam Mansur? You did not tell me this!"

"Well, the subject never came up before," said Ivan, a bit defensively. "I wasn't trying to hide anything, though."

"Are you crazy?" Marina cried. "This Imam Mansur is dangerous man. He thinks only good infidel is dead infidel. Everyone knows he gives infidels one opportunity to accept Allah, and if they don't do this, he has them killed. Did he try to convert you?"

"Well, sort of, but…"

"And what did you say?"

"Bottom line? I said no, of course."

"Then he will have you killed, too. They will slit your throat, like slaughtered lamb. Just like Akhmad."

"But I couldn't just pretend to convert."

"I know. You don't have to explain. But we must be very, very careful now. We must watch everything we do. What did we say in my office before we found bug?"

"Ali. We were talking about the waiter at my hotel, a man called Ali."

"That's right. I said he was Muslim, and that Akhmad was killed by Islamist extremists because he was traitor to jihadist cause when he said that Chechnya needs agreement with Russians. But how else can there be peace? He only wanted peace. That was his terrible crime!"

"Imam Mansur claims that there can only be peace when everyone lives under Sharia law. I suppose the jihadists were furious when they found out that Akhmad was advocating the idea of living in peace under the rulership of infidel Russians."

"They saw him as traitor two times under," said Marina. "Traitor to country, and traitor to Islam."

"Two times over, you mean."

"What?"

"It's an idiom, I guess. We say *two times over.*"

"You can say what you like, but traitors work under the cover, not over it. They are deceitful, and they like to hide under and behind."

"So you think Imam Mansur was behind it, then?"

"He is behind everything. He is top leader in shadowy world of Islamist politics. He has more power than you can understand or imagine. He is dangerous man, and now bug has told him we know what he has done to Akhmad. We are in great danger. You should go home. Go home, Ivan. As quickly as you can."

"I won't go without taking you with me. I'm not going to let you face this danger alone."

"How can I leave job? How will I live? What will I do?"

"Leave it to me, okay? I'll take care of all the details. Just remember, as far as Imam Mansur is concerned, a good professor is a dead professor."

CHAPTER TEN

Ivan looked at the address on the card that Kahnsultan had given him at the breakfast table that morning. He remembered the street from the long walk he had just taken with Marina. He retraced his steps, walking more quickly now that Marina wasn't with him. He located Kahnsultan's bullet pock-marked building, found the listing for Akhmatov, and rang the bell. He was buzzed in, and a male voice directed him to go to the third floor at the back.

When Ivan arrived at the landing, he saw Kahnsultan waiting for him at the door of his apartment. He stepped inside, feeling as though he had been transported to a place straight out of the Arabian Nights. Cushions, pillows, and draperies were all in blended shades of brown and green. Ivan liked the upscale tent effect, although cushions on the carpeted floor were not particularly comfortable for a man of his size.

Kahnsultan, dressed in a white caftan, was as hospitable as any Arab potentate. When his host left to get the food, Ivan continued to look around. A large hookah stood like a silent sentry in one corner. An impressively carved ancient brass tray rested on the carpet, surrounded by a collection of throw pillows. Evidently it was there to receive the strong coffee that was usually served in small glasses in Arab homes or in their desert tents. The effect made Ivan feel that there ought to be belly dancers and concubines sprawled among the cushions.

Who was Kahnsultan, anyway? His name struck Ivan as some historical cross between Kublai Khan and an Ottoman emperor. Was he just a misplaced rich nomad merchant?

What was his relationship to Simeon Montcalf and the U.S. State Department?

Kahnsultan returned, carrying a hand-worked brass tray with several bowls and assorted implements on it. The meal consisted of the omnipresent lamb in a tangy sauce, some chureks, pita bread, and a huge bowl of goat milk yoghurt. Everything was excellent, and certainly of better quality than the restaurant food he had had in Chechnya. The yogurt, however, was quite tart, as though the starter needed changing. Ethnic yogurt-making involved using some of the previous batch to start the new batch of yogurt, and this could go on for months at a time. Ivan knew from his own experiments with making yogurt at home that one must use fresh starter on a regular basis, otherwise the yogurt becomes sour and develops an off-flavor from the accumulation of extraneous bacteria over time. If Ivan had been the yogurt maker in the family, he'd have changed the starter much sooner.

"Please tell me about your lessons with Imam Mansur," Kahnsultan said, as they were enjoying their meal. "Were you disturbed by anything in your meeting with him?"

"Not really," Ivan said. "I think I was actually a bit more concerned about your warnings over breakfast this morning. You described Imam Mansur as an extremist – a man whose purpose in life is to make sure that the world is eventually dominated by Sharia law. I had the impression that you felt he would stop at nothing, not even murder, to see that his dream is eventually realized. I hope I didn't misinterpret your meaning."

"No, you are quite right, I'm afraid. I am indeed saddened by the course of recent Islamist movements. There were certain times in the course of human events when leaders were faced with choices that changed the face of history. If Henry VIII had chosen Catholicism over divorce, the story of England would have been different. If the Pharisees had acknowledged Jesus as their Messiah, there would have been no Christianity. When it came to Muslim history, if Muhammad had delineated a clear system of succession there would have been no conflict between Shia and Sunni Muslim believers."

Kahnsultan hesitated, suddenly realizing that although Ivan was listening politely, he seemed restless and eager to have a chance to talk himself.

"I am being very rude," Kahnsultan said. "I apologize. I am an old man, and I tend to talk too much. Please tell me what has transpired in your fast-moving life since we had breakfast this morning."

"Well, for one thing, I had a long talk with my friend, Marina Kortikuova."

"The professor of Russian history, am I right?"

"Yes. She's worried that I might have gotten into some deep trouble with Imam Mansur because I criticized the veracity of the Koran, and I also made it obvious that I wasn't interested in converting to Islam."

"This could be a problem, depending on how much time the imam believes you need before you are convinced that Allah is the one true God and Muhammad is his prophet."

"Well, the other thing is, we discovered that Marina's office and her apartment have been bugged. But before we found out about the bugs, we talked rather indiscreetly about how we believed that Akhmad was killed by Islamist jihadists who might have thought he was a double traitor for appeasing the Russian establishment in Chechnya and for showing a low commitment to the jihadist cause. I suppose now they think they should kill us too, since we were close friends of his."

"This is indeed a dangerous situation," Kahnsultan said. "It needs to be taken care of by the right people. I suggest you call Mr. Montcalf right away."

Ivan looked at his watch. "It's one o'clock here. That means it's only six o'clock in the morning in Washington."

"I think you should call him anyway," Kahnsultan said firmly. "I would not like you to risk having your throat slit to protect Mr. Montcalf's early morning slumber."

Ivan looked dubious as Kahnsultan handed him a cell phone. He had assumed that only land lines could be made secure.

"Please don't worry at all," Kahnsultan said, noticing his expression. "This is a secure cell phone, and there are not many in Chechnya. Just press *One, Talk*."

Kahnsultan left the room so he could do the dishes and give Ivan some privacy.

Ivan held the tiny instrument in his very large hand, and placed the call. He soon heard Montcalf's familiar voice.

"How are you, old boy?" he said, jovially.

"I'm fine, just fine. How about you?" Ivan said.

"Dandy. Tell me what you've been up to in Chechnya."

"I'm in Kahnsultan's apartment. He just served me a very nice dinner in his elegant living room. I feel like a pasha. Have you ever been to his place?"

"I've been in several of them. They've all been very much the same. Kahnsultan is like an Ottoman Romanov. You know, an effete product of a regal bygone age that has been deposed by an ignorant bunch of ruffians. He himself is timeless; he would have made a good Roman senator. Kahnsultan has the reclining position mastered, and nobody appreciates the finer things more." Montcalf chuckled. "He may be from the old school, but he has character. We could use more of that these days. He is honorable, and totally reliable. You can trust him with your life. Now, tell me everything you've been up to lately."

Ivan told Montcalf that he felt that the trip had been very worthwhile and that he had found a thesis topic that would blow the doors off Harvard's Widener Library, but he needed to develop the idea more before speaking about it. Then he told Montcalf that he could use a little help.

"What can I do for you?"

"Well, it would be great if you could check out an imam I've had some dealings with. The name he's using here is Imam Mansur Shamil al Fatihoun. He told me he has an MSc degree in electrical engineering from MIT. Also, if you can find any information from people who knew him when he was in Boston, that would be helpful to me too. He may have used a different name then. In fact, I'd be willing to bet that the name he uses now is not his real name. The name *Mansur* means *Victor. Shamil* is the name of a famous early separatist leader. These two names together, therefore, seem appropriated to me, rather than conferred by family. He speaks Chechen, Russian, Arabic, and English. He's a striking figure. The title *Imam* in most cases means the prayer leader of a mosque, but it also can mean an infallible successor to Muhammad, or one descended directly from the Prophet, which would make him a caliph."

"A caliph, eh? I'll see what I can find out, and I'll let you know through Kahnsultan. Anything else?"

"One more thing. This place is totally paranoid. Just asking questions can get you killed. I told you about my friend Akhmad. The police thought I murdered him and I was arrested and questioned, but then they let me go. I also told you about his history professor, who might be in real danger. Someone has bugged her office and her apartment. Can you make some inquiries to see if we can get a visa for her to come to the States when I return? Please see if you can find her a teaching job. Things could get hot for her around here if we piss anyone off."

"What's her name?"

"Marina Kortikuova. I'll send you her CV, and perhaps you could forward it to potential employers."

"Hold on. How do you spell that?"

"K-O-R-T-I-K-U-O-V-A. We're pretty sure it's not the Russians who planted the bugs, although you never know. Can you check with them just to make sure?"

"No problem. Anything else?"

"I guess not."

"Okay, I need you to do something for me now."

"What is it?" Ivan asked.

"I'd like you to go to Tolstoi-Yurt. The Russians are building a new petroleum separation plant there in order to placate the separatists."

"They'll separate the petroleum for them if they promise not to separate the country," Ivan noted. "That's a nice one."

"It's their way of making amends for having blown the country to smithereens in 1999 and 2000. The Chechens are desperate for cash flow. The separatists are either waiting for a chance to blow it up, or else they're planning to work a little protection racket on the oil companies. We're not sure what they're up to. I'd like you to go there and size up the situation."

"It just so happens that Akhmad, the dead student, is from Tolstoi-Yurt. Marina and I are going to attend his funeral, so we have a cover story for being there.'

"Well, if you can find out anything, let me know."

"I'll do that."

"Tell Kahnsultan you'll need to use his phone a few more times in the next week. Call me any time you have something to tell me. I'll be working on your requests in the meantime. Take care of yourself, and your girlfriend. 'Bye for now."

Ivan said goodbye to his gracious host and made his way back to his hotel. To keep his mind off the possible peril that he and Marina were facing, he began to think about ways of bringing peace to the combatants in Chechnya. It seemed to him that the problems would probably be solved by attrition more than logic. After the uninterested but well-equipped Russian soldiers, along with their less numerous but spirited opponents, had exhausted themselves and lay panting in the streets of Grozny, perhaps then some not yet assassinated politician might remind both parties that dead people cannot be converted to any point of view, so everyone had better try making their arguments less strenuously. Ivan remembered how Akhmad had looked as he lay in the morgue with his blood-drained face emptied of any convictions, waiting to be buried along with his hopes and dreams.

"May I offer you some baklava and coffee?" said his kind host, interrupting his disturbing reverie.

"Thank you so much," Ivan said. "But it's getting late, and I have to leave early in the morning to go to Akhmad's funeral with Marina. But I'll come back tomorrow right after the funeral, and I look forward to that. Montcalf sends you his best wishes, by the way."

The next morning Ivan woke up feeling depressed. He remembered his destination, and thought how differently he would feel if he were going to see a live Akhmad instead of a dead one. He put on a clean shirt, located his darkest, most conservative tie, knotted it, and went across the lobby to breakfast.

Ali, the ever-present guardian of things culinary, seated him at his usual table. He mentioned that he had missed him at dinner the night before. He asked solicitously after his health, as though insinuating that if he didn't eat regularly at the hotel, he might very well start feeling a little under the weather.

"I had dinner at a friend's house, and I'm feeling fine," Ivan said reassuringly.

"I am glad that you have already made friends with someone you can visit," Ali said obsequiously. "And in such a short time, too," he added.

The bugging discoveries had pushed Ivan a long way down the road to paranoia, so he thought Ali might well be part of the massive effort to track his every move. He decided to find out what he could about Ali by keeping an eye on him in return.

At five minutes to eight, Ivan got up and walked to the hotel entrance. He was prepared to wait for Marina, but she was already waiting for him in an old red mini car called a Kompakt Nani. Ivan knew right away that he was in for an uncomfortable ride. The Ukrainian-manufactured vehicle was a "people's" car, meaning it was a cheap minimalist automobile designed for the common man, and Ivan was a lot longer than the commoner the manufacturer had in mind. He carefully folded himself into the passenger seat, just barely managing to close the door on his wide shoulders. With his knees under his chin and his head jammed against the ceiling, he was not going to be the poster boy for this car model.

They spent most of the trip talking about the industrial areas they were passing as they wended their way toward Tolstoi-Yurt. As he expected, Ivan was stiff from being cramped inside the Nani. When Marina found a parking space and pulled up the emergency brake, he had to struggle hard to wrestle himself out of the car.

Just as they started to walk toward the mosque on the other side of the square, a coffin-bearing procession of about fifty people turned a corner, heading in the same direction. Marina and Ivan joined the procession. The parade of mourners entered an outdoor courtyard, placed the wooden coffin on a table, and formed themselves into lines behind it. The local imam moved to the front of the lines, and stood before the coffin. He then recited verses from the Koran and said prayers in Chechen, which neither Marina nor Ivan understood.

After a time the pallbearers lifted the coffin and, followed by all the men, continued the procession toward the cemetery. It was apparently customary for only the men to attend the actual burial. Ivan decided to stay with Marina, and they followed the women out of the courtyard and up the street. The group made a right turn along the narrow stone road that divided the connected low residences on both sides of the street. Half a block further on they stopped by an ordinary building, indistinguishable from all the others. One of the women stood with her back to the door, receiving condolences from the group. She was obviously Akhmad's mother.

Marina and Ivan, who were the last in line, reached the grieving mother and did their best to express appropriate sentiments of regret. Marina explained that she was Akhmad's professor, and Ivan was an American friend from the University. The mother was hospitable in spite of her loss, and invited her son's friends to have tea with her. They tried to decline, but she was insistent.

"I can speak English," she said, looking at Ivan. "Not very well, but I learned it from radio. VOA, and BBC."

As she moved around making tea, she told them that her name was Sawdah, after one of the Prophet's wives. Ivan remembered her as the one Muhammad married after Khadijah's death, and mentioned that to Sawdah. She was surprised that he knew the early history of the Prophet of Islam. When they inquired if Sawdah had other children besides Akhmad, she told them that she had once had seven children, but now only four remained alive. Her husband and two of their sons had been killed fighting for the separatists against the Russians. Marina uneasily received this bit of information. Sawdah knew that her son's professor was a Russian, but she seemed to bear her no malice. She had come to the end of the hate boundaries.

"I have only one son now," she said. "I also have my girls, and now twin grandsons. I didn't believe that Allah wanted me to suffer any more. I encouraged Akhmad to go to university to learn how to make peace. And now after all the sacrifices my family made, they killed him."

Ivan looked down at this frail, suffering woman.

"The Bible says, *blessed are the peacemakers, for they shall be called children of God.* I am sure that Akhmad is one of God's children now."

He took the mourning woman in his arms and hugged her for a long time. When they separated they both had tears in their eyes. Marina thought that was a special thing for Ivan to have done, and her respect for the huge man increased.

As the afternoon light began to fade, Ivan and Marina took their leave of Sawdah and headed towards the new plant that was under construction in the outskirts of the small city. They could see the building from a distance, as it towered over everything around it. As Marina drove past the sentries, Ivan could see that they were bored young Russian conscripts playing at soldiering. Maybe they would never be battle tested. Ivan hoped this was the case, as he didn't think they'd stand up well against experienced, motivated fighters. He wondered if there were any young men left to fight on the side of the separatists.

As Marina bumped her way around the perimeter of the immense plant, she approached a building which seemed to be more or less completed. From the condition of the suddenly smooth road and the size of the huge gates, they deduced that this was the main entrance to the complex. As they drew nearer they could see that a large black car was discharging its four passengers at the gate. One of the four was a tall bearded man in a dark business suit and carrying a briefcase. The other three men were dressed in abas. They surrounded the businessman, looking alertly in all directions as they walked to the gate. As they got closer, Ivan, who had thought the man with the attaché case looked familiar, was now sure of it. It was Imam Mansur. What was he doing here? And out of uniform, so to speak?

There was absolutely no way that Marina could have stopped the car so he could have a better look. Not there, and not in these times. A suddenly stopped vehicle might well have spelled out "suicide bombers" to one or more of the boy soldiers. What little training these young soldiers had been given included a course in "hate-the-Chechens." As a result, if they had suspected that the little car contained terrorists, they would surely have killed the occupants before ascertaining who they were. It would not have disturbed them very much, either. Their officers would have praised them for their quick thinking, and rewarded them with some leave time and perhaps a bottle of vodka. The Russian military officers did not dare to make mistakes. As a result, everyone they killed was a Chechen rebel, terrorist, or spy, with no exceptions.

"Marina, that man at the gate was Imam Mansur."

Marina looked at Ivan with a quizzical expression.

"Why is he here?" she asked.

"I can think of several possibilities, but of course I don't really know anything for sure. Still, maybe he's here so they can bribe him not to attack this petroleum complex. Then again, maybe he's in league with the mafia, and they're paying him not to preach against them in his sermons in the mosque. Or perhaps he is being wined and dined by the Russians so that he'll support piping the oil to Azerbaijan according to their plan, instead of flowing it to Turkey so the Americans can control it."

"It seems strange to me that religious cleric is involved with political and economic affairs," said Marina.

"Ah, but when you consider that Muhammad himself was not only the head of state, but also the commander-in-chief of the military as well as Allah's choice as spiritual leader of the Islamic peoples, on top of which he wrote the Arab's book of business practices, then maybe it's not so strange," Ivan pointed out. "You realize, Marina, that imams are held by Muslims to be not only the prayer leader of a mosque, but also divinely sinless, and appointed to be a successor to Muhammad himself. Shiite imams claim to be in the direct line of the Prophet through Ali, who was Muhammad's cousin as well as his son-in-law. Most Shiite practitioners live in Iran and Iraq."

"And the Sunnis? What is their claim?" Marina asked.

"The Sunni's claim, since Muhammad had no living sons, is that their imams descend from the first caliphs, who were the first disciples of Muhammad, and were elected to the leadership of Islam. That's the main difference between the two divisions of Islam. Naturally different customs and practices developed in various parts of the world, but these are relatively minor. There seems to be a definite move afoot these days to bring Islam together. In any case, as any Muslim will tell you, they consider Muslims of the other sects to be brothers. They are closer to other Muslims than they are to members of any other religion. The Chechen people have been influenced by a mystical group of Shia Muslims known as Sufis, but they are Sunni nevertheless, as is 95% of the Muslim world."

"What do you think about all this?" asked Marina.

"I think that something very strange and odious is going on in Chechnya, and I don't believe it stops at the border. It has a far greater global significance than just Chechnya. I've also had another flash of intuition that expands my original hypothesis."

Marina looked at him with raised eyebrows.

"Let me put it this way, then. The central theme in the symphony of mankind is the search for power. We distract ourselves from the main theme by embroidering it here and there, but we inevitably return to the basic theme of man's search for the power to rule over his environment and his fellow men. In effect it's his attempt to be not only like God, but to replace God altogether. The cleverest themes of the power symphony are those that suggest that it's God's will that they take power in his name. They insist that we all behave as he wishes, which just coincidentally happens to be also to the advantage of the power seekers."

"Well, who are these power seekers?"

"There have been lots of them over the course of history, but the ones who have the very highest aspirations today... I suspect that they are a body of elected, self-sustaining caliphs that form a sort of council. This council might be located in Mecca, their holiest city—I don't know. But I suspect that these caliphs are patiently but incessantly exerting pressure on the population of the earth to grant them the power to rule. This council is content to make small strides when it can't make great ones. So long as growth continues they are satisfied to wait as long as it takes to complete their work. They'll be absolutely ruthless and feel completely justified in any action they take to push on with their plan of conquest. This group is committed beyond life and death. The little way stations of Chechnya, Afghanistan, and Iraq are relatively inconsequential as long as their universal plan continues and eventually succeeds."

"But wait. How do you know that the supreme power mongers in this world are Muslim caliphs?" Marina asked.

"When we see enough similar examples of behavior patterns over centuries of time and huge expanses of territory, we're forced to suspect that a coordinating force is present."

"If is true what you say," Marina commented, "it could have great influence on my field. So you actually think there is secret council of caliphs that pulls world strings behind scenes?"

"That's pretty much it," Ivan said. "But I'll have to prove it, of course. "Right now it's just a hypothesis."

Marina frowned and thought about all the things Ivan had just told her. What would become of him if he so much as mentioned the covert conspiracy of the council of caliphs? And what would become of *her* if she were known to have had a part in the development of his theory? In spite of her desire not to blame herself for Akhmad's death, she still wondered if she was in any way responsible.

Ivan read her mind. "Dangerous, isn't it?"

"Yes," she said with feeling. Her blue eyes were on the road, but the tears in them were for her young student, now in his plain box in the ground.

"Have breakfast with me tomorrow, Marina," Ivan said, hoping to cheer her up. "Come to my hotel."

"All right. I come at eight o'clock."

They fell silent as they continued their drive back to Grozny. Marina grieved for the Dudaev family, while at the same time her troubled thoughts dwelled on the future of the world. She had visions of a large feline prowler crouching in the shadows, ready to pounce on a wobbling globe. Ivan, for his part, was thinking of his second dinner invitation with Kahnsultan.

Neither of them was thinking about the car following along behind them on the road.

CHAPTER ELEVEN

After Marina dropped him off at Kahnsultan's flat, Ivan rang the bell and got a weak buzz in return. He climbed the stairs to the third floor and entered the pasha's apartment, greeting the old gentleman with a hug. Both men were genuinely pleased to see each other.

"Here is my cell phone," said Kahnsultan. "Please sit down and make yourself comfortable. I will look after things in the kitchen while you call Mr. Montcalf."

It wasn't long before Ivan heard the familiar voice of his cheery sponsor.

"How are you, Welland?"

"I'm fine, thanks for asking."

"What are you up to these days?" Montcalf wanted to know.

"I've just come back from Tolstoi-Yurt. Marina and I attended the funeral of our friend Akhmad Dudaev, as I told you we would. We met his mother there. She's a Chechen patriot with not a trace of foolish fanaticism in her. She lost her husband and two sons in the fight for independence, and now another son is dead, for I don't know what reason. Even on the day of her son's funeral she was composed, hospitable, and had many intelligent things to say. She was someone special, and I'm glad to have met her. She's exactly the kind of Muslim who could easily make this a much better world."

"Dudaev, you say? Is her name Sawdah Dudaev?"

"That's right."

"I'm familiar with that name. It seems to me Dudaev was President when Chechnya tried to secede after the collapse of the USSR. He was killed later in the fighting, I believe. Could your friend's mother be his widow?"

"She is, but she never mentioned anything about her late husband. She lives very humbly now in a house that's only one step up from a hovel. There's something about her, though. She has a certain presence about her. She gives the impression of being considerably more than her circumstances indicate."

"What else did you do in Tolstoi-Yurt?" Montcalf wanted to know.

"We went to the petroleum complex and drove around it. It's huge, and it's all walled in. There are armed sentries guarding the place almost every few feet. We were afraid to stop even for a minute, for fear they would think we were suicide bombers."

"Who was guarding the place?"

"They were mostly young conscripted soldiers. They seemed nervously trigger-happy to me. The only peculiar thing we saw was the arrival of a man and his bodyguards, who happened to be passing through the front gates of the plant at the time we were driving by. The guy was dressed in a business suit, and he was carrying an attaché case. There wouldn't have been anything unusual about that, except that the man was Imam Mansur."

There was silence on the other end of the phone, and then Montcalf spoke again.

"I had the boys at the CIA check him out. He seems always to be somewhere near the hot spots, wherever they are, but we have no hard evidence of his connections to any group. He's either very slippery, or it's a coincidence. What do you think?"

"This guy is no victim," Ivan answered. "He may have created some victims, though, but I'm not sure yet."

Something in Montcalf's voice indicated to Ivan that he was not divulging everything he knew about Mansur. He couldn't help wondering why, so he decided to dig further.

"What do you think the imam was doing out of clerical uniform, so to speak? And what was he doing going into an oil refinery? Why would a man of the cloth need three very large bodyguards? Why would the Russian managers of the oil refinery be expecting a visit from the leading Islamic cleric in Grozny? Are American interests involved in this refinery?"

"Slow down, slow down!" Montcalf exclaimed. "Those are good questions, Welland, but I haven't the faintest idea what your imam is up to. I'd be very interested to know, however, as you can readily imagine. Try to dig up anything you can."

"What about the oil?" Ivan asked.

"What do you mean?"

"Are we involved?"

"Of course we're involved. We're always interested in oil, no matter where it comes from. We need it to keep us going, and we need to know who has it. Our President can call the Russian President by his first name if he likes, but when it comes to oil, our two countries go separate ways. OPEC would love to have Russia join the organization. The Russians have their hands full with the Islamist terrorists, however, and I don't believe they'd be willing to give over control of their oil to any group that's strongly influenced by the Arabs. In any case, Chechnya is in the middle of all these issues. We'll talk about it when you get back."

"I look forward to it," Ivan said.

"By the way, I looked into the employment possibilities for your girlfriend, and I've got some good news for you. I spoke to the Chairman of the History Department at Harvard, and he'd actually be glad to interview her. One of their full professors suddenly died of a stroke, so they're in a tough bind. They need a one-year replacement as soon as possible. No promises, you understand, but there's a good chance they'll take her… if she can sell herself. Is she serious about this?"

"I'll have to let you know tomorrow. But meanwhile please take care of her travel documents, both U.S. and Russian. We have only eight hours in Moscow between train and plane, and I don't want to spend them dealing with the Russian bureaucracy. These documents are essential if we're going to leave this forsaken country. If I've done anything to make the cartel or the caliph or the clan mad enough to kill her for associating with me, then... well, let's not even think about it."

"Don't worry," Montcalf said. "I'm on it."

"I must tell you, Montcalf, that I get the feeling you sent me to Chechnya to be some sort of flak attracter, or possibly a sacrificial lamb."

"Now Welland, don't be churlish. We've subsidized your education, and when you get back you'll be seen as an expert on Chechen affairs. No doubt you'll have gathered enough material for an interesting article, too, or maybe even a thesis."

Ivan couldn't deny that he was getting very familiar with Chechnya and that the material would be essential to him when the time came for him to write about his experiences when, and if, he returned. It was the *if* part that bothered him the most.

"Tell me something," Ivan went on. "Did you find out if it was the Russians who bugged Marina's apartment and her office?"

"The Russians disclaim any responsibility for that. They told me, though, that they'd be interested in knowing who *is* responsible. They wondered if you could take the device with you when you check out. I think they want to see who made it. They probably think it's one of theirs that was sold into the black market by one of their own agents, and they'd like to find the operative responsible. That's the trouble with the Russians, my boy. You can't depend on them not to be entrepreneurs."

"That's ironic. I suppose they were well prepared by their communist system."

"They're starved for liberty, that's the problem. Anyway, call me tomorrow and let me know whether your girlfriend is coming to the U.S. with you. I'm going to ring off now. It's five in the morning here, and I'm going back to bed."

Ring off indeed. What made him use such a British term? Ivan wondered what Montcalf's background was, and what his job was, exactly.

Just then Kahnsultan returned with a tray of sandwiches and some beer for Ivan, as he drank no alcohol himself. The two of them spent the next hour happily discussing politics and religion, the taboos of all polite conversation.

"How much effect do you think the Arab influence on Islam has had on the religious practices in Chechnya?" Ivan asked him.

"Well, as you know, the origins of Islam in the Caucasus are Arabic, but I don't believe that Arabs today hold any sway over Chechnya's religious life."

"I think there might be more Arabic religious influence than you believe. After all, Islam uses the Koran as the inerrant textbook of life."

"That's true. But I believe that Chechens know more about the spirit of the law than the Arabs do. The Arabs are far more interested in the letter of the law and how it can help them get power over the people."

"I have no doubt about that," Ivan agreed. "By the way," he continued, "do you know if there's a central authority in Islam, like the Papacy for instance?"

"A central authority? You mean like the Caliphate of ancient times?"

"Yes, that's exactly what I mean."

"Well, my answer would have to be no. I've never heard anything about a central Islamic authority."

Ivan decided to leave it at that. He didn't want to discuss his theory of a covert caliphate with anyone yet.

He finally said goodnight to his friend and walked back to his hotel, conscious of everyone he saw on the streets. He didn't want to end up like Akhmad.

When he arrived safely at his hotel he went directly to his room, undressed and went to bed. His mind was full of the events of the day and the various implications of his theory. Eventually he drifted off to sleep in a miasma of troubling complexities.

Ivan was clear-minded again when he awoke the next morning. He wondered if his room had been searched while he was in Tolstoi-Yurt. If it had, he could see no signs of it. When the maid cleaned the room she could have searched it. But how would she know exactly what to look for? Could any ordinary maid read several languages and interpret what might be technically difficult material? What would she do with it, anyway? Scan it, take pictures, call the cops, what? If she were a spy, wouldn't she be underachieving during the time she was acting as a maid?

No, his room would have to be searched by people with higher skills. What would they be looking for? Ivan was a writer, not a smuggler or a foreign agent. They could search all they liked. He had no guns or explosives. It occurred to him that if he was supposed to be a writer, perhaps they wanted to see what he knew about them, and what harmful things he might say about them in the press.

The only things they would find in his room were a few books and a couple of translations of the Koran with some highlighted passages in them. Maybe they would think the passages contained coded information. He laughed and thought that would give the perpetrators something to work on, as the marked *Surahs* were those he had found to be most unclear or problematic.

"Let *them* wrestle with those verses," he chuckled. He had just reached the part in his thinking that suggested that the intruders might be there to plant something in his room, and not to find something, when there was a knock on the door. Ivan opened it, and found Ali standing there.

"Pardon me Mr. Welland, but your professor lady is here. I thought you would like to know."

"Why, thank you, Ali," Ivan said. "I'll be right along."

Ivan wondered how Ali knew Marina was a professor. He ran a comb through his thick brown hair. It helped a little, but he needed a haircut. He was considering whether to go to a barber in Grozny or wait until he got home to Cambridge. Either way, it was no bargain for the barber, he thought. He swung open the door and headed across the lobby to the dining room.

"Good morning, Marina," he said cheerily. "How are you doing today?"

"I am fine, thank you. We have much to talk about, ya?"

"Yes, but we can't cover everything here," he said. "By the way, did you happen to tell the waiter, Ali, that you were a professor?"

"No," Marina said, "I did not tell this to him. Why?"

"Well, he knocked on my door just now and told me that my professor friend was here."

"He said that your professor was here? I said nothing to him except good morning, table for two please," Marina declared.

"Well, evidently Ali thought you should not be kept waiting, so he dashed across the lobby and told me that *my* professor was here. He must be a romantic. I think we should encourage him. He's not the only one who has linked us in this way."

Marina blushed a little. "What do you mean?"

"People think we're seeing each other."

"What means this *seeing each other*?"

"They think we're lovers, or at least working up to it." He gave a little chuckle, as though he thought this was a silly assumption. He looked carefully at Marina to see how she would react to this information, but she was wearing her best inscrutable expression.

As Ali approached the table, Ivan reached across and took Marina's hand very firmly so that she could not have pulled it away even if she had tried. She did not try. He let her hand go so Ali could place the meal in front of them.

The gesture did not escape Ali's notice. Marina's response was another matter. Was she interested in him in that way? Ivan was shy, he knew that about himself, but he was a very good actor and other people usually chose to believe his acting. He looked across the table at her and waited until their eyes met.

"I think our investigation may go better if we pretend to be lovers," he said. "If public opinion in Chechnya is on the side of Cupid, why should we disappoint them?"

He thought he saw a tiny flicker of disappointment in her eyes. This game of pretending was probably not going to be easy if real feelings were involved. He thought he had put the situation in the best light. It was open-ended enough so that she could totally reject it if she wanted to. She could play along, or she could be serious. It was up to Marina. He leaned forward and spoke to her in a whisper.

"My source in the U.S. told me that Imam Mansur is, in fact, suspected of being connected to the Islamist terrorists, because he's always nearby when an attack occurs. But they have no real proof of his involvement."

"I see," said Marina.

"How serious are you about taking a job in the U.S.?" he asked her, in the same hushed tone. "We touched on the subject yesterday, and I took the opportunity to see if there are any suitable positions available for you there. My contact told me the chairman of the History Department at Harvard would like to interview you. One of their full professors died suddenly of a stroke recently, and they're looking for a one-year replacement right away. They'll pay your expenses."

"Really? Is this true?" Marina said, with a mixture of surprise and controlled excitement.

"Of course it's true. If you're interested in pursuing this position, you must let me know at once. You must also understand that this is an interview and not a job offer. If you decide to come to the U.S. with me, travel documents and transportation will have to be arranged. I must leave as scheduled in order to get back to my classes, so everything has to be accomplished within the week."

Marina, looking thunderstruck, stared at Welland. The whole course of her life would change drastically if she accepted his proposal. As she contemplated the effects such a move would have on her life, she wasn't sure if she was thinking about a leap of faith or a fall from a great height. She was a person who usually welcomed new challenges, but this one was as big as they got. Finally she achieved a modicum of dispassion and began thinking in practical terms.

Would she be cutting off her career in Russia? Not if she presented it the right way. She would emphasize the research aspects. She could say she was going to write a book analyzing the differences between the Russian and the American point of view regarding various historical events. Since she would not be draining the departmental budget of even one ruble, she thought she would be given permission to take a sabbatical on short notice.

The academic year was coming to a close, and there would be only two or three more lectures for her to give. One of her colleagues could be assigned to teach these classes. She would tell him that she would grade all the exam papers if he would just mail them to her. Her graduate students could get along for a while without her physical presence. They were all writing their theses anyway—all but Akhmad, that is. If she handled it properly she would not be burning her bridges.

On the personal level, she was single, childless, and had no reason to stay in Grozny or Moscow. Her relationship with Ivan was totally due to propinquity. Was it the planning of an unseen, all-knowing God that had put Ivan Welland in the seat next to hers on the train? If it was a plan, she could afford to let it play out a little further. After a couple of minutes, she broke the silence.

"All right, Ivan," she announced. "I will go to United States of America."

"Good," said Ivan, his eyes lighting up. He did his best to hide the excitement he felt when he heard that she was willing to go with him. "If we can get our chores done this morning, we should be able to have one of our long walks this afternoon."

Marina understood his meaning to be that they should not discuss other matters until they were in the open air. After Ivan had straightened out the bill with Ali, they got up and left the dining room. Ivan took Marina's hand in a casual way as they entered the lobby, but he was quite sure the nosy waiter had noticed.

As they strolled towards the hotel door, Ivan whispered to her that he would stop by her office at lunchtime and bring some sandwiches. Then, at the door, he firmly pulled her to him and gave her a kiss on the lips. She hadn't expected it, but he was so large there would have been no use resisting anyway.

"We mustn't disappoint anyone," he said in a low voice as he pulled away from her. "See you later," he added more loudly.

As they both went their separate ways—Marina to the University, and Ivan to Kahnsultan's apartment—Marina wondered if the kiss was a ruse or if it had lasted just an instant too long, indicating something more. She felt that as the "older woman" she should be in control of the situation, but this Ivan Welland was not easy to figure out. He was boyish, but at the same time manly. He was intellectually gifted and business-like about his ideas, but emotionally she did not know what to make of him. She didn't know if he was a typical American. Were they all so reticent? Marina did not have a vast experience of men, but she had known a few. Mostly they had been pushy. Even when they were trying not to seem too anxious, she felt they were guiding her persistently to the bedroom.

Marina went directly to her office. Everything seemed to be in order. Her papers and books were as she had left them, and so was the electronic listening device. She had two beginning history classes to teach that morning, but the material was very familiar to her. She had taught similar classes many times during her career, so she didn't need to prepare for these classes. She gathered up her notes and the textbook, and then walked purposefully down the hall to the chairman's office.

He was an ambitious man of very average abilities— another florid, vodka-drinking product of the Communist period. As an historian, he was more of a propagandist for the Soviet system than an actual scholar, but because his superiors in the education system trusted him not to be creative, he had risen to the limit of his capabilities, perhaps even slightly higher. As a result of his peasant background and his fondness for alcohol, he had begun to resemble a soft, aging potato. His rotund body, sallow complexion, and sunken eyes betrayed his self-satisfaction. The man was a joke, but he was a dependable joke.

Marina knew that she could get anything she wanted out of him, as long as she pointed out the advantages of her requests. She told him she would like to take a sabbatical leave in order to write a book, which would redound to the benefit of the university's history department's reputation. She claimed that she had been offered a one-year, non-tenured position as a visiting professor at the famous Harvard University. When she returned, her CV would reflect this fact, and would make his department look good.

She pointed out to him that her expenses would be paid by the Americans, and therefore his departmental budget would not be affected. She suggested that her colleagues could take over the few remaining classes of the semester. She would prepare the exams and grade the papers and mail them in so they wouldn't be overworked. The only slight problem was that she must be ready to go by the end of the week.

After a few moments of squirming and simulated pondering, the chairman agreed to let her go, providing she made it clear to the Americans that Russia was correct in its policies in Chechnya.

CHAPTER TWELVE

Ivan strode purposefully toward Kahnsultan's apartment block. He wanted to call Montcalf as soon as possible so he could make arrangements for Marina's departure. She thought of it mainly as an opportunity, but to Ivan it was an exit strategy, otherwise known as an escape.

He observed in the windowpane of a store that he was being followed. A short, overweight, middle-aged woman was trying to keep him in sight by propelling herself down the street as fast as her short little legs would carry her. Ivan lengthened his stride, and after a few blocks he lost her. He wondered if Marina was also being followed.

Ivan hoped Marina would not mind his suggestion that they pretend they were lovers so that the spies in their lives would not wonder why they were spending so much time together. His idea of a lie was to stay as close to the truth as possible. He wanted the vipers that killed Akhmad to think of him as a fool who had fallen for the first woman who came his way. He also wanted Marina to be regarded as a weak woman, not worth thinking about or killing. If they were seen as impotent, insignificant idiots, that suited him just fine. He hoped Marina would not mind being painted with this brush. If he was lucky, she would never know.

His mind was fully engaged in bringing order to a host of possibilities. His theories were equivalent in intrigue to the papacy of five hundred years ago. The web that his brain was spinning was as complex as that of any spider, visible only to him as the weaver of his as yet unrevealed theory about the council of caliphs. He wondered to what extent the inheritors of Muhammad's religion might have emulated the heirs of the Roman Catholic Church by trying to do the same things, but in a consciously different style.

He recalled reading somewhere that at one time there were only twelve cardinals. Even with this paucity of numbers it had taken them three years to elect one of them Pope. Ivan could see no reason why the Muslims might not have been equally testy about the governance of Islam. The advantage of having a single declared and recognizable head of the church in the person of the Pope was also its disadvantage; you knew whom to take orders from, but you also knew whom to assassinate, or whose death to patiently anticipate. Ivan had read that there was some controversy about the identity of those Popes who came immediately after Peter. It seemed appropriate, then, that Abu Bakr, Muhammad's long-time friend, should succeed him as head of Islam.

However, like the Catholics after Peter, the Muslims after Abu Bakr had disputes about who should lead the expanding new faith. The early Muslims and Christians had similar problems, but the Muslims had the advantage of six hundred years of observing the Christian mistakes before developing Islam. The Christian progression from disciples to the formal, centralized papacy is a well-documented passage. The spread of Islam, too, is historically understood in a political sense. Less well known is the internal system of governance employed by the Muslim clerical hierarchy.

Ivan felt this mysterious system of organization existed, but was intentionally kept secret. Logic told him that there were just too many similarities in policy among the Muslim nations of the world for it to be accidental. What was the organizational glue that kept the Muslims together? Ivan understood the Koran and the Hadith, (the sayings and actions of Muhammad). What he did not understand were the other two sources of Islamic Law, the Ijma (the consensus of Muslim scholars) and the Qiyas (new case law coming from Sharia judges). He didn't know how the information was disseminated from mosque to mosque, and from country to country. He didn't understand who decided policies that would affect nations, no matter what political system was in use. Yet he knew with every fiber of his being that there was a coordinating force at work.

Ivan believed that Muhammad knew all along that Islam could not survive if the commitment of its adherents was weaker than that of its Christian opponents. He made his canon as simple as possible so that the majority of Muslims could clearly understand it and practice it. He selected monotheism, settling on Allah (one of the many gods in the Ka'bah) to be the one and only God of Islam. He wiped the other idols off the face of the earth.

In order to avoid having any opposition on this point, he claimed to have received the rulebook directly from Allah. Only he could speak for Allah. He continued to simplify the doctrine for Muslims so the practice of the new religion was reduced to the five pillars of Islam. Now he had something sturdy to build on. He was a practical man, so he did away with those aspects of Christianity that were complex and could only be accepted on faith. So the resurrection, the trinity, and the concept of salvation by grace had to go. He needed his people to earn the right to Allah's approval and acceptance by doing what Allah's messenger commanded.

Ivan was certain that Muhammad and his acolytes must have known that in order to install the one true God, they must have a cadre of leaders that could direct Islam so it could overcome the infidels. It must have been at this point that the prophet had a revelation that is never spoken of by Muslims, yet Ivan knew from his analysis that it must have existed. The revelation was that the politics of Islam must be ruled by an anonymous small group of Muslim clerics, a sort of inner circle of caliphs who would never be identified or questioned. This secret group of powerful nabobs would implement their directives through the existing sheikhs, imams, mullahs, and tribal leaders. Using the authority of

Allah's name, the wealth of Islam, the wisdom of the council of caliphs, the guidance of the Koran, and the threat of terrible retribution, these leaders have built Islam into a world religion.

Ivan was quite sure that the latest terror tactics of Islamist extremists that led to suicide bombing had been designed by a centralized effort, and not by coincidence. The Arab press had invented the conspiracy of the Elders of Zion, and in so doing invited the question of a possible conspiracy of caliphs. If their Semitic cousins, the Israelis, had a secret plan to wipe out the Palestinians, why mightn't the Arabs have a secret plan to wipe out the Jews and the Christians? How else could the car bombings occur all over the Middle East? The knowledge of how to manufacture such bombs, and the ingredients necessary to make them, had to come from someone with the knowledge and ability to disseminate it—someone who had the wherewithal to buy weapons and explosives, as well as the organization to distribute them.

Who was that someone, and what was that organization? The only one in Chechnya that Ivan knew was the imam of victory, Mansur.

Could it be that simple? Or was it beyond good and evil? The establishment of peace and democracy in the world was clearly a multidimensional problem. The three monotheistic religions were battling for control of the hearts and souls of mankind. Intellectual secular humanists were arguing firmly that there's no God. Many other nations were seeking to perpetuate their authority over their people, some of whom wanted nothing more than freedom and independence. National economic rivalries were battling corporate interests. Rich and powerful people wanted to continue to hold sway over poor and powerless ones. Oil, needed for perhaps another fifty years until a new energy technology could be implemented, continued to be the lingua franca of the world. Human rights issues like equality for women, free elections, systems of modern governance, improved literacy and education—all these ideas competed fiercely for the attention of contemporary economists and politicians.

But the eternal conflicts always had self-interest as their cause, and violence as their effect. Ivan thought he could express the laws of human relations in the same way as the axioms of geometry, but he didn't have time right then. He made a mental note to develop this line of reasoning later, but first he had to finish his business in Chechnya. The plan for his doctoral thesis was developing in his head, but he didn't want to write anything down in Chechnya that could be found and read by anyone there. That was an issue of self-interest, too.

Ivan arrived at Kahnsultan's building feeling invigorated by his ponderings. He took the stairs two by two up to the third floor and knocked on the door.

His host greeted him at the door. Eager to get Montcalf working on Marina's arrangements, Ivan asked if he might use the phone again. Kahnsultan nodded and passed it over to him. As usual Kahnsultan headed for the kitchen while Ivan punched *Two, Talk* on the cell. In a minute Montcalf's unmistakable voice came through.

"Hello, Comrade Welland, how are you this morning?"

"I'm fine, Mr. Montcalf. I've talked to Marina, and she definitely wants to teach in the U.S. So could you please go ahead with the arrangements?"

"I can and I will," said Montcalf. "You are a fortunate young man and Marina is lucky too, for it usually takes a year or more to get an appointment to a professorship. The only one who wasn't lucky was the Harvard chap who died, leaving the Department of History short one person. Marina can get a one-year appointment immediately if she does well in her interview with the chairperson.

"Good. That sounds like just the ticket for both Marina and Harvard. We've got to get out of here soon. She's being bugged, as I mentioned before, and I think my room is being searched, too. I was followed today. Someone out there is interested in us. We're pretending we're lovers to keep them from taking an even more determined and paranoid interest in us."

"Why pretend? You're young and free, just make believe you're in Paris and have a good time."

At that point Ivan was concerned mainly about his exit strategy. He didn't like the fact that the train was just about the only way to get out of Chechnya. With no commercial flights, with checkpoints on all roads, with mountainous terrain populated with hostile tribal fighters, and with only a twice-weekly connector train to Moscow, it would be an iffy proposition to get out of Chechnya safely. Short of a military evacuation, Ivan and Marina would be stuck in Chechnya if they were detained by even one of a number of unfriendly factions.

"There are lots of hurdles and roadblocks in our way," Ivan grumbled. "It's going to be difficult to get out of here, you know."

"Don't worry, dear boy. Such are the vicissitudes of life. You'll be fine. When have I ever let you down?"

Ivan was not reassured by Montcalf's attitude.

"I might need some extra money in case I have to bribe my way around of some of those roadblocks."

"Just ask Kahnsultan for any reasonable amount of cash you need, and he'll give it to you without question."

"Well," Ivan thought, "at least Uncle Sam is consistent about continuing his policy of buying his way through the world."

Ivan guessed it was cheaper than fighting in most cases, but it annoyed him that the corrupt gangster nations and their minions were so adept at wringing those bucks out of the Americans. Whatever happened to Jefferson's policy statement, where he says, *"Millions for defense, but not one cent for tribute?"*

When Ivan and Montcalf finished their conversation, Ivan was more convinced than ever that he was on his own. He began to formulate a plan that he hoped would cover the bases of his retreat from Russia better than Napoleon had covered his.

Now that he was with Kahnsultan, he resolved to enlist his help in implementing his plan. When Kahnsultan arrived with his usual tray of excellent food, the two men sat on either side of the small table and began to talk.

"Mr. Montcalf said you'd be able to give me some cash to help get Marina and me out of the country," Ivan began.

"That is no problem at all," Kahnsultan assured him. "How would you like the cash? In twenty dollar bills?"

"That would be fine. A thousand dollars in twenties should do the trick."

"I shall give them to you before you leave."

"Thank you so much. Now, I have another question."

"How may I help you?"

"I noticed a copy of the Koran on Imam Mansur's table. It didn't look old, but there was something about its green cover and its general size and shape that communicated that it was different from the usual publications of the Koran, but not so different that it stood out. Anyway, are you familiar with the edition of the Koran that the imam uses?"

"This Koran that you speak of is a special version used by all the imams in the world. Apparently no one but an imam is supposed to possess or use this particular edition."

"Do these special Korans ever come on the market?"

"No, they never do. They're passed from imam to imam, and never fall into the hands of rare book dealers."

"Is it possible to find a similar volume somewhere?"

"Must it be a Koran?

"Not necessarily," Ivan said. "It would help if it were, but it should look as much as possible like the real thing."

"Do you want me to look around for such a book?"

"Yes, if you can. I'll need it as soon as possible."

"No problem. Is there anything else I can do for you?"

"Yes," said Ivan. "Do you think you could make me another sandwich? I'd like to take it with me when I leave. Also, I'd like to discuss some aspects of Islam with you."

"Fine. I would be happy to make you another sandwich. I'm pleased that you like my food. We Muslims are taught to be hospitable to everyone, strangers as well as guests. Now, what would you like to know about Islam?"

"I'd like to know why you seem so at peace with Islam, when all I hear from Islam is blood-thirsty diatribes against the Israelis and the Americans," Ivan said.

"We have our extremists, just as the Jews and Christians do, but they are in the minority. I, for instance, belong to a very large, peaceful segment of Islam called Ahmadiyya. It started in the late nineteenth century, in Lahore, Pakistan."

"Ahmadiyya. I didn't know it started in Pakistan."

"Yes, and we are also eager to get our message across to the rest of the world. We try to use reasoned arguments to convince human minds and hearts of the truth and beauty of Islam. We use Muhammad's other name, Ahmad, which symbolizes his tenderness and mercy."

"Yet a lot of terrorism is associated with Pakistan, too."

"That's true. Pakistan is home to the fundamentalist thinking that resulted in the Taliban, but the right wing Islamists never got more than 6% of the vote in democratic elections. There are 150 million Muslims in India, the largest Muslim minority in the world. Aside from a few local flare-ups, these people have lived in peace with Hindu neighbors for many years. So Islam *can* coexist with other religions."

Ivan had wanted to have a conversation like this with Imam Mansur, but it never came about because the cleric was totally convinced that his cause was right, and he was not going to listen to the other side of the argument.

"But this coexistence," Ivan observed, "can only happen in a democracy, as you said yourself. So do you think the problem with Islam is caused by lack of freedom?"

"Yes, I do. Lack of freedom combined with tyranny. Unfortunately the prophet of Islam gave his people a model of autocratic leadership in which he was the commander-in-chief, sole arbiter, and holy man. This example caused the twenty-two Arab nations to evolve various systems of governance that are more concerned with self-perpetuation than with solving their own problems."

"Do you think it's getting worse?" Ivan wanted to know.

"The Arab states have about 280 million inhabitants. If birthrates continue, there will be about 460 million by 2020. I read the UN's Arab Human Development Report, which analyzes this problem in a brutally honest fashion. It points out that the reasons that all Arab nations trail behind Spain in their GDP is due not only to soaring birth rates, but also to lack of freedom, a shortage of education, and the absence of women's rights."

"This report was prepared by Arabs?"

"It was. And for the first time it doesn't blame the lagging development in the Arab states on the Arab-Israeli conflict or on the Americans. It faces the fact that the Arab region has the lowest degree of freedom in the world in civil liberties, political rights, government accountability, and independent media."

"What about literacy? And the status of women?"

"Both are abysmal. The whole Arab world translates only three hundred books annually, while a small country like Greece translates five times as many. In spite of some progress, there are still sixty-five million illiterates, most of them women. The Arab world wastes half its potential productivity by keeping its women at home."

"Isn't it time that Islam had a reformation?"

"Yes, I believe Islam is overdue for a reformation like the one that brought reform to the Christian church. But this must come about from within. It can't be imposed. It will be hastened by tolerance, but the enemies of reform will be strengthened if outsiders bring pressure for change. There are strong proponents for change working within Islam right now, and I am sure that reform will come about as a result of these efforts."

"But don't you think the U.S. should continue to do everything it can to help the process of democratization?"

"On the socioeconomic side, if democracy succeeds in Iraq and Afghanistan it will be hard for the rest of the Arab states to ignore it. The hopelessness and poverty of the young people in the Arab world must be addressed, or disillusion and despair will create more Bin Ladens and Saddams. Our people have great abilities, and our lands contain resources, but our leaders have often squandered our wealth and let our people down."

"So isn't there anything that can be done about all this?"

"The bad news is that the Arabs have dug themselves into a deep hole, and it is going take a long time for them to dig themselves out. Islam is made up of people from many lands, not just Arabs, so you must not expect homogeneity among Muslims any more than you can expect it from Protestants."

"Why is it that terrorism is practically non-existent in the world except in an Islamist context?"

"Desperation must account for that," said Kahnsultan. "Muslims live under repressive regimes, where women are not empowered, and youth have no voice in their future. It is in this environment that the fanatical clerics can whip them into fighting frenzies, or give them visions of an immediate paradise if they become martyred suicide bombers. If we can change the political context in which Muslims live, we can change the way they act. You seem to insinuate that Islam is morally responsible for terrorism. I don't agree. If you hold that idea you must wonder why a professed Muslim like me is working with Mr. Montcalf."

"Well, it had occurred to me," said Ivan.

"I thought so. I would compare the situation of Islam in today's world with that of Christianity in Roman times. It took hundreds of years of miserable conditions under the heel of incompetent and immoral Roman Caesars before Christianity became the religion of the Roman Empire. During that period many were martyred in Christ's name. Some Christians did not rebel and fight the Romans; they patiently served by keeping the faith, waiting for the cream of truth to rise to the top. So it is with many Muslims. We live our faith, and wait for the awakening of others."

"And is the strategy working?" Ivan asked.

"Islam has now overtaken Catholicism, and it continues to grow stronger throughout the world every day. I believe Islam is bigger than politics, and it will succeed no matter which type of political entity rules it, and that includes Western democracy. As an example, how many mosques are there in the U.S.?"

Ivan thought for a minute. "Many, perhaps thousands."

"You see, we *are* invading your hearts and minds. We don't need bombs and armies, we need time. Democracy offers us freedom of religion, and I, and many Muslims like me, are content to take it."

"What about the terrorists, then?"

"The hot-heads among us are not content with small gains. They want everything right now, in a blaze of glory, but this is wishful thinking on their part. Allah's creation is a continuum. It took thousands of years to move from the Neanderthal caves to the cave on Mount Hira where Muhammad (praise be unto him) received the first Surah. Only Allah knows how long it will take for the true religion to be received by all his people."

"So the terrorists are on the wrong track."

"Yes, of course. You know this yourself. Allah wants converts, not corpses. Terrorists are acting out of anger. Their pride is hurt. They feel degraded, disgraced, and humiliated by the failure of their governments to bring them success in the modern world. But unfortunately they have chosen to buy into the propaganda of their leaders, who say the cause of their problems is the Israelis and the Americans.

A psychiatrist would say they are in denial. It is always more difficult to see your own faults than to see the faults of others. So these fanatics hate Americans more than they love their own hopeless lives."

"This is tragic," said Ivan. "A true Islamic tragedy, for both the children and for their parents, too. But tell me, Kahnsultan, do you have no family yourself?"

Kahnsultan grew pensive. "I had a wife and son once, but they were killed."

"Forgive me for asking, but how did they die?"

"They were killed in Iran during the Israeli bombing of the nuclear plant there some years ago."

Ivan looked thoughtfully at the kindly Muslim gentleman, understanding, at last, the cause of his sad demeanor. He must have wrestled with the impulse to hate those who had taken the joy out of his life. No doubt he had come to pacifism the hard way, by wrestling with his anger until forgiveness won out and gave him peace. Ivan respected Kahnsultan more than ever.

"What are you doing in Chechnya?" Ivan asked him. "Or to put it another way, why did you leave Iran?"

Kahnsultan did not seem to mind telling Ivan that his father, a Chechen Sufi cleric, had left Chechnya just before the Germans invaded in WW II. He moved to Iran to avoid danger and to avoid the religious persecution he believed would follow, regardless of whether the Germans or the Russians emerged victorious. He met his wife in Teheran and they settled there permanently, or so they thought. Then Kahnsultan came along, and later his younger brother. Eventually Kahnsultan grew up and married an Iranian woman, the choice of his father, as was the custom in Iran. She became his beloved wife, and bore him a son, and both were killed in the Israeli attack.

"Collateral damage, they call it now," said Kahnsultan, shaking his head. "I was away on a trip to Pakistan where I had been sent to buy equipment that was needed during the construction of the nuclear plant. After a long period of depression, during which time Iran overthrew the autocracy of the Shah and replaced it with the tyranny of the Ayatollah, I could stand it no longer and I decided to leave Iran. My father and mother had died of natural causes by this time. I inherited an old apartment in Grozny, which had belonged to my father's family back in Chechnya."

Ivan and Kahnsultan were sitting in this apartment now. Mr. Montcalf had known his father from international business contacts and had come to see Kahnsultan in Grozny years before. They became friends, and eventually Montcalf hired him to be a sort of friendly agent in Chechnya.

"Forgive me for boring you, Mr. Welland. Simeon, or rather Mr. Montcalf, may have already told you all this."

"No, actually he told me nothing about you. He just gave me your name and said you would contact me to see if there was anything I needed. He said I could trust you."

"It was nice of him to have confidence in me. It was also kind of him to allow me to use my discretion about meeting you. Unfortunately there are Muslims here, as well as every-where, who have chosen to construe the meaning of some passages in the Koran for their own violent purposes. These hard-liners would not pause for an instant to kill a fellow Muslim who stood in their way. I suspect that they were responsible for what happened to your friend Akhmad. We must take care not to share in his fate."

"I am against all killing on general principle, but when I am the scheduled victim I become enormously defensive."

"And so you should, Mr. Welland. So you should."

"I must go now. I've enjoyed talking with you."

Kahnsultan handed Ivan a paper bag with a sandwich, a piece of date loaf, and a roll of American $20 bills inside.

"I'll have a green book for you soon," said Kahnsultan. "I have a friend who binds books. I will have him make a cover just like the imam's Koran. Do you have a preference for what book should be bound by this cover, perhaps a Tom Clancy, or an Aidan de Vries novel?"

"It's a temptation," Ivan said, with a chuckle. "But I think I'll just stick with the Koran. It seems like the safest thing to do under the circumstances."

Kahnsultan smiled and nodded his head.

The two men hugged, and then Kahnsultan accompanied Ivan to the door. He watched the young American from his window as he walked quickly down the street.

CHAPTER THIRTEEN

After leaving Khansultan's apartment, Ivan headed for the University. Along the way he opened his lunch bag and pocketed the roll of twenties that Kahnsultan had given him.

It was lunchtime when he arrived at Marina's office. He knocked at the door, and was relieved to hear her tell him to come in. He realized that until they were out of this God-forsaken country he would continue to be anxious, always half suspecting that something was about to go wrong.

"Hi Marina," Ivan said. "I've brought you a sandwich."

"Mmm, is delicious. What is it?" she asked.

"I have no idea."

"You brought me mystery sandwich? How can you not know what is it?"

"A friend made it for me. I didn't want to ask."

"You are here for only one week and already you have ladies making sandwiches for you!"

"You are the only lady in Chechnya who has ever made me a sandwich."

"Ah, so cook is *man*. Then maybe you should introduce me to him. I need man who likes to cook."

"Let's go for a walk in the park," Ivan said, pointing to the microphone above and behind her chair.

"Okay, big American guy," she said playfully. "But I have to be back in one hour to teach my classes."

Ivan attempted to take her arm as they were leaving the building, but she shook him off. She didn't want anyone on campus to start a rumor about her and the tall stranger. Ivan, on the other hand, wanted everybody to think that they were lovers. Nothing in Chechnya seemed above suspicion, even a man and a woman walking together. He didn't know who liked intrigue more—Russians, Chechens, or Muslims—all he knew was that he detested it. But if he was to get some proof to substantiate his theory, he knew that he would have to play the game reserved for those whose business was espionage.

"Why are you being so quiet?" Marina asked him as they walked along. "What you are thinking?"

"I'm trying to think how to get a copy of Imam Mansur's Koran. His personal Koran."

"Are you mad? Why do you want his Koran? What is wrong with your own Koran? It is exactly same one."

"No, that's the point. It's not exactly the same at all. I've found out that there's a special one that's passed from imam to imam, and never sold on the open market. So I think it's possible that instructions to Muslim activist groups through-out the world are transmitted in a code that references passages in those special Korans that belong only to the imams."

"You think Korans of imams have secret code?"

"I'm not sure. I have no proof. But the only way for me to find out is to switch a similar Koran for a real imam's Koran, and that's what I propose to do. If I can smuggle it out of the country when we leave, I can have our cipher decoders examine it, and perhaps I'll finally have proof that a council of caliphs is pulling the terrorist strings all over the world."

Ivan was wound up again. He wondered why Marina had this effect on him. He wanted to convince her that his theory was right. He hoped he was clear-headed and fair-minded enough to value the truth more than the impression he was evidently trying to make on her. He continued on, outlining how there were too many similarities between the various terrorist attacks occurring in different nations for them to be simply coincidental.

"Take the Abu Ghraib prison in Baghdad, for example," Ivan said. "How could forty to sixty insurgents show up all at the same time to attack the prison without directions from a command and control center? They had to be organized. Fifty or sixty heavily armed men with RPGs, automatic weapons, and car bombs made it through the crowded Sunni neighborhood without attracting attention. How do you suppose they did *that?*"

"There must have been collusion by citizens."

"Exactly. The attack continued for four hours. Four hours! That many men firing for that long would need a truckload of ammunition. Eighteen U.S. servicemen were wounded in this battle, as well as several Iraqi prisoners inside the jail."

"Russian military tell similar stories of their encounters with Islamist insurgents," Marina said.

"I'm sure they could. But how do these terrorists always have weapons and explosives? Where do they get them? This kind of stuff is not available at an Army Navy store in the U.S. or in Russia. Yet the list of places where a car bombing or a suicide bombing has occurred is as long as the membership of the UN."

"This is true."

"We may not have found weapons of mass destruction in Iraq," said Ivan, "but what we did find, and what we're *still* finding, are what amount to masses of destructive weapons. Isn't that essentially the same thing? They definitely have enough weapons in Iraq to kill masses of people. But where do they come from? Who sells them? Who pays for them? These arms dealers, whoever they are, should be tried for crimes against humanity."

Ivan told her about an article he had read just before leaving the U.S. which claimed there were 39,000 Madrasa schools in Pakistan now. The young people emerging from these schools would have no knowledge of anything except the Koran, and would therefore be ill-prepared to participate in the modern world. They would no doubt end up parroting their teachers, and blaming the world's problems on the Americans and their allies. Iran has 50,000 pledged suicide bombers in their army. If there was anything that he and Marina could do to expose the fraudulent, hate-filled mendacity of this portion of the doctrine of fundamentalist Islamist extremists, then they had to find a way to do it.

"What you think we should do, then?" Marina asked.

"We'll do what we were educated to do. I'll write a thesis about Chechen culture and literature, and get my PhD. You could write a history of Chechnya, if you want to. We'll publish them in our respective countries, and we'll try to shed light on some very arcane, evil forces that need to be driven out into the open where they'll be exposed to the sunlight."

"I meant today, and tomorrow."

"Well, right now we should be packing our bags," said Ivan soberly. "We both should be ready to go on a minute's notice, so pack as little as you can. Take only a few clothes and whatever papers are absolutely necessary."

"What about books?"

"You'll have access to any printed matter you need, once we get to Harvard. So clean up your apartment, but leave enough stuff in storage to make it clear that you'll be back after a year. But for now, once you've packed what you need and you feel you're ready to leave everything else behind, come to my hotel for dinner. And be prepared to stay the night."

"What is this all about?" Marina said, a bit huffily. She had spent her life getting to a position where she seldom had to take orders from a man, and never from one younger than she was. But some of Ivan's instructions sounded more like orders to her.

Ivan knew his thoughts were running ahead of his ability to express them as clearly as he would have liked. He knew he was being a bit curt with Marina, and he wondered if he did this with other people as well. His mind was racing ahead. He would try to be more patient. Perhaps too much ego and self-confidence was his fatal flaw. After all, Marina could not know what he was thinking.

"I'm so sorry, Marina. I didn't mean to sound like a drill sergeant, but I'm a little distracted right now. I'm going to take something that doesn't belong to me. Furthermore, I'll be stealing from someone I think is very dangerous. If I'm lucky, the theft may not be discovered for some time. But if I'm not lucky and the theft is traced to me, I'll be in very serious danger.

"I don't like you to be in danger."

"And I don't want *you* to be in danger, either. So I'm trying to protect you by having some plausible way of explaining our relationship, so I thought it would be a good idea to use love as our excuse for being associated with each other. I hope you can understand why it's important for us to have the kind of cover story that will appeal to the prurient natures of those who pry into our personal lives. I'd like them to think we're getting on the train to Moscow to have a romantic tryst. If they suspected we were leaving with a copy of their stolen code book, they'd be a bit more antagonistic than if they believed we were just a couple of immoral infidels. Do you agree?"

"Yes, I agree," Marina declared. "But it seems little bit melodramatic. On other hand, I remember Akhmad, who never harmed anyone, and yet they slit his throat. He was Muslim, too, so I can imagine that to kill infidels like us would be easy for them."

"My sentiments exactly," Ivan said.

Their wanderings had taken them back to the University grounds. Ivan put his arm around Marina's shoulders as they approached her building.

"See you tonight," he whispered, and headed off to his hotel. Marina went up to her apartment to get ready.

During the time she was packing her things, she had plenty of time to think about Ivan and what was happening between them. Their original meeting had been a totally random accident, and she had not considered it in any way a romantic one. In the early stages it was their age difference that had prevented her from moving beyond friendship. After they had shared some experiences, however, she had grown to like and respect him as a person. Staying overnight in his hotel room, though, would definitely move things to another level. Yet she had agreed without protest, and she was trying to understand her motives.

In turning over in her mind what possible reasons she might have for giving herself to this foreign boy, she considered the physical side as honestly as she could. He was certainly not unattractive, though his height might be awkward for her to deal with. Marina had not had sex in more years than she wished to count. She had been approached, but not by anyone she wanted to be involved with. She felt herself to be a normal woman, and she did want to enjoy sexual relations with a man, but over the years she had become very selective in choosing a partner.

What it came down to for Marina was not a matter of sex at all; her decision was based mainly on the character of the man in question. She asked herself if she believed that Ivan was kind and honorable. When she decided her answer was yes, she asked herself what tangible evidence she had to support that opinion. She thought about their time together and how he had always behaved like a perfect gentleman. He had been respectful, considerate, generous, and cheerfully pleasant at all times and in all circumstances. As far as character was concerned, Ivan was more honorable than any man she had ever been even remotely interested in, and he towered above them in more ways than one.

She continued to mull over Ivan's good and bad points. Marina liked his personality. He was funny and intelligent. His only bad point was his age, and maybe that was not so bad either, as he probably wasn't going to present her with a long, dark history with women. What Ivan said and how he behaved indicated that he was certainly mature for his age.

She had not given much thought to the ticking of her biological clock, but now that her mind was on the subject of sex, she began to think about it seriously. If she was going to have a child she would be well advised to start soon, but there had been a distinct shortage of husband material in her life up to this point. She considered Ivan as the possible father of her child, and the more she thought about it, the better she liked the idea.

When Ivan arrived at his hotel he went to the desk clerk to see if he had any messages. He really hadn't expected any, but there were two. He went to his room and opened the first one. It was from Kahnsultan, notifying him that his book would be ready to be picked up any time after ten the next morning. The second message was written on the back of a business card from a Mr. Wilson Bagwell, Chairman, Alpha Group Energy Corporation, United States Division. The message said, *"Mr. Welland, please meet me in the dining room at 5 p.m. It is important."*

His curiosity piqued, Ivan decided to meet this man, if only to find out how Bagwell had heard of him. He reviewed the possible ways that might account for the fact that a total stranger was summoning him to a meeting in a place like Chechnya. He looked carefully at the man's business card. He worked for an energy corporation, which to Ivan's way of thinking was a euphemism for an oil company. Up to this point Ivan had not yet met even one other American in Chechnya, so it had to be more than a mere coincidence that an American oil man should come out of the woodwork to seek him out. Ivan's paranoia had just deepened due to this new layer of complexity. He felt he had to sort out the under-lying motives of all the participants in order to understand the labyrinthine nature of the political forces vying for hegemony over the Caucasus.

The political view of the Chechens was simple enough to understand. For most of the local people it was a question of freedom. Language, geography, ethnicity, and history demanded that the people of the Caucasus region be a separate entity. The Chechens believed the oil in the Caspian Basin belonged to them and should be used to fuel the economic development of their region. They had the example of the dissolution of the Soviet Union foremost in their minds. Many nations had sprung from that convulsion. Why should the Chechens be any different?

Ivan also thought he understood the Russian position, which was that the mountainous region of the Caucasus was a part of Russia, and the oil went with the territory. To appease the residents of the area, they had allowed them to be a mostly self-governing republic within Russia, but the issue of independence through secession was unthinkable. The Russian politicians were suffering from the ego-crushing experience of the breakup of the Soviet system and their fall from superpower status. They were not going to tolerate any more nationalistic defections.

American interests in the area had everything to do with sourcing oil for their vast industrial needs. The U.S. was no doubt interested in having a new supply source to rival the Arab oil cartel and keep the price down through new com-petition. If they could tweak the Russian bear's nose while obtaining the oil, so much the better. This was how Ivan saw it, anyway.

The wild card in this situation was Islam. Ivan was still not certain what their position was, although he harbored a great many suspicions. The more the various players tried to hide their real agendas, the more Ivan worried about the outcome of their talks. The Arab leaders had squandered much of the wealth they had gained from their oil resources. No new oil discoveries were being made in their region. It was possible that the finite supply of oil and the eventual run-out that must inevitably occur was at last beginning to be understood by the sheikhs.

Ivan felt that this might account for the desperation that was evident in the terrorist attacks of recent history. But was it the flailing of a body in its death throes, or was it a coordinated, aggressive plan for the future takeover of the minds of men by bloodthirsty conspirators? Ivan was mulling this over when five o'clock came around. Time to go and meet Wilson Bagwell.

Ivan recognized Bagwell instantly, though he had never seen him before. It was not a great accomplishment, as there were few well-dressed American executive types in the country, let alone in this one dining room. He went immediately to the oil man's table and introduced himself.

Bagwell was not a small man by any means. He was over six feet tall, and very broad. He looked about fifty. His face was even-featured, but it was hardened in a gladiatorial fashion.

"A line backer," Ivan thought, as he grasped the wide hand that had been extended.

The two men seated themselves across from each other. Their pleasant expressions did not completely cover up the competitive measurements and calculations that occupied their thoughts beneath the gentlemanly surface.

"I'll come straight to the point," Bagwell said in a hearty voice. "I need an interpreter to help me through a meeting that I'm scheduled to attend. I contacted the U.S. State Department to see if they could recommend someone, and Simeon Montcalf called me back and gave me your name."

Bagwell listed the biographical details of Ivan's background that had been supplied to him by Montcalf.

"So," Bagwell continued, "I'm prepared to offer you $2,000 to verbally translate the proceedings of an oil supply negotiation that is scheduled for tomorrow. So are you interested?"

"I'd be happy to take you up on your offer. Where does the meeting take place?"

"At the Grand Mosque in Grozny, two o'clock sharp."

"I'll be there," said Ivan.

Ivan had been thinking for days about just how he was going to steal the imam's Koran. This providential meeting would give him the opportunity he needed to switch the books, although the exact moment of the switch would have to be determined later. Meanwhile, he looked forward to observing how these big international oil deals were conducted. The two men agreed to meet the next day in front of the mosque at 1:50 p.m.

Ivan returned to his room to wait for Marina. He lay on the bed, thinking of the physical details of the imam's office. He wondered if he could arrange to be seated near the right hand corner of the large desk nearest to the Koran. Would the imam have cleared his desk off prior to the meeting? If so, would he, Ivan, be able to locate the volume? He decided that the imam would leave the Koran in an obvious place on his desk, as the mere presence of the volume would add the lofty authority of Allah to his role as negotiator for the oil interests of Islam.

It seemed strange to Ivan that a cleric would even be present, let alone be a participant, in such a high-level business meeting. This would never happen in the U.S., but it was not a problem for those adherents of Islam. After all, their beloved prophet had often presided over such matters. Perhaps the imam's purpose for being at this meeting was to act as a mediator between the parties. Ivan visualized the stern, bearded visage of the imam, and thought how unlike a mediator he really was.

Bagwell had told him that the attendees at the meeting were to be, in addition to the imam, the Russian Minister of Energy, the leader of the insurgent Chechen Independence Party, the head of the Grozny Energy Company, and a mysterious unallied Russian. Ivan was entertaining himself by imagining how this disparate group of strongmen could ever be in the same room together, let alone negotiate an oil deal. Bagwell would have his hands full with this cast of characters. He wondered if Bagwell would be wearing a bulletproof vest to the meeting. Even more, Ivan wondered if Bagwell would bring along a vest for him, too.

His thoughts were interrupted by a knock on the door. It was Marina. He let her in, noticing a whiff of cologne as she passed by him into the room. This was the first time he had ever detected any scent on this usually intentionally asexual woman. He tried to resist drawing any conclusions about her cologne. He quickly suggested that they go for dinner.

Once out of the room, Ivan took her arm and guided her across the lobby to the dining room. Ali, the omnipresent waiter, tried to seat them at their usual table, but Ivan told him that he wanted a little more privacy that evening. As a result, they were seated in the back of the room at a table against the wall. Ali quickly appeared with wine, opened the bottle, and poured two glasses for them.

"I have good news," said Ivan, leaning close to Marina. "Tomorrow I'm going to earn $2,000 because I had a Russian grandmother. Is your Russian grandmother going to provide you with an equal opportunity?"

"What you mean by this? I do not understand you," Marina laughed flirtatiously.

"My grandmother taught me to speak Russian, and now I'm going to be paid to use that skill tomorrow at an oil conference. I'll be doing some simultaneous translations."

"That is very wonderful, Ivan. This will buy you many chureks."

They laughed and chatted, ordered dinner, and drank the wine as they went over their departure plans for the next day.

Ali, who was hovering around nearby, thought these two foreigners seemed like an old married couple. Where was the heat in their relationship? He knew they had known each other for only a few days, so how was it that they were so comfortable together? He wished they would do something so that he could report it to his supervisor. Ali's career as a spy would never advance if all his surveillance subjects were so composed and dispassionate.

After collecting for the dinner check, Ali watched with narrowed eyes as the couple crossed the lobby, went into Ivan's quarters, and closed the door firmly behind them.

CHAPTER FOURTEEN

When dawn came, Ivan opened his eyes wide and found he was looking down at the top of Marina's tousled blond head. She was curled up against him, still asleep. He began to gently untangle himself from her, intending to let her sleep a bit longer while he got up to take a shower. In spite of his good intentions, Marina woke up. Realizing he was trying to get out of bed, she playfully grabbed a handful of his hair and pulled him back down beside her.

"Do not try to sneak away," she said. "Come back."

What Marina needed was a reality check. She was not sure that the night before had been real, or that her memory of it was true. Because of Ivan's youth, Marina had not expected that he would, in one unforgettable night, redefine her womanhood and provide her with a completely new understanding of the joy of sex. Would things be the same in the light of day as they had been in the dark? She was a mature woman at the height of her sexuality. She needed to be certain that what she had felt the night before was indeed something special. She wanted to know that it was not the wine, or the sexual deprivation over a long period of time that had made her respond this way to a man as young as he was. Ivan was more than happy to prove to her once again that the joy of their relationship was real, even in the light of day.

After their morning ablutions, Ivan and Marina walked across the lobby to the restaurant, chatting contentedly and looking like any ordinary couple going to breakfast. Ali held Marina's chair for her as she sat down. He knew she'd spent the night in Ivan's room, and he had already reported this fact to his superiors. He was thinking how nice it would have been if they had been authorized to capture on video the activities in their room. He would have enjoyed watching that, but unfortunately these people were only important enough for audio surveillance, not video camera observation.

"I'm going to get that look-alike Koran from my friend," Ivan said in a low voice. "I'll need to have it with me this afternoon when I do my gig as a translator."

"I will be in office, finishing last day of work," Marina said. "Is Friday, so is end of workweek and last day before beginning of sabbatical year."

"Thank God for that," Ivan said happily.

Marina ran her foot up and down his leg under the table. "I am so very glad to go to America with you," she purred, "especially since we have reached new level of personal understanding. Come to my apartment after your meeting this afternoon. I make you nice dinner. Maybe we can raise eyebrows in my apartment block, now that we have already done so at your hotel."

Ivan chuckled and readily agreed to assist her with this project. They ate their breakfast hungrily, but dawdled a bit over their coffee, as they didn't really want to separate.

Finally Ivan called for the bill. Ali had a dirty, knowing little smile on his face as he brought it to the table. Ivan would have liked to wipe that smile right off his smug face, but he chose instead to show his displeasure by leaving a smaller tip than usual. He wondered if the insensitive little snitch would even know why his tip had been reduced.

They left the dining room hand in hand, speaking to each other softly. In the lobby Ivan saw Wilson Bagwell, no doubt on his way to breakfast in the dining room. Bagwell nodded, and visually appraised Marina's physical attributes in a less than subtle fashion. Ivan threw him a stylized gesture of salute in recognition, but he inwardly felt the first pangs of jealousy.

Once they were on the street, they kissed and went in separate directions—Marina to the university, and Ivan to Kahnsultan's apartment. As he walked along, his mind was on Marina and on their relationship. When he had first encountered her in the seat next to him on the train to Grozny, he assumed that she was too old to be interested in him. The age difference, plus the fact that she was very professorial in her demeanor, had led him to dismiss the idea of being close to her. He had felt like a college student on a spring break overseas. She had seemed like a self-confident woman of the world traveling on business.

Yet things had turned out very differently from the way he had expected. On the subject of love, neither one of them was an expert, but it seemed to him that their roles had been reversed. He was now the experienced man, and she the timid girl.

This was quite different from Ivan's previous experiences with the opposite sex. From puberty onward he had always needed the intellectual company of persons older than himself. Yet it was incongruous to be using his mind to solve difficult quadratic equations, and then moments later be participating in some inane bit of flirtatious nonsense with a teenage girl. As a result he had been between a rock and a hard place when it came to matters of the heart. But Marina had turned out to be the answer to his problem. He never would have imagined on the train that they would end up in bed together. Ivan guessed that she was equally surprised.

"God works in mysterious ways his miracles to perform," he thought, quoting to himself one of his mother's favorite sayings.

Marina, meanwhile, was busy bustling around her office packing her personal things, writing notes to her students, and generally clearing up the various the details concerning her imminent departure. Thoughts dealing with the apparent randomness of life occurred to her as well. Who would have guessed that sitting next to a boy on a train would result in the changes in her life that she was now about to embark upon? How could she have known that this boy would turn out to be more of a man than any she had ever known before? What a wonderful surprise! She felt blessed that he seemed to be so attracted to her. Marina was used to thinking of herself as a woman who knew men, and one who could take them or leave them. In her career she had found men to be competitive, mean-spirited, and demeaning to women. The Russian men who had been interested in her seemed to fall into two categories. There were the ones who liked her because she had a steady job and could contribute to their life style, and there were the ones who were confident that they could subdue her independent nature.

Ivan, however, was unlike either of these types. He was interested in her career, and had helped her by actually going out on a limb to find her an exciting opportunity to advance it. He was not interested in money. He didn't try to dominate her. He was encouraging in every aspect of their relationship.

She had more or less given up on the idea of having children. Russian society was a mess, and Chechnya even worse, so who would want to bring children into these situations? Marrying some idiot she didn't love or respect just in order to have children wasn't her idea of a desirable family life. But at her age she knew that she had to think seriously about reproducing, or it would be too late. Was she crazy? She had only known Ivan for a few days, and already she was thinking about the unthinkable. She had successfully beaten back nature's imperative so far, and now she was having maternal thoughts for no reason except that she had been with Ivan. Was she weakening? She must be crazy. For the first time in her life she felt a strange physical sensation in her lower abdomen. The feeling was emptiness.

She knew without a doubt that she wanted to have a baby, and she wanted Ivan to be the father. Was it possible that he understood this about her without anything having been said? How could they have had unprotected sex in this day and age without a word of discussion? Ivan must have assumed that she was on the pill. He probably thought she was a much more experienced woman than she really was. She pondered her behavior for a while. She knew she had made no attempt to avoid getting pregnant.

His tail this time was a man. Ivan lost him by following a woman into her building, walking through the hallway and out the back door while his pursuer was locked out at the front door. Ivan wanted to do what he could to protect Kahnsultan. There were those who were so curious about Ivan's business that they tried to follow him everywhere he went. They might get interested in Kahnsultan if they found out that he was linked to him, and he didn't want to endanger his friend.

He was becoming familiar with Kahnsultan's building. He held the entrance door open for an elderly woman with a shopping bag who was on her way out. As a result he had not needed to ring Kahnsultan to gain admittance. He bounded up the stairs and knocked forcefully on the door.

"Who is it?" said a familiar voice.

"It's me, Ivan Welland."

The door opened a crack and an inquisitive eye peered out, making sure it was indeed Ivan who had knocked so officiously.

"Come in, Ivan," said Kahnsultan, holding a large, shiny black pistol in his right hand.

"Are you going to shoot me for being early?"

"Not this time," the elderly gentleman said. "You are looking particularly sprightly this morning. Have you been at the spa?"

Ivan was not sure if this question was a veiled comment based on some knowledge of his activities the previous night, or if he really looked healthier than usual. Either way, he did feel particularly well, and if that was in any way attributable to his night with Marina, then so much the better.

"I've never seen a spa in Chechnya," said Ivan.

"My boy, you can get anything here if you know where to look, and if you can afford to pay. But never mind that. I have good news for you. I have the book you asked me to get for you. I also received an envelope for you containing tickets and travel documents for a Dr. Marina Kortikuova. Evidently you are intending to export one of our professors to America."

He put the pistol in the pocket of the elegant jade-colored silk robe that he was wearing, and went off to find the book and the envelope that Ivan had come to get.

"I understand you are leaving Grozny tomorrow night," Kahnsultan said, when he returned with the items. "It has been a short visit, Ivan. Too short. I feel we could have had many interesting discussions if you had stayed here longer. By the way, I noticed how you looked at my pistol when you came in. Was that an admiring look? Would you like to have it? It is a very fine handgun."

He put the pistol on top of the green-covered book so that Ivan would have the choice to leave it or take it.

"I was just surprised to see it, that's all," Ivan said. "I have no experience with guns. I can't tell a Berretta from a Bazooka, but if you say so I'm sure yours is a good one. Guns make me nervous, though. When I was a kid, a child at my school was killed by a playmate using a pistol his father had left lying around the house. It was traumatic for the whole neighborhood, and gun control legislation picked up a few rare votes in Texas as a result of this incident."

Ivan hesitated for a moment and looked carefully at Kahnsultan.

"Do you have some hidden reason for offering it to me? I mean, you don't really think I need it, do you? If that psycho detective catches me with a gun, he'll arrest me for sure. I'm bound to be searched before boarding the train here, and again before getting onto the plane in Moscow. So it'll either be taken away from me, or I'll have to get rid of it before tomorrow night. I'm only going to be here for the rest of today and tomorrow. How much trouble can I get into in that short a time?"

"This is Chechnya, my boy," Kahnsultan said. "The current is running strong in these waters. Do as you wish, but if you take the gun you mustn't allow it to be traced back to me. I can assure you that any people here who wish to cause you trouble will be armed. This gun is only to equalize things."

Ivan still wasn't sure if Kahnsultan was offering him the gun because he knew something, or if it was just a safety precaution. His general inclination was to stay far away from any situation in which guns were involved, but the death of Akhmad changed things, and now he had Marina's safety to think about as well. At the last moment, just as he was about to bid Kahnsultan goodbye, he picked up the pistol, saw that it was loaded, checked the safety catch, and quickly put it in his pocket. He looked directly into the older man's eyes.

"Thank you, Khansultan. Thank you for everything," he said with feeling. "If it were up to just us the trouble between Islam and Christianity could be solved quickly."

He left the old man's apartment carrying the Koran, the tickets, and the gun, and headed back to his hotel. He felt relieved to get there, for he needed time to strategize before he left for the meeting at the mosque.

When he arrived at his quarters he found the door partly open. The maid was inside, making up the room. He had seen her once before. She was the same woman who had followed him until she couldn't keep up any more.

She pretended she had never seen him before. She spoke with a Russian accent, but she didn't sound like the other Chechens when they spoke Russian. Ivan guessed she was a native Arabic speaker. She excused herself and said she would be finished in a minute. Ivan waited and watched her puttering around the room. He had the distinct feeling that she was not a real maid. She was simply too inefficient. Anyone who had cleaned rooms for a living would not have needed to walk back and forth quite so much. Besides, she looked like one of Osama's forty-five sisters, and not like a Chechen woman.

"I have finished now, sir," she said at last. "I hope I have served you well," she added, closing the door behind her, sure that Ivan hadn't recognized her.

Ivan looked around the room. Nothing seemed out of place. If the bogus maid had searched the room, she must have finished just before he arrived. He was glad he was staying at Marina's that night. At least no one would have a passkey there.

He took off his jacket and hung it up. He carefully examined the copy of the Koran that Kahnsultan had given him. It was in Arabic. That was good. As far as Ivan could tell it was a dead-ringer for the one he had seen in Imam Mansur's office. It seemed to be a typical version of the Koran that could have been used to make the Russian and English translations that Ivan used. If he was lucky enough to exchange the books without being caught, would Mansur be able to tell the difference? He made a tiny, nearly invisible dot on the back cover with a pencil so that he could identify this particular book. Then he took the book and stuffed it into his pants under his belt along his lower spine. He walked around to see if it would stay in place. To his surprise, it stayed very well. That took care of the book problem. At least he hoped so.

Next, he began to think about whether he should take the gun to the meeting. He remembered the three goons who had accompanied Mansur in Tolstoi-Yurt. They would never let him into the meeting if they knew he was armed. But how would they find out? Would they pat him down? How could they do that without seeming overly suspicious? Maybe they would have a metal detector, but that was not likely, even though some mosques had been threatened in the past. Still, Mansur had been an electrical engineer earlier in his life, and being an important imam in one of the most dangerous places in the world, his mosque might be expected to be in the forefront of security technology. Ivan finally concluded that it would not be a good idea to walk into this meeting packing a gun. He wasn't sure how paranoid to be, however.

He decided to take a walk over to the mosque to look the situation over. The Friday noon service would begin in an hour. All over the Islamic world this was the one service of the week at which the imam always delivered a sermon. There would be crowds of worshipers everywhere. If he was lucky, perhaps he could find a hiding place for the gun before the meeting started.

Ivan put the gun in a paper bag. He stuffed the Koran into the back of his pants, tightened his belt, and put his jacket on. He looked in the mirror to make sure the book wasn't showing.

He left his room and walked to the mosque. Leshenko's man trailed behind at a safe distance, but Ivan knew he was being followed. He went all around the perimeter of the building, looking carefully at the details. He hoped he would not have to enter the mosque, as his height was just too obvious a feature. If he went inside, someone would be sure to notice him.

On his second trip around the outside of the mosque the eerie call to prayer from the minaret began. In no time at all people were coming from every direction, flocking to the mosque for the weekly high service. When the call to prayer began, Ivan looked up to see where the speaker was that amplified the call. As his eyes were returning to ground level he noticed the imam's office window. It was open for ventilation purposes. Just below the window sill there was a stone ledge that was part of the building's structure. Between the ledge and the bottom of the sill there was a space that was large enough to hold a small object like a gun. It would be nearly invisible from the street. The only problem was that the ledge stood about ten feet off the ground.

In a very short time the street had become deserted, since all the people were inside the mosque. Ivan could hear the imam beginning his microphone-enhanced sermon in the local Chechen dialect. He hoped he wasn't telling them to be on the lookout for a very tall American guy wanting to hide a gun in their mosque.

For the first and only time, Ivan wished that he had played basketball in school. He had heard that some of the guys in the NBA had standing vertical jumping skills up to four feet. He knew he was not one of those guys. He could touch the rim of the basket if he jumped as high as he could, but he had never been able to get above the rim and dunk the ball down into the basket. In order to place the gun on this ledge he would have to make the leap of his life. He walked around the mosque one more time. When he was sure he would be out of the view of the man tailing him for a few seconds, he took the bag with the gun in it and held it in his fingertips at arms length over his head. He bent his knees in a crouch and leapt straight up with all his might, and wonder of wonders, he was able to set the gun over the edge of the ledge—and it stayed there.

Ivan turned away from the window, very happy in the knowledge that he would at least have access to a gun in the unlikely case that he needed one. He was in the clear, unless Leshenko's man was taller than he was and could jump higher as well as see around corners.

He walked back to his hotel by a different route. He had gotten used to having the book pressed against his spine. It had stayed in place even after his record jump. If anyone caught him he would say that it provided support for his back and freed up his hands. He could say he used the holy book because of its curative powers. That might win him some points if his captors were Muslims.

When he got back to the hotel he asked if there were any messages. This time he had none. When he got to his room, the door was ajar. He opened it quickly and went inside. The same faux maid was there. She apologized again, saying that she hadn't wanted to bother him earlier when he was in the room, so she had departed before she replaced his soap. He knew this was a lie, but she handled it coolly, too coolly for a maid. He was very glad he hadn't left the book, the gun, or the tickets in the room.

He stretched out on the bed, closed his eyes and tried to think of all the possible things that could happen at this meeting. He knew he was going to be the least important person there. That might buy him a few seconds if violence broke out. He knew the layout of the imam's office, too. That might be worth something as well. He doubted that the others had ever been in Imam Mansur's private study.

Ivan felt he had to position his chair so it was nearest to the right hand corner of the desk as one faced it. That was the side where the imam kept his secret Koran. "Hidden in plain sight, like the Purloined Letter," Ivan thought.

If the imam left the room for any reason, Ivan would expect the worst. His plan called for him to pick up his chair and throw it with all his might through the window. On his follow-through he would knock the Koran to the floor behind the desk and dive after it. Once on the floor he would get on his knees and reach out the window to the ledge a few inches below and retrieve the gun. He would switch the books while he was near the desk. If all went well and he was still alive, he would either shoot his way out of the room or jump out the window.

The killers would not be prepared for either alternative, he felt sure. Granted, it was very risky, but it was a plan even so. Nobody but those in attendance knew that Ivan was at this meeting. If everyone died but him, nobody would ever know that he had even been there. The imam, of course, would not be dead, unless Ivan killed him. He didn't know if he could kill someone, but if what he suspected the imam was up to turned out to be true, this man would be number one on his hit list. If the hellish scenario Ivan was conjuring up turned out to be the real thing and he didn't manage to kill the imam, then he would be hunted down. Worst of all, Marina would likely also be killed if she was with him. He prayed that all the thinking he was expending on his worst-case scenario would prove to be unnecessary, and that the oil bigwigs would be able to divide the spoils peacefully.

It was time for him to go. He was nervous, but resigned and ready.

CHAPTER FIFTEEN

There was a knock on the door a few minutes before Ivan was ready to leave for the mosque. When he opened it he found a bellboy holding a package in his hand. He took the package, tipped the boy, and went back to his room. When he opened it he found another business card from Wilson Bagwell. On the back was written, "Wear this to the meeting."

"The guy must have an inexhaustible supply of these cards," Ivan thought grimly. "But I'm afraid he has only one grammatical mood—the imperative."

Under the card was what appeared to be a white dress shirt. He shook it out and held it up. Amazingly it appeared to be about his size. When he looked more closely he noticed that the shirt had several layers of fabric thickness in its front and back panels. The fabric was also strangely unfamiliar to him. It was woven very tightly and had a slightly metallic feel in the thickest places.

He took off his old shirt and hung it in the closet, then put on the new shirt. As he looked in the mirror, the location of the thicker panels told him that this shirt was some sort of bulletproof vest. He smiled when he remembered that the first time he met Bagwell he had wished for a bullet-proof vest. He thought he was being humorous, but he was actually being prescient.

He retied his tie and adjusted his belt around his waist to make sure that his holy spine protector was in place. He went to his bedside table and removed the rubles he had left in his Gideon's Koran, shoving them into his pants pocket. He didn't know if he would ever return to this room again. He looked around one last time to make sure he hadn't left anything important behind. Then he opened the door and turned to meet an uncertain future.

Ivan walked the familiar half-mile or so to the mosque. He waited for Bagwell by the main door as he had been instructed. In a few minutes a chauffeured car drove up, and Bagwell got out. The two men shook hands.

"Good, I see you got my present," Bagwell said. "It's the latest style in defensive clothing. Montcalf told me to make sure I didn't let you get killed."

"That was nice of him. And you, too. Thanks."

"No problem," Bagwell said. "Tell me, Welland. Would you like to have your clothes shipped back to the States? If so, it can be arranged. You might not want to go back to your hotel later."

"That would be fine," said Ivan.

"Good, then it's settled. If you give me your room key I'll arrange to have everything packed, and I'll pay your bill as well. I'll deduct the amount from your interpreting fee, as that's going on Montcalf's budget, not mine. I'm assuming you have another place to stay tonight," he added, with a suggestive, knowing smirk.

Ivan disliked his snide way of talking, but he gave his key to Bagwell, who then handed it to his chauffeur with a few instructions.

"You're right about tonight," Ivan said evenly. "I have a place to stay, and I leave on the train tomorrow night. When are you leaving?"

"Right after this meeting."

"How can you, though? The next train doesn't leave till tomorrow."

"I'm going by helicopter. I don't do trains any more."

Ivan liked the sound of that comment, not because he was impressed by Bagwell's self-importance, but because if there was going to be a chopper waiting for him, his company or the government must be assuming that he would be alive to use it. He hoped the same would apply to him, as well.

"Is there anything you think I should know about these negotiations?" he asked Bagwell.

"Only that this is not the first meeting we've had with these gangsters. It's the first meeting in this location, though. I was surprised when it was suggested as a venue. We in the West are of the opinion that a religious structure is a sort of sanctuary. In Iraq we learned that a mosque could also be an armory. In this case I suspect it's the latter, but let's look at the bright side."

"Which is?"

"That these bozos will take the billions of dollars that we're offering, and get fat and lazy. They don't have to like us to take our money, and we certainly don't like them. I'm bringing our last offer to the table today. It they're smart they'll take it, but if the crazies among them prevail, who knows what will happen? We know they're not stupid, but too often they let their fanatics dictate policy. You can't bargain too well with a bomb."

Ivan was quite sure that Bagwell had had more intimate relations with bombs than with women. The guy struck him as one part special ops, one part CIA agent, and one part linebacker. Ivan was much more cerebral than gung-ho, but in the end he had to agree with G.K. Chesterton, who once said that "My country right or wrong," is something no patriot would ever think of saying except in a desperate case. It's like saying, "My mother, drunk or sober."

Ivan worried that he was entering a Kafka-like labyrinth in which all the other characters were masters of deceit. Dealing with the devious was his least favorite thing to do. He was not looking forward to getting any enjoyment from knitting together a plan that would unite the diametrically opposed interests of those attending this meeting.

Ivan and Bagwell were patted down thoroughly by the imam's bodyguards before being allowed into the office.

These were the same men that Ivan had observed entering the huge oil separation plant with Imam Mansur in Tolstoi-Yurt the day of Akhmad's funeral. As he was the first to enter the office he sat closest to the desk, and closest to the Koran, which was in its usual place on the imam's left as he sat at his desk.

Bagwell sat next to Ivan. The chairs were arranged in a semi-circle, facing the desk. Ivan noticed that the window was open just as it had been before, so the gun on the ledge had probably not been discovered. While Bagwell's attention was riveted on the searches being done on the other people attending the meeting, Ivan stepped over to the window. He looked out. There were no people on the street. He could see the reflection of the office in the window glass. No one was watching him.

He quickly grabbed the gun off the window ledge, slid it out of its bag and into his right-hand jacket pocket, and sat back down. He had put a few hard candies in the bag with the gun for just this purpose. When Bagwell noticed him fidgeting with the paper bag, he offered him one of the candies.

"So far so good," he thought.

The other men entered the room a moment later. Ivan was glad he'd managed to get the gun before the meeting started. It would save him valuable seconds, and perhaps his life.

After everyone had found a seat, the imam swished into the room. Evidently Mansur thought he would seem more important if he came in last. Ivan had expected that as the host he would be there first, to greet and welcome the others. Evidently that was not the Arab way, or at least not the imam's way.

Ivan's mind was racing with possibilities, as the others made light conversation. His first thought was that the imam, dressed in his clerical robes, and hosting the meeting in a mosque, was trying to play the part of a peacemaker among the others. Ivan was not taken in. He believed Mansur was putting up a front. This religious holy man had been a tribal warrior in the desert, and Ivan felt his present position was a cover-up for the true soldier of Allah that he pictured himself as being. Mansur's name was a give-away, or so it seemed to Ivan. This guy was all about victory—total, uncompromising victory. He had the home court advantage, as he was the only one in the room who had not been searched. He was also the only one who had henchmen close enough to help him.

On Bagwell's left sat the Russian Minister of Energy, a chubby, self-important bureaucrat and high-level flunky. Ivan sensed that this man had been rewarded with his position for his loyalty to his leader more than for his ability. He felt his main motivation was to do nothing to embarrass the President. If he succeeded, he would keep his job, his beautiful wife, and his spacious house near the President's residence outside of Moscow. The Yukos corruption scandal had brought him to power. His job was to see to it that the new breed of Russian oil capitalists didn't walk off with the golden goose, in this case 100,000 barrels a day of Caucasian revenue-producing black gold.

Sitting next to him on his left was one of the worst of the Russian oil barons. He was trying hard to seem like a gentle-man. He was thin and tanned from having spent hours in the spas of the rich. He wore a very expensive Italian suit with a rose in his lapel. As opportunistic as any free-booting pirates in a bygone age, this robber baron and his ilk had managed, through shady privatizations, to gain control of Russia's oil businesses in just the few years that had passed since the end of the Soviet era. No wonder the Russian President was hard-ening his position against unbridled free enterprise. Twenty-four percent of Russia's gross domestic product was now in the hands of thirty-six billionaires. Moscow was now home to the largest number of billionaires of any city in the world. This robber baron was one of the chief offenders as far as the Minister of Energy was concerned. It would be interesting to see how these two enemies, who were sitting next to each other, would react during the negotiations.

On the other side of the robber baron sat the Chechen insurgent leader. The Minister of Energy was secretly livid at having to leave his gorgeous wife to come down to Grozny and sit down in the same room as this archenemy of the Russian State. Why hadn't the army been able to get rid of him? The Chechen insurgent leader was an idealist who wanted his country to be separate from Russia. He wanted an independent democratic Chechnya, and he was willing to die to get it. Ivan liked him, and thought him the best of a sorry lot of vultures wanting to pick the flesh of both Mother Russia and Chechnya down to the bone. The insurgent leader had been hiding and living a life on the run. He was gaunt, with a stubbly beard. He had dirty fingernails and poor, locally-made clothes. Evidently insurgency did not pay well.

The last man was a merciless racketeer, who headed up the Russian mafia. He was also the last man that Ivan would choose to sit next to, if he had a choice. He was the Slavic version of Al Capone. He even had a facial scar to complete the caricature. Organized crime was the result of the vacuum that existed between the time of the Soviets and the present capitalist system. The police were unmotivated and corrupt. As the space between the police state and the unpoliced state widened, unemployed workers and local tough guys joined together to rip off anyone they could. The Russian racketeer rose to the top because he could stomach anything, and he was smarter than most of the others. Nothing much ever happened in Russia unless the mafia was paid off not to interfere, and old Scarface was the man to see.

Ivan was deep in thought. He was thinking about each participant's motives and character to see if he could figure a way out of the complications they had gotten themselves into. Money was the obvious thread that wove these guys into a pack. Like the voracious wolves they were, each man in the room wanted to be the alpha wolf.

Ivan was brought out of his reverie when the imam called the meeting to order. Mansur greeted them, and took a few moments to outline the unsuccessful discussions of previous gatherings. He told them what they all knew, that this was the last chance for an amicable settlement. He suggested that each man present state his position on the disposition of the oil money. He asked them to do this in two scenarios—one if oil were permitted to flow through Chechnya to the Americans, the other if it flowed to the Russians. He asked the Russian Minister of Energy to begin.

The Energy Minister presented the Russian position, stating that the oil was in Russian soil, and that included Chechnya, which belonged to the Russian people. His government represented the people and his job was to defend their interests. The economic benefits of having the oil processed in Russia were frankly enormous, and it was unpatriotic to even consider allowing the Americans to get their hands on it. He said that the Caspian Basin had the largest known oil reserves outside the Middle East. It was estimated to be on the order of 200 billion barrels. He cited the fact that Russia had poured billions of rubles into its smaller republics to help them develop economic strength, and they could keep this up only if the oil resources were kept in Russian hands. He continued his panegyric to the Russian motherland, even though no one in the room was the slightest bit interested in his version of patriotism.

When he finished his opening statement, the imam asked the Russian oil baron to present the position of his company. The robber baron had become an experienced public speaker. He presented his case competently, stating that now Russia was a nation functioning in a free market environment. He explained that the best way to succeed was to allow the corporations to do what they do best. The inefficiencies of the communist system were legion, and private enterprises like his energy conglomerate were now clearly the way of the future. International oil companies functioned in the most modern countries in the world. The Russian Republics would not be able to move back into a leadership role among the nations unless they developed their own corporate entities. He told the others to keep in mind that oil in the ground is not gasoline. The oil must be processed before it becomes gasoline, and his company owned and operated the largest refineries in the area. He pointed out that the U.S. was planning to build a pipeline that would move the oil through the Caucasus to Turkey. If they were allowed to do this, he warned, the oil would simply pass through both Chechnya and other Russian Republics, and the economic spin-offs would be lost.

The leader of the Chechen insurgents spoke next. He would without doubt become President of Chechnya if his independence movement succeeded in divorcing itself from Russia. His army was strong enough to prevent any pipeline from moving through his territory. They were fighting for freedom. When they finally succeeded, it would be time to discuss who would pay the highest price for the oil. Russia deprives Chechnya of its right to be free, so Chechnya, in turn, will deprive Russia of Chechen oil. The Americans do not help Chechnya in its fight for freedom, so why should Chechnya care about their need for oil?

Ivan had been merrily translating the speeches from Russian to English so Wilson Bagwell could understand what they were saying. It was Bagwell's turn to speak now, so Ivan had to switch to translating from English to Russian. He was now delivering the American position.

Bagwell was blunt. He told them that the U.S. needed oil to keep its industries and its transportation system going. He pointed out that his company had already opened a pipeline across Georgia to the Black Sea. They had the experience and the money to do another pipeline across Chechnya. He stated that his company was in business to make money, and not to get involved in political struggles. His company was offering to undertake all the costs of building the pipeline, in exchange for exclusive rights to buy the product at fair market value. How the other interests around the table divided up the spoils was up to them. He reminded them that alternatives to oil as the primary energy source were coming along rapidly. If they didn't refine and sell their oil while they could, they might very well be stuck with it. His deal was on the table now, but Bagwell couldn't leave it there forever. He needed a go ahead in a month, or his company would move on and find other sources.

Ivan suspected that the American position, one that he was advocating by being Bagwell's translator, was at least partly a lie. He was sure that Bagwell was putting forth this position so that Russia would be forced to cooperate more closely with Eurasia, and therefore be kept out of OPEC. The organization of petroleum exporters controlled a huge portion of the available world oil supply. The Arabs controlled OPEC, and if Russia could be persuaded to join them, they would have a nominal monopoly of the world's oil. Then they could, if they wished, shut down the U.S. military/industrial complex. There were quite a few world leaders who would enjoy seeing the fall of the American empire. Ivan disliked that attitude because it meant the end of social and economic improvement. If winning is not accomplished by getting better, but comes about instead because the leaders are pulled back into the pack, then it's no longer a race, it's a stampede.

The next person to take the floor was the notorious Russian mafia leader. He said in no uncertain terms that no labor would be available to anybody unless his union was satisfied with the deal. Ivan translated his comments to Bagwell, who grunted that this gangster was like Billie the Kid demanding a government check every month in return for not robbing the mint.

Finally Imam Mansur rose to speak. Ivan was not sure what to expect. He put his hand on the gun in his pocket. The imam began by saying that his message was a religious one.

It came straight from the heart of Islam. The people around the table began to relax, thinking he was going to speak about matters of peace and compromise. What they heard was the furthest thing from peace that they would ever hear, and for most of them the last thing they would hear. He told them that Allah gives nothing to infidels, but gives everything to faithful Muslims. Allah offers everyone a choice to convert to Islam or die. Ivan's hand tightened on the gun.

Mansur was ranting about how these negotiations were an abomination to Allah. The selfish ambitions of men and nations are trivial in the eyes of Allah. All must bow down before the Creator and confess "There is no God but Allah, and Muhammad is the Messenger of Allah." He ordered everyone in the room to get down on the floor in the Muslim praying position. Everyone present was stunned, and nobody moved.

The imam reached into the folds of his aba and took out a pistol. Ivan could hear the sound of men approaching outside the door. Wilson Bagwell heard them, too. He pretended to move to the floor, but he never went all the way down. The imam's attention was divided for just an instant. Ivan pulled out his gun and shot Mansur twice in the chest at close range. Then he dove under the desk, as he had rehearsed it over and over in his head, taking the Koran with him. He switched the books, then he picked up the desk chair and hurled it through the window.

Bagwell ran over to the door just as the first bodyguard entered. He grabbed the man's gun hand and slammed it backwards into the doorframe, breaking the guard's wrist. With his right hand he held the man's throat and crushed his windpipe. He picked up the gun that the guard had dropped when his wrist snapped. Bagwell quickly crawled around behind the desk. In the time it took him to do that, the remaining two guards shot everybody else in the room with their automatic weapons. Then Bagwell shot the two guards from his kneeling position.

"Bagwell! Follow me!" Ivan called out to him, jumping out the window.

Bagwell was right behind him. Ivan knew exactly how far down it was, and he landed well. Bagwell landed harder.

"You okay?" Ivan asked him, stretching out his hand.

"I'm fine," Bagwell assured him, lumbering to his feet.

The two walked away from the mosque as unobtrusively as possible, acting as though they were engrossed in their conversation.

"You were great, kid," Bagwell said.

"Don't tell anyone that I shot Imam Mansur," Ivan said hastily.

"Don't worry. Nobody will ever hear it from me. Listen, you want an airlift out of here?"

"Do you have room for Marina, too?"

"Marina, is that her name? She's the one I saw you with in the lobby of the hotel?

"Yes, and we could sure use a ride out of here."

The mounting pressure of being followed, bugged, and interrogated was making Ivan feel uneasy. Montcalf had told him the Russians had denied being responsible for bugging and tailing him. That was an outright lie. He felt Inspector Leshenko had shown an instant dislike for him, but he had no idea why. If he were to be in any way connected to the incident at the mosque now, he and Marina would never get out of Chechnya. It was a good thing that they had train reservations. Leshenko would check and find that tickets were issued. He would have to assume they were on the train to Moscow.

"Sure, kid, we can take her." Bagwell held the door of his car open. "Get in and we'll go pick her up. I can take you as far as Moscow, then you can get a commercial flight home."

Ivan was relieved that he and Marina were going to be able to get out of Grozny immediately. He was not a big believer in luck or good fortune, but he was profoundly grateful to be walking away without a scratch from a gun battle in such close quarters. By his count, eight men had just lost their lives. Perhaps it would be more accurate to say that eight men had been shot. He couldn't help hoping they were dead so nobody could ever place him at that horrible scene.

He was sure that his mind would be on instant replay for a long time to come, even though that was the last thing he wanted to think about. The two bright red blood spots that stained Imam Mansur's blazing white robe, and his contorted facial expression when he realized it was he, Ivan, who had shot him, would be permanently etched on his memory.

What was it all about, anyhow? The questions remained unanswered. Who would control the oil? Would Chechnya be a free, independent nation? Would Russia continue to dominate the Caucasus? Would terrorists continue to operate in Chechnya? Everything was in the same mess as before, only now eight more men were dead.

PART TWO

Cambridge, Massachusetts

CHAPTER SIXTEEN

After a turbulent but uneventful helicopter ride from Grozny to Moscow, Ivan thanked Wilson Bagwell for getting them out of Chechnya safely and landing them with all their baggage right at the departure terminal of the Sheremetyevo 2 International Airport.

"My pleasure," said Bagwell, as they shook hands and said goodbye. "Take care kids, and have yourselves a safe journey back to the States. If I didn't have to stay here in Moscow on business, I'd go right along with you."

Ivan didn't show it, but he was profoundly relieved to be leaving Russia without repercussions from the Grozny Grand Mosque incident. As they were walking through the terminal he noticed the newspapers were all carrying stories about the shootings. It was a hot issue all over Russia by now.

When they got to the check-in counter, Ivan was notified that a certain Mr. Wilson Bagwell had requested that they be bumped up to first class.

"What a guy!" exclaimed Ivan, as the attendant handed them their tickets and checked their baggage. "You're going to love this, Marina!"

They passed through security with no problem. Ivan had been a little worried about this, as he was still carrying the stolen Koran tucked into the back of his belted trousers. He knew the metal detectors couldn't pick it up, so he felt pretty sure that he would pass through the electronic arch without setting off any alarms. But if someone happened to notice it and questioned him about it, he would say he was using it as a temporary support for his back, which had been bothering him lately. Everything had gone smoothly, however, and no explanations were required.

Now they were sitting in the boarding area holding hands and waiting to be called to the flight that would take them to the United States. Ivan was closely examining Marina's hand, which was large and strong for a woman. Her healthy nails were short, well trimmed, clean, and unpolished. Her fingers were slightly longer than average, and with nicely squared tips. He loved her hands. He thought they were beautiful. They spoke to him of her capability, practicality, and honesty. They were feminine, but not fragile.

He was just getting ready to study her palm when from the corner of his eye he saw two men in the uniform of the special anti-terrorist police approaching the boarding lounge. They started at one end of the room, examining the papers of those preparing to board the nonstop flight to New York. Two by two they quickly looked at the passports and travel documents of the passengers. They were obviously looking for a particular person. They were coming closer and closer to the seats that Ivan and Marina were occupying. Ivan feigned calmness, in spite of the rapid beating of his heart. He was glad that he hadn't told Marina anything about his part in the mosque affair. That way she could act genuinely surprised by anything the police might say.

The police approached a dark-haired man with a bushy moustache who was sitting several seats away. They looked at his papers, and told him to please follow them. Evidently they had found their man, and Ivan managed to relax.

When they boarded the airplane, the first class flight attendant directed them to their seats. "God bless Bagwell," Ivan said to Marina, as he sank into the wide seat. The flight attendant asked them if they would like some champagne.

Ivan said *yes* for both of them. He didn't see the man the police had been questioning, so they must have stopped him from boarding. Was he a known terrorist, a bomber, maybe?

The engines were roaring and the aircraft was backing away from the terminal when the champagne arrived. They were told that the hors d'oeuvres would be served as soon as the plane took off. The huge plane rolled along the runway faster and faster until it lifted off at an amazingly steep angle for a plane that heavy. They were airborne, and Ivan's mood soared along with the plane. He had had his adventure in Chechnya, and it was time to go home. He had the copy of the Koran, but he had not had time to study it. He was eager to see if he could figure out how the Islamist jihadists might be using these Korans as code books to coordinate their efforts to rid the world of infidels.

He was also looking forward to finding out how his new approach to Russian language-teaching was progressing. He needed to write his thesis proposal so he could get his topic approved. He had promised Marina to co-author an article with her on the topic of modern Chechen history and politics. He had promised Montcalf a written report about his findings and reactions to the situation in Chechnya. He was also eager to show Marina everything that was great about the United States. He needed her to be happy in America, because he certainly didn't want to live in Russia. Those were just some of the things he had to attend to when they got home.

Marina was hungrily munching on the appetizers. Ivan advised her not to fill up too much on the starters or she wouldn't be able to eat her real meal when it came. He thought she might not realize how much food is served in the first class cabin of an international flight. They really hadn't eaten properly for two and a half days, so they were hungry when the lobster bisque was served with some warm rolls. Then along came a Caesar salad, followed by filet mignon, accompanied by mashed herbed cauliflower and petit pois. They had a white Riesling with the soup course, and a sturdy

Cabernet with the meat course. For dessert there was straw-
berry shortcake. Coffee and an aperitif finished the meal off
in grand style.

"I have never had so marvelous meal before," Marina said
enthusiastically. "My belly is so full, I cannot believe there is
not baby in there!"

Ivan showed her how to recline her seat. He asked the
flight attendant to bring pillows and blankets, and he put one
of the blankets over her.

"It's not quite as good as a real bed," he said, "but it's
heaven compared to sitting up all night in tourist class. In the
morning we'll land in New York."

Marina answered him with a gentle snore.

It was still dark when Ivan and Marina were awakened by
lights and some fussing in the galley. Marina went to the
head. When she returned she told Ivan how impressed she
had been with all the soaps, lotions, tampons, towels, and
bathroom articles that were crammed into such a tiny space.
He got up and took his turn in the bathroom. When he came
back there was orange juice and coffee waiting. Omelets,
toast with butter and jam, and more hot coffee came along in
short order.

"You'd better not get used to eating like a commissar," he
said quietly, "because when we get to New York we'll be
treated like peasants. The flight to Boston only takes an hour,
so we'll be lucky to get a bag of pretzels and a Coke."

The dawn had come, and it was a clear day. Ivan leaned
close to Marina to enjoy the view of New York City from the
air as the plane circled to make its landing. Commercially-
minded people appreciate large, crowded cities because there
is a greater market there for their wares. But Ivan's view of
them was more romantic, almost religious, a kind of *City of
Zion on a hill* idea. He saw cities as the central bastions of
thought, the hubs of human institutions, and the places where
civilizations gathered to put their stamp on history. In the
hubbub of a city there was always a chance that human

synergies will lead to great things. Ivan liked cities, and to him New York was the living mother of all cities in our age. That no doubt explained why the Imam Mansurs of the world hated it so. They wanted Mecca to have the honor of being the greatest city in the world, and they were prepared to tear down all the other cities in order to bring this about.

"We'll explore New York some other day," Ivan said to Marina. "Our connecting flight to Boston is scheduled to leave in an hour, and the gate is pretty far away."

"Is pity," said Marina, with genuine disappointment. "It is hard to see famous city from air and then not have time to know it on ground. I can tell it has great, pulsing spirit. I would like to be completely enveloped in it."

Marina was clearly star-struck. Ivan was glad she felt that way. He wanted her to love the U.S.A. Mansur was afraid that the American lifestyle would come to dominate his culture, but that was because his world called for Muslim domination under Sharia law. The ideal of the melting pot was a concept with acceptance and tolerance at its center. It didn't demand the obliteration of all other ideals. Peace through submission: *Islam.* Peace through love: *Christianity.*

Ivan sang his version of *On the Road Again* (*On the Plane Again*) to Marina as they prepared to board the plane bound for Boston. She didn't know the original song so she missed the humor, but she was surprised at how beautifully Ivan sang. She thought how wonderful it was to be in love, and to be finding talents and depths in her man that she didn't know existed.

They sat in the plane in their usual places, she by the window, and he with his legs in the aisle. Having been with Ivan constantly for several days, Marina realized what a lot of discomfort he had to endure because of his size. Nothing seemed to be made to fit him. She resolved to take his height into consideration when she did any planning for their homes in the future. She would play in a giant's house, and not in a doll's house. She was looking forward to seeing his "digs," as he called his apartment. Marina knew, as everyone does, that you can tell a lot about a person from the way he lives.

The plane landed at Boston's Logan Airport. They picked up their luggage at the baggage carousel, and Ivan loaded the suitcases on a cart and wheeled them to the taxi stand. He told Marina they could take the MBTA (subway) train to his apartment, but he thought they had done enough traveling in crowds for the time being.

They stood in the taxi line, and when their turn came a yellow cab pulled up, the trunk lid popped open, and a little middle-aged man wearing a turban came around to help with the bags. Marina almost laughed aloud because it was so funny to think of this man, who was half Ivan's size, helping with the luggage. Ivan gave him his address in Cambridge and the driver took off at break-neck speed. Twenty minutes later he pulled up to the curb in front of a small, nondescript apartment building.

Ivan and Marina trudged up the stairs and stood by the apartment door while Ivan fished around for the key. When he finally managed to open the door, they pushed themselves and their luggage through the opening, entered the hallway, and closed the door behind them.

Marina looked around the one-bedroom, one-bath apartment, trying to take it all in at once. It was a typical Boston apartment, with a large living room and a dining alcove at one end. It had a small U-shaped kitchen with an open space and a counter. It was adequate, as Ivan had told her, and he was right when he said that she wouldn't be able to escape from him in these "digs." Fortunately, she thought, she didn't want to escape.

Ivan had a workstation along one wall of the living room. He would rig up a similar station for her in the bedroom. That way they wouldn't distract each other when they were working. He cleared half the drawers in the dresser so she could put her clothes away. They could share the bedroom closet, which providentially was quite large. Coats, boots and shoes could be kept in the hall closet near the door. They had quite a few details to work out concerning household and domestic matters, but those could wait until they conquered the jet lag that they were both feeling.

It had been several days since they had made love. They were both a bit nervous again, almost like the first night in his hotel. In time the need to be both naughty and nice found resolution, and the two discovered joy in each other's arms.

Marina sat up in bed the next morning and said, "Ivan, I think I have put you into serious relationship with older woman before you are ready. We have not known each other long enough under normal time-frame to become engaged. Now I have invaded your home and your bed. You can have very little privacy with me here. If you like, I can find my own place, or if you have changed mind about me, I can go back to Russia after few days and probably get old job back. You do not need to feel obligated to me because we have been intimate."

Marina was looking at him imploringly, with a worried expression on her face. Ivan snuggled close to her, and held her in his arms.

"First of all, and above all else Marina, I love you. That's not going to change, ever. It doesn't matter where in the world we may be—it will always be the same between us."

"But I am old, Ivan. I am ten years older than you."

"I see this as a good thing," Ivan assured her. "I was never interested in girls my age because they were girls, and not truly women yet. But you, you are all woman, with just an occasional girlish moment thrown in to keep us both young. I think you're just having a momentary feeling of insecurity. It's true we've known each other for only a short time, but we know each other very well nevertheless, and after a while we'll know each other even better. I didn't bring you here to push you away from me, but to bring you closer. I've already had plenty of privacy. What I need now is cohabitation. This apartment and this bed are no longer mine. They belong to both of us."

Ivan felt her body relax.

"Thank you, Ivan, for all wonderful things you have said and done for me. I try to be little less insecure in future. Maybe if you are lucky I make lunch, right now in present. But I make second breakfast for lunch instead. I am not hungry for big meal. Is good? I think I have jet leg. My belly is mixed up."

"Okay," Ivan smiled. "We'll have a second breakfast, then."

"Do you have food in apartment? It makes two weeks that you are away."

"I keep bread in the freezer, and orange juice, too. There are eggs in the fridge, and the milk is UHT, so it'll be fine."

"What is this *UHT?*" Marina asked.

"Ultra high temperature. It lasts forever."

"Ah. This is good, ya?"

"Yup."

Ivan went and sat down at his computer. Marina made a simple breakfast of juice, boiled eggs, toast with marmalade, and black coffee. Then she walked up behind Ivan, kissed his neck, and told him to come and eat.

Just then the phone rang. They both jumped in surprise, as they hadn't heard a phone for more than a week. Ivan picked it up on the third ring.

"Hello?"

"Welland? This is Montcalf. How are you?"

"I'm fine, thanks. I'm getting back into my routine."

"I want you to come down to D.C. for a few days."

"When?"

"As soon as possible."

"I can't make it till the weekend. I've got classes to teach, and Marina is here and I can't just up and leave. Also, I've got to be back to work on Monday again. Marina has an important interview on Monday afternoon."

"O.K., just come for the weekend then," Montcalf said. "You know civil servants at my level work weekends, too. And feel free to bring Marina with you. I know when her interview is. After all, I arranged it, remember? Don't sweat it, Welland. She's a shoe-in. I'll send plane tickets, and I'll have reservations for you at the Marriott."

"Okay. Sounds good."

"I'm looking forward to meeting Marina. I hear from Bagwell that she's got a killer body. I'll send a car for you at ten on Saturday morning. Be in the lobby, the driver will find you. See you Saturday. 'Bye."

Ivan sat still, looking straight ahead.

"Is something wrong?" Marina called from the alcove.

"No, it's okay. Do you want to go to Washington D.C. for the weekend?"

"Is good. I like to see your nation's capital. But why we go there so suddenly? Who was that on telephone?"

Ivan told her about his scholarship sponsored by the U.S. State Department. He explained that this scholarship would allow him to go to study in Russia for two weeks every year, and she would be able to go along and visit her family.

"So if the State Department wants to see me," he said, sitting down at the table again, "and they pay my expenses, I guess I can't refuse."

"This is good, ya? I will love to see my parents every year."

"That reminds me. I must call my mom and dad. They're probably worried."

Ivan called his parents to tell them he'd arrived home safely. His dad asked him how his schoolwork was going, and Ivan told him he would probably finish sooner than expected. He also told them about Marina, and if everything worked out he'd bring her home with him in the summer.

When he hung up he asked Marina if she wanted to call her folks. She called home and talked to her parents for about fifteen minutes. She told them that she had arrived in

Boston and had a nice little apartment near the university. She said she had found a special man and she would bring him home next year, and yes, he spoke Russian.

While Marina was talking to her parents, Ivan checked his e-mail and found a cryptic note from Wilson Bagwell. *Welland,* it read, *check your snail mail tomorrow. Bagwell.*

"How about a pizza for dinner tonight?" Ivan asked when Marina hung up. "Or we could go grocery shopping and fix something later at home."

She opted for shopping, as she was eager to see a super-market. Ivan reminded himself that Marina had grown up shopping the communist way under the Soviets, and that meant shortages and long lines. It had improved lately, but Chechen grocery stores were a long way from American supermarkets. Ivan thought it would be fun to see Marina's face when she beheld the giant market about four blocks from the apartment.

Marina was duly impressed by the quantity of available food and the amazing varieties to choose from. She had taken an unofficial inventory of Ivan's food supplies so she had a pretty good idea of what was needed. They pushed their cart around the store and she selected the items she needed for her meal preparations.

"You don't have to do all the cooking, you know," said Ivan. "But if you do, I'll do all the washing up, okay?"

"You are only man I ever wanted to cook, so you should enjoy it while it lasts," she said with a chuckle.

"To cook *for,* you mean."

"No, I cook only one man, not four."

CHAPTER SEVENTEEN

Ivan's Calvinistic work ethic drove him out of bed at the first light of dawn. The pattern of his previous years had been: *wake up, get up, clean up, eat up, and go to work.* It was difficult for him to loll about in bed, but of course Marina's presence made it a whole lot easier. Marina liked to cuddle, be close to him, feel his warmth, and sense his vitality. She had never had her own man—one whose body she could explore in detail without shame or reservation.

He was thinking these things, and trying to evolve a strategy to get out of bed that morning without making her feel that he was trying to escape her clutches. The problem was solved when she got up herself and ran to the bathroom and ducked into the shower.

Ivan picked up the stolen Koran, and the two other copies he had worked on in Chechnya, and placed them on his small desk. He planned to begin work on them after breakfast. Marina came out of the bathroom wearing a white terrycloth robe that hung down to her feet. While Ivan was cleaning up and shaving, Marina made breakfast for them.

"What we are doing today?" she asked.

"I'm going to begin working on the stolen Koran. I have to find out if my theory has any validity. Can it be demonstrated that there is a council of caliphs that communicates with terrorist cells all over the world, using a coding system found in certain Arabic Korans? I need to find out, but I'm not quite sure how."

"What you are doing first?"

"I wish I spoke Arabic, but I do speak mathematics. The Arabs are good mathematicians, so maybe I can make some headway using math to break the code."

"This is good. Meanwhile I do some notes for my article on Chechen history."

After a couple of hours, Ivan went down to the lobby to see if the mail had come. He returned in a few minutes with a handful of bills, and one personal letter. He opened it and read, *Welland, my company appreciated the translating job you did for me in Grozny, and so they are sending you a little bonus. Thanks buddy, you saved my life. Bagwell.* Inside was a check for $10,000.

"Yes!" Ivan exclaimed. "Happy days are here again."

Marina came over to see what he was talking about. He handed her the note and the check.

"Ivan, this is wonderful!" she exclaimed. "But what does he mean, you saved his life?"

"Oh, it's just an expression. It means I did a good job."

"But Ivan, that is too much money."

"Don't you think I deserve it for being a good translator?" he laughed, ruffling her curly, wet hair.

"Yes, you do deserve," she said, looking contrite.

Ivan checked his watch. "We'd better get dressed. We'll get a bite for lunch, then afterwards we're going to buy you a laptop computer. Then we'll come back here and I'll get you set up. We can't have you lollygagging around here being a sex kitten. We have to get some work out of you. Then we'll get dolled up and we'll go out for a fancy dinner. When you are slowed down by food and wine, we'll come home and I'll chase you around the bedroom. How does that sound?"

"That sounds too good to be true, a day of high living in America. And thank you for laptop and fancy dinner. But, my friend, beware of last part of plan. Claws come out when animal is cornered in bedroom."

"By the way, where did you get that bathrobe?"

"It is yours. Do you think I would buy robe that is so long that I trip on top of it?"

"If it's mine, I'm taking it back. Give it to me now," Ivan said, trying to strip it off her. She scuttled away and made it to the bathroom, closing the door in his face. Ivan went back to his desk and continued looking at the Koran. A little while later she came out dressed up in a conservatively revealing open-necked tan sweater and a dark brown form-fitting skirt.

"Oh, God," said Ivan. "You're wearing my favorite outfit. You're going to drive me nuts."

He gave Marina a kiss before they left and told her how proud he was to be seen with her. They stopped at the bank and deposited the check, and then they stopped at a Subway for a sandwich. After they finished he led Marina toward the electronic superstore, while she protested that he should not use his hard-earned money to buy her things. She figured that he hadn't really had a chance to earn much money yet because he was still a student.

"I can use university computers when I start job."

"That's true, you could. Don't forget, though, that we can claim part of the $10,000 back as a tax break from the Internal Revenue Service, so it isn't such a bad idea to buy that laptop. In the U.S., remember, an auto mechanic or a tradesman is expected to buy his or her tools and bring them to the job. So since a professor is expected to publish or perish, your writing tools are necessary for the practice of your profession. The tax department recognizes this fact, so you should be able to deduct the cost of your home office from your tax return. Therefore some of the cost of the computer will come back to us as a tax deduction."

By the time they arrived at the huge electronics store, Marina was convinced that it was all right to spend the money this way as long as they got most of it back in the form of reduced taxes. Ivan knew what Marina needed in the way of hardware and software, so the purchase of her system went easily and quickly. He bought her a nice carrying case and they left the store with everything she required.

When they got home he plugged in the various wires and downloaded her software. In an hour or so she was ready to go. Ivan left her to play with her new toy.

About an hour later he got up and stretched.

"There's a disc I forgot to get from the computer store. I need to download it now, so I'll just run out and get it."

Marina looked up. "You want me to come?"

"No, it's okay. It won't take me long."

"All right. I see you later."

Instead of going to the computer emporium, Ivan headed straight for a jewelry store. After a careful search, he picked out a one-carat diamond ring that he thought would look great on Marina's hand. He paid the store owner and put the ring in its little plush box into his pocket. He planned to give Marina the ring that evening during dinner. Now that he had received Wilson Bagwell's generous compensation for his "translating" services, he could afford to buy an engagement ring for the woman he loved.

When he got back to the apartment Marina let him give her a kiss, then returned to her typing. She said she was writing an outline for an article, adding that she had eaten so much at lunch time that she was too full to go out to dinner that night, and did he mind if they postponed their dinner plans for another evening? Ivan, a bit disappointed about the change, decided he would give Marina the ring later that evening. He returned to his analysis of the Koran.

The Koran was not giving way easily to Ivan's attempts to crack any code that might or might not be hidden in its Arabic calligraphy. He regretted not having learned Arabic. He might very well need help with this project, but he hated to admit it because he much preferred to work alone. He noted the presence of some twenty-eight different characters, which he presumed represented letters. He promised himself that he would go to the library the next day and borrow a copy of a beginning Arabic textbook and get to work on it.

Ivan bet the Israeli Mossad would have people who could help, but if he brought his suspicions to them they would just take over the project and he'd never know the results. The CIA was also capable of doing the work, but they wouldn't share the results with anyone, either. He would have to retain control of this idea until it was proved or disproved that a council of caliphs existed, and that it directed all violent Islamist activities.

The trouble with the Hebrews and the Arabs was that their religions were exclusionary, which led to the separation of peoples such as the Jews and the gentiles, or the Muslims and the infidels. The beauty of Christianity, on the other hand, was its *in*clusiveness. If he was able to decipher the Koranic code, which he still intuitively believed existed, then the walls between Muslims and others could be torn down and some progress could be made toward establishing peace.

Hebrew scholars and mathematically-inclined oddballs had been trying to understand the scriptures since medieval times by applying mathematical tools of analysis in mystical ways. Ivan wanted no truck with the fringes of religion that were trying to prove the existence of God or communicate with him through mathematics. The cosmologists had been bad enough. He merely wanted to prove that his Koran, and others like it, contained the codebook of the Islamic internal communication system that was used everywhere to unite Islamist terrorists with Muslim strategists and policymakers.

"Would you like just fruit instead of heavy meal tonight?" Marina called to him from her work station.

"That's fine by me," Ivan said. He wasn't an aggressive gourmet. He loved good food once he had it, but he would never actively pursue exotic foods or gourmet concoctions.

Marina washed the berries while Ivan got out the bowls and spoons, and put them on the table. They sat down and ate, happy just to be together.

"So explain to me the mathematics," said Marina, pouring cream on her berries. "Why you change fields?"

"The truth is, when I was in college I went about as far as I could go in math. I felt sort of like a very good chess player who wasn't good enough to be a grand master or a world champion. So I figured that if I was never going to be able to contribute something original to the field, it would be better for me to do something else that I was really good at."

"I think I know what is that," she said, suggestively.

He smiled, but remained serious as he explained that he chose Russian literature as a field mainly so that he could be free to use his mind for other things.

"Not that Russian literature doesn't have its challenges," he added quickly. "I like the field very much, but I feel more sympathy for the Renaissance men than for the specialists."

"We go to bed early, ya?" Marina said. She didn't want Ivan to get too excited about Renaissance men just then.

"Not yet," Ivan said. "I have something very important to ask you before we go to bed."

She was puzzled. He got down on one knee in front of her chair, reached into his pocket and took out the little plush box, opened it and offered it to her.

"Marina, I love you with all my heart. Will you marry me?"

Marina was astonished, as she was not entirely familiar with the cultural practices in the U.S. Ivan was always pulling these wonderful surprises out of his hat. She looked at the ring, she looked at Ivan on his knee, and burst into tears.

"Yes," she said. "Yes, with all my heart, yes."

She stood up, and so did Ivan. She clung to him and her tears of happiness soaked through his shirt. Ivan didn't cry, but he was happy just the same. He slipped the ring onto her finger.

"The diamond smiles," she said, wiping her tears.

"I should have bought it sooner," Ivan admitted. "I should have given you a ring when we were in Grozny, but where would I have found a ring suitable for a princess in Grozny?"

CHAPTER EIGHTEEN

The morning was sunny and bright. Ivan and Marina sat at the breakfast table eating eggs with buttered toast, and drinking orange juice and coffee.

"After my class this morning we could go for a walk and do some more sightseeing if you like," Ivan suggested.

"I like," Marina said enthusiastically. "I work with my computer until you come home."

Ivan was a very good teacher—humorous, but strict. He quickly learned that although these Harvard students were bright, they did not exceed him in experience or linguistic ability. As a result he became a well-loved and respected teacher, and his students worked hard to excel.

When he had finished teaching his class, Ivan headed for Widener Library. He had lived in libraries all his life so he felt very much at home, even in the magnificent Widener. In a short time he had gathered together three books that he felt would be helpful with his Koran analysis project. One of them dealt with the topic of Arabic writing, printing, and calligraphic penmanship. The second was a tome about the history of the Koran, but it had a chapter on publishers that looked interesting. The third book was an Arabic grammar.

Ivan hurried home, dumped the library books on his desk, picked Marina up off her feet and swung her around a couple of times.

"Go and get dressed, Marina. It's a nice spring day, and we're going to have a good time this afternoon."

They usually spoke English together, as Ivan wanted to help her work on her pronunciation.

He told her that at times her accent made her sound like an actress playing the role of a czarina in an American movie epic. She observed that he sounded like an actor playing Rasputin when he spoke Russian, and he looked like him, too.

"Rasputin, wasn't he that crazy mystic who advised the czar during World War I?"

Ivan knew exactly who Rasputin was, but he wanted to hear what Marina had to say about him.

"Yes, that is Rasputin. His enemies tried to kill him many times, but he refused to die. But they finally got him. He had reputation for having huge private part, so after he was dead they cut it off. It had fourteen inches in length. I tell you this because now you do not mind to be compared to Rasputin. So you see what can happen to man if he does not keep czarina happy."

"Whoa! I'll be super careful from now on."

They walked out onto the sidewalk and headed towards the Charles River to take a look at the rowers in their sculls. They watched a few stiletto-like rowboats being pushed through the water by tanned, husky young crews, encouraged by coxswains with megaphones. Marina had only glimpsed this sport on TV during the Olympics. She thought the men were handsome and had great muscles. Ivan decided not to hang around there anymore.

They took the subway to Faneuil Hall, the enormous food court in Boston. Ivan saw to it that Marina tasted all the Boston specialties.

"I like very much these Boston baked beans and brown bread," said Marina. "They remind me of Russian dish."

After sampling the food in Faneuil Hall, they took a walk around historic Boston. Ivan told Marina that every school child in America knew the story of Paul Revere and the Old North Church, the Boston Tea Party, and the battles against the British at Concord and Lexington.

"I do not know these events," Marina declared.

"You're kidding."

"American history not so popular in Russia. This must be obvious, no? We never learned what you recounted to me."

"Well then, I guess I'll just have to brainwash you in the American style."

"Ya? Then I tell you about Ivan the Terrible. I think you are named for him."

The apartment was already beginning to feel like home to Marina. They hung up their jackets, kicked off their shoes and sat down on the couch, intending to relax and have a little chat. Marina stretched out and rested her feet in his lap. Ivan began massaging them with his strong fingers.

"I know what is you think," Marina said.

"I know you do."

Marina patted the arm of the couch and told him to lie next to her. He took the back cushions off the couch and put them on the floor, and she scrunched over to make room for him so they could lie side by side. He put his head on the arm of the sofa next to hers. His long legs, of course, extended beyond the end of the couch. He folded one under him and stretched the other out so that it rested on the arm of the sofa.

"This is not comfortable for you," Marina said.

"It's okay for a while."

"I love this quiet feeling of intimacy."

"Enjoy it while you can. I have the feeling it's going to lead somewhere else."

"Do men think that intimacy must always end in sex?"

"Well, let's see. If you want to know what I think, I'd say that most men would be very disappointed if intimacy didn't go all the way. Men are not particularly complicated. We just want to get straight to the bottom line and then go and find something to eat."

"Ivan! Be serious. I ask you important question."

"I *am* being serious. But women usually like to do it backwards. First they like to be wined and dined while a

Hungarian waiter plays the violin, and *then* they're ready to go home for an evening of unforgettable love."

"We do not go backwards," Marina objected. "We go step by step forwards, until it is time for fireworks."

"Yes, of course," said Ivan, wisely agreeing with her. "What was I thinking?"

He retrieved his hand from the resting place where she had put it. He couldn't help sliding his fingers over that incredibly smooth patch of inner thigh as he pulled away. Nothing, nothing, *nothing* could ever be as physically enticing to him as the surfaces of her female body.

"You will not regret to wait," she promised, blinking her eyelids and striking a flirtatious pose. Ivan gave her a love pat on the behind just as she turned and ran to the bedroom to change for dinner.

"Leave my bottom line alone!" she called to him over her shoulder.

She put on a colorful, silky skirt and a blue blouse that matched her eyes and showed off her cleavage without revealing more than decorum allowed. Ivan noticed the action of her skirt as she strode along the streets of Boston. There was just the slightest undulation of the fabric as her feet touched the ground step by step, first one side then the other. He could have watched her walk around in that skirt forever. She wore inch-high block-healed strapped shoes that revealed her straight, strong toes with their unpainted nails. If Marina, with her well-developed calf muscles, had been wearing high heels, Boston would have ground to a halt to watch her walk by. As it was, she turned quite a few male heads. Ivan thought if Marina had a tan to go with the high heels, and with her proud way of walking that bounced her curly hair, she would surely be kidnapped by some Arab sheikh and added to his harem.

In fact, as he appraised her appearance, he wondered how it was that he ever got out of Chechnya with her. She was the national treasure of that poor land, but he had her now, and he wasn't sending her back. As he thought about the clothes he had seen her wear, he concluded that she had very good taste. Given a little money and some elegant stores to shop at, Marina would be right up there with the handsomest women he had ever seen.

For a woman in this day and age Marina was unusual in that she had no interest at all in wearing jeans or pants. He suddenly realized that he lived with her and he didn't know for sure if she even owned any pants. As far as he was concerned he preferred skirts and dresses anyway, but he was always the odd ball, and he was sure women in pants were here to stay. He remembered clearly where his hand had been only a few minutes before, and he thought to himself that it wouldn't have been half the memory if she had been wearing jeans. He had been quiet for so long that Marina asked him what he was thinking. He told her, all of it. She blushed a little, then a little more.

"You make me feel like teenager," she said.

"If you were, I could be arrested for what I'm thinking."

Ivan had decided to go to a favorite restaurant of his in Boston, called *Legal Sea Foods*. He didn't remember why it had that peculiar name, although he recalled that it was not because they only dealt with licensed fishermen. It was a modest restaurant, but the fish was always excellent and very fresh. They started with raw oysters on the half shell and cold beer. Marina had never had an oyster before, and Ivan only very rarely had eaten them.

"In America we say that oysters are supposed to increase sexual potency," Ivan said, "but I can't recall if it's males or females that benefit most from eating them."

"I do not think you need help from bi-valve, Ivan, but perhaps you eat extra one, just to be sure. In Russia caviar is famous aphrodisiac, but is too expensive."

Ivan ordered a Maine lobster, and Marina had salmon.

"Russian bears like salmon," she observed. "I feel like Mama Bear when I am with you, so I eat salmon, too."

"Well, I feel like Papa Bear, so maybe next time you have salmon you'll have your Baby Bear with you."

After their meal they walked along the Boston harbor front for a few minutes before they headed home.

The MBTA train let them off at Harvard Square. Ivan put his arm around Marina and held her tightly against his side as they walked down the street. It was a pleasant night, but still somewhat chilly. Marina was glad to feel his warm arm against her shoulder.

They strolled along until they came to their building.

"Do we need anything from the store?" Ivan asked.

"I go tomorrow."

Once the door was safely closed behind them, Ivan enfolded Marina in his arms and kissed her. He told her how beautiful she looked that night, and how every day she became more attractive to his eyes. He looked down into her face, the face he had thought reasonably attractive the first time he saw her on the train in Moscow. Now that face had become the most beautiful face in the world.

"Whatever spell you have cast over me, it has worked," he said. "I feel as though you've put a love potion in my drink."

"I have no mercy," said Marina, standing tall. "I will make you into love slave."

"At last," thought Ivan. "At last we're going to do what always comes first for me."

In the morning Ivan told Marina he was going to keep trying to break the Koran code. He quickly reviewed the grammar rules for Arabic, then he looked at the book on calligraphy. Were all the copies of the Koran printed in the same printing plant? If all the Arabic language Korans were printed in the same place, then more than likely the imam's copy was, too. He needed to get another Arabic copy to see if it differed from his. There are many thousands of mosques throughout the world, and an even greater number of imams. Ivan wondered if there was a list of the names of the practicing imams. He was sure the Vatican could compile a list of priests if it had to, so why not the Muslims? When the designers of the Koranic code distributed the special volumes, did they mail them? Maybe they distributed them during Ramadan. Maybe pilgrims making the hadj were given these Korans to take back home for their imams.

Ivan had a whole lot more questions than answers. He was worried that he might need some CIA cipher experts to help him uncover the devious communication method being used by the covert leaders of the Islamist jihads. He was feeling inadequate to handle the task.

Then suddenly he had an idea. What if Koranic references by chapter and verse were related to instructions contained in the Hadith? Muhammad's sayings, actions, and approvals are recorded in separate collections. Ivan would need to find a copy of the Hadith as well. He would have to go back to the Widener Library and dig out some more books. Would the Hadith exist in an accurate English translation? Barring some eureka-like revelation, Ivan was afraid he might have to turn to Montcalf for assistance with his theory.

Marina was busy with her new computer, updating her résumé. She wanted to have a copy or two ready for her interview on Monday afternoon when they returned from Washington. She asked Ivan to look at her C.V. and tell her what he thought of it.

It took Ivan only one minute to read and absorb the two pages. He was happy to have this opportunity to check her background, just in case someone in Washington might ask him about her.

"It's very impressive," he said, handing the curriculum vitae back to Marina. "Good schools, lots of publications, and excellent teaching experience."

She beamed with pleasure. She wanted him to be proud of her accomplishments.

"But you left out the most important part," he added.

Her expression froze. "What part?"

"You forgot the sexy bits about being engaged to Ivan "the terrible" Welland.

She swatted him with the papers and shooed him away.

Ivan laughed and went to the hall closet for his coat.

"I'm going to the library to get a copy of Al Bukhari's nine-volume Hadith. I'll be back as soon as I can."

"Wait! What is Hadith?"

"It's a great big collection of the sayings, teachings, and approvals of Muhammad during his lifetime, as related by his wives, disciples, and adherents."

Marina looked heavenward. "Are you reading *all* this Hadith?

"Maybe. But I'm going to start out by plugging them into my algorithm and test them against Koranic references by chapter and verse to see if there's any evidence of a logical correlation system. Later I'll examine sermons emanating from the Ljma to see if references to Ayats and Surahs in the Koran can be related mathematically to form a systematic code, in which case there would be evidence of an existing system of communication between Muslim clerics throughout the Islamic world."

"That sounds like much work."

"It will be. But even if I can prove the existence of such a code, I'll have to identify who the users are. I'll also have to substantiate that it's used to transmit orders to be obeyed, and not just for sermon topics. Then I might have to correlate a sufficient number of terrorist events with these messages sent in the Koranic code to prove by a statistically valid sample that my theory is factual, not just fanciful, and that it's being used by a group of unknown culprits to control the actions of jihadist terrorists."

"So they are like organized group of terrorist leaders?"

"Exactly. But there's no point in going to the trouble of identifying the existence of these people unless I can also prove somehow that they're engaging in some sort of a monumental crime against humanity."

Ivan was concerned lest he get so enthralled by his own theory that he overlook or misinterpret the results of his research. He had seen evidence of scientists who became so enamored of their own ideas that they threw science out in favor of a personalized solipsism. He would do everything in his power to stick to the facts and keep his ego out of his research.

He gathered some books and materials, threw on his jacket, and went over to Marina to kiss her goodbye.

"I am glad you work so hard to understand tactics of terrorists," Marina said as he left the apartment. "They must be stopped, before everything goes too far. The longer we wait, the stronger they become."

After spending the rest of the morning at the Widener Library, Ivan checked out the volumes he needed and went back to the apartment, where he found Marina still where he'd left her.

"You will break your back with so many books!" she exclaimed, getting up to greet him. "Are you hungry? You might find something in refrigerator."

When he opened the fridge he was surprised to see a beautiful Waldorf salad next to a stack of bagels and lox with cream cheese.

"How did you know about Waldorf salads?" Ivan asked her, as he took the lunch over to the table.

"I did not make it," she laughed. "Serving girl prepared salad, the one who looked after you before I was imported to do job."

"But I still don't see how…"

"You have cookbook in cupboard, silly. It has beautiful, colored photographic picture of Waldorf salad."

They ate their lunch, bantering back and forth as lovers do. Then they retired to the bedroom for a little nap, after which they went back to work in a perfect mood to tackle the problems of the world with clear minds and peaceful hearts.

Washington D.C.

CHAPTER NINETEEN

Ivan and Marina had each packed only one small suitcase for their three-day journey, so they decided to take the subway to Logan International Airport in order to save cab fare. One of the best things about living in Boston is that the airport can be reached via the subway. In most cities one has to take a cab ride for twenty miles or more. In New York it is normal to pay up to $100 for taxi rides to one of the three airports.

When they were traveling in Russia, Marina was the tour leader. Now that they were in the U.S., it was Ivan's turn. At the airport the two of them got into a conversation about the differences in security checking. Ivan thought it was similar to the differences in the justice systems of the two countries. In Russia he had the feeling there was always a presumption of guilt, whereas in the U.S. one is presumed innocent until proven guilty.

"I have the impression that the Russians are mostly guilty," Ivan said, "so the law has to work that way."

"I think *you* are guilty of presuming Russians are always guilty."

"Yes, but the Russians have to be guilty because after all the trouble they had with Rasputin, they picked another Putin to be their leader. When we get you to Washington you'll have to explain this to the State Department."

"I am engaged to comic man. What will become of me?" Marina moaned.

It was a clear day when they boarded the plane for Dulles International Airport. At cruising altitude they could almost see all the way to Washington, D.C.

"Looks like one huge, long city stretching along coast," said Marina, looking down at the Northeast Corridor.

Ivan had to admit that she had a point. The relief map of the future would be a map with no relief from urban sprawl. The cities expand into the suburbs. The suburbs become towns. The towns become villages. Then the reverse occurs as a new city appears over the horizon.

"Civilization seems to be largely a game of filling in the blanks between cities," Ivan observed, a bit wistfully.

"I think new definition of progress should be growth and expansion," Marina remarked. "Nations want always to grow in population and expand their space. But space is finite, at least on this planet. Population growth may be finite too, but we have not yet reached maximum density. Science and technology have kept us going. Perhaps they always do this, so when we reach point where population growth is no longer sustainable on Earth, we can simply export excess people to moon or other planet. Science fiction writers have anticipated this for long time now."

"I think that won't happen for a while, though."

"On Earth our people struggle politically, same as in dark ages," Marina went on. "Some countries have tried peaceful methods of land expansion such as how the clever Dutch people have reclaimed land from sea using their dikes to create polders. Some countries have used detritus left by populations in landfills, which expand their land bases. History of world is being written every day, which is why I love to study it."

Marina was in fine form, and just warming up to her subject.

"Where you think human species goes?" she asked.

She waited for a few moments for his answer, but after a while she became impatient with his thoughtful silence.

"Why you not answer when I ask you question?" she said, nudging him with her elbow.

"Well, it's a pretty big question, don't you think? I need at least two full minutes before I can formulate an answer about where the human species is headed. The truth is we haven't been able to find a good method of including all the peoples of the world in our version of progress. As a result, huge areas of our land and populations have not enjoyed the so-called progress of the modern nations. Unlike all the other species on the globe, mankind knows that death awaits all of us. The time constraint of having only one lifetime makes people hurry desperately to achieve a lifestyle that's equal to that of the most successful of their neighbors. But the aspirations of enormous numbers of the world's population are not going to be met during their lifetime, though, in spite of how hard they may try to achieve par with the Western democracies. If the purposes of national governments could be kept pure, and the welfare and progress of their peoples were the true aim of administrations, then perhaps some good could be achieved, but unfortunately civilization is still battling the most primitive human selfishness in its fight to distribute its benefits fairly among the peoples of the world."

"So you think all is futile in this world?" Marina asked him sadly.

Just when she was beginning to wonder whether or not Ivan had heard her question, he continued describing his thoughts about the future of mankind.

"I once read an address," he said, "given by C.S. Lewis at Magdalen College, at Oxford University, during World War II, entitled *De Futilitate*. In this speech Lewis refutes an ultimate futility and encourages mankind not to throw our imperfect justice aside. He thought it was best for us to go on using it, just as a pupil advances to more perfect arithmetic not by throwing his multiplication tables away, but by using them till he can advance further. So, to answer your question, I really don't know where our species is headed, but I do know that we were all meant to keep on trying to do our best, right up to the end."

It was Marina's turn to fall into a thoughtful silence.

As the plane began to land, Ivan pointed out to Marina the principal monuments and buildings in Washington. It truly was a grand sight, and Marina was excited to be able to see it so clearly. She thought to herself that many of the Russian leaders that she had studied about had landed at this same airport. She hoped that she and Ivan could accomplish some small work that would foster peace. She took Ivan's hand in hers. How much better things were going to be, she thought, now that she had a humble, open-minded partner to share the search for the help they needed to offset the futility of their own frail efforts.

When Marina and Ivan reached the front of the taxi line, they directed the driver to take them to the J.W. Marriott Hotel on Pennsylvania Avenue. When they arrived, the doorman helped Marina out of the cab, taking subtle but appreciative note of her strong, shapely legs as she stepped onto the sidewalk. Ivan paid the driver, and together they followed their baggage to the registration desk. When Ivan gave the clerk his name, he was told that his suite was on the twelfth floor.

A bellboy took them up to their room, which turned out to be the elegant two-room Lincoln suite. After showing them their room and receiving his tip, the bellboy left. Ivan and Marina looked at each other in amazement. The surroundings were elegant to an extraordinary degree. Neither of them felt important enough to be occupying such quarters, and they wondered why the taxpayers should be paying for this extra-vagance. They decided that since they had no choice they would enjoy the luxury while it lasted.

A basket of fruit and a bottle of fine champagne were on the table with a card from Montcalf, which welcomed them to their nation's capital. He informed them that there had been a change in plans, and he would see them at 8:00 a.m.

for breakfast in their room. The card was signed "Simeon Montcalf."

This was the first time Ivan had known Montcalf to use his first name. He couldn't help wondering why he was getting such special treatment. After all, he was only a poor graduate student and Marina was an unemployed professor. What sense did it make?

"I feel as though I'm being recruited for a special job of some kind," he remarked to Marina. "Well, I guess we'll find out tomorrow what it's all about, and in the meantime let's just be tourists."

"Can we be lovers, too?"

"I'll have to get permission for that, but I'll ask someone soon," he smiled, delighted that she was putting first things first. "Meanwhile, perhaps we can take a walk up the street past the White House, and then have lunch somewhere. What do you say?"

"Is good," she agreed.

They unpacked, hung up their clothes, washed up and took the elevator down to the palatial lobby. They strolled down Pennsylvania Avenue until they arrived at the White House. They had to admit that it was an impressive sight. No matter how many times they had seen it in the news, it was still awe-inspiring to be standing at the door, so to speak, of the most powerful person in the world. Ivan was reminded of the quotation from the Book of Revelation where Jesus says, "Behold, I stand at the door and knock…" He wondered if he would ever be invited to the White House.

Since bread is the staff of life, especially for Russians, Ivan and Marina decided to have lunch in a quirky, slightly chaotic restaurant called "The Bread Line." Fortunately for them it was just after the lunch hour or they might not have been able to survive the experience of getting a sandwich in Washington D.C. during the midday rush of government workers. They had a tuna sandwich on the best baguette they had ever tasted, and the coffee perked them up enough to encourage them do a little more sightseeing.

They were both great walkers, and Washington D.C. is the perfect city for long distance walking. Everything in the city is large in scale and generous in its proportions. They circumnavigated the rectangle formed by the White House and the Ellipse by walking down along 15th Street, across Constitution Avenue, then up 17th Street to Pennsylvania Avenue. They had a peek at the National Theatre, which was next to their hotel, and they prowled around the expensive shops in the National Place Mall. They could tell that they weren't going to put much of a dent in the tourist potential of the nation's capital in just one weekend. They resolved to come back sometime to see the things they were going to have to miss on this trip.

"White House not largest building of its type, but is more cheerful and less austere than Kremlin, or Hermitage, or Schoenbrun Palace. Is good that democratic leader of world has such small, simple home."

"Well, I'm about ready to go back to our small, simple room at the hotel," Ivan said. "Listen, would you mind if we have room service send up our dinner tonight? I'd like to work on my algorithm a bit more. What do you think?"

"Is good," Marina declared, taking his arm. "I walk long enough. I throw away my shoes and read book this evening while you work."

They entered the hotel's four-story lobby atrium with its marble columns, mahogany trim, and Asian rugs, and went up to their suite. The wood furnishings with burgundy and cream-colored accents were too formal to be homey, but everything about the place was first class. They felt overly pampered and therefore a bit less comfortable than they otherwise might have been. This environment was about as far from Chechnya as it was possible to imagine. Their social consciousness did not allow them to feel completely without guilt about living this way while others existed in dangerous and poor conditions such as those they had left behind in Grozny.

Ivan was quite capable of making general conversation while his mind was simultaneously turning over difficult problems. During his walk with Marina he had had several ideas that could be worked into his program to analyze the Arabic scriptures. He was anxious to get to work, but he didn't want Marina to feel neglected. She seemed perfectly all right about being left to her own devices, however, and he greatly appreciated that about her. His method of working demanded occasional periods of protracted concentration, and a serious relationship with a dependent woman would not have been possible for him.

Marina, for her part, liked her work, and she didn't mind being left alone to do it. Most of the Russian men she knew could not even imagine that a mere woman was capable of pursuing anything seriously worth doing. She always thought this was a peculiar attitude on their part, for those same men were usually borrowing her notes, asking her opinion, and often following her advice. How could they have such a split view of her worth as a scholar? How many centuries was it going to take to get real gender equality? On the personal level, however, she had now come across the one man who was so totally unaware of stereotypical gender prejudices that she had to believe there was hope after all. Marina believed that Ivan's fair-mindedness was so rare that she didn't know whether to guard it jealously and keep it for herself, or share it openly so he could serve as an example to other men.

Ivan worked away furiously on his computer for a couple of uninterrupted hours. It seemed to Marina that he was making some important progress, so she didn't bother him even once.

Finally Ivan stopped and stretched.

"You hungry?" he asked.

"Not very much. And you?"

They ordered shrimp cocktails and a salad from room service and were startled by how quickly the food arrived. The waiter deftly placed the items on the table, arranged the chairs, and left.

While they ate their dinner, Ivan explained to Marina what he was doing. Aside from the technical proof that his analysis would provide, there was the question of how breaking the code would be used. Would it merely supply intelligence so that vengeful attacks could be made? This would guarantee some victories, but eventually the leaders of the Muslim insurgency would realize that their code had been compromised, and they would evolve another method of secretly communicating with their terrorist cells.

Ivan wanted to make sure that the spotlight would be thrown on the council of caliphs that was hijacking the Islamic faith. Muslims must be encouraged to see how their religion had been used to falsely enflame hatreds in order to fulfill the ambitions of a few power-hungry elitist extremists. He knew the reform of Islam had to come from within. He hoped that if the motives and the secret, violent operations of the caliphs were exposed, the great mass of Muslims would revamp their doctrines and make their objectives peaceful.

"I must stop you for one minute," Marina interrupted. "I cannot discuss peace in world until I first pee in bathroom."

"Go right ahead. I wouldn't want you to pee anywhere else," Ivan chuckled.

"There is small swimming pool in bathroom," she said when she came back to the table. "This is unbelievable."

"It's called a Jacuzzi," Ivan told her.

"I think we should explore its features together. It needs to be subjected to careful scientific investigation."

"You're absolutely right," Ivan agreed. "It's pointless for Uncle Sam to provide such a luxury if we don't use it."

Ivan hadn't had this type of plumbing in the dormitories, nor was the Jacuzzi commonly found in Chechnya. Marina had heard of luxuries of this type, but had never had the opportunity to try one. After reading the instructions he ran the water, tested and adjusted the temperature, and waited for the huge tub to fill.

In the meantime they undressed in preparation for the new experience. Marina walked to the edge of the tub and stuck her toe into the water to make sure it wasn't too hot. Ivan watched her do this and knew for certain what inspired Degas, Renoir, Cézanne, and the other impressionists to paint women bathing. He would have dearly loved to paint Marina, but sadly he had no talent for painting or drawing. He did have the ability to appreciate art, however. To his eye her body was perfectly proportioned. Any artist would give anything to have such a model.

She sank into the warm water as he stood at the edge of the tub looking down at her. She held up her arms to signal him to get into the water, too. The tub was clearly designed for two people, but unfortunately it was designed for two normal-sized people. Ivan could not flatten his long legs, so his knees were forced to poke out of the water like twin volcanic islands in the sea. When he sensed that Marina was about to kid him about his long legs, he turned the pump switch on and jets of water shot out of the holes in the sides of the tub, creating a whirlpool of warm water and providing him with a diversionary conversational subject. Ivan put his arm around her, and they sat peacefully enjoying the warm water massage caused by the roiling water around them.

In fifteen minutes or so they felt totally relaxed. Ivan got out of the Jacuzzi and grabbed a fluffy towel from the pile nearby. He held it up for Marina, and when she stepped out of the tub he wrapped it around her, giving it a little rub here and there. Then he toweled himself off, wrapped the towel around his midriff, and brushed his teeth. Marina did the same. While she was brushing her teeth, he slipped his towel off and climbed into the king-sized bed to await her. In a minute or two she slid into the bed and snuggled up to him.

"We can sleep late tomorrow," said Ivan, happily. "Mr. Montcalf isn't coming until eight o'clock."

"He is coming here?" Marina asked.

"Didn't I tell you? There was a note from him when we got here, saying that he would have breakfast with us here in our suite."

"Is good, ya? Then we do not have to get up extra early and travel to meet him somewhere across city. This means we have permission to make love all night, ya?"

"That's right," said Ivan, drawing her warm body close to his own.

CHAPTER TWENTY

W hen Ivan heard someone knocking at exactly eight o'clock the next morning, he opened the door and found a cheerful Simeon Montcalf waiting in the hallway.

"Hello, Welland. How are you, old boy? What have you been up to lately?"

"Good morning, Montcalf," Ivan smiled. "And I'm fine, thanks for asking. Please come in."

"Marina Kortikuova, I presume," said Montcalf, not waiting to be introduced. "I'm glad to meet you, dear lady. Welland hasn't seen fit to tell me about you, but we'll get to know each other anyway, I'm sure."

"I am pleased to meet you too, Mr. Montcalf. Ivan has not told me about you, either," said Marina, playing along with him.

"Please call me Simeon," Montcalf requested.

Ivan could see he was going to be pretty much out of the picture at breakfast. What secret pheromone did Marina emit that immediately turned these middle-aged men into such womanizers?

"I didn't order food. I didn't know what you wanted."

"No problem, Welland," Montcalf said brightly. "I took care of it myself."

Marina was very relaxed and chatty. She described the things that she and Ivan had done since they arrived. She thanked Montcalf profusely for helping her to come to the U.S. on such short notice, and for arranging an interview for her at Harvard. She promised she would do her best in the interview. Montcalf could see what a genuine person Marina was, and it certainly crossed his mind that she was a poised and attractive young lady.

"What do you do," Marina asked him, "if you don't mind me to be curious about you, Mr. Montcalf? I mean to say, Simeon?"

"Well," he began. "I work for the federal government and I am a lookout, or scout. Some people refer to me as *the recruiter* because my job is to find and hire the most talented, capable, best-trained people to work for the U.S. government. Basically I work for the State Department, because often the people I seek are in some specialty that would be helpful in the fields of international relations, history, and politics. Take young Welland here, for example. I became interested in him because he's fluent in Russian, and highly trained in mathematics and physics. If the State Department were negotiating a treaty with Russia that included scientific details, we might call upon him to help us out with technical or linguistic details. Do you follow me?"

"Yes, Simeon. I think you have best job in whole world. You are sort of like God's personnel man."

"Correct," Montcalf said, looking pleased. "I like that title, God's Personnel Manager. I shall use that title, if you don't mind, when I speak with my colleagues."

Ivan noticed right away how Montcalf had promoted himself to *personnel manager* from Marina's suggested *personnel man.*

Just then the room service waiter arrived with a cart loaded with food. He set the table with plates, silverware, glasses and napkins. He pulled the trolley close to the table, and when everyone was seated he displayed what was under the stainless steel covers and offered to serve them. It was as if everything on the entire menu had been loaded onto the cart and sent up to their room. Ivan was sure that the tenant up the street at 1600 Pennsylvania Avenue was going to go without breakfast because they surely must have delivered his to Ivan's room by mistake. When they had loaded up their plates, Montcalf dismissed the waiter and told him not to come back until he called.

"So, Mr. Montcalf, am I to assume I'm being recruited?" said Ivan, coming straight to the point.

Montcalf smiled and delicately wiped his lips. "Indeed. You've already been recruited, as you put it. Did you think we were going to pay your whole tuition and send you on a vacation to Russia just because we found you charming? You were asked to mix with the local people and get a reading on how much dissatisfaction exists among them. You are still expected to give me a written summary of your trip. Subsequently you were asked to do a little translating job, and I am pleased to say you did very well, according to Bagwell. So you are moving up on my popularity list. I like the personal recruiting job that you did, too," he added, looking at Marina with doting eyes. "Now, after we finish breakfast we're going to a debriefing over at the State Department building. I've asked an associate of mine to escort Marina around Washington for sightseeing, shopping, or whatever she would like to do. We'll try to get you both back in time for supper."

Montcalf pulled a cell phone from his pocket and punched in a number.

"Please have my car brought around, my dear," Montcalf said. "Then come up here and I'll introduce you to Professor Kortikuova." He snapped the phone lid closed. "If you want to use the washroom," he said, turning to Ivan and Marina, "now would be a good time."

Marina ducked into the bathroom. Ivan put on a jacket and tie and grabbed his laptop. When Marina emerged from the bathroom, she heard Montcalf talking to someone at the door. Ivan and Marina exchanged a kiss in the bedroom and went back into the living room, ready to go.

Montcalf introduced Marina to his assistant, a sweet and unassuming young woman who looked like a Swedish farm girl. Marina sensed that this woman, who was about her age and single, could tell some stories about the men she had worked for that would be similar to her own. The four went down in the elevator together, but went their separate ways in the lobby.

Ivan and Montcalf climbed into a black car that was waiting in front of the hotel. Montcalf told the driver to take them home. Evidently home for them was the office. They drove along Constitution Avenue until they got to 23rd Street, where they turned right and stopped in front of the huge Department of State building. Montcalf hopped out and led Welland into the building where he was processed through security and given a visitor's badge. He would have liked to be shown around, as the history in this place was absolutely palpable, but Montcalf seemed anxious to get to the meeting room.

When they arrived at a less prepossessing part of one of the upper floors, they entered a large conference room. Inside were four men, who evidently had been waiting for Ivan and Montcalf to arrive. Montcalf took charge, making introductions all around. There was a security agent, a diplomat, a man with a Russian accent whose job was unclear, and a Chechen émigré with a rebel political past.

Montcalf and the others conducted what Ivan assumed was a debriefing. They wanted to know Ivan's opinion about the important streams of thought in Chechen politics at the moment. Ivan told them everything he could think of except his code theory and the details of the fatal meeting in the mosque. After about an hour or so they seemed to run out of questions, so the meeting broke up and the four other men left the room to Montcalf and Ivan.

"Why didn't you say anything about the events in the mosque?" Montcalf asked.

"They didn't ask me about that."

"Are you trying to be cute, Welland?"

"Suppose you tell me what you know about the incident at the mosque? What did Bagwell say?"

"That's not how it works, Welland. I ask the questions and you answer them."

"Sorry, Montcalf, but I'll answer any questions having to do with the purpose for my visit to Chechnya. Anything other than that is personal, and I won't discuss it with anyone until I know by whose authority I'm being asked these questions, and for what purpose my answers will be used."

Montcalf was growing annoyed by Ivan's recalcitrance, but he didn't want the situation to blow up. He felt Ivan was a valuable asset, and he didn't wish to lose him. In a way he admired the mental toughness of this young man, and also his cautiousness. What he didn't know was that Ivan felt an obligation of loyalty to Wilson Bagwell. He didn't want to confess to a murder, or witness to anyone else that Bagwell had been forced to commit it in order to save their lives. If either Ivan or Bagwell had acted any differently that day in Grozny, then neither of them would be alive to tell the story. Talking about it now without Bagwell being present was out of the question.

"I won't talk about the incident at the mosque unless Bagwell is with us," Ivan told Montcalf. "Furthermore, I'd like to speak to the Secretary of State in person for a few minutes before I talk to anyone else. It's about a different matter of great potential value to the United States. And I'd also like to suggest that you arrange for me to speak with Bagwell as soon as possible. I realize it might be difficult to get an appointment with the Secretary on short notice, but the matter is urgent. In the meantime, I'll stay put right here and work on my computer until Bagwell and the Secretary show up."

"I can't arrange an appointment with the Secretary without telling her what it's about," said Montcalf, trying to control his annoyance at being given instructions by this presumptuous nobody.

"Tell her it's about the council of caliphs," said Ivan.

"What's the council of caliphs?" Montcalf bellowed.

"Just get me in to see the Secretary. If she wants you to know, she can give me permission to tell you. Meanwhile I have nothing further to say."

Montcalf stalked out of the room, fuming. He decided to give Bagwell a call before he attempted to break into the Secretary's schedule. He dialed a number and said, "Wilson, is that you?"

"Yeah, who's this?"

"It's Montcalf at the State Department. I've got a problem here. Ivan Welland is being debriefed, but he refuses to say anything about the incident at the mosque in Grozny unless he talks to you first. Can you come down here right away?"

"I'm afraid that's not possible. I'm in Denver right now. But I'll talk to him on the phone. Put him on."

Montcalf went back to the conference room. "Bagwell is in Denver and obviously can't just drop by. He wants to talk to you." He handed the phone to Ivan.

"Is this a secure line?" Ivan asked.

Montcalf nodded.

"Could you leave me alone for a minute while I talk privately to Bagwell?"

Montcalf left the conference room with murder in his heart.

"Is this Wilson Bagwell?" Ivan asked.

"Of course." Bagwell sounded concerned. "Say, what's going on down there, Welland?"

"Did you tell Montcalf about the incident at the mosque?" Ivan asked him.

"Sure I did. Why not?"

"Did you tell him who shot the imam?" Ivan asked.

"He thinks I did it," Bagwell admitted. "I never told him anything about you except that you did a terrific job translating, and that we escaped together."

"You realize, Wilson, that if they got pissed at you they could get you extradited back to Grozny for murder," Ivan said. "Or else maybe they could leak the information to some terrorist and he'd try to assassinate you. I'm worried about your vulnerability as a result of this matter. I was impressed by the way you handled the gunfight at the O.K. Mosque, and I felt I owed you a debt of loyalty. So before I talked to Montcalf I needed to know what you had already told him."

"You're a good man, Ivan. I was impressed by the way you handled yourself that day, too. But you don't have to worry about me, I'm licensed to kill."

"What does that mean, you're licensed to kill?" Ivan asked him.

"It means I have a contract with the government that says they won't prosecute or extradite me for any killings that happen when I'm on a mission. You know, like 007."

"Oh, so I can blame all my killings on you, then."

"Yeah, you do that, brother Welland. Listen, I've got to run. Nice talking to you."

Ivan went to the door and called Montcalf back in.

"Okay. I spoke to Bagwell and he said he told you all about the event at the mosque. So what more do you want me to tell you?"

"Is it true?" Montcalf asked, still seething about the kid seizing control of the situation.

"Yes, it's all true. We both would have been killed if Bagwell hadn't acted as he did. I merely threw a chair through a window and we made our escape by jumping out before the security guards came in."

"So why couldn't you have told me that before?"

"Well, he saved my life and I felt I owed him a debt of loyalty before I told you or anybody else information that could lead to a murder charge in some courts. What he did was brave and in self-defense."

"So we're square, then. We can cancel our meeting with the Secretary, right?"

"No. What I have to speak to the Secretary about has nothing to do with the shooting at the mosque. Please set this up for me, Montcalf. You won't be sorry."

CHAPTER TWENTY-ONE

Montcalf was amazed at his own success. He had approached his boss, the Under Secretary, and together they had managed to persuade the Secretary's secretary to pencil in ten unscheduled minutes with the third most powerful person in Washington. Welland had better have something special to say, or it would be highly embarrassing for God's Personnel Manager.

Montcalf liked to think of himself as the yeast without which no successful fermentation could take place. He loved putting talented, intelligent people together to see what they could do as a team. Even though he didn't always understand in great detail the specialties of his discovered ones, he strongly associated himself with their accomplishments. If the work they did was recognized for its distinction, then Montcalf had his reward. The fame of his recruits was his finder's fee.

He didn't know Ivan well enough yet to be absolutely sure that he would bring honor down upon himself, and therefore upon the great facilitator that Montcalf believed himself to be. Nevertheless, Ivan had an inner confidence that exceeded the level of the usual graduate student's by a mile, but at the same time he seemed to have little or no personal ego. Ivan had stood up to Bagwell, the imam, and to Simeon Montcalf. He was, after all, sleeping with the next best thing to the Czarina. Perhaps he was the real McCoy.

Montcalf was proud of his ability to recognize future leaders while they were still in their cocoons. Maybe this time he'd go to the next level. He was hoping this long shot would have a big payoff for him. Nevertheless, he didn't like not knowing what Ivan was going to say to the Secretary. Montcalf was silently mulling all these things over when he and Ivan approached the formidable office of the Secretary of State of the United States of America.

In fact, Montcalf had never been in the Secretary's private office, but he announced to the receptionist in his deepest basso profondo that Simeon Montcalf and Ivan Welland were there for their appointment with Madame Secretary. The receptionist asked them to be seated, and told them the Secretary would be ready for them in a few minutes.

When they finally entered the office of the Secretary of State, it was difficult for the two men not to be in awe of the one responsible for the foreign policies of the greatest power in the world. Ivan was immediately at ease with the small woman who had risen to this high office. Montcalf was not as relaxed, perhaps because ultimately his job depended on this woman having a good impression of him.

The Secretary told the men to have a seat. She came out from behind her desk to join them. She could have been aloof and used her large desk as a buffer between herself and her visitors, but she was used to putting people at ease. A lifetime in the field of international relations and a steady progression of increasingly important jobs had enabled her to meet and interface with powerful world leaders. She was on her home turf, and in no way threatened by men, even men as tall as Ivan.

"What was so important that you had to see me at once?" she asked, contemplating them with an expression of friendly curiosity.

Montcalf would have liked to be the first to speak, but the truth was he didn't know what Ivan was going to say, so he had to defer to him. Ivan began the conversation by thanking the Secretary for seeing them. He explained how Montcalf had found him at Harvard and had sponsored his trip to

Chechnya. He credited God's Personnel Man with finding exceptional people to contribute their skills to their country.

"The reason I came to see you," Ivan continued, "is that while I was in Chechnya I uncovered something that was so important that I'd like to speak to you in private about it."

He asked if Montcalf could be excused from the room for a few minutes so he could speak to the Secretary alone. She looked thoughtfully at Ivan for a few moments before finally asking Montcalf if he would step out of the room. Ivan found himself alone with the Secretary of State of the United States of America.

"Madame Secretary," he continued, speaking in hushed, deferential tones, "while I was in Grozny looking for a thesis topic, I did quite a lot of thinking about the influence Islam has had on the violence in Chechnya. I decided to study the Koran and the history of that religion in the Caucasus and in Arab lands in general. I read copies of the Koran in their English and Russian translations, comparing them to each other in order to better understand the passages. In the course of my reading I happened to uncover a few inconsistencies. I felt I should consult a Koranic scholar who knew Arabic, to determine what the true meanings were. I went to the Grand Mosque in Grozny, therefore, and asked to see the imam. He seemed like a man who was a good deal more accustomed to being obeyed than questioned. In fact, everything about him was regal, far beyond what you'd expect of a cleric in a place like Chechnya. When I inquired about him later I was met with a silence that could only have been fear-driven."

"Was this the imam who was shot in the Grand Mosque a short time ago?"

"It was," Ivan replied.

"Go on."

"The bottom line is that I believe I've discovered a con-spiracy that uses for its cover the Muslim desire that their leaders be direct descendants of Muhammad, or caliphs, as they call them. I believe these caliphs have formed a council which now controls and coordinates Islamist terror groups all over the world. My examination of the Koran and the Hadith has led me to believe that these men communicate by means of a code hidden somewhere in these religious writings. I suspect that certain specific volumes of the Koran that are in the sole possession of the Muslim imams, contain the key to decoding these instructions. I was acting as Mr. Wilson Bagwell's interpreter at the meeting in the Grand Mosque at the time the imam and seven other men were killed. In the confusion I was able to remove the imam's personal copy of the Koran. I've now developed an algorithm to expose the workings of the code as well as the workings of the council of caliphs. I've brought my analysis along. I also have the imam's personal Koran here."

"How many people know about this now?" the Secretary asked.

"Three. My fiancée and I, and now you," Ivan said.

"What do you think should be done about your theory?"

"Ideally I think a small group of experts in deciphering codes should be formed to help me finish what I've started. In this group there should be someone absolutely fluent in Arabic and English, and thoroughly familiar with the Islamic religion. There should be a computer expert with a heavy background in statistical analysis. There should be someone who has access to security files, particularly as it applies to Arabic terrorist events worldwide. All these people should have the highest security clearances, and I would hope I could be the project leader."

"What about your fiancée? Should she be involved?"

"No, I don't think so. It's out of her field, but if you want a briefing about the Russian aspirations in Chechnya, she is an expert. She's been teaching modern Russian history at the university in Grozny for the past two years, and has written a book about Russia's adventures in the Caucasus region. You might like to meet Marina. Marina Kortikuova is her name."

"Well, I tell you what I think. This matter is potentially too important and too complicated to consider in the time we have allotted to our meeting today. I suggest we have dinner together tonight and discuss this in depth. I'd like to meet Marina, and if it's possible I may be able to bring along someone I have in mind to examine this project. In the meantime, I should tell you that I find you a very interesting young man. You did the right thing in choosing me as the first person to discuss your theory with. If you had chosen to approach my colleague in the Defense Department then your theory, if true, would have produced some military victories in the short term, but it would not have altered the long-term prospects for peace. I can approach him anyway, should we have need of military support. I recognize that if this theory of yours proves to be correct, the political value we gain may turn Islam from its present destructive course to one that may bring us lasting peace."

"Thank you, Madame Secretary."

"My first name is Julia. From now on we'll proceed on a first name basis, and behave as the friends I hope we will soon become. You are staying at the J.W. Marriott, is that right?"

"Yes."

"Fine. They know me there, so I can arrive unobtrusively. We'll have dinner in your suite, if that's all right with you. I'm afraid I have a target painted on my chest. The press, the paparazzi, and violent radicals of every stripe are in constant pursuit, so we'll be having a secure meal tonight."

The Secretary of State rose to her feet, and Ivan followed suit.

"We'll be delighted to have you as our guest," he said.

"The honor is mine," she answered graciously. "When you leave, please send Montcalf in to see me. I'll instruct him to look for candidates for your little task force. I think your idea is worth pursuing. The worst that can happen is that your theory will be proven wrong."

"Thank you for letting me go forward with it. I appreciate it very much."

"See you tonight, Ivan. By the way, you can describe your project to Montcalf. He's cleared for security at this level, and I'm sure he'll function better if he knows what's going on."

Ivan went to the outer office and told Montcalf that the Secretary would see him now.

"I'll wait for you here," Ivan said to him, but Montcalf didn't bother to answer.

When Montcalf came out, Ivan asked him if he would call his assistant and tell her she could bring Marina back now. He would also be grateful if he could ask his driver to take him back to the hotel.

Apparently the Secretary had told Montcalf something good about Ivan, because he was full of newfound respect.

"I'll take care of those items at once," he said politely.

Marina had not yet returned when Ivan arrived at his room, so he sat down on the couch and turned on the T.V. As he flipped through the channels he was surprised to find such a high proportion of them showing political programming. There were pundits proffering predictions. There were pollsters picking probabilities. There were politicians posing for photographers, and there was a plethora of perennial prevaricators unrivalled in any city in the world. Welland was just wondering how performers had pre-empted philosophers in political prowess when Marina let herself into the suite and saved him from his ponderings. Ivan loved words and word games, but he loved Marina more.

"I'm home," she called out, as she closed the door behind her.

Ivan smiled at her, thinking how wonderful it was to hear the woman he loved declare that she was home.

"Did you have a good day?" he said, taking her coat.

"Yes," she said eagerly. "We went everywhere."

Marina and Montcalf's assistant had visited some of the most expensive galleries and boutiques in Washington, but the sticker shock had forced her to keep her wallet tightly closed.

"So, you take me to dinner tonight?" Marina asked coyly. "I want to listen to romantic Hungarian with violin."

That reminded Ivan of the dinner plans that Marina knew nothing about. He began recounting to her the events of the day, and especially his meeting with the Secretary of State and the excellent impression she had made on him.

"She was the first politician I've ever heard of who saw the big picture, and wasn't completely locked into one-sided party politics," he said, admiringly.

"Perhaps your interest in older women extends to politicians who have age of Secretary," said Marina, in a teasing tone.

"You'll like her too," Ivan assured her. "You're going to meet her tonight. She's coming here to have dinner with us."

Marina was completely taken aback by this news. "What? Secretary of State of United States of America is having dinner with *us*? Where? At this hotel?"

"Right here in our suite. She wants complete privacy."

"Perhaps I go, then. I will disappear so you can be alone."

"No. She wants to meet you and get your opinion on Chechnya. She'll probably bring someone else with her, but I don't know whether it's a personal friend or someone she wants me to work with on the caliph project."

"You do not kid me about all this, ya?"

"Of course not. Why would I do that?" He looked at his watch. "You'd better go and change your clothes. She'll be here soon."

"What shall I wear?"

"Wear that skirt that undulates. That way you won't have to worry about any competition from the Secretary of State."

Just then the phone rang. Ivan picked it up and a woman's voice said, "Hello Ivan, this is Julia. May I come up?"

"Yes of course, Julia. We've been expecting you."

"Is too late!" Marina exclaimed. "I have no more time! I cannot change clothes!"

"Don't worry. You look beautiful just the way you are."

"You call her Julia? How well do you know this woman?"

Ivan chuckled. "Honestly, I just met her today. But she particularly asked to be called Julia, so I was just being obedient, exactly the way you like me to be. You should call her Madame Secretary, though, until she asks you to call her Julia, too."

There came a rap on the door that was so loud it startled them. A bulky man in a dark blue suit and tie was standing in the doorway. Behind him were the Secretary and two other men.

"Ivan, these men are my security guards," said Julia. "Is it all right if they come in and check out the room?"

"Of course." Ivan said.

The hefty man came in and walked around each room, looking from place to place. Ivan and Marina had no idea what he was looking for, but after a minute or two, he left to join his partner to stand guard outside the door.

The Secretary came in, then, along with a slim man in his thirties. Julia introduced the man as David Feingold, her cipher and computer analyst. Ivan and Marina shook David's hand and welcomed him.

Then Ivan introduced Marina to Julia saying, "Madame Secretary, I would like to introduce you to my fiancée, Dr. Marina Kortikuova."

"It is great honor for me to meet you, Madame Secretary," Marina said respectfully.

"Never mind that Madame stuff, call me Julia. I get called Madame so often I sometimes think I'm managing a bordello instead of a madhouse. You must know the feeling, Marina. May I call you Marina?"

"Yes, of course," Marina said. "It must be relief to just relax after long day of formalities."

"Exactly so," Julia agreed. Then, looking at Ivan, she spoke as though she were back in her office again. "I had to take the liberty of getting a background check on you and Marina before I came here. I'm sorry, but it's just routine security these days. I'm pleased to say that you qualify for secret clearance with my endorsement. Marina, of course, is a foreign national and therefore can't be cleared to work on your secret project. But you told me this afternoon that Marina has at least some information about your theory and its possible consequences. That is true, isn't it?"

Marina nodded and Ivan said, "It is."

"Do you intend to remain in the United States, Marina?"

"My first desire is to be with Ivan. Is most likely that he will find employment in America, so therefore I expect to be with him and to find job here myself. I have interview for position at Harvard on Monday afternoon. So we see what is happening."

"Ivan appears to be on the trail of something that could have great political consequences. I would like to help him explore his theory, but until it's proven, we can't let this get out of the room. Ivan is a United States citizen, employed as a consultant to the government. As such he will sign certain documents that ensure that he maintain silence about this work. You should understand that if you violate the terms of this agreement you can and will be sent to prison. I will ask you to sign this paper too, so that Ivan's work can begin at once. Will you do that, Marina?"

"Of course. I wish to help Ivan in every way. I agree not to discuss his secret work on project with anyone. A situation like this would be no different in Russia."

Ivan and Marina signed the papers while Julia and her computer specialist, David Feingold, looked on. Then Ivan ordered dinner without wine so that he and David would be clear-minded as they formulated the methods to be used to do the work of exposing the covert conspiracy of the council of caliphs.

Simeon Montcalf had recruited David Feingold from City College of New York's doctoral program in mathematics. David wasn't much to look at, with his unkempt hair and thick glasses, but his mind was a thing of beauty and a joy for Ivan. He later described David's creative mind to Marina as "Feingold's fine gold." Ivan liked this strange worm that had come out of the Big Apple, and he winked at Julia to let her know that David was a good find for the project.

By the time the room service waiter arrived with the food, Ivan and David had been working on the computer, using Ivan's algorithms as if they were born teammates. They hardly skipped a beat in their conversation about statistical methods and the mathematics they might use to decipher the imam's Koran.

The two women had also developed a personal rapport as a result of their protracted discussion while the men were busy.

"I think you two young people should consider moving to Washington," Julia said. "I could offer Ivan a job that would be exciting for him. When it comes to problems of scale and significance, nothing can rival the government, and I believe your big man needs big things to grapple with or he won't be challenged."

It was getting late, so the group decided to call it a night. It was agreed that they would let Montcalf work his magic in finding the other members needed for the team. Meanwhile, everything that could be done at this stage had been agreed upon, so the Secretary and David Feingold said good night and left, with their security officers in tow.

"How did you like Julia?" Ivan asked Marina, when they were alone in the suite. He hung his coat in the hall closet and turned to look at her. "I never had a chance to hear what you two were saying. What did you talk about while David and I were at the computer?"

"I like her so much," Marina said. "She is like older sister to me. She is wise and yet earthy. Your American President must be very wise man to appoint her to be in cabinet."

"So my male instincts were right in identifying a woman friend for you," Ivan remarked, rolling the dinner cart out the door.

"Yes," Marina admitted. "I think she likes me, but she does not have time for us to become real friends. She is busy woman. But you, Ivan, I think you have obviously bowled her down."

"Bowled her over."

"You are good grammar teacher," she frowned. "You are always so quick to correct my English."

"Sorry, sweetheart. It's just force of habit. But tell me about Julia."

"She spoke very much about you. She likes you, darling. She already knows you are genius. That is because she is very intelligent woman."

"I doubt that she thinks I'm a genius."

"If I know, then she knows too," Marina insisted. "We are both intelligent women. She told me that she wants you to work for her someday."

"Well, we'll have to give that some serious consideration. A job offer coming from the Secretary of State is nothing to sneeze at."

"What are you saying to me? I do not sneeze. What are you talking about?"

"It's just another one of our silly little expressions. If you sneeze at something, it's supposed to mean that you think it's not very important.

"I see," Marina said, nodding seriously.

"Right now, though, I think we really ought to go to the bedroom so we can put things in the right order. You are my top priority, followed by imams, terrorists, affairs of state, and world peace."

Ivan bent down and put his arms around her, lifting her up so that her head was almost touching the ceiling.

"And just what kind of an animal are you?" he said. "You've climbed to the top of the social pile in no time flat! Your head will be in the clouds soon, never mind the ceiling, my little Czarina from Muscovy."

He let Marina slide slowly down his long body until her toes touched the floor. He held her close and whispered, "Now that you have had your dinner you will have to put out for me."

"What is this, *put out?*" she asked, a little suspiciously.

"It's an American expression that means *to do it.*"

"I suppose I do not need to ask what," she said, testily. "As for this putting out, I do not put out unless I want to."

"And how do you feel about it now? Ivan asked.

"It happens that I feel good about it," she replied. "But right now I clean up."

Marina emerged from the bathroom a little bit later, carrying her clothes over her arm. She laid them on the chair and then slid into the bed next to him. She smelled fresh and clean. She looked Ivan in the eyes and said, "I will put out now."

Ivan burst out laughing. Marina looked at him quizzically, feeling confused and slightly offended by his reaction to her statement. She expected him to be pleased, not amused.

"I'm sorry," he said. "Please don't take it personally. I'm laughing because it's only young, single men who use that term. I'm sorry I didn't explain it clearly enough to you."

She pretended to pout for a moment, and then she relaxed.

"Is all right. Is not important. I do not sneeze."

Ivan laughed again.

"I was only kidding when I used that term," he told her. "It was a stupid thing for me to say. I would never seriously think about our sexual relationship in such a crass way, because it implies it's *quid pro quo.*"

"What is *squid pro quo?*" she asked quickly.

"*Quid pro quo,*" he corrected her.

"That's what I said," she frowned.

"It means *this for that* in Latin," he said.

"It sounds like Turkish bazaar to me," Marina remarked.

"Yes, well it does have a sort of transactional element to it," he explained. "Kind of like a business arrangement."

"We both put out for each other, ya?" she whispered. "But do you grow tired of me now that we are together so often?" Marina asked him.

"Never!" Ivan declared, with great conviction. "As far as I'm concerned, the sexual part of our relationship is more like a homecoming."

"But you can only come home once."

"What do you mean? Why only once?"

"It is everybody's destiny to find their way home. And when they succeed in it, they are so happy to be home they never want to go away again, so they cannot have any more homecomings. Homecomings? Is that how you called them? Do I pronounce it right?"

"You pronounce everything beautifully," Ivan assured her, holding her against his chest.

"Then why you want to leave me?"

"I don't want to leave you at all!"

"Then why you speak of coming home?"

"I'm always at home when I'm with you."

"We go in circles. Circle has no beginning and no end, just like engagement ring."

Ivan suddenly lifted Marina off her feet, twirling her around and around.

"You see? We're going in circles, and yes, they have no beginning and no end. That's how I love you. I've always loved you, and I always will."

They kissed each other, and then Marina said, "Come home, Ivan Welland."

"With pleasure," he said.

"You will give me a squid," Marina said happily, "and I will make you a pro."

Ivan laughed again.

"Why you laugh?" Marina asked.

"You don't have to try to make me a pro," he chuckled. "I already know a few things."

"You do, is it?" she said admiringly. "Then you make *me* a pro, please."

Ivan started by giving her a very long kiss.

CHAPTER TWENTY-TWO

In the morning Ivan and Marina decided to get in as much sightseeing as possible. They dressed and went down to the Avenue Grill that was located off the lobby of the Marriott Hotel, and helped themselves to the buffet. Their plan was to walk to all the monuments and museums within range, so as to do a quick survey of every one of them. That way they would know which ones to visit again the next time they were in town.

With breakfast safely tucked inside them, they headed out of the hotel in the direction of the Mall—an open, grassy area with an elongated, rectangular shape. At one end is the tall obelisk that is the Washington Monument, towering over everything in sight. On the other end is the Capitol Building, which houses the Senate and the House of Representatives. The two main avenues that lie parallel to the Mall are lined with museums and federal government buildings.

Ivan and Marina arrived at the Smithsonian Museum of Natural History and checked out the animal displays, starting with the huge African bull elephant that dominates the lobby. The Smithsonian Museum had grown to encompass many buildings, each dedicated to a different subject matter.

Next, Ivan decided that he should do something about Marina's ignorance of American history, so they stopped at the American History Museum and did a quick pass. It was obvious to them that all the museums would be worthy of extended visits. Both of them were gluttons for knowledge and could have easily spent the rest of their lives visiting all the archives, museums, galleries, and historical buildings in Washington. They agreed to return as often as possible so that they could continue to enjoy what was being offered absolutely free to any visitor.

They were on their way to the National Gallery when Ivan's cell phone announced a caller. It was Montcalf, and he was back to his usual self.

"Welland, how are you, old boy?" he said.

"I'm fine, thanks. We're fine," said Ivan.

"Good. I've found someone for your project. I'd like you to meet him today. Can you do it?" Montcalf asked.

"You bet! No problem."

"Are you okay for dinner?"

"Dinner?" Ivan repeated. He looked over at Marina, who nodded. "Where shall we meet, and when?"

"How about seven o'clock at the Old Ebbitt Grill? It's just a block from your hotel on 13th Street."

"Sounds good. We'll be there," Ivan said, snapping his cell phone shut. "He's amazing, that guy," he continued, pocketing his phone and turning to Marina. "He's already found another fellow for the project. He has tentacles all over the place."

They continued walking west down Constitution Avenue, stopping at the Sculpture Garden for a quick look around. Up the avenue a bit further they entered the National Gallery, which houses an invaluable collection of artwork of all kinds. Some philanthropists donated huge sums of money, as well as their personal art collections, to get the magnificent gallery underway. After wandering around the museum for about an hour, they located a small, upscale restaurant and sat down at one of the tables. It seemed to be dedicated to the well-heeled patrons of the museum, if the prices on the menu were any indication. They decided that a spinach salad, shrimp scampi, and a cappuccino in a quiet corner was just what they needed.

It was four o'clock by the time they got back to the hotel. They had a couple of hours to kill before their dinner with

Montcalf, so they decided to try to take a nap. They partially undressed and put on the terrycloth bathrobes that seem to be *de rigueur* in the better hotels these days. They were able to sleep for an hour, leaving them rested and with time to clean up before dinner.

The Old Ebbitt Grill, a fixture in Washington's culinary circles, was only one block west and one block north of the Marriott. They asked the *maître d'hôtel* for Montcalf's table, and they were guided right to it immediately. Ivan spotted Montcalf sitting there with another man, talking over drinks.

"Ah, there you are, Welland," said Montcalf, rising to his feet. "Let me introduce you, please, to Mr. Damian Rutledge. Damian works for the CIA as a sort of historical archivist."

After the introductions were made, Ivan and Marina sat down and ordered bloody Caesars. Then Ivan turned toward Rutledge, who was seated on his left.

"If you're with the CIA, Damian, how can you work on my project?"

"I can have him seconded to the State Department for the length of the project," Montcalf said, before Rutledge could open his mouth. "I can arrange it, if you need Damian's services."

"I'd like to know more about the kind of work you do, Damian, but I'm aware that there are certain aspects of it that you're not at liberty to talk about."

"It's okay," said Rutledge, who had shown no irritation about Montcalf's pushiness. "I can keep it simple. A lot of folks like to call me *Doctor Disaster.* My job is to record all the details of every terrorist attack in the world. I document them by plugging them into a database that's kept over at company headquarters."

"Could I tap into your database?" Ivan asked, pleased to know that there was a single source of such information.

"I can arrange it for you Ivan, don't worry," Montcalf said. "I can easily get clearance for the inter-departmental information transfer."

"I'd appreciate that," Ivan replied, then he turned back to Rutledge.

"Do you know David Feingold, by any chance?"

"I know him from written and phone communications I've had with him, but we've never met in person."

"You may meet him soon, if you join our team."

Dinner came, but the men went on talking business without noticing the delectable, aromatic dishes that were put before them.

"I'm trying to prove that there's a conspiracy at work that controls worldwide Islamist terrorism," Ivan explained to Rutledge. "I strongly suspect that terrorist leaders are using special editions of the Koran and the Hadith as the basis for coding messages between a council of covert caliphs and their operatives in terrorist cells around the world. If we can break this code we might be able to relate the orders sent to the cells to the events themselves, and hopefully identify the source of the orders."

"Sounds intriguing," said Damian. "Go on."

"I've discovered some clear differences between the editions of the Koran used by the imams and those used by the general public. David Feingold and I are evolving some algorithms to analyze the Arabic texts to determine if these differences are hiding a system used to encode messages. If so, we need a *Doctor Disaster* to correlate the orders to the events. If we decipher the order for an attack, and correlate it with the actual attack, we will have proof that a coordinated control group exists. Then we must find out who and where these people are."

"Well, I certainly have the means to do that," said Rutledge, with growing interest. "How did you come up with all this?"

"An insight became a series of deductions, then they developed into a theory, and now it all has to be proved," Ivan said.

"You know, it's interesting. I've occasionally had the feeling that there have been many incidents that were related too closely to one another for them to be accidental, but it was only a hunch. I had no proof, and no knowledge of a secret code. Now it looks as though I might be able to do something about those hunches. I'd really love to work with you on this project."

By the end of the meal it was clear that Ivan had found his second man for the team. Now all that remained was the Arabic scholar. Montcalf had succeeded again, and Ivan thanked him.

"Two down, and one to go," he said to Simeon.

Ivan was brushing his teeth the next morning and thinking happily about the more or less sleepless night he had spent with Marina, when he was brought back down to the earth by the insistent ringing of the phone.

"Can you get that?" he called to Marina in the bedroom.

He was rinsing out his mouth when he heard Marina's voice.

"Is for you. Is Simeon," she called back.

He picked up the bathroom extension.

"Hello?"

"Welland?" It was Montcalf's familiar voice.

"Yes," Ivan replied sharply, annoyed at being called so early.

"I've found your third man," he said triumphantly.

"What? How could you have found him so quickly?"

"While you were sleeping, or not sleeping, as the case may be, I was busy making phone calls."

"Good for you," said Ivan, with mixed feelings. He was irritated with Montcalf for implying that he had wasted *his* time by sleeping the night away in the arms of his beloved, but he was thrilled that he'd soon be meeting a potential number three.

"The best thing of all is that he works at State, so we don't have to borrow him from any other department. What time would you like to meet him?"

"The sooner the better. When are you both free?"

"We're free now," said Montcalf. "What about you?"

"We were just about to go down to breakfast."

"Good. We'll meet you in the lobby restaurant."

"What? You're downstairs? *Now?*"

"I told you, I don't waste any time. Tell Marina I'll keep her company while you two talk."

He hung up.

"Montcalf thinks he's found the third man," Ivan said to Marina, toweling off his face. "He wants you to know that he'll keep you company while I talk to his candidate. I could almost hear him licking his lips in anticipation. Disgusting old goat."

"Goats are nice."

"Not this one. He's a dirty old man, but he's very good at his job."

"This is what counts, ya?"

"Yes, but I don't like it that he has a crush on you. He's joined the ranks of your accidental conquests."

Marina was standing in her bra and panties, holding up one of her dresses and looking at herself in the full-length mirror.

"What do you think I should wear?" she asked him.

Ivan looked away.

"What is wrong?" she said, looking worried.

"Nothing's wrong. Everything is just right. You look so perfect to me, I can hardly keep my eyes off you."

"Good. I do not want you to keep hands off."

While he hurriedly knotted his necktie, Ivan wondered what Montcalf's new recruit would be like. He hoped the chemistry of the group would help them work together and achieve the proof he needed in order to expose the council of caliphs and their terrorist plans.

When they arrived at the lobby restaurant, the *maitre d'* led them to a round table in the corner, next to a window. Montcalf and his guest rose to greet Ivan and Marina, and introductions were quickly made all around.

"Meet Abdul al Sharif," said Montcalf, beaming with pride. "He is a disaffected Iraqi, the son of a sheikh from a tribe that was particularly in disfavor with Saddam Hussein."

Montcalf continued speaking as though Abdul were not even present. "He has been in the U.S. since about the age of ten, so by experience and education he is American. After getting his BA at Brown University, he moved into the PhD program in Near Eastern Studies at Yale. After he got his doctorate he was hired by the State Department to do some complex Arabic-to-English translations and some political analysis. Now, you can take it from there," he concluded, "while I attend to the lovely Marina."

Ivan shook hands with Abdul, who seemed not to mind or even notice Montcalf's haughty manner. He was an olive-skinned Arab in his late twenties who, Ivan thought, could easily have played the Mahdi in *Laurence of Arabia*. About six feet tall and with dark, hooded eyes, Abdul was what today's girls would call a "hottie."

"What level of clearance do you have, Abdul?"

"Secret clearance. There should be no problem."

"I'm not worried. I'm sure I don't have to remind you that you can't mention a word about this project to anyone."

"I understand. I've worked on secret projects before."

Ivan sat back and outlined his conspiracy theory. He told Abdul how he and the other team members were preparing the methodology to prove his theory.

"Now what we need," he said, "is someone who is fluent in Arabic and has a good knowledge of the Koran."

"I could be your man," said Abdul. "Obviously I'm fluent in Arabic, and I'm also quite familiar with the Koran, which goes well beyond what we were expected to know at Yale. I have a personal interest, of course."

Ivan pulled out his copy of Imam Mansur's Koran and showed it to Abdul.

"Do you notice anything unusual about this particular copy of the Koran?"

Abdul looked at the book on all sides. Then he opened it and checked out the first few pages.

"This is an imam's copy," he said, with some surprise. "Where did you get it?"

"Chechnya," Ivan replied.

"You realize that only an imam may touch this book. If you were caught in possession of it you could be killed."

"I'm not worried," Ivan said. "I'm giving it to *you* now."

Abdul paled.

"Please start working on this Koran right away," Ivan continued. "Compare it to the usual editions. Note the places and the ways in which it differs from the normal books. Get a copy of the Hadith, the one with nine volumes. See if the Arabic in the imam's Koran could in any way be making references to the Hadith. In the meantime Feingold, Rutledge and I will be doing statistical analyses to coordinate with your findings. I'll come down to Washington next weekend and we'll go over our progress. Here's my cell phone number if you need me before next weekend. This project has the personal support of the Secretary of State, and I'm anxious to get her some results ASAP. I needn't remind you not to let this Koran out of your hands. There are implications here that concern the future of our world, so let's bring this project to a successful conclusion."

Every once in a while Ivan glanced over at Marina to see how she was reacting to Simeon Montcalf's non-stop flow of conversation. As far as he could tell from Marina's eyes, she seemed to be holding her own with the old windbag. He hoped that she was heeding his advice about not allowing herself to be taken in by his old-world charm.

"I'm sorry, I didn't mean to interrupt your thoughts," Abdul was saying, "but I need your e-mail address."

"Of course," said Ivan, handing him a business card that Montcalf had had printed on his behalf. "It's all there."

The two young men discussed linguistics for a while, looking for some esoteric connections between Russian and Arabic. There followed a long discussion about the relative advantages and disadvantages of Harvard and Yale's PhD programs, and other matters peripheral to their core purpose. As Ivan observed Abdul, he wondered if he was being totally open about his feelings concerning the project. Ivan thought he might have some reservations about their work in that he feared that any information they discovered would be used to kill Muslims.

"You understand," Ivan told him, "that the information we collect is going to be used in a peaceful fashion to help recapture Islam from the secret council of caliphs that's holding it captive. That's why I gave the project to the State Department and not to the military, so that we can try to find a purely political solution to the enmity that exists on the part of fundamentalist Muslims towards Christians and Jews."

"It would be nice if it could work out that way," Abdul said, looking a bit gloomy.

"The problem with Islam is coming from deep within itself. If we allow a small group of desperate, power-hungry men to secretly manipulate Islam away from a peaceful existence by turning every Muslim they can get their hands on into a radical, suicidal fighter, the world will be a horrible place."

"What they're doing is not supported by anything in the Koran," Abdul pointed out.

"That's right. These extremists are hijacking Islam and using it as a license to kill. So obviously, they have to be stopped. Your own family serves as a good example of what can happen to anyone who ever protests against the rule of these despots, and in a personal way you have more at stake in this than any of us. You've lived in America and benefited from her generosity and liberty, so you above all people should know that there's no element of racial, ethnic, gender, religious, or political prejudice in our philosophy of government, and there'll be none in this project, either. Our purpose must be to expose these tyrants so their criminal actions can be seen by those who love a peaceful Islam."

"I'm with you on that," Abdul agreed.

"I have no doubt that once this conspiracy of the caliphs is exposed, the Muslims themselves will handle the situation. Our job must be merely to shine a light on the nest of vipers that's trying to use and pervert Islam for its own purposes."

Abdul was convinced of Ivan's sincerity, and promised to put his mind to work on doing his part to decipher the code.

They stood up and said their goodbyes. Abdul took his leave and went home, saying that he hoped to hear from Ivan soon.

"You have an amazing ability to locate the right people for the job that I have in mind," Ivan said to Montcalf.

"You liked Abdul, did you?"

"I did," Ivan nodded. "He has enough Arab left in him to keep the rest of us from falling into stereotypical thinking."

"I never thought of that," said Montcalf, with a cryptic smile.

"I'll bet," said Ivan. "Look, I want to thank you for breakfast and for kindly entertaining Marina while I talked almost exclusively with Abdul."

"Think nothing of it. The pleasure was all mine."

Before Ivan could think of a rejoinder, Montcalf was already talking about travel arrangements for the following weekend. He would arrange for accommodations in the same hotel, and he'd have the airline e-mail their tickets to them.

Ivan and Marina walked Montcalf to the front entrance of the hotel, and the bell captain called him a cab. When Montcalf drove away, they turned and went back into the lobby.

"What did you talk to Montcalf about?" said Ivan, as they waited for the elevator.

"We talked of many things," she said.

"But not cabbages and kings," Ivan said.

"Of course not. Why should we talk about cabbages and what? Kings?"

"It's a verse from a famous poem by Lewis Carroll. It's called *The Walrus and the Carpenter.*"

"Why is walrus with carpenter?" she asked, as they got into the elevator.

"They were talking of many things," Ivan smiled. "The poem goes like this:

> *The time has come, the walrus said,*
> *To talk of many things:*
> *Of shoes, and ships, and sealing wax,*
> *Of cabbages, and kings,*
> *And why the sea is boiling hot,*
> *And whether pigs have wings.*"

"What is ceiling wax?" Marina asked, looking up at the ceiling of the elevator for signs of wax.

"Sealing wax," Ivan said. "It's for sealing envelopes."

"Walrus discusses with carpenter how to seal envelopes? What does walrus expect carpenter to do? Nail the envelope shut with hammer? You Americans are mad."

"The British. It's the British who are mad."

"Why the British?"

"Lewis Carroll was born in England."

"Well, *you* memorized poem. You were born *here*. So Americans are mad."

"Mad about Russian women, maybe.

"With little push maybe from Secretary of State," Marina reminded him as they got off on their floor. "Is thanks to Mr. Montcalf, remember, that I am here with you."

"I do thank him for that," Ivan said. "I thank him most sincerely," he added, inserting his card into the slot on the door of their room. Then he suddenly lifted Marina off her feet, backed into the door to keep it open, and carried her over the threshold.

Cambridge, Massachusetts

CHAPTER TWENTY-THREE

I van was sitting at his desk in the Cambridge apartment, hard at work on the feedback he was getting from his little team in Washington. He was so deep in thought that he was startled when the door flew open and Marina burst into the room.

"How was the interview?" he asked, turning around.

"Professor Burbidge says I have job," said Marina, her eyes shining. "But first I must get rubber stamp from Dean."

"I'm sure he'll give you all the stamps you need."

"I am glad for job. I like to contribute to our bank account."

"I'm happy too, my little czarina."

"And how are your algorithms?" Marina asked.

"I've made good progress. I think I'll be able to make some test runs this weekend in Washington. I'll call Feingold and the others in the morning to find out how they're doing."

"This is good, ya? I make dinner now to celebrate all good things that happened to us. I make lamb chops to remind us of Chechnya, when we ate lamb every day."

Later, when they were enjoying their celebratory dinner, Marina suddenly put down her fork and looked at Ivan.

"Why," she asked, "is meat always tender in America?"

"The U.S. can't take credit for the lamb. Most of it is grown in New Zealand."

"Americans cannot grow lamb here?"

"It's not that we can't. It's just cheaper."

"This is amazing, ya? Meat cheaper from other side of world. Global village getting smaller every day. Soon Americans will do nothing for themselves except to make hot dogs and ice-cream."

"Hey, now you're talking. If you haven't planned anything else for dessert, I'll take you to Brigham's for ice-cream with jimmies on top. What do you say?"

"What are these jimmies?"

"Little pieces of chocolate that they sprinkle over the ice-cream."

"I will ask them for take-home jimmies, then, and later I sprinkle them all over *you.*"

Returning to Cambridge meant coming back to chores and obligations. Ivan had final papers to correct and grades to get over to the registrar's office. Marina wanted to create lesson plans for the classes that she would teach in the fall. Ivan needed to tell his thesis advisor that he was ready to take his oral exam as soon as possible, and to discuss his thesis topic. The week was crammed full of expectations, and every day brought something new to be dealt with or celebrated. Their flight to Washington was arranged as promised by Simeon Montcalf. They would leave on Friday morning, so their work week in Cambridge was shortened by a day, which added to the pressure to handle their mundane but necessary duties.

By the time Friday morning rolled around, everything was in readiness. Marina had signed her employment agreement, and Ivan had spoken on the phone several times with his team in Washington. Each of the men had reported some progress, but Ivan wanted to knit their efforts together. His algorithm was the key to processing the huge amounts of data that needed to be analyzed. He was sure that if his logic was correct, patterns would emerge that would enable his team to decipher the caliphs' code, and in so doing, prove the existence of the ignoble conspiracy that had stolen the heart of Islam.

As they were packing for their weekend trip to D.C., Ivan noticed that Marina was looking a little sad.

"What's wrong?" he asked her.

"Is menstrual period. It started this morning."

Ivan held her and comforted her to the best of his ability. Apparently there was little relationship between how much they loved each other and the random nature of procreation.

"I once knew a young couple who tried to have a baby for years," he told her. "Finally they gave up and went to China to adopt a baby. She was the cutest little girl in the world, and smart as a whip. Then right after that, the wife became pregnant with twins."

Marina had heard similar stories, and although she had a rational understanding of the matter, she still felt sad. It was probably hormonal, she decided. She thought about the finite number of ova she had been assigned from the time of her birth. She calculated that her body had given her 240 chances so far, and she had willingly wasted them until Ivan came into her life. In the light of those statistics, she felt pressured to get pregnant before it was too late.

"I know how much it means to you to have our child," Ivan told her. "It means everything to me, too. But give it some time. Everything will be all right, you'll see."

The flight to Washington from Boston was routine. When they arrived at the Marriott, they were quickly recognized by several of the hotel's staff. Ivan guessed it was because of his height. He chuckled to himself when it crossed his mind that they probably remembered his beautiful fiancée more than they remembered him. After they registered, the concierge personally took them up to their suite.

"Mr. Montcalf called, sir," he said, as they rode up in the elevator. "He'll be here at four o'clock."

"Four o'clock? What time is it now?" Ivan asked.

"It's ten past three, sir."

When he was sure that everything was in order and his guests were comfortable, the concierge closed the elegant double doors of their suite and left them alone.

They had just finished unpacking when there came a knock at the door. It was Simeon Montcalf. He greeted Ivan with a quick nod, then swept right past him and made a beeline for Marina.

"My dear young woman, it is such a pleasure to see you once again," he said, planting a delicate kiss on the back of her hand. "Do you have everything you need?"

Marina nodded and smiled.

"Well, if you want anything, just let me know. I'll be glad to accommodate your every whim."

"You are very kind," said Marina, demurely.

Montcalf finally turned and faced Ivan. "Are you ready for your meeting tomorrow morning, dear boy?"

"Yes."

"Very good," said Montcalf, turning his attention right back to Marina. Ivan thought that Marina was like catnip to Montcalf. He was asking her in detail about her interview at Harvard. He seemed genuinely happy for Marina, and they were talking to each other like old friends.

Ivan was amazed at his capacity for jealousy. He was completely certain of Marina's fidelity with regard to any relationship that involved something worth being jealous over, and yet he was bothered by Montcalf's attentions. He watched Marina as she talked with him. She was vital and responsive, but in no way coquettish or sexually overt. She had the natural charm and confidence of an intelligent, mature woman, without even a hint of the imperiousness of a social climber. He was astonished, however, at how the average male behaved towards Marina. Men of a certain age, those who were on the down side of their prime but felt they were still in the game, just worshipped her.

Since he was totally left out of the conversation between his fiancée and Montcalf, he had plenty of time to ponder the subtleties that resulted in his exclusion from social conversations between Marina and "her men." Was her attention the prize in itself, or was the game supposed to symbolically capture the woman of a younger competitor? Somehow these older guys were trying to make him feel as though he had unfairly kidnapped the princess from the royal castle. Ivan realized that any show of jealousy or pique would work to his disadvantage and make him seem petty and immature. His ripostes had to be calculated to obscure any hint of ill will. He felt certain that Marina's "men" were working on his age and lack of experience by emphasizing their own sophistication.

"Montcalf can do what he likes," Ivan thought sourly, "but even with the age difference, I'll be a bull to his calf."

Just then Montcalf managed to peel himself away from Marina long enough to direct his attention to Ivan for a brief moment.

"By the way, Welland," he said, almost as an aside, "the Secretary wants you to call her. Do you have her number?"

"I have Julia's private number," Ivan told Montcalf, stressing the word "private" just to tweak his nose.

"Excellent!" exclaimed Montcalf, beaming. "Well, I have to get back to work," he added, looking at his watch. "If you need anything, Marina," he added, looking fondly in her direction, "just call the concierge and tell him that Mr. Montcalf approves."

"Thank you," said Marina. "You are very kind."

"No amount of kindness is sufficient for a delightful, charming, gracious young lady like you," said Montcalf, unashamed to be openly flattering her in this way.

To Ivan he said, "A car will fetch you at 8:30 in the morning and take you to the State Department. The others will be there waiting for you. I'll look after Marina while you're gone."

He opened the door and let himself out, bowing from the waist and waving to Marina as he left.

Marina looked at Ivan and raised her eyes heavenward. "He intentionally snubs you, ya? Why he does that?"

"I think he's jealous. I know he hated it that Julia and I got on friendly terms so quickly. He thinks I'm a neophyte and shouldn't be getting ahead so rapidly. He uses you to get at me because he knows you're older than I am, so he believes you'll be more interested in him than in a kid like me. I'm sure he's just waiting for me to blow my cool so he can exploit my so-called childish jealousy. But don't worry. I won't lose my temper unless he really gets out of line. On the other hand, don't think I'm going to step aside and just let any other man take you away from me, because that's not going to happen."

"I do not know why these men behave like this, but now you know why I waited to love you. You know in your heart that I belong to you. For always."

Ivan kissed her. "You're a beautiful woman, Marina. It shouldn't surprise me that they're all attracted by you."

"Sometimes I think men are angry because you are so tall that you make them feel small," Marina remarked.

"I've been conscious of that reaction in many men, but in this case it's a secondary reaction. It's not about me, it's about you. There's a ripeness about you that summons men from everywhere. Like fruit flies arriving from who knows where, the minute the fruit is on the table."

Marina giggled. "You make me sound like soft pear waiting to be eaten by the next gentleman who passes by."

"Ah well, you do have a soft pair," Ivan said, as he cupped her breasts in his hands.

"Young man, you must stop your instincts for now. Call Julia right now. You should not keep her waiting." Marina reached over to the desk and handed him the phone.

Ivan dialed Julia's number, and her secretary answered.

"Hello, this is Ivan Welland. The Secretary asked me to call."

"Oh yes, Dr. Welland. She's in a meeting right now, but she asked me to invite you to a party at her house this evening. She told me to tell you that it was Russian night, and she thought that Dr. Kortikuova might be interested in meeting some of her countrymen in the diplomatic corps. She asked you to be there in business dress at about eight, and she instructed me to have you picked up at your hotel at seven. Is that all right?"

"Why yes, of course," Ivan said. "Please tell her that we accept her kind invitation, and we'll see her later."

"What did she want?" Marina asked when he hung up.

"We're invited to a party at her house. She wants us to go and meet some Russian diplomats. She's sending a car for us at seven o'clock. I'm supposed to wear a business suit, so I guess you should wear a cocktail dress. Did you bring one?"

"Yes, I brought dress I wore in Russia on very special occasions. Is from Czarina's collection," Marina said.

"I see," said Ivan. "Does it undulate when you walk?"

"I do not know. Why you ask?"

"Men always keel over when they see you in that dress. I just wanted you to be prepared for the Russian fruit flies."

"I try to hide my ripeness to the most I can."

Later in the evening they dressed for the party—Ivan in his best blue suit with the requisite presidential-looking red tie, and Marina in a green shift with a string of pearls at the neck and pearl earrings to match. She had on black high-heeled shoes, and carried a small black purse. Ivan was surprised at how sophisticated she looked. She clearly had much more experience than he did in handling social occasions. When all was said and done, he was really only a Texas country boy who wasn't terribly at home in fancy duds. He kissed her on top of her blond head and told her that she was his *bella donna*. Just then the concierge called to tell them their limo was waiting, so they headed to the elevator, feeling like pampered royalty.

They both felt guilty as they alit from Julia's limo in front of her gorgeous stone house in Georgetown. They didn't think they deserved to be treated with so much deference. Many of the guests, however, had no such reservations. Indeed, Ivan felt the pomposity factor had exceeded its normal Washington limits by a large margin. Evidently Julia thought so too, as she looked almost relieved to see them appear on her doorstep.

"Thanks for coming," she said, smiling at the two of them as she led them inside. "I'd like to see you privately later," she said quietly to Ivan.

Julia was in her usual fine spirits. "You're not going to find many relaxed, normal conversations here in D.C.," she said. "But you should circulate and try to let the air out of some of the stuffed shirts anyway."

"We'll do our best," Ivan smiled.

"Meeting the Russian embassy staff may be of some help to you in your work, Marina," she said.

She escorted them over to the Russian Ambassador. She introduced Marina as Dr. Marina Kortikuova, Professor of Modern Russian History at Harvard University.

"Marina is engaged to be married to Dr. Ivan Welland, Your Excellency," said Julia. "Their union is the purest form of glasnost. I think you will find that they represent the very best of the young people of both our countries."

Julia left them with the Russian Ambassador, and went on with her duties as hostess. Marina and the Ambassador talked for a while in Russian. They felt each other out as expatriates do when they meet in a foreign country.

After a short period of small talk he passed Ivan and Marina over to his wife, making the introductions in a broad English accent. The ambassador's better half was a middle-aged, appropriately frumpy woman, obviously a steely-eyed veteran of the communist political system. Having few or no accomplishments of her own, she took it upon herself to denigrate those who did. She showed her claws as soon as she laid eyes on Marina. In Ivan's mind she was like the wicked stepmother in *Snow White* who, with a very inflated opinion of her own attractiveness, tries to eliminate the real beauty. Nothing in the world was uglier than the envy of one woman for the beauty of another, he thought. Ivan guided Marina away at the earliest opportunity.

Since they had not eaten dinner, they were only too happy to visit the buffet table, where they found some enticing examples of international culinary excellence.

"Oh, look at *these*," said Ivan, helping himself to some iced prawns. Having already had two glasses of *vino*, Ivan's *veritas* lay in the solid nourishment offered by the food.

Marina popped a bacon-wrapped scallop into her mouth and handed the toothpick to Ivan.

"You may dispose of this any way you wish," she said, with an imperious smile. Then she moved away from the table to make room for some hungry Russian guests whom she had not yet met.

A handsome young man approached Ivan and told him the Secretary could see him now. "This way, please," he said. "Bring your drink and your food with you," he added, when Ivan tried to find a place to put them down. Ivan presumed the man was a secret service agent.

Ivan followed him to an antechamber where he found Julia seated at a table, nursing a glass of champagne.

"Please, have a seat Ivan," she said, indicating the chair across from her. The secret service agent backed out of the room and closed the door behind him.

"I can't leave my guests for very long, so I'll get right to the point," she said. "How is your project coming along?"

"Montcalf came up with a team of three young men to work for me," Ivan replied. "You probably know who they are. We're going to meet tomorrow morning to go over my

algorithm for decoding the messages sent by the caliphs to
their henchmen all over the world. And if, as I suspect, it
turns out that there *is* a code present, then the proof of that
leads to other important questions."

"Such as?" said Julia, leaning forward.

"Who is sending the messages, and can we decode them?"

"So you'll be devoting your full attention to the project."

"I certainly will. Right now the other team members are
processing data, so it's best for me to concentrate on my
academic work. But I'll definitely be on hand to supervise
and contribute to the analysis of the data, and to determine
the direction of the future work. I'll see to it that things move
along as quickly as possible."

"Is there a deadline for your doctoral dissertation?"

"No, but I'd like to go ahead with my wedding plans, so
I'll need to find a teaching position. I can't expect to get a
job without a PhD, of course, so I'll just have to finish the
dissertation as soon as I can."

"You wouldn't need a PhD to work for the State Department," she said. "You could finish your thesis in your spare
time. How do you feel about that?"

"I'd be flattered to consider the offer if it were extended. I
should tell you, though, that Marina has just signed a contract to teach at Harvard for a year."

Julia looked thoughtful. "That shouldn't be a problem, she
said finally. "She could come down here on the weekends.
It's not uncommon for people to commute from Boston."

"I'll talk it over with her," Ivan promised.

"Fair enough," Julia said. "You'd better join her now. She
might need to be rescued from the red menace."

Ivan found her talking with a man who broke off what he
was saying when Ivan approached. Marina introduced him as
an attaché, but Ivan thought it was more than likely he was a
secret service agent. He couldn't help feeling that most of the
people at this party didn't harbor any great love for the
United States. Envy and suspicion were the main attitudes

that prevailed among the members of the Russian diplomatic corps.

"I'd like to leave soon," Ivan said quietly to Marina.

"Montcalf wants to show me city tomorrow."

"I'm sure he'd be very happy to do so," Ivan said sourly.

They wended their way through the people who were still left in the room so they could say goodbye to their hostess.

"What were you talking to the so-called attaché about?" Ivan wanted to know.

"He is typical suspicious Russian investigator. Always he asks questions, but never answers any himself. Probably makes dossier about me. I think he wants to find out how great is my loyalty to mother Russia. He likes to know if I drop my Russian citizenship now that I work here in the U.S. and I prepare to marry American citizen."

"And what did you say?"

"I tell him is too soon to make decision."

"Nosy little bastard."

"Why Julia talks to you alone in library?" Marina asked.

"She was just testing the waters to see if I would consider taking a job in her department."

"What you tell to her?"

"I said I'd consider it if she made me an offer, and I left it at that. I told her I'd like to write my doctoral thesis before everything else in the world gets in the way, but she thought I'd have no trouble writing it in my spare time. We'll just have to wait and see where this goes."

"I am at Harvard for a year," Marina reminded him.

"Yes, of course. Let's just wait until we have an offer in hand before we get into this too deeply. Julia knows our situation. We can trust her to understand."

When they got back to their hotel room, Marina went to the bathroom to brush her teeth and get ready for bed. Ivan took off his suit and hung it up along with his shirt and tie. Marina came out of the bathroom wearing only a pair of bikini panties. Ivan passed near her and gave her a pat on her barely covered behind on his way to the bathroom.

When he came back she was in bed with the covers up to her chin. He went around to the other side and slipped in beside her.

"You have ended my long years of being monk," she smiled.

"Nun, you mean."

"None of what?"

"A nun of a convent. A convent for women."

"You want to send me to convent?"

"Not unless I can come with you," Ivan said.

"Is shocking thing to say! You cannot come to convent! You cannot come *in* convent, either. What would nuns say?"

"Now, now. *None* of that," said Ivan, pulling the covers down and admiring her perfect body.

CHAPTER TWENTY-FOUR

Ivan opened his eyes. He was conscious of Marina's even breathing next to him. He looked at the electric clock on the bedside table. Six o'clock. Two hours to go before he had to be downstairs to meet his ride. As he lay waiting for Marina to stir, he turned his thoughts to his upcoming meeting. He felt totally prepared. He was sure he had the analytical blueprint that would in time break the code of the caliphs. He was clearly dealing with masters of deceit. How else could they have stayed in the background for so long, perhaps centuries, without being discovered? Well, they were going to be exposed now. He was eager to get started, but he lay still for Marina's sake.

At six thirty Marina's eyes slowly opened.

"Hi," she said. "Is time to get up?"

"I'm afraid so. Shall we have breakfast sent up?"

"This is good idea, ya?" she said. "Gives me more time to get ready for Simeon. He comes here at ten o'clock."

"And I leave in an hour," said Ivan, glancing at the clock.

"You take shower then, and I order breakfast."

She called room service and placed an order for two, then went into the bathroom and began brushing her teeth. Ivan was conscious of her presence, so he looked out over the glass doors of the shower and saw her standing in front of the sink, energetically brushing her teeth while her bare breasts jiggled from the motion of her arm. He watched her for a minute. When she raised her head she noticed his forehead and eyes looking at her over the shower rod. She gave a little shriek.

"Why you peek at me? You are voyeur! I call manager!"

Actually she liked it when he looked at her, although she wondered what a psychiatrist would say about it. She threw a towel over his head and left the room. When Ivan was dry he came out to find her in one of the hotel robes waiting for the food to arrive. She held up his bathrobe for him, while pretending to avert her eyes.

When breakfast came they sat down to eat, still dressed only in their robes. They were hungry, since they had only eaten canapés for dinner the night before. A cheese and onion omelet had never smelled so good.

After breakfast Ivan put on an old sweatshirt, a pair of Dockers, and running shoes. Marina was surprised by his casual attire, but he told her he was going to work, and he worked best when he was relaxed and comfortable.

"Have a good time with Simeon," he said, grabbing his laptop and briefcase, and giving her a quick kiss as he left the suite.

His chauffeur was waiting for him when he stepped out onto the street. Although he had never seen the driver before in his life, the man seemed to know who he was and called him by name. Ivan guessed someone had to have told him to look for the tall guy.

The hotel doorman opened the rear door for him, but he decided to ride in the front seat next to the driver. He didn't like being the recipient of all the special treatment. That was Montcalf's game, not his. He didn't think the representatives of democracy should be cavorting around in limousines as though they were royalty, especially at the taxpayer's expense. One of the advantages of growing up in an average houschold was that he hadn't become accustomed to being served. When he was waited on hand and foot he felt uncomfortable and unworthy of such treatment. Montcalf thought he shouldn't feel that way since the servants needed jobs too, but Ivan was unconvinced.

Welland was let out at the reception area where he was patted down, his computer case searched, and his name and ID checked against a list. Then a uniformed security guard led him to a conference room that had been assigned to his team for the day. When he opened the door he found his three co-workers already at work, with their papers and computers spread over the table.

"Good morning everyone," he said cheerily, putting his laptop on the table.

Feingold, Rutledge and al Sharif returned his greeting and stopped working, staring at him as if they were expecting some sort of introductory speech. Ivan cleared his throat.

"Gentlemen, if we're successful with our project, we'll help to clean out the most devious nest of vipers the world has ever known. The glory, if there is any, will no doubt go to others. But we four, who are pledged to secrecy, will know what a great thing we've done, and our reward will be the satisfaction we gain from the knowledge that we have helped to win this war. Now, we're only concerned at this point with two questions. First, is there a secret code hidden in the Arabic scriptures? And second, can we decipher that code? Actually, right now we're only interested in the *how* of the matter. The *who* and *why* questions will come later. Is that understood?"

The trio nodded their agreement.

"Good, then." He connected the power cord to his computer and set it at the end of the table so they all could see the screen. "Now, let's look at the criteria I've used for my algorithm. Please feel free to comment or to ask questions at any time."

Ivan began by confessing his totally abysmal lack of knowledge of Arabic, and pointing to Abdul al Sharif to acknowledge that his expertise would be invaluable. He told his team that in looking at Arabic in some older styles of printing he was taken by its likeness to seismographic chart tapes in that there seemed to be a lot of spikes and valleys.

Subsequently he had come across some analytical software that was used to compare the seismographic output of geological events such as earthquakes. He was able to adapt that software so that it would compare the peaks and valleys of various different types of Arabic script one to another, as if they were tremor recordings.

"Even though I had no idea what the writing meant," he said, "the program helped me match two different versions of the Koran and point out the aberrations and places where there were differences. This will allow Abdul to go directly to those places and see what the changes are. Since we're dealing with ten fair-sized volumes, Abdul would have had to read each book word by word to discover the anomalies, and we don't have time for that. But if I'm right about the seismology approach, Abdul should be able to tell us in a few hours if the pattern recognition software is helpful in identifying the paradigm that I suspect exists."

Ivan whipped a disc out of his attaché case and handed it to Abdul. He had already asked him to scan his personal copy and the imam's copy of the Koran into his computer. Ivan's disc would let the computer scan and match each version to the other and italicize the passages that didn't match up perfectly. He delegated that portion of the project to Abdul and told him to get started at once. Abdul was to make a preliminary run and report back at one o'clock for lunch and discussion of his results.

Ivan handed David Feingold a disc with his criteria for evolving his algorithm, along with the mathematics he had used to produce it. He asked David to flash it up on his computer and blow holes in it if he could. Ivan told him it was essential that this project must be done correctly, and no amount of ego was to get in the way of the math.

"Don't change anything," he said to Feingold. "Just make a note of whatever suggestions you have that would improve my work, and report back when you're done."

Feingold left, leaving Ivan with Damian Rutledge.

"You and I will work on the history of Islamist terrorism over the last ten or twenty years," said Ivan. "Show me what you've got."

Ivan sat down beside Damian so he'd have a good view of his computer screen. Damian called up his database and began displaying the statistics concerning thousands of Islamist terrorist attacks all over the world. *Doctor Disaster* was no misnomer. Damian had the information classified and cross-referenced by country, target, casualties, suspected culprits, date and method of attack, and arrests, if any.

"Have you been able to identify any trends or patterns in the attacks?" Ivan asked.

"There were some incidents that bear the stamp of certain groups or individuals. If David could provide me with the dates when those coded messages were sent, I'm sure my data can correlate them with known attacks. If we could get a big enough statistical sample of coded orders and actual attacks, we could certainly remove coincidence from the equation."

At one o'clock the door opened and two waiters appeared with trays of burgers, fries, and cokes. Abdul was right behind them with his computer and a sheaf of papers.

"Did the seismic software work?" Ivan asked him. He was almost holding his breath in anticipation of his answer.

"I'm glad to report that it worked very well," said Abdul, trying to contain his excitement. "It'll save me months of time-consuming work. Your idea to adapt seismographic analytical methods to Arabic script was very creative. I ran scanned versions of the Koran against the pattern recognition capability of the seismic software, and sure enough, it brought up all the disparities. I didn't draw any firm conclusions, but I'm sure I can come up with some preliminary ones by the end of the day."

"Yes!" Ivan exclaimed, making a fist and bringing his elbow down sharply in a triumphant gesture. His elbow hit the table rather hard, but he managed to keep his cool in spite of the pain.

"How about you, David? Did I pass my math exam? Will my algorithm work?" Ivan asked, attempting to be inconspicuous as he rubbed his throbbing elbow.

"I believe the math is correct. I think we may be able to depend on statistics to prove that a code exists, and I also think we probably can decipher it. What I can't find out, of course, is who the guilty ones are, and how we can get rid of them."

"Don't worry about that," Ivan said. "As I mentioned this morning in my opening remarks, it's not up to us to deal with the results. Our job is to grind out the proof in such a way that it becomes undeniable."

"I'll keep 'er coming," David promised.

"David, you do a web search and see if there's informational software about the Koran, like Strong's *Concordance*. Bible scholars have created data banks that can tell you how many times certain words appear in the text, and where to find them. See if the Koran has a similar concordance, and give it to Abdul. Then see if you can get a complete list of e-mails sent from the organization of Muslim scholars in Mecca to any imams, and get copies as soon as possible. I am particularly interested in sermon topics suggested for preaching in the mosques on Fridays. Go to work on this stuff right away, and get back to me ASAP, okay?"

"I'm on it," said David.

"Damian and I will take a whack at writing a program to match dates of terrorist attacks with dates of e-mails. The Secretary of State has given our project a high priority and she's expecting a progress report from me tonight, so let's roll up our sleeves and produce something worthy of the brain power here."

Ivan was feeling secretly worried, and quite frustrated. The results that his program turned up from Damian's events calendar didn't make any obvious linkages between the events. There was no doubt that the same people had been involved in several of the terrorist attacks, but they couldn't prove the orders had come from headquarters somewhere else.

It wasn't until David Feingold came back with a sequential list of dates on e-mail messages sent out from a group in Mecca to some, and sometimes to all imams throughout the world, that matches began to show up—always within forty-eight hours of the date the messages were sent. David told Ivan there was indeed a Koranic database comparable to a Bible concordance, and he had given Abdul the site address.

"*Now* we're getting somewhere," Ivan exclaimed, looking pleased. He pumped his fist like Tiger Woods after making a forty-footer, but this time he was careful to keep his elbow well away from the table.

"David, get me a statistical fix on the number of hits that occurred within forty-eight hours, as compared to how many terrorist events took place overall."

"Gotcha," said David.

Just then Abdul came back into the room, looking excited.

"What have you got, Abdul?" Ivan asked him.

"It looks good," he said, his eyes sparkling. "I produced a computer-generated list of all the variances in the two texts. Then when I started reading them I noticed a pattern. First, I have to explain that according to Islamic law, every time the name Muhammad is mentioned it's considered irreverent if the letters PBUH don't follow his name. PBUH stands for *Peace Be Unto Him*. So when I was reading the imam's copy of the Koran, I happened to notice that in some cases the PBUH was left out. I have to admit I was stunned by this omission. This would never happen if it weren't intended, I assure you. It's got to be some sort of key. Maybe when it's left out, the reader is supposed to refer to something else, possibly in the Hadith. Maybe the reference will be to some action of the Prophet as described in one of the books. If we can find the specific referencing system and match it to your terrorism events calendar, we may end up finding the proof we're looking for."

The men sat there in silence for a moment, then suddenly they all began speaking at once. They were all excited about this latest development. It was beginning to get interesting, *very* interesting.

"Okay everyone," Ivan said above the hubbub. "It's ten o'clock. We're going to have to break it up now and go home and get some sleep. I have to call the Secretary of State now and give her our progress report. We'll all meet here tomorrow at nine sharp."

The three men gathered their papers, closed up their laptops, and quietly filed out of the room. Ivan dialed the private number of the Secretary of State.

"Is this phone secure, Julia?"

"Yes. Go ahead, Ivan."

"We've got statistical confirmation now to back up my theory that there's a flow of orders moving from Mecca to all the imams in the mosques of the world. I'd like to show you the numbers and explain what we've done. Are you up for it tonight?"

"Yes, by all means. Fire away. No, on second thought, I'll come right down. I'd rather talk to you in person. I'll be there in a minute."

She was as good as her word. A minute later she appeared at the door, looking as fresh as she did at the start of the day. Ivan excused his own disheveled appearance. He thought he'd have time to change before making his report. Julia told him not to stand on ceremony, and to describe what his team had come up with. He summarized the work they had done up to that point, and told her about the conclusions they had drawn.

"In the last ten years there've been about 1,600 terrorist incidents in the world that can be traced to Islamist extremists. Of those 1,600 incidents, approximately 1,500 occurred within 48 hours of the local mosque receiving an e-mail message from a certain source that calls itself *The Prophet's Proclamations*. These numbers are statistically significant, and rule out any possibility of coincidence. The messages seemed benign and ordinary, and dealt with sermon topic suggestions. But Abdul noticed that in various messages the honorific *Peace Be Unto Him* was missing. This is very important."

"Wait, let me get that down," said Julia, scribbling as fast as she could go. "Did you say, *Peace Be Unto Him?*"

"That's right."

"Got it. Okay, go on."

"Okay, so Abdul told us that the words *Peace Be Unto Him* always appear after the name of the Prophet. He said they'd never be left out of any Arabic language message, especially one from a group with a name like that. He felt this omission in certain messages was a key that told the local imams on the receiving end to search for the coded information."

"Have you broken the code?" asked Julia.

"No, not yet. In fact we don't know for sure where to look for the coded information, but we're working on it and we hope to have something further for you tomorrow on this. One thing is certain, though—there's a controlling group in Mecca that's ordering cells in Muslim centers around the world to perform these terrorist attacks.

"This is fascinating," Julia said. "But how did you know this controlling group was in Mecca?"

"Through electronic surveillance. We determined that the e-mails were being sent out from the *Ka'bah*, where the Muslims are encouraged to make their pilgrimage, or *hadj*, once in a life time."

"You mean that black square building that you see every year in the newspapers? Where millions of people walk around in circles, and some of them get trampled to death?"

"That's the one."

"Good Lord," said Julia. "Who'd have thought that they'd operate *there*?"

"That's just it," Ivan said. "The terrorists specialize in the unexpected. Who'd have guessed they'd take down the twin towers by slamming into them with our own jet planes?"

"Exactly so."

"Well, we're also trying to figure out which computer is originating these messages. It's not too much of a stretch to think we may be able to identify the person who sends them. He may be only a clerk, though, following the orders of the leaders of this conspiracy. I'll contact you tomorrow with another progress report, and we'll discuss where to take it from there."

"Good work, Ivan," Julia said. "I'm extremely pleased with what you've done so far. I'm stunned, actually, that you made so much progress so quickly."

"Thanks for your support and your confidence in me," Ivan said. "There's still one thing I'd like to ask you."

"What's that?"

"I realize that the uses to which this information will be put are questions of policy, therefore not in my jurisdiction. But I'd be grateful if I could take part in the discussions about the plans for the use of my findings. Could you look into that for me? Or could you put in a good word on my behalf to the right people, whoever they are?"

"I'm not sure I can arrange anything like that," she said, hesitantly. "I'll definitely consult with you to formulate my presentation and my suggestions for how your information should be used. However, this kind of information is going to find its way to the President, the National Security Advisor, the Secretary of Homeland Security, and possibly the cabinet, the Joint Chiefs, and the appropriate majority Senate and House leaders. It will be vital to U.S. global strategy, and although it has much to do with international relations, I'm not certain that I can control the tenor of the deliberations when all the important contributors voice their various opinions. In the end it will be the President's call."

Ivan nodded his head. He rightly worried that the hawks would want to order a strike on the conspirators responsible for so many thousands of deaths. Ideally Ivan felt the proper way to rid the world of these merciless killers would be for the Muslims to do it themselves. But unfortunately Islam had allowed these terrorists to operate behind the scenes for decades, and maybe even centuries. How likely was it that Islam would purge itself of these power-mad conspirators by using information received from the U.S. government?

Ivan was struggling against these pessimistic feelings. It was not in his nature to think the worst of people, but the proponents of suicide bombings, beheadings, and jihads did not leave him any choice. The civilized world of the twenty-first century simply could not tolerate this kind of murderous behavior.

Marina jumped up and greeted Ivan when he finally got back to the suite at the Marriott. She told him all about her sight-seeing day with Simeon Montcalf, which had turned out to be absorbing and exciting for her. She had collected a lot of information that would be useful to her in writing her book.

"I'm so glad you had a good day, Marina. I wish I could tell you about what we did, too. All I can say is that we're making some great progress, and we're all very excited. I'll have to work all day tomorrow, and then give a full report to the President. Will you be all right while I'm gone?"

"Of course, darling! Don't worry about me, I am just very fine. Tomorrow I go to Jefferson Memorial. Jefferson is my favorite President."

"Really? Why?"

"He arranged to have country explored and mopped."

"*Mapped*," Ivan said. "He had the country mapped."

"*Thank* you Ivan," said Marina, with a hint of impatience. "He also expanded country by making Louisiana Purchase from Napoleon, and moreover, he defeated Barbary pirates. They were terrorists, too. But he was very brave man. He refused to pay them tribute when they attacked European business ships. In fact, he sent American navy to chase them out of Mediterranean. We should do same."

"*Millions for defense, but not a cent for tribute.*"

"What?"

"That was Jefferson's motto. He refused to allow his country to be held for ransom by those pirates. He never hesitated to spend whatever was necessary to wipe the hornets right out of their nests. I'm glad you reminded me of all that."

"I love American history. But right now I am sleepy history professor, so we go to bed."

"You don't have to twist my arm," said Ivan.

"I am not even touching you, you big baby."

CHAPTER TWENTY-FIVE

A t five o'clock in the morning, Ivan was at his computer again. He was like a bloodhound on the trail of an escaped prisoner. Like so many of the world's great discoveries, positive results were due mostly to hard preliminary work, with a light sprinkling of inspired thought at the critical points.

In Ivan's case the "Eureka" came while the rest of the world slept. He was searching the Hadith for a way that might lead to the secret of the caliphs' code. There were nine volumes, each volume holding a number of books, and each book containing hundreds of sayings or reports from the early observers of the Prophet's preaching and actions. The task of combing through this material for clues to the code appeared daunting to Ivan because of the sheer volume of information that might have to be read and analyzed. He was working from an English translation of the Hadith when he came across an index that listed the subject matter to be found in each book. In volume 4, book 52, he found 323 separate sayings on the topic of *jihad*. As he read these verses, he believed that *it was possible to interpret these old admonitions as instructions for modern day acts of terror.*

Ivan's heart was beating faster. He would get Abdul to analyze these verses to see how they applied to the e-mails being sent out of Mecca. He was almost certain that the code was some sort of cross-reference system between the Koran and the Hadith. If all the terrorist attacks could be classified and assigned a number corresponding to one of the 323 verses, then by mentioning the verse in the material to be included in the imams' sermons, in combination with the absence of the PBUH (peace be unto him), the imam or cell leader could receive the order to carry out a specified kind of terrorist act.

When Marina awoke at 7:00 a.m., she got up and found Ivan sitting at his laptop with a beatific smile on his face.

"How long you are up, Ivan?" she asked him sleepily.

"A couple of hours."

"And why you are smiling to yourself?"

"I've solved the problem I've been working on," Ivan said, barely able to contain his excitement. "I know how they're doing it, and I know how to advise Julia so she can stop them."

"This is good, ya? Tell me about it, please."

"You know I can't tell you anything, but it will make this a safer world for Hieronymus to grow up in," Ivan chuckled.

"Who is Hieronymus?"

"Why, our son of course. When we have one."

"You cannot name son Hieronymus!"

"Why not?" Ivan said, with a straight face. "It's a famous name, with Latin origins.

"I will never consent to this name," declared Marina, her hands planted firmly on her hips. "Answer is *no.*"

"Listen, Spunky," Ivan said. "Hieronymus is a terrific name. How about Hieronymus Bosch, the famous painter?"

"No, no, and *no,* I will not consider it. And what is this Spunky?"

"Spunky is my nickname for you," Ivan said.

"Yes? And what means Spunky?"

"Spunky means *spirited,* and that's what you are."

When he arrived at the conference room in the State Department for the second day of meetings, Ivan was gratified to find his team already hard at work. He called to them to hold up for a few minutes while he explained his early morning revelation. After he outlined his theory, he asked them to delve into volume 4, book 52 of the Hadith and see if they could determine the pattern being used to encode the various types of terrorist attacks that the caliphs were ordering their forces to perform.

The men divided the 323 sayings equally among them, and then they began looking for cross-references. Did attacks take place immediately after e-mailed messages containing numbered Hadith references went out? Which of the sayings were used most often? Did they correlate to specific types of attacks?

Ivan quickly developed a spreadsheet to record and tabulate the results. It became clear that the preferred method of terrorist attack in Iraq had become the car bombing. Sometimes the car bombings were accomplished by suicide attacks, and sometimes remote detonators were employed. Assassinations, kidnappings, and ambushes were classified and counted. Proved and suspected perpetrators were recorded in an effort to match them against the Hadith verses that were used in suggested sermon material sent by the group calling themselves *The Prophet's Proclamations.*

In a short time it became obvious that there was going to be a pattern, but they completed their work to be absolutely certain. They had to be statistically accurate so that their results would bear the most severe scrutiny. The men were almost tingling from the intoxicating effect of their up-coming success. They'd deciphered the code of the caliphs, and all that remained now was to test the results by sending a false message.

Their excitement aside, they all knew that the next stages would move their project out of their sphere of intellectual inquiry into the hands of political and military activists. They could proceed no further without exceeding their authority. Ivan asked each member of the team to write a coded false message. He would then gather them and they could discuss the pros and cons of each one, and then decide by consensus which false message to pass along to the higher-ups.

By lunchtime they were all finished. They decided that Damian's version of a false message should be the one that Ivan would recommend to the Secretary of State. Ivan called Julia on her private number and requested an immediate meeting with her. The others were impressed that he had her number and thought nothing of calling her at home on a Sunday. Actually Julia was not at home, but in her office in the same building where they were meeting. She told Ivan she would come right down and they could make their report as soon as she got there. The young men put on their jackets and tidied up the table.

When Julia arrived, Ivan arranged the seating so that she could see the computer screen. He explained the logic of the code, and its method of transmission. He demonstrated how it worked, and then showed her the overwhelming statistical evidence to support the validity of the now broken secret code of the caliphs. Ivan wanted to be certain that Julia understood that his team's accomplishment was one based totally on mental work. They didn't have any tangible hard evidence to prove that they were right. He suggested that they test their idea by sending out a false message to see if the instructions would be carried out.

"Here is Damian's proposed test message," he stated, handing it to Julia. "Would you authorize us to send it out?"

Julia read the message, and then looked at the little group.

"If this gets sent out it might result in some deaths."

"No," Ivan said. "We can't let that happen. We'd warn the people in harm's way to secretly leave the target area."

"I see," said Julia. "It's risky, though. We'll have to make sure we find a good reason for clearing the target area before the attack, or the terrorists will suspect their cover was blown and they'll change their methods of intercommunication."

"Meanwhile a lot of deaths are occurring every day as a result of the messages that the caliphs *are* sending out," Ivan reminded her.

"You're right," Julia agreed. But I'll have to get approval from the President before I allow you to proceed. How do you plan to do this?"

"David will electronically slip the false message into one of the real transmissions in such a way that they will never know where it came from. Abdul will translate it into Arabic, and use the same writing style as the caliphs. We can then clear the target area just before the attack and make it look as though we got lucky. Not every one of their operations is a success, so they will just chalk it up to bad luck. Hopefully they won't notice the mission wasn't authorized by *The Prophet's Proclamations*. If they do notice, they'll just assume it was executed by an overly enthusiastic cell acting on its own initiative.

"Wait a minute. Let me get this straight," said Julia. "Have you already gone so far as to choose a target area?"

"Well, it would have to be authorized, of course, but we've been talking about the Turkish naval base in Izmir as the site for the test because Turkey is a Muslim country which is on good terms with us. We can warn them of an impending attack, and they'll clear the area without the terrorists' knowing. I'm sure the Turks would be glad to cooperate."

"I'm sure they would," Julia agreed. "The Turks and the Arabs are not that close, even though they're all Muslims."

Ivan knew that the Turks were a nation of 66 million people, a member of NATO, and about to gain admittance to the European Union. At one time The Ottoman Empire was huge, and included all the Arab tribal sheikhdoms. But the Turks in general didn't admire the lack of civilized accomplishments of the desert nomads, who but for their oil would still be driving camels instead of Mercedes. The Turkish government had worked hard to regain the respect of the world, and they were not about to give it up to support an Arab jihad.

"You've done a marvelous job, all of you," Julia told them. "Someday soon history is going to be changed because of your good work." Then, turning to Ivan she said, "I'd like you to come with me to see the President. You'll need to prepare an effective presentation for POTUS, and I'd like you to do it now."

She turned and left the conference room so she could call the President for an appointment. When Ivan and his team deemed that the Secretary was out of hearing range, they all exploded into whoops and hollers.

"She told us we're going to make history!" David said.

"Don't let it go to your head," Damian warned him.

"POTUS," said Abdul. "What does that mean?"

"President of the United States," said Ivan

"Get outta town," said David, giving Ivan a playful poke on the arm. The young men had never felt as close as they did at that moment. They had become a real team.

They were all astonished at how fast the Secretary was acting on their work. They discussed the best way to present their findings and recommendations to the President. Ivan listened carefully to what they had to say, and then he incorporated their suggestions into a PowerPoint presentation. He was just finishing up when Julia called to say the meeting with the President would take place at five o'clock in the West Wing of the White House.

"Are you up for this?" she asked Ivan.

"I just did a PowerPoint presentation for him."

"Good. I'll pick you up at 4:30, and we'll go together."

Ivan dismissed his team, but told them to stay close to their cell phones in case they were needed. Then he called Marina and told her that he was going to make a presentation at the White House, and he didn't know when he would be home.

"This is exciting, ya?" Marina said. "I am happy for you and I am proud of you, too. And do not worry about coming home late. I am with Simeon, and he has been very sweet in allowing me to choose the historical things I want to see."

Ivan cringed to think that for once he was actually grateful to Montcalf for looking after Marina.

Julia stopped by at the appointed time and took Ivan with her in the official limousine. Ivan felt conspicuous and overly pampered in a limousine driven by a secret serviceman and accompanied by a motorcycle escort. They pulled up at the visitor's entrance to the White House and passed quickly through the security check. Julia, of course, was familiar with the White House and led Ivan straight to the President's outer office. She announced to his receptionist that the Secretary of State had come to see the President. They seated themselves and waited to be admitted.

After five minutes or so they were told that they could go in. The President was seated behind his desk in the Oval Office. He rose to greet Julia, calling her by her first name. Julia introduced Ivan, and the two men shook hands.

It was exactly five o'clock when Ivan started his presentation, and he managed to get through it in ten minutes. The President's mood changed from genial to pensive. Ivan asked the man with the toughest job in the world if he had any questions.

"What should be the next step?" the President asked.

Ivan suggested the false message ploy as a method to insure that they had indeed fully deciphered the code. He described the Izmir scheme, and why he had chosen Turkey for his test site. He explained to the leader of the free world that he believed the risk involved in sending a false message was minimal for the United States.

"Presuming we successfully order a terrorist attack on the naval base in Izmir," Ivan said, "and presuming the Turkish security officers are able to clear the target area before the attack and arrest or kill the insurgents, we could then prepare a plan to clean out the vipers that are passing their hatred off as *The Prophet's Proclamations*."

The President removed his glasses, looked at Julia, and ordered her to work out the details with the Turks.

"Don't tell them anything except that our intelligence people have gotten wind of a planned attack on their naval base," said the President. "Tell them that we have no other details. Neither you, nor Dr. Welland, nor his staff, are to leak any of this to anybody, effective immediately. Madame Secretary, you and your staff have done a terrific job in bringing this to my attention. Now I'd like you and Dr. Welland to prepare a scenario to illustrate the way that we can best use this information to our own advantage. Keep me up to date on this one," the President instructed Julia.

"Yes, Mr. President."

"Good work, Dr. Welland," he said to Ivan, as he rose to return to his desk.

Ivan and Julia also got up.

"Thank you, Mr. President," they said, almost in unison.

The Marriott Hotel is close to the White House, so Julia dropped Ivan off on her way home. During the ride Ivan told Julia that he'd call David Feingold and have him insert the Izmir message into the Prophet's next proclamation, and then he'd leave in the morning to return to Cambridge as planned.

"I'll try to work out some ideas while I'm there," Ivan promised her. "I'll come back to Washington as soon as I'm needed. In the meantime, my team will prepare a decoding manual."

"Good. I'll let you know about all the developments as soon as they happen. Take care now, and stay in touch."

Ivan let himself into the suite and found Marina perched on the sofa, with Montcalf sitting across from her in the easy chair. They had been talking about the contrasting habits of Russian and American women. Marina had already decided that Russian and American women of her age were more alike than they were different. Older women of Russian origin were reading from another page, however, and the page had already been turned. The status and accomplishments of their Russian husbands determined the importance of many women in Russian society. The loss of so many men during World War II had forced the nation to educate and use the talents of women more than at any other time in the past, but Russian men resented the progress they made. American women had obtained a higher degree of equality through the use of democratic laws, though not without a fight. Marina had finally concluded that American women had a better chance of getting ahead. Both Ivan and Montcalf were very glad to hear it, because neither of them wanted her to go back to Russia.

"So, how are things going, my friend?" Montcalf asked Ivan after he sat down next to Marina on the sofa.

"Things are progressing," he said, cryptically. "By the way, could you book me a flight for next weekend? I'll cancel it if it turns out I'm not needed. But it's better for me to have the ticket just in case."

"No sooner said than done," said Montcalf. "And now, may I entertain the hope that you will be my guests for dinner?"

"You're very kind," said Ivan, "but I've been up since four o'clock this morning and I'd like to go to bed early."

"Then I shall take my leave," said Montcalf graciously. He didn't want to wear out his welcome with this young couple, for he always enjoyed basking in the reflected glory of having discovered them. They were moving quickly to the top of the Washington hierarchy, and he wanted to be sure that his career benefited from their progress. If he had known that Welland had just come from the White House, he would have realized how right he was to stay on Ivan's good side

Simeon could not help feeling, however, that Welland was an upstart, leading a charmed life. He had moved too easily from Texas to Harvard. Then, even before finishing his degree, he had the Secretary of State wrapped around his little finger. To top off his good fortune he arrived back home from Chechnya with Marina, who, if she had been the Czarina herself, could not have been any more eye-catching. On the way down in the elevator Montcalf was thinking how much like the Frankenstein story it all was. It was he who had created Ivan Welland, and now the monster was getting all the attention.

Cambridge, Massachusetts

CHAPTER TWENTY-SIX

Immediately after leaving the airport in Boston, Ivan's mind was at work remembering all the things he had to do now that he was home again. He wanted to take his oral exam, and he hoped it had been scheduled for this week. He promised himself that as soon as he got to the apartment he would put the Prophet out of his mind and put Pushkin in, put Turkey out and Turgenev in, detonators out, Dostoevsky in, and all the literary alliterations he could get his batty brain to drum up.

"You are very busy lately, Ivan," Marina said, as they rode back to their apartment in a taxi. "I miss you, and Bernard too."

"Bernard? Who's Bernard?"

"Is my nickname for your comrade," she told him.

"I don't have a comrade. I'm not Russian. Well, not 100%, anyway."

"Is true," Marina said. "But through close collaboration with him, Bernard is now comrade."

"But why *Bernard*?" Ivan had finally got her meaning.

"Because he reminds me of Saint Bernard," Marina said.

"A Saint Bernard? The dog, you mean?"

"Yes, Saint Bernard. Big and friendly."

"I see. Well, I'm very grateful that the Czarina didn't dub him *Charlie the Chihuahua*."

"Bernard Welland. I hope to meet him again soon."

"You can count on it," Ivan assured her.

Once inside their Cambridge apartment, Marina looked after the unpacking while Ivan checked his e-mail.

"What is new?" she asked, after she finished her chores.

"Well, let's see. My orals have been scheduled for Friday morning. And there's a message for you to call the History Department to make an appointment to go over your course description. There's another one for you from Montcalf, saying he enjoyed conversing with you. He has arranged ticketing and accommodations for this weekend, and he looks forward to showing you around Washington again. So, that's it for now."

"We must both get back to work," said Marina, with a little frown. "I need to write book on Chechnya."

"Good. And I'm going to review for my orals."

Ivan was a bit annoyed to have to read so much of what the critics said about the great writers. The only purpose that he could find in reading the criticism was to know what others had already written in order not to repeat anything without crediting them in a footnote. None of this seemed like a meaningful existence to Ivan. He did like teaching, though, but he realized that if he didn't publish a profuse number of arcane articles he could never get tenure at a highly-regarded university. He hoped that Julia would make him an offer he couldn't refuse, and save him from the inbred halls of academe. Marina seemed to be able to hack it in academia, but her field was different.

After writing her book for about two hours, Marina began to make lunch. They both enjoyed working and writing at home, each knowing that the other was nearby, and stopping once in a while for meals and chat time. After lunch they returned to their work until late afternoon.

Ivan went out to the mailbox and found a letter from Marina's parents and one from the U.S. State Department. He took the mail upstairs and gave Marina her letter, and then opened the correspondence from the State Department.

His envelope contained two communications: one from the Human Resources Director for the State Department, and the other was a personal letter from Julia in long hand.

He read Julia's letter first. She said she was establishing a new section within the State Department to interact with other government agencies, particularly those concerned with security issues worldwide. She told Ivan that at a level below hers there was a serious lack of cooperation and coordination. Many of the agencies acted as if *they* were in charge of making foreign policy for the U.S. government.

"They think we're soft because we don't wear guns," Julia wrote. "They think we're only capable of throwing parties and spreading B.S. As a result of this and other diplomatic errors, the country has lost a tremendous amount of credibility in the world. We're no longer trusted to the same degree by other nations. We're perceived as a country that shoots from the hip, and unfortunately this is largely true. So I'd like you to come to work with me and help me restructure our department, our image, and our country's future. Enclosed you will find a formal offer of employment. If you accept it, you'll be placed in charge of the new section, which I'll call the *International Security Coordination Section.* I'm open to another name if you can think of a better one. Especially if it's shorter!"

Ivan's mind began to race. What a superb opportunity to make a difference and be useful! All his training and all his education could at last have some practical value.

"I know you have expressed concerns," Julia continued in her letter, "about being able to complete your PhD thesis before settling into a new job. Unfortunately I don't think the country can afford to wait. You can write your thesis on your own time. Marina will have to fulfill her contract with Harvard, but I'll help her find a job for next year in the D.C. area. One or the other of you can commute. It's only a short flight, and it takes no longer than many people spend driving to and from work in rush hour. So please think very carefully about my proposal. I'd like you to picture me in an Uncle Sam suit pointing my finger at you and saying, 'Aunt Julia needs YOU.'"

Ivan thumbed through the employment contract, noting the handsome salary and other perquisites. Marina had just finished reading the letter from her parents, and was looking at Ivan as he sat next to her, deep in concentration.

"What you think about?" she asked.

"Why don't we just switch letters? It's easier that way."

Ivan read in Marina's letter that her parents missed her and were very proud of her. The job at Harvard University was wonderful and would advance her career when she returned to Russia. There were some family news items, and lots of love being transmitted through the mail. Her parents were both relieved that she was in Cambridge now, instead of Chechnya.

"This is wonderful news, ya?" Marina exclaimed, looking up from her reading. "You are now very important man in Washington! I walk with chin up, like queen."

They spent the next hour discussing the job offer from Julia. No matter how they squirmed about the commuting and the separations, they had to agree that her offer was too good to turn down. It was the chance of a lifetime, and they both knew it.

"I'll call Julia tomorrow and accept, but right now I think we should go out and celebrate. How about it?"

They had a fine meal at a local bistro, complete with wine and Ivan's favorite dessert, *crème brulée*. After dinner they held hands and sauntered along the quaint little streets of Cambridge.

"What a momentous day this has been," said Ivan.

"Day not finished yet."

"What do you mean?" He knew what she meant, but he asked her anyway.

"Bernard needs to be canonized."

Ivan laughed. "Then we should run right home."

But they walked, they didn't run. They were too full of good food.

At breakfast the next morning Ivan asked Marina if she had any reservations about his accepting Julia's job offer.

"No, I still feel like yesterday. Is perfect opportunity, darling. You take it. I commute. I do not mind."

Ivan called Julia, and her assistant put her on.

"I have some interesting news, Ivan. You'll be happy to know the imams received your false message and acted on it. They clearly thought it was from caliph headquarters."

"We did it!" Ivan exclaimed. "We cracked their code!"

"Yes! I'm sure the terrorists just loved your idea. They thought they were going to sink a frigate in the harbor at Izmir and disable the entire port for incoming and outgoing vessels, including the coast guard and the fishing fleet."

"But you warned the Turks. Nothing happened!"

"Right. When the Turkish Embassy got our message they immediately called the port authorities, who quickly caught a couple of divers planting some mines in the neck of the harbor, so there was a bit of a kerfuffle about that. The Turkish government's anti-terrorist force arrested four other men in Izmir. The men all had Greek passports, but the Turks don't believe they're Greeks."

"That was smart of them," said Ivan.

"You bet. The Turks are pretty savvy, I'm sure."

"No, I mean it was smart of the terrorists to pretend they were Greeks. The Turks and the Greeks have been at each other's throats over the Ionian Sea for thousands of years. So the terrorists want the Turks to think the Greeks did this in order to monopolize the fishing this year, or worse, to start a war. If they can keep the Turks busy worrying about the Greeks they'll be free to organize the Islamist radicals."

"Devious little bastards, aren't they?"

"You bet. The caliphs are already trying to play the religious war card so they can marshal as many Muslims as possible to believe in their version of the so-called jihadist cause. If they can do that, it'll be a very big coup for them. They've already got the younger, disaffected men eating out of their hands. They all buy into this martyr business. It's a sad, sad thing to see."

"Well, thanks to you and your team, Ivan, we can at least have some control over the messages that are sent out to all those imams," Julia said.

"For a while, anyway," Ivan agreed.

"So what about my offer?"

"I've talked it over with Marina, and I accept."

"Bless you," Julia said, sounding greatly relieved. "I need you more than ever. Get on a plane and come down!"

"I'll come tomorrow, as soon as my oral exam is over."

"There's going to be a strategy session in the War Room on Saturday morning, and I want you to go with me to that meeting. Please call as soon as you arrive in Washington."

"I'll do that."

"Good. Then I'll say good-bye for now."

Ivan and Marina discussed the details of yet another weekend in Washington. Marina thought she would visit the National Archives and have a look at the Constitution, and perhaps visit the Library of Congress as well.

"I make chart for students," she told Ivan. "Is time-line to compare American and Russian history. It shows events that preceded, then happened during, and then followed American Revolution. Is good for students to draw conclusions based on reasons why Czars are able to keep power for more than one hundred and fifty years, while British and loyalists lost power very quickly."

"I like the sound of your course description."

"I must get enough knowledge of American Revolution by September to teach material. To be in Washington gives me good opportunity to review American history. So if you decide to send me back where I come from, at least I am able to teach American history to Russians."

"I won't be turning you in for another model."

"Do you feel well prepared for your exam?"

"I know the material pretty well, I think, but I suspect the professors are going to try to give me a hard time."

"Why you say this?"

"They know I go to D.C. a lot. It probably makes them think I'm not really serious about my academic career."

"Is hard to be good at many things," Marina observed. "Less talented people complain you have divided loyalties. Makes them feel good about themselves to criticize others."

The two scholars worked away at their respective desks until sundown. Then Ivan stood up, stretched, and turned on the TV. CNN was reporting the details of a foiled terrorist attack on the Turkish seaport city of Izmir. Ivan smiled to himself, wishing he could tell Marina how he and his team had orchestrated the whole thing. The Turkish security agency officials, however, were happily taking all the credit for uncovering the very serious terrorist plot. No mention was made of their having received a tip from the CIA. He was pleased, however, that the U.S. had been left totally out of the equation. He had delivered the proof that the code existed. He had been able to insert an order into *The Prophet's Proclamations* that triggered a terrorist attack that might have been successful but for the warning sent to the Turks. Ivan was confident that his suspicions had been confirmed. Now all that remained was to put these guys out of business.

The meeting that he would attend on Saturday would be devoted to deciding how to do it. He worried that the final decision might be influenced too strongly by hawkish military leaders. In the end it would be the President's decision, of course. Ivan hoped that Julia could successfully present the idea that the statesmanlike approach would be the best way to handle terrorism, and he would help her make this point. For the moment, though, he was not going to let the terrorists keep him from passing his oral exam.

When Ivan awoke the next morning, he was surprised to discover that his mind was fastened on his upcoming trip to Washington, and not on his oral exam. He was certain that his professorial examiners would make him pay for having chosen a career in government over one in academia. If he were to be successful, however, his work in Washington would ironically help to ensure the future of academia, so the professors should really be showing some support for his work, rather than acting as though he were some kind of a traitor. He suddenly remembered one of his favorite quotes from Mark Twain: "It is better to deserve honors and not have them, than to have them and not deserve them."

For some time Ivan had been thinking about the exact means that could be used to rid radical Islam of its corrupt manipulators. Unfortunately he was not yet privy to the list of assets the U.S. had in Saudi Arabia. He needed to know how many operatives were functioning near Mecca and what their specialties were so he could plan a successful surgical strike. His thinking had taken him this far, but the future operations might require men more like Wilson Bagwell than himself.

Marina, always conscious of his morning efforts to escape her bed, changed his train of thought by inquiring how he was feeling.

"Thanks to you and our activities last night, I feel totally relaxed," he said. "I also feel extremely energetic," he added, making a lunge at her.

"Get up, you impossible man," she cried. "Get up, or you are late for oral examination."

Ivan decided to wear his best suit and dress shoes to his exam. He felt his inquisitors might think him older and more impressive if he dressed as formally as possible. He had to take the suit to Washington anyway, and wearing it was easier than packing it. He noticed that Marina was packing his favorite skirt; the one that he felt displayed her derriere in such a tantalizing fashion when she walked.

"I hope you're wearing that for me," he said to her, "and not for Montcalf."

"I bring it because I do not have to iron."

She prepared a quick breakfast of fruit, toast, scrambled eggs, and coffee.

Five minutes later Ivan wiped his mouth and stood up.

"Give me a good luck kiss before I go," he said, drawing her close to him.

"You look so handsome," said Marina, "but I look like poor, used, slatternly housewife."

"*Slatternly*? Where did you learn that word?"

"I study classical literature in English. Is not good word?"

"You're the most beautiful slatternly housewife in the world," Ivan said, looking at her fondly. "I can't get enough of you."

Marina opened the door and shoved him out.

Ivan walked rapidly to the seminar room in Boylston Hall where his knowledge and understanding of Russian literature was to be examined. He found the room empty. There was a table with five chairs on one side, and one chair on the other side. Obviously that one was meant for him, so he sat down and waited. At the exact hour, Vasili Fedorenko entered the room, followed by four serious-looking professors from the Russian Department. Vasili sat in the middle chair, forcing two of the others to pass behind him to find seats.

"He never misses an opportunity to show his status," Ivan thought.

The chairman spoke first. He outlined the purpose of the meeting and advised all those present that the proceedings would be taped. Ivan assumed this was done so that if the examiners wanted to revisit an answer, or if the applicant complained about the procedures, the statements could be reviewed.

Fedorenko held up his hand for silence, turned on the tape recorder, and announced that the examination of Ivan V.

Welland would be conducted by the faculty of Russian
Studies of Harvard University to determine his competence
to continue his work for the degree of PhD. The names of all
those present were listed, and then the chairman began the
proceedings with the first question. It concerned *Boris
Godunov*, by Pushkin. Ivan answered clearly, and quoted
verbatim from the 1825 work:

> *A day will come when some laborious monk*
> *will bring to light my zealous, nameless toil,*
> *kindle, as I, his lamp, and from the parchment,*
> *shaking the dust of ages, will transcribe my chronicles.*

Each professor took a crack at embarrassing the neophyte
academic, who was thought to be deserting the ship. Unfortunately for the egos of the four professors, Ivan was very
knowledgeable and the equal of any of them. Eventually they
eased up on him and returned to their main occupation,
which was trying to impress one another.

It was lunch time when they finally ran out of questions.
Ivan was dismissed and told that he would be notified later
as to whether he had passed or failed the exam.

When he got home, Marina was at the door to greet him.

"How was exam?" she asked him eagerly.

"I feel pretty sure I passed. I knew all the material, so I
don't see how there could really be any problem. They only
tripped me up once. It had to do with some little detail about
Barakov, but I'm certain they won't hold that against me. In
fact, it might even have been a point in my favor, because
Vasili was delighted to show the others how he could set me
straight."

"They do this to me, too, when I take oral examination at
University of Moscow," Marina declared. "Is opportunity for
them to show off. Professors are same everywhere."

During their direct flight back to Washington D.C., Ivan worked furiously on his laptop. He was doing his best to put himself in the place of the caliphs. Did these immensely rich and powerful individuals actually believe the fundamentalist doctrines of the Taliban and Al Qaeda and the various other extremist religious groups? If, in fact, they didn't believe in a Muslim theocracy, then they were clearly just using Islam, but for what purpose? They were undoubtedly among the most important power brokers in their society already, so what more did they want? Perhaps the caliphs were seeking temporal power, but it was the royal family that held all the power in Saudi Arabia. With 6,000 members, the royal house of Saud was coup-proof. There would always be a successor to the king, so the traditional Arab tactic of assassination was unavailing.

But if a theocracy could be established by the clerics who believed that the Prophet and his heirs were intended to lead both the secular and the spiritual aspects of life, then they, as caliphs (the direct descendants of Muhammad), would be installed as the leaders of Islam worldwide, outranking all others. Since the U.S. supported the Saudi royal family in order to keep the oil flowing, perhaps the caliphs believed that if enough enmity for America could be developed, the hatred would spill over on the king and his family and they would be deposed for their unholy alliance with the infidel Americans.

In any case, no matter what their objectives, the caliphs controlled the jihadist terrorism that was plaguing the globe. The salient question still remained: What was the best way to rid the world of these power-mad caliphs? The best scenario would be to expose them as plotters attempting to hijack the legacy of Muhammad, so the Muslims themselves would do the removal job in whatever way they chose. The second best scenario would be for the caliphs to have an internal insurrection and kill one another off. The third best would be a surgical strike of some sort that killed the caliphs. And last would be a counter-terrorist strike against any global cell that could be suckered out into the open by issuing counterfeit orders from the group calling itself *The Prophet's Proclamations,* and using the code Ivan had deciphered. By the time he had considered all these possibilities, the plane had landed at Ronald Reagan Airport.

While Marina waited for their luggage at the carousel, Ivan called Julia's office at the State Department to let her know that they had arrived in Washington.

"Good evening, Mr. Welland," said her assistant. "I'm afraid the Secretary is in a meeting right now, and she'll be busy for the rest of the evening. But she asked me to tell you that she'll pick you up at the Marriott on her way in from Georgetown tomorrow morning at 8:30."

"Yes!" he exclaimed, turning to Marina with a glowing face. "I won't be seeing Julia until tomorrow morning. We have the whole evening for each other!"

"But we are not alone," Marina said.

"What are you talking about?" Ivan said, a little heatedly. "Are you meeting *Montcalf?*"

"No, I speak of Bernard. I make him very happy."

"Now you're talking! But first I'll give you wine and roses, along with a gourmet dinner in a dark corner of a quiet little restaurant somewhere. I can't promise you that I'll come up with a Hungarian playing a violin, though, but I'll do my best."

Washington D.C.

CHAPTER TWENTY-SEVEN

I van was rested and happy the next morning when the Secretary of State pulled up to the Marriott to take him to the strategy meeting.

"Well, Julia, did you have any brain waves since we last spoke?" Ivan asked as he got into the car.

"Not really. We'll just have to see what happens. The men in the military are going to want to take your discovery and use it to blast every mullah, ayatollah, and caliph out of their minarets."

"I sympathize with them in a way," said Ivan. "The terrorists have it coming. But much of the rest of the world thinks we're just as bad as they are. We have a problem here, and if we don't handle it properly we'll have a heavy price to pay."

They both understood the stakes, and they talked about some of the consequences as they walked through the White House to their meeting in the War Room. The discussion was to be chaired by the President's National Security Advisor. Everyone was seated at exactly 9:00, and the chairman called the meeting to order. The majority of people around the table were senior military officers whose uniforms were covered with ribbons.

"Even the oak leaf clusters come in clusters in this company," Julia whispered.

The Chairman outlined the purpose of the meeting, which was being held at the request of the Secretary of State. Julia was called upon to brief those in attendance about the broken code, and the inevitable conclusion that there was a covert council of caliphs in control of global terrorism. Julia praised the work of Ivan and his team for discovering, and then deciphering, the code that was used to order terrorist cell groups into action. Then she introduced Ivan and turned the floor over to him.

Ivan spent some time explaining how he had suspected a centralized planning structure when he was in Chechnya. He had delved into Imam Mansur's Koran, and had determined its place in the scheme. He told them that until the recent Turkish success in Izmir, everything he had done was academic and purely theoretical. He explained that the terrorists in Turkey had been ordered to attack the fleet in Izmir by Ivan's team, using the code of the caliphs. Of course the Turks had been warned in advance of the impending attack and had prevented the mining of the harbor. But the test in Turkey was proof positive that the decoding had been successful.

"As I see it," Ivan concluded, "our job is to evolve a strategy that is more than just individual tactical actions."

With these words he paved the way for Julia to explain her hierarchy of desired diplomatic results.

Julia took over the meeting temporarily when she produced the first scenario that she and Ivan had worked out together.

"My main point is that for every good reason in the world it would be better if the Muslims themselves cleaned up the mess that the caliphs have made, and that they not use some sort of American expeditionary force to do this. I don't have to remind you that the 9/11 tragedy was a great victory for the terrorists. From the point of view of the caliphs, that attack was probably the most cost-effective battle in the history of jihadist warfare."

Julia told the military figures in the room that she, too, would like to annihilate the terrorists, but she wanted the American revenge to come in a more elegant way. She informed them that her assistant, Dr. Ivan Welland, had come up with a strategy that she wanted them to carefully consider. Before she turned the floor back to Ivan, she told them that his plan would involve very little loss of American lives or military materiel. So-called "collateral damage" would also be minimal.

"I would especially like to emphasize," Julia concluded, "that all inter-service and all inter-agency rivalries must be set aside. We must all be on board with this plan, or it just won't work."

She yielded the floor to Ivan, who thanked her and turned to address his audience. He was an imposing figure when his long frame unfurled itself from the chair.

"It's important to understand that every terrorist attack up to this moment has occurred in a city with at least one mosque. This doesn't mean that every Muslim worshipper is a terrorist, or that the majority of the people of Islam sympathizes with them or supports terror. What it does mean is that the terrorist cells receive their messages from the imam of the mosque that they attend—their *home* mosque, so to speak— with or without the imam's knowledge. I have no doubt that in certain Islamic countries the ordinary citizens know a great deal more about the terrorists than they dare to admit. There can be no doubt that people who live in these rabbit warren neighborhoods in Iraq are aware of the influx of terrorists, foreign insurgents, Baathist hardliners, and Islamist extremists. There is no way they can be unaware of the masses of destructive weapons being moved around in tractor trailer loads in their neighborhoods.

"So how can we get Islamic countries to act against their own people as they continue their terrorist activities?" Ivan asked rhetorically. "Our job is to release disinformation that convinces Islamic nations that the terrorists are going to use atomic weapons. We will leak false information that reveals that Islamist jihadists have acquired radioactive materials from corrupt dealers in Russian cold war nuclear contraband.

We'll insinuate that the knowledge of how to use these devices has come from Pakistani scientists. All Islam must be made to shake in its boots for fear that the fall-out will kill them. It might come from their own dirty bomb, or it might come from nuclear reprisals from the U.S. or Israel, but whatever the source, they must believe that the end is near. Only then will they act."

It was obvious to all present that Ivan was correct. If the Arabs could be encouraged to clean up their own house it would be infinitely better than if the democratic nations were forced to do it for them. The savings in lives would be enormous if the terrorists could be rooted out from within. Furthermore, unless the Muslims who were sympathetic to the cause of extremist Islam could be made to change their minds, the U.S. and its allies were going to have to continue operating in a miasma of death and destruction forever. If the infidels could be kept out of it there would be no loss of face for Islam either, and that was the most important considera-tion in establishing a basis for future international relations.

Everyone agreed that there was nothing to lose and much to gain by implementing the Secretary's plan. It was decided that each branch of the government represented at the tactical meeting would prepare a plan to support the principal strat-egy through the use of the resources under its command. Ivan was appointed to be the inter-agency coordinator. His job was to pull all the efforts together into one unified plan, and then when the master plan was completed, to present it to the President for his approval, and then if approved, to supervise its execution. He would set up tactical meetings with the directors and staffs of the CIA, the Chiefs of Staff of the three branches of the military, and the press officers from the State Department and the White House.

Ivan scheduled his first meeting with Tim Morrison, the Director of the CIA. He asked Morrison to bring along his best Middle East tacticians and be prepared to work on roughing out the details of his agency's part in the plan. Ivan set up a meeting for the next morning with the Chairman of the Joint Chiefs and his staff, requesting that the Army's best psych ops officers be present.

The press officers from all the agencies were to assemble in the afternoon after his meeting with the military. He told the department heads to get the spin-doctors to figure out the most convincing way to persuade the nabobs of Araby that they had to take steps to save themselves from the holocaust that their extremist brothers were perpetrating.

"In five days we will schedule another meeting to discuss progress, and interconnect the pieces," Ivan told them. "What you are embarking on is the most important mission that has come along in many years. More than likely you will never be able to discuss this mission, never get a medal or ribbon for your work, but you'll have the satisfaction of knowing that you have served your nation and your world."

Ivan asked them to think of a basketball team, every member of which is a team player. Each teammate must be at least as interested in assists as he is in scoring.

"No *hot dogging,* please, and no victory dances either—assuming we're successful," he warned them.

Finally he turned to Julia and asked her if she had any-thing else to add. She reaffirmed what he had told them, and added that she wanted the detailed plan rolled out for the President's approval by next Friday. Then she adjourned the meeting.

After a quick lunch, Ivan went to the meeting he had arranged with Tim Morrison, the Director of the CIA, who in turn had summoned the relevant Middle East experts at Langley to join him for the session. Ivan didn't want to usurp his authority as Director of the CIA, so he allowed Morrison to introduce him to his staff and outline the purpose of the meeting. When it came down to specifics, Ivan was invited to discuss the breaking of the code, the fact that they could now use the code to order terrorist activities in places of their choosing, and that whatever they did it had to be part of the larger plan, which was to convince the Arab leaders that they had to stamp out their own terrorists before they got them all killed. He also told them about the council of caliphs, whose existence he only knew about because of the messages that were emanating from the Ka'bah under the banner of *The Prophet's Proclamations*. He suspected that they had the opportunity to pull off one of the biggest coups in the history of espionage.

Ivan requested a full discussion of the resources, both human and material, that were available in the Arab world. He told the CIA officers that he didn't trust Islam to get rid of the caliphs. He strongly believed that the kings, sheikhs, and emirs would never openly challenge the caliphs, who were operating in Muhammad's slipstream and carried the power of the Prophet's name.

"Many Islamic worshippers favor a theocratic caliphate as the preferred method of governance," he explained. "No good Muslim would ever allow any disrespect to fall on a caliph, let alone any harm to come to one. Therefore, it will have to be up to the U.S. to put an end to the covert council that's usurping the spirit of Islam and wreaking havoc throughout the world. If the caliphs were removed, there would be no challengers to the secular rulers, and the ruling families could proceed to weed out the terrorists without fear of being overthrown by the caliphs and the clerics who support them. Hopefully in the future these medieval realms can be slowly converted to democracy, but for the time being we can't have them overthrown by something far more insidious and dangerous."

There were a few murmurs from the men around the table as they conferred quietly among themselves.

"I would like to hear suggestions as to how we can remove these devils from their perch in Mecca," Ivan said.

The room became silent again, and Ivan continued.

"Ideally it would be best if the U.S. were not in any way implicated in the scheme. Has anyone here ever heard of the existence of these caliphs?"

No one seemed to know anything about any caliphs.

"Well, I have reason to believe that they have their summit meetings in the Ka'bah itself. As you all know, the Ka'bah is to Muslims as the Vatican is to Catholics, so it is very clever of the caliphs to carry out their nefarious plots from such a holy site. They know very well that nobody in the West would guess this was going on in that particular place. So, are there any questions up to this point?"

Ivan waited a moment, then continued.

"Well, I have a few questions myself. Do we have anyone in Mecca who has observed or can observe the comings and goings in the Ka'bah? If meals or food are being carried inside, especially fancy meals, it might be a tip-off. An electronic scan might reveal what equipment is being kept inside this supposedly holy place. We have seen the arms caches that were stored in mosques in Iraq, so why shouldn't weapons and electronic equipment be kept in the Ka'bah? How about young women entering the building? How about hookahs?"

There was a pause, and then a ripple of laughter.

"But seriously," Ivan said, turning to Morrison, "does the CIA have the means to determine if a water pipe, for example, is being smoked in the Ka'bah?"

"We have the means," said Morrison.

"I'd like to request twenty-four hour surveillance of the site."

"We can do it via satellite and human observation."

The penchant of the Arabs for fine things and rich palaces led Ivan to believe that the caliphs were living the high life in their secret hideaway. So much of Arab pride is based on position and wealth that it just wasn't credible that these icons of Islam weren't living in luxury. If a brute like Saddam Hussein once had so many palaces, surely the caliphs had some interesting digs, too. Luxurious living requires servants, and caliphs in Mecca were no exception.

"Could we track the servants coming and going, and note what it is they are bringing in and taking out?"

"I'm on it," Morrison said.

"The next time we meet, I'd like to have every piece of information you can get for me about the Ka'bah and the men we suspect of heading up a worldwide network of terrorism. These caliphs live safely in the Ka'bah because they think no one would ever dare invade the holiest place of Islam."

The Director and Ivan both stood up to indicate that the meeting was at an end. They shook hands and agreed to meet on Monday morning to consider procedural recommendations from the CIA.

Ivan called David Feingold and told him to round up Damian and Abdul, and meet him in an hour at their temporary office in the conference room in the State Department building. The four men got together at the appointed time, and Ivan briefed them on what had happened at the meeting in the White House.

"The best brains in Washington have been assigned to our project," he said. "So you can start working right away on a new set of orders to be sent out by *The Prophet's Proclamations*. When we go into the Ka'bah to get the caliphs, we'll want to substitute a totally new set of attack orders to replace the ones they've already issued. The idea is to clean out all the terrorist cells at one time, from top to bottom."

"Whew," said Damian. "That's quite a tall order."

"Maybe so, but we only have one chance. We'll have our military on full alert, as well as whatever allies we can muster. It's up to us to let our guys know what to expect."

"Can you outline for us what sorts of things you want us to put in the Friday sermon, then?" David asked.

"Lace it full of big talk about nuclear weapons. We want everyone in the Middle East to believe the terrorists have acquired an atomic bomb. This is important. We want the Arab-in-the-street to be shivering in his boots now that he thinks the extremists will use it. No one except the caliphs will know that they don't have a nuke. But the caliphs won't want to contradict those who say they do have a bomb, because having it accords them tremendous status. So we're counting on the fact that the Arab sheiks will find the resolve to cooperate with us to arrest the terrorists who have been operating right under their noses."

"What makes you think that the Arab governments will cooperate?" Abdul asked.

"The relief of having the terrorists gone will be felt all over the world, especially in the palaces of the kings, emirs, and sheikhs. The secular leaders have always been afraid they'll be overthrown someday by Islamist fundamentalist clerics and their hordes of blind followers. These political leaders don't want any fanatic clerics setting up caliphates to replace their authority."

"You know, we just might pull this off," said David.

"Just remember that if you do the job right," Ivan said, "there'll be no atomic weapons, no terrorists, no caliphs, and no Americans to either blame or credit for the events."

When Ivan let himself into his suite at the Marriott, he found Marina hard at work on her book. She jumped up and gave him a hug and a kiss.

"I like to be good, concerned woman and ask you how was your day," Marina said, pretending to pout. "But I cannot ask, because with you everything is big secret."

Ivan understood how she felt, but he didn't have any answer for the problem that didn't include platitudes and vagaries.

"Everything went more or less as expected," he told her, nuzzling her hair. "Now, would you like to have dinner sent up? I'm afraid I'm going to have to work afterwards, though. I hope you don't mind."

"Of course I do not mind, Ivan. I call room service."

Marina was amazed at how easily Ivan seemed to adapt to his increasingly challenging tasks. In the last twenty-four hours he had moved, undaunted, from the position of student examinee to advisor to the Secretary of State. His strategy for confronting world terrorism was being considered by the leaders of the most powerful nation on earth. He was working in the White House with the leaders of his country, and yet he seemed not to be intimidated by either his new colleagues or his surroundings. She hoped his increasing power and responsibilities would never go to his head. She would see to that, if she had to.

CHAPTER TWENTY-EIGHT

When he got into the limo the next morning, Ivan had a few minutes to collect his thoughts. He had never been in the armed services, and aside from what he had learned from a few movies, he knew nothing about the military mind. He wished he had graduated from the War College, the Staff College, or at least one of the academies. On second thought, however, he realized that if he had had a little knowledge he might have embarrassed himself with the brass, whereas this way he could just come clean.

Ivan called the meeting to order and reviewed the purpose of the gathering. He made the point that his part was to coordinate matters and to assist with planning where it was deemed necessary. He might ask them if something was possible, but he would never give orders to the armed forces. Then he went over what was known about the caliphs and the way they had organized their jihad.

"There is much work to be done, gentlemen," Ivan told them, setting up his computer so he could illustrate various items on the agenda with a PowerPoint presentation. "Here is a photo of the Ka'bah. As you all know, it's located in the center of Mecca, in Saudi Arabia. Every good Muslim male is expected to come here at least once in a lifetime to pay his respects to Muhammad. Here you see them on their hadj, walking around the Ka'bah."

"Check it out," said one of the men. "There are millions of them!"

"We have reason to believe that the caliphs are directing their personal reign of terror from beneath the Ka'bah," Ivan continued. "This is a very tough spot to reach with a surgical strike, because it's *the* Islamic religious holy place. Unlike in the U.S., where we encourage Muslims to put up mosques across the street from Christian churches, no non-Muslim is permitted to enter the city, let alone the Ka'bah. It's the most important holy place they have. If we were to put boots on that holy ground in Saudi Arabia, every Muslim in the world would rise up in anger."

The men agreed unanimously.

"So we're going to have to get rid of the caliphs some other way," Ivan told them. "My team will send false coded messages to key terrorists around the world. These men will assume the information is genuine, and sent by their leaders in Mecca. That way we'll get the jihadists and insurgents to attack in places and at times of *our* choice so we can be waiting for them."

The group of men around the table began chattering fervently among themselves until Ivan held up a hand to request silence.

"I need you to make up a list of places that you would like to use to ambush these terrorists, and we will coax them out for you. If we handle the public relations correctly and demonstrate how these evil caliphs have used and abused Islam for their own purposes, we can gain the support of the citizenry. We've always had the support of the Arab leaders, kings, emirs, and sheikhs, who have long feared that the clerics would depose them in favor of a caliphate. At last, with some help from the locals, we may be able to clean up the vipers in Iraq and Afghanistan, where we have had to keep troops stationed. In countries where we have no troops, the idea will be to get the Arabs to do their own dirty work. For too long now we've failed to exact a price from those who murder our citizens, and from those who dance in the streets to celebrate these acts. We must be prepared to offer support to government security forces in those countries where we have no troops on station. We can have our advisors operate out of our embassies. Naturally we mustn't expect any credit or any thanks for bringing peace, but the end of this jihad crap will be reward enough in itself."

"Amen," the men murmured.

"Gentlemen," Ivan continued, "the Ka'bah has been built and rebuilt up to as many as twelve times over the 1,400 years since Muhammad participated in a reconstruction project during his pre-prophet life. The last renovation was in 1996. It's my contention that during the period of re-construction a good deal of unrecorded work has been done. We're trying now to ascertain if there is a foundation, basement, or tunnel below the cube-shaped form of the structure. We need to know if electricity has been installed. My team has reason to believe that the e-mail instructions to terrorist cells, which are sent in code to imams in mosques around the world, emanate from the Ka'bah. We've been maintaining surveillance around the clock on this structure, as well as on the huge mosque right behind it."

"What part, exactly, do you think the armed forces should play in this boondoggle?" asked a four-star general seated near Ivan.

"Well, I'd say it would have to be reconnaissance in act one, back-up in act two, and big time ambushes in act three," Ivan told him. You must plan for a great many small battles in all sorts of different places. This war is not like the con-ventional wars of the past, so massed armies are ineffective now. As far as I know, this is the first time in history that guerrilla warfare has been waged on a worldwide scale. So as you can appreciate, we have to prepare for them now in a completely different way."

"Guerrilla warfare on a worldwide scale," mused one of the generals. "I like your way of describing it. That's just what it is. Guerrillas always have the advantage of knowing where and when and how they're going to strike. That leaves us in the impossible position of having to be mind readers. Meanwhile, we're constantly being criticized by our own citizens for not knowing what they're going to do next. But of course, we'd have to be psychic to foil those psychos."

"That's it in a nutshell," Ivan said. "But now we don't have to be psychic. We have the advantage of knowing what targets the enemy will attack because *we'll* be the ones selecting them."

"Yes!" said another general, banging the table with his fist.

"It's also a very good opportunity for training our battle commanders to deal with the new urban terrorist wars," Ivan said, "while at the same time we rid the world of most of the cells that have succeeded because the element of surprise was in their hands. This time *they'll* be the ones who walk into the traps."

"About bloody time, too," someone said.

"I hope the Dastardly Deeds Department will take care of the caliphs," Ivan went on. "If we're going to call all the terrorists out at approximately the same time, the army will have to arrange many warm welcomes for them. If all goes well, we should be prepared to take a great many prisoners."

"We'll need to have a coordination session very soon," Ivan concluded. "Don't forget, we're scheduled to present our various recommendations to the President next Friday morning."

The Chiefs and their staffs adjourned. They would take the strategy development to the next level in their head-quarters at the Pentagon.

Ivan's next meeting was with the disinformation experts, and was scheduled for right after lunch. He hoped he could persuade all the public information officers, the PR people, and the press secretaries to present a unified disinformation program to convince the various Arab nations that fanatical fundamentalist terrorists had acquired nuclear capability and were planning to use it. He would have to be at his most convincing if he hoped to get all the spokespersons to set up a unified and convincing propaganda smokescreen sufficient to put the fear of God into the governments of the Islamic nations.

When the fourth estate, the propagandists, and the spin-doctors were assembled, Ivan proceeded to tell them about how he had uncovered the covert council of caliphs, and the secret code by which they directed the terrorist activities throughout the world. Since those present at this meeting had not attended any previous sessions, they needed to be brought up to date. Ivan made sure that they understood that the success of the plan depended on them. They must leak false information to the right sources in such a way as to make the governments of Islam believe that their own Muslim sources had uncovered a plot by the fundamentalists to use newly-acquired nuclear materials in terrorist attacks. Ivan told them he was counting on them to manufacture some totally believable evidence to indicate that suicide bombers were very close to being able to set off several cataclysmic nuclear explosions that would bring the West to its knees. It would also be appropriate to leak the information that the United States would not allow such an attack to go unpunished.

"We want every Saudi royal, every emir, every sheikh, and every government official in Islam to think that the U.S. has a retaliatory nuclear missile pointed at their palaces. Let's make sure that every tin pot nabob knows that the U.S. will hold him responsible for any Islamic involvement in the nuclear age of terrorism that takes place from now on. It's my belief that if they're threatened with total destruction and certain annihilation, these leaders will turn inward and put an end to the influence of the fundamentalist clerics and the caliphate that these two-faced cowards have allowed to hijack their nations and their religion for the past number of years."

"What do you want us to do, exactly?" said a reporter.

"Ladies and gentlemen," Ivan continued, looking around the table at all the expectant faces, "the pen that we believe to be mightier than the sword must now move into the nuclear age. We must dig out the terrible photos of the victims of Hiroshima and Nagasaki and see to it that the pictures appear in every possible Arabic media source. Fantasy time is finished for fundamentalists. The first requirement for a sovereign is that he has control over his people. The Arab leaders have allowed a covert viral strain of poisonous religious extremism to infect their lands. Up to this point they've merely thrown up their hands, saying that they can't control the religious passions of their people who, after all, have many bona fide quarrels with Israel and the Americans who support her. But now it's your job to inject realism into the minds of the Arab leaders. They're not living in the time of the Arabian Nights. A fantastic, and rationally purposeless, mission like 9/11 is never going to result in the defeat and destruction of the United States. Furthermore, the nuclear line in the sand, once crossed, can never be redrawn.

"But shouldn't we at least try to negotiate with them?" someone asked. "We're a civilized country, after all."

"No amount of coddling the Islamist extremists will do any good once a mushroom cloud comes rising up from their next target. The Arab leaders already know this and have, in their half-hearted fashion, been moving in the direction of trying to put a lid on their most cuckoo clerics. What we need now is to goad them into decisive action. You folks are the wordsmiths. Your country, in fact the whole world, is depending on you to make the case that life imitates your art. It's ironic that no one will know, at least in your lifetime, that you created a powerful, imaginary masterpiece that sheathed the scimitar of Islam."

Ivan told them they had two days until the next meeting, and that folks from Langley and the Pentagon would be present.

"I must have a fully coordinated strategy to present to POTUS by 0930 on Friday. Please put your minds to work on this at once, as it has top priority from the cabinet level."

Ivan asked them to remember the Apostle Paul's admonition to the Ephesians: *For we wrestle not against flesh and blood, but against principalities, against powers, against the rulers of the darkness of this world, against spiritual wickedness in high places.*

The meeting adjourned. For the first time in days, it seemed, Ivan's mind had a few minutes to touch on personal matters. He could clearly see that his job was going to move into a position of top priority in his life, at least for the time being. He was feeling guilty about what this would mean to Marina. He had brought her to the United States so they could be together, and now he had arranged things so they wouldn't even be in the same city for the majority of the time. He wondered if life was getting ready to play one of its *now you see it, now you don't* sleight-of-hand tricks. He was engaging in some mental role-playing, thinking about what he would say to Marina. But he knew he wouldn't be able to tell her what he was really doing, which was another complicating factor.

He wondered how the great men of history had handled issues of government secrecy. Did Harry Truman discuss the Manhattan Project with Bess? Did Lady Bird Johnson have input into Lyndon's Vietnam decisions? Did Bill Clinton let Hillary in on his al Qaeda training camp air strikes? Ivan was pleased that Marina understood and accepted the bond of trust that his position carried. He was sure that she would never push him for information that he was unable to share with her. Still, it was a peculiar situation that mustn't be discussed with the one person whose opinions were most trusted, and to whom absolute candor had been promised. If Marina were the one in possession of the secrets, would Ivan be able to refrain from asking about them? Presidents had advisors, but who advises the advisors? Not their wives, evidently. It was time to go back to the suite and tell Marina that she would be returning to Cambridge alone.

Marina seemed to be plowing right along with her book when Ivan arrived back at their hotel room. They embraced, and Ivan's nostrils were filled with the familiar smell of her shampooed hair. As he held her close, he felt the electric zing of desire surge through him. He resisted the urge to pursue his instincts. He wanted to clear up all the personal issues that needed discussing so there would be no distractions later.

"Would you like to go somewhere special for dinner tonight?" he asked her.

"Is too late now. We go to restaurant downstairs, ya?"

Seated at a table away from the other diners, Marina ordered a glass of wine, and Ivan had a beer. When the server came with their drinks, Ivan took a long swig of his Heineken's, wiped his lips, then looked at Marina.

"I'm going to be very busy for the next few weeks, so I won't be able to go back to Cambridge with you this time."

"This is not so good, ya?" said Marina. "I must teach in summer school, so I cannot stay here with you."

"I'm sorry I've moved so fast, but I couldn't help it."

"I know. Is not your fault."

Although neither of them liked the idea of a separation, they had already prepared themselves for the inevitable inconveniences to be endured during the following year.

"I leave on morning flight, then," Marina said.

"And I'll stay on here at the Marriott for now. When you come back next weekend, we can look for an apartment. You can keep my apartment in Cambridge until you finish your contract with Harvard, and that way we'll have a *pied à terre* in both cities for next year."

"Can we afford two apartments?" Marina asked. It was hard for her to imagine such extravagance.

"We'll work something out. Just leave it to me."

They put their heads together over dinner and roughed out a plan for their separate and conjugal lives. They promised they would call each other every night. They planned to guard their weekends together so that they could have some time alone. Ivan promised he would finish his thesis in the evenings, and Marina agreed to spend her free time writing her history book.

They discussed money matters and agreed that Marina should take care of Cambridge expenses, while he handled their costs in DC. By the time they finished their dinner they had worked out most of the mundane details of the dual existence they were about to embark upon. They charged the meal to their room and went up to their suite to spend their last night together.

Once inside the suite, Marina told Ivan she wanted to pack most of her things so she would be ready to leave in the morning. Ivan brushed his teeth and got ready for bed. When he had finished washing up, he undressed and got into the king-size bed, and Marina took his place in the bathroom. After some splashing noises and a few shadowy movements visible through the partly open door, Ivan saw Marina's naked figure as she turned off the bathroom light. She hopped up onto the bed and slid between the sheets.

"I ovulate in Cambridge while you are in Washington," she said sadly.

"I thought of that, but there isn't much we can do. I think you'll be ovulating for two or three days at least, so there's hope. Besides, it's difficult to make accurate predictions anyway, so you never know."

Ivan lifted up the sheets and peered at Marina's body.

"I just love looking at you naked. No sexy clothing, no cosmetics, and no jewelry could ever improve the way you look. My apologies to the cosmetics industry and to the lingerie manufacturers."

Marina raised herself up on her elbow and kissed him. They touched each other everywhere, and every touch increased their need to be together.

CHAPTER TWENTY-NINE

Morning came all too soon to suit Marina. When she opened her eyes, Ivan was nowhere to be seen. She knew he would never leave without saying goodbye, so she decided he must be in the other room. She got up, peeked around the door, and discovered him sitting in the swivel chair at the desk, working at his computer. He was completely naked. She guessed that he had not wanted to take a chance on waking her prematurely by opening the closet door to find a bathrobe, or by turning on a light in the bathroom, so for her sake he had remained in the outfit he had worn to bed.

Marina watched him as he typed away on his laptop. She could see his flattened rump through the space between the backrest and the seat of his chair. As she watched her lover at work, she was reminded of all those other Christian heroes who had fought against Islam in the past. Her mind produced a list of historical figures—Richard the Lionheart battling Saladin, Charles Martel combating the Saracens, Charles V saving Vienna and Europe from Suleiman, Ferdinand and Isabella driving the Moors from Spain, Thomas Jefferson standing up to the Barbary pirates, and Ivan Welland facing the caliphs. None but a female historian in love could ever draw parallels between her lover's naked behind and the endless procession of Islamic threats that the heroes of history had repelled.

Eventually Ivan became conscious of being watched. He swiveled around in his chair and caught Marina staring at him.

"Come out and let me have a good look at you," he said. "I won't be seeing you for a few days, and I want you to be fresh in my memory."

After some persistent beckoning, she stepped into the room.

"You're beautiful, Marina. You make me so happy."

Ivan put his arms around her and drew her onto his lap. They kissed, and he held her close. He fondled her breasts, and kissed them lovingly.

"Your breasts have tremendous character. They're possessed of a womanly confidence, and yet they have retained a healthy portion of girlishness."

He held first one, then the other, and spoke to them in turn. He whispered to the left one that she was cute and jaunty, pointing upwards a millimeter too high in a proud sort of way, while simultaneously favoring the left side by a millimeter, as if she were being more playfully carefree. He cupped her right breast, telling her that she was the reliable sister, always responsive to his touch.

Marina looked at him as though he were crazy.

"You must not get these ideas," she scolded him. "No time now. We must eat breakfast, and then I go to airport."

"But the left one is pouting. She needs to be consoled."

"Ivan, you are hopeless case," said Marina, drawing away from him. "You must wait until next weekend. Be happy with last night. Is not enough?"

"It's never enough. Never."

"Well, I take shower now. You must behave yourself and start to think about important things."

Dressed, packed, fed, and loved, it was time for Marina to go downstairs to catch her cab. They kissed a long, lingering kiss, and then Ivan opened the door to let her roll her suitcase out.

"You belong to me now," he said, "and I want you to remember that. I'll call you tonight. Have a safe trip. I love you."

The elevator came and she was gone. Ivan went inside and closed the door. He had nothing but work to do, and tons of it. He decided he would write up the plan of attack as if it were a stage play. It would have a prologue, three acts, and an epilogue. Each act would have its own timeline. The part that each character (in this case, group) played would appear as stage directions. He would write temporary acts using his own ideas until he received the actual plans from the military, the propagandists, and the intelligence operatives. In this way any ideas of his that were useful to the three main groups could be merged with their suggestions and blended into the final plan that would be presented to the President.

He spent the entire day working on his script without seeing another soul except for the maid, who came in to make up the beds. He did receive a call from Julia, who wanted an updated progress report. David Feingold also called, requesting an opinion on a technical matter.

At about dinner time he got a call from Montcalf, who was disappointed to hear that Marina had gone back to Cambridge to begin teaching her summer school class.

"I didn't know she was teaching in the summer school program," he said. "This is very interesting."

Ivan thought he could sense the wheels turning in Montcalf's head as he tried to invent a reason to go to Cambridge himself. He was about to create a project to keep Montcalf in Washington when the old sycophant mentioned that he had hoped to escort Marina around town on Tuesday, because he had to fly out to the West Coast for the rest of the week to do some interviews at Stanford and Cal Tech. But it appeared that scheduling conflicts were going to keep him away from Marina after all.

"Too bad," said Ivan. "I'm sure Marina will be sorry."

He intentionally failed to tell Montcalf that Marina would be back in Washington the following weekend.

After he hung up, Ivan decided to order a small steak from room service. He realized that he had skipped lunch altogether, but he wanted to work some more without losing time by scrounging for food outside the hotel.

While he was waiting for his dinner to arrive, he decided to call Marina to make sure she had arrived home safely. He was annoyed to find that the line was busy. His suspicious mind immediately jumped to the conclusion that Montcalf had called her as soon as he learned she was in Cambridge and not with him. He missed Marina, and the truth was that he resented the fact that Montcalf had gotten through to her before he did, if indeed that was who she was talking to. If only he had called her before ordering dinner, he thought. It was his penchant for efficiency that had prompted him to get his meal in motion before calling her.

A few minutes later he finally reached Marina. She was happy to hear from him, and she asked him to guess who had just called her. Ivan felt she was a little disappointed that he immediately assumed it was Montcalf.

"I just finished talking to him myself," Ivan told her. "I figured he'd call you as soon as he realized you were alone."

"He says to me he must go to California for few days," she explained. "But he likes to see if he can change schedule so he can come to Cambridge. He tells me he is worried I am lonely."

"So what did you say?"

"I thanked him for this concern, but I told him I am not lonely because I must teach classes and make preparations, so I cannot spend time with him anyway. I hope I convinced him. But maybe he comes here anyway, in spite of protests."

Ivan sighed. "Well, I hope he soon finds some other guy's woman to moon over. Maybe he'll get lucky in California."

Marina reminded him that Simeon was a gentleman, and never touched her or suggested anything untoward. She found him knowledgeable and definitely harmless. There was no need to be jealous or annoyed about his attentions. Outwardly Ivan knew there was nothing going on between them, but inwardly he wished the old coot would just drop off the edge of the earth.

"I meant to tell you that I won't be able to meet you on Friday when you get into the city. I'm scheduled to be at the White House then. I'm really sorry."

"I understand. You must not worry. I know my way now, so we meet together in hotel later."

"I'm still in the same suite. I'll be there as soon as the meeting is over. Julia says hello, by the way."

"This is good, ya? Give her some greetings for me."

At three o'clock in the morning Ivan finished writing the material that he would be outlining to the President later that day. He went to bed to grab a few hours of sleep so he would be fresh and clear-minded for the meeting. As he fell asleep his mind was whirling with questions. Did he forget anything? Was his presentation clear? Did he put everything in the right order? Did he leave out any important details?

He had decided to call his presentation *The Council of Caliphs,* which he had written in the same structure as a play. The prologue was in two parts. The first part dealt with his experiences in Chechnya, his connection with the imam, his observations about Islam, the discovery of the code of the Koran, and the deciphering of the code. The second part described the terrorist organization headed by the caliphs in Mecca, their objectives, their modus operandi, their effect on Islam, the necessity of their removal, and the overall plan to bring about their downfall.

He wrote each of the three acts as descriptions of the actions to be taken in order to achieve the destruction of the covert Council of Caliphs. A well-coordinated plan could bring down the secret organization that was plaguing the world with its deadly doctrines and evil actions. Ivan wrote each act as a rough draft. He didn't believe he knew enough about counter-terrorism to make detailed plans for professionals with years of experience in the field. He did feel, however, that some of his suggestions might be valuable to the experts. Ivan suggested that each group of experts be in charge of performing one act of the plan.

The first group, under the command of the President's Chief Security Advisor, would amend or improve Ivan's draft of *Act One*, which described how disinformation could be spread around to ensure that the leaders of the Muslim nations were convinced that terrorists had acquired nuclear capability.

The second group, working under Tim Morrison, the Director of the CIA, was to take Ivan's draft of *Act Two* and turn it into a viable undercover plan for the capture or the assassination of the caliphs. Ivan's description of this operation was based on his speculations about how the caliphs were conducting their evil business from under the Ka'bah in secret quarters built in 1996 during the last reconstruction of the ancient building. Ivan's suggested scenario called for the hookahs used by these men to be laced with anthrax or some other deadly poison so that when they smoked the water pipe they would die. If this could be accomplished in a *sub rosa* fashion, the United States would not be implicated. Even if the CIA were suspected, Ivan's draft of the plan provided no evidence of their involvement. Furthermore, when the spin doctors of the first group got through painting the horrible picture of how the caliphs had hijacked Islam and subverted the authority of the rulers to gain power for themselves by conducting a phony holy Jihad, everyone would be so overjoyed to see the end of the caliphs that few questions would be raised about the methods used to rid the world of them.

The third group, under the command of the Chairman of the Joint Chiefs of Staff, would take over the military operations that would take place in *Act Three* of the plan. Ivan's own team of code breakers would work in concert with the military to order terrorist cells to attempt strikes that would be intercepted by previously alerted military forces. Every branch of the military at one time or another had taken losses caused by sneak terrorist attacks from Islamist extremists, and they all lusted for revenge. The growing importance of the Special Forces in these days of grim warfare had resulted in the creation of various units that were highly effective in combating the shadowy tactics of the Mujahideen, Hamas, Hezbollah, and al Qaeda. Ivan was sure that if the terrorists could be lured out into the open, the military would make short work of them. Removing the enemy was what the Special Forces were all about. Ivan welcomed their help, knowing that this was the last court of appeal when it came to dealing with fanatics.

Each of the groups would be expected to present an inventory list of manpower, ordnance, or other special needs. The analogy of the play continued on in Ivan's mind as he equated the cast of characters, property list, and epilogue with the information to be supplied to him by the three participating groups. He hoped that the President, after analyzing the plan, would be the actor who read the epilogue by way of authorizing the performance. He was also hoping that the powerful leaders who attended the planning sessions would accept the playwright's structural format for the plan. Ivan thought of himself as a Pirandello whose characters were in search of an author, but different in that these characters had to write their own acts, as the author had developed only an outline of the play along with a few suggestions for a plot.

Now it was time to make sure the backers were signed up for a long, successful run. His driver was downstairs waiting to take him to one of his country's most important planning sessions, and he mustn't keep history waiting.

It only took Ivan a few seconds to discern that his three groups had taken their planning seriously. Papers, books, and laptop computers were spread out over the tables as he walked to the lectern. He called the meeting to order and outlined what he hoped to achieve during the course of it. He explained that he was a professor of literature, and thus the ideal person to plan a military Special Forces operation. That drew a few laughs.

"However," he went on, "having read more books, plays, and poems than anyone else in the room, I have a great deal of knowledge about the construction of plots. That being the case, I've taken the liberty of writing you a play in three acts. It's not a real play, but I've structured the material as though it were. You will be divided into groups according to your specialties, and each group will take one act and criticize, amend, or rewrite it, so each act will fit the plot perfectly. We'll know we've done our jobs superbly when they're justified by the epilogue, so the President can read it aloud to us on Friday."

Ivan distributed copies of the three acts to the appropriate groups, and told them to go to work turning their plans into one cohesive plot that could be acted out to the accolades of the world at large. Ivan allowed them time to read the act that he had assigned to each group. He was glad to see them all go to work just as he had instructed. Evidently they found some of his ideas intriguing, as a good deal of conversation was generated.

Throughout the morning Ivan walked among the three groups, spending time in half-hour increments with each one. He was gratified to see that his idea of structuring his overall plan in the form of a three-act play had turned out well. Now that they were in the planning stage, the strategists actually liked the play format. Ivan was pleased that somehow his academic training had proved to be of some practical use in the all too real world of geo-political shadow warfare. He thought his father would be surprised and pleased to be getting some practical payback from his son's switch from science to liberal arts.

At noon Ivan collected the rough drafts of each act that the three groups had interspersed with his original ideas.

"Gentlemen," he said, addressing them from the front of the room, "I've ordered a buffet lunch to be served next door. When we reconvene, we'll pass the drafts around so that each group will understand what the others are planning. In this way everyone will be up to speed, and surprises will be few."

Cross-fertilization of ideas was to be encouraged, and Ivan planned to have a period of open discussion at the end of the day. Each group would then hand over their portion of the plan in writing to Ivan by noon the next day. He would read them and then write his epilogue, using the plans they submitted as the basis for the finished copy of *The Council of Caliphs*.

"The epilogue will be a summary of what we can expect to accomplish if the President orders the implementation of the plan. So we all have to roll up our sleeves and get to work. The epilogue must be ready to send to the President so he can read it before the Friday meeting. If he approves it, we could be asked to begin the implementation stage early next week. I think it's time we had a name for the plan described in *The Council of Caliphs*. I suggest we call it *Operation Playwright*. At least that way nobody will guess what it's all about."

After lunch the teams reassembled. Ivan distributed the plans to the three groups, and for the next hour they read them and discussed them. A few good suggestions evolved from their conversations, and by the end of the afternoon everyone was satisfied that the plans were well conceived and were ready for them to put in writing.

"All right," Ivan said. "You have your work cut out for you. I look forward to seeing the results. Remember, your deadline is noon tomorrow."

Ivan thought he would walk back to the Marriott to give himself some fresh air, now that the meeting had concluded its business for the day. He would be relatively free until the noon deadline the next day, but he didn't know how time-consuming the implementation stage would be. It was a huge project, and he was already feeling guilty because he would probably have to leave Marina alone much of the time. He would have to call her and talk it over with her. Perhaps she might want to stay in Cambridge to give him time to devote all his energy to the project, but there was no way he could go there to join her. If he read her intentions correctly, she would want to be with him as soon as possible because of the timing of her ovulation. Maybe he could find a way to meet her over the weekend. After all, the President wouldn't be getting his finished copy of *The Council of Caliphs* until Friday, so he would need the weekend himself to read it and ponder it.

Ivan plodded along, thinking about Marina and the work he had to do. When he passed by a *Victoria's Secret* lingerie shop he suddenly remembered his promise to himself that he would buy her some silk underwear when he had the chance. He entered the store feeling very self-conscious, and it got worse from there. The advertising artwork, the mannequins, and the merchandise displays were all calculated to promote prurience. He was the only man there, and not of a size to go unnoticed.

The young clerk who approached him was obviously a believer in the merits of her own merchandise. From Ivan's altitude he could see through her liberally-flaunted cleavage halfway to the basement.

"May I help you?" she asked.

It was the first time Ivan had ever heard those ordinary words uttered in such a suggestive way. It was clear to him that he should never have come into the store, but it was too late now. All he could do was try to remain unflustered.

"I would like to make my wife a present of some soft, comfortable underclothes."

That was probably unnecessary information in this store. The information that *was* necessary—her sizes—he did not know. He told himself that the great planner should have planned this operation a whole lot better.

The clerk knew that she wouldn't be able to make a sale to Ivan that day, but she hit upon what he thought was an intelligent strategy. She gave him a copy of the latest catalog and told him to choose what he liked from among the items pictured.

"After you figure out what you want to give her," she said, "you can look in your wife's lingerie drawer and find out what sizes she wears in those items."

"That's a very good idea," Ivan muttered, surreptitiously slipping the catalog into his briefcase lest anyone see him with it. "Thank you for your help."

He headed quickly for the door, convinced that the clerk and her friends would have a giggle about his ineptitude with ladies' lingerie after he left the store.

Ivan suddenly remembered another errand that he had to take care of. He had spoken to Marina about marriage, but had made no concrete moves to make arrangements for their nuptials. He should determine what the civil requirements for marriage were in Washington. He knew he needed a license, but where did one need to go to get one? What other requirements were there? He knew they wanted to be married by a minister, but who would that be? They hadn't yet found a church in Washington. He would have to talk with Marina about whom to invite, and when, and where the ceremony would take place. It all seemed much more complicated to him than saving the world.

It was only a short walk along Pennsylvania Avenue from the White House to the J.W. Marriott Hotel. A surprising number of hotel staffers greeted him by name as he entered the lobby and proceeded to the elevators. He was sure that someone was giving friendliness lessons to the employees, and he was perhaps very recognizable because of his height, but it did make him feel at home there.

When he got up to his room he removed his jacket and tie, put his attaché case with his laptop in it on the desk, and kicked off his shoes in favor of his slippers. He removed his computer from its case, and in so doing he revealed the *Victoria's Secret* catalog. While he thought of it he decided to implement the clerk's strategy to find out Marina's bra and panty size. His plan was foiled when he discovered that Marina had packed and taken all her underclothes with her to Boston when she left. He hoped that his plans for the demise of the secret caliphs would go forward with fewer snags than his misadventures in the veiled world of *Victoria's Secret*.

Ivan picked up the phone and called room service. After placing his dinner order, he dialed Marina. His call came a bit earlier than she expected, but she didn't mind. They told each other that they missed being together, and they looked forward to their reunion on the weekend. Marina led off with a description of her exploits as a new lecturer at Harvard. Ivan could not respond with any information about his work, so he just told her he was very busy.

"There's one thing we *can* talk about, though," he said. "Our wedding plans. We both have jobs now, and soon we'll both have apartments, and with any luck we'll have a child, too. So I think it's time we tied the knot, don't you?"

"We tie knot long time ago," Marina laughed. "But we can make it legal when you like."

"I want to now," Ivan replied. "But there's so much to do. I don't even know where to begin."

"Men are so helpless without women."

"It's just that… you can't imagine all the work I have, and I can't tell you, either."

"Is not good for wedding to be in your head when you have so much work. There is only one way to eliminate this worry. I make it surprise, ya?"

Ivan had no idea what she meant, but he knew he'd better say yes, so he did. It seemed to him that from that point in the conversation she couldn't wait to say goodbye.

"Call me tomorrow to receive instructions," she said, and hung up. That was Marina, Ivan thought. Direct, quick, and unpredictable. His dinner arrived and he sat down to eat it, wondering what his mysterious wife was up to.

As soon as she was off the phone with Ivan, Marina called Julia at home in Georgetown. After the usual small talk, she got straight to the point.

"Ivan and I wish to be married, but with his new job and my job too, we do not know when we can arrange wedding, so I am ready to take cow by horns and do it on Saturday," Marina said breathlessly.

"On Saturday! Why the rush? Are you pregnant?"

"Not yet, unfortunately. But Ivan is busy and he must not have wedding in head when he needs head for big thoughts. Best solution is we get married before he can begin to worry and waste time on plans and duties."

"I see," said Julia, smiling. "Well, it all makes sense, in an unconventional sort of way. What can I do to help?"

"Is Ivan free on Saturday night?"

"Yes, as a matter of fact, he is. He's actually going to be free on Saturday and Sunday as well, so I see no reason why you shouldn't get married this weekend."

"This is good, ya?"

"I would say it's excellent, yes. You picked the perfect time. Anything else I can do?"

"Can you recommend small church and pastor to marry us? He can be Protestant or Catholic, we do not mind. And then can you explain to me nice restaurant that we remember forever after our wedding dinner?"

"Is that all?"

"Yes, that is all. Oh, and maybe your advice about florist. There must be flowers, ya?"

"I would say so," Julia agreed.

"So what do you think? Shall I call you later for ideas one, two, and three, with subtopic florist?"

"You academics are all alike," Julia laughed. "Crazy as loons. But we love you anyway."

"I am very glad this is so," said Marina.

"How about witnesses? Are they subtopic B?"

"Would you be witness for us?" Marina asked timidly.

"I'd be honored," said Julia, with genuine pleasure. "So now here's my idea. There's a stunning little country inn in Virginia, called *The Inn at Little Washington.* I know the chef there. Patrick creates the most sensational dishes you can possibly imagine. They also do weddings. They have a wedding director, and one of the staff is a pastor. They'll arrange all the details of your wedding for you. All you have to do is say the word. How does that sound?"

"Which word do I say?" Marina asked.

"Just say *yes.*"

"Then I say *yes,* with all my heart."

CHAPTER THIRTY

Ivan lazed around the hotel suite, reading his notes and trying to relax. There was not much he could accomplish until he received the completed plans from the three groups, which were due at noon. He had his breakfast sent up, and when he was finished he showered and shaved.

It was still early, so he decided to walk over to the White House, where he would receive the final plans. He was eager to write the summary of actions to be taken which would then supply the President with a detailed explanation of what he had decided to call *Operation Playwright.* If the President approved the plan, Ivan's play would move from fiction to fact.

The phone rang just as he was about to leave.

"Dr. Welland? You have a phone call from the Secretary of State. Would you hold on, please?"

Julia wanted an update on how things were going. She had been out of touch for a while, and wanted to know what he had been up to. Ivan told her everything relating to the finalization of *Operation Playwright.*

"Why did you call it that?"

"Because I did the first draft of the plan in the form of a play. And secondly, because the name says nothing about where or what the operation is all about, and thirdly, because no one will forget the first planning session, with its play format. It's better than calling it *Murder in Mecca,* don't you think?"

"I hear you. When do I get my autographed copy of this play of yours?"

"I intend to finish the final draft by 1700 hours this afternoon. I'm on my way to the White House right now to pick up the pieces, so to speak. It's up to me to write an epilogue that will summarize the plan and pull it together, including an assessment of the results to be expected when the operation is completed. If I do my job right, the President could authorize the operation any time after 1100 hours on Friday. If you like, I can personally deliver your copy to you this evening."

"I'd like that," said Julia. "I look forward to reading your play. I'll see you later, then."

Ivan greeted the security guards at the entrance to the West Wing of the White House. The guards knew him now, but a thorough search was *de rigueur*, so Ivan submitted to it cheerfully. Once inside the building, he went immediately to the conference room and set up his laptop on the table. He was fifteen minutes early, but the courier from the first group was already there, delivering his vital package of papers containing Act One of the *Council of Caliphs.* Ivan signed for the large envelope, dismissed the courier, opened the envelope, and began reading.

He had just finished reading the first part of the plan when a Marine sergeant in dress uniform arrived with Act Two. Ivan signed for the envelope, thanked the sergeant, opened it up and began reading it. The military portion of the plan was much harder to read and digest because Ivan was not familiar with their terms, acronyms, and hierarchical responsibility levels. The large sheaf of papers contained the plans for forty different small military engagements, as well as pages of statistics estimating losses, attrition rates, assignments of flag officers' responsibilities, and all manner of details expressed in a crisp military jargon that tested Ivan's patience. They had been thorough, however, and they must have worked long and hard to prepare the document in such a short time.

Ivan was about one third of the way into the second act when the courier from the dirty tricks section of the CIA arrived with their contribution. After signing to acknowledge receipt of the documents, he opened the envelope containing the third act. It was this package that would include the method by which the caliphs would be dispensed, and was the key to the whole plot. If this portion of the plan were to be unsuccessful, all the rest would go for naught.

He quickly got to the method that would be used to kill the caliphs. In his short consulting sessions with the CIA planners he had sensed that they liked his suggestion that they poison the hookah, but they were concerned that the plan contained no back-up measures to ensure its success. Ivan was pleased to note that they had included several additional layers of silent killers in their plan. By the time he finished reading the Third Act, he had developed a new respect for the CIA. He pitied anyone who found themselves in their cross hairs.

Now, with all three segments of the plan on the table, Ivan sat down at his laptop and began writing his epilogue. He justified the necessity of the plan, summarized the actions that needed to be taken, and predicted the results that would come from implementing *Operation Playwright*. It took him most of the afternoon, but when he was satisfied with the results, he printed off six copies. He put the completed sets of the plan into six large envelopes and addressed them to the President, the Secretary of State, the three group leaders, and kept one copy for himself. He put a personal letter in the envelopes for the group leaders, thanking them for their timely and well-reasoned contributions to the plan. He used the top-secret courier system to deliver the documents.

When he had finished his work, it occurred to him that he had been totally consumed by the caliphs for more than a month. He had managed to get through his orals, but aside from that he hadn't read a scholarly book or worked on his PhD dissertation since he'd left Cambridge to go to Grozny. He had no regrets, for he knew the importance of the work he had been doing, but the stress, especially in the last week or so, had been considerable.

He got up, collected his things, and headed out to the State Department building to give Julia her copy of the plan. Now that he had his credentials as an employee of the State Department, the admittance procedure was a whole lot easier from a security perspective than it had been at the White House. He went immediately to the Secretary's office and announced himself.

"The Secretary mentioned that you would be coming along at about this time," said Julia's assistant. "Please take a seat, sir."

She called Julia to announce his arrival. After a few minutes she told him that the Secretary would see him. He entered the office, and as usual could not help being awed when he thought of all the historical people who had been in this room.

"Please have a seat," Julia said, scrutinizing the contents of her envelope. "This weighs a ton. You've just provided me with a whole night's work."

"I hope you like it. If you find any flaws, please call me and let me know, no matter what time it is. Many heads are better than one. If the operation goes awry, we might all be in more trouble than we ever imagined."

Her expression grew serious. "We have to take a tough stand to deal with all this killing and despair. Your plan is the best hope I have for doing something worthwhile during my term as Secretary of State. So thank you for all your good work, Ivan. You're doing okay for a guy who's only been on the job for a week."

Ivan thanked her for the compliment, but hoped it wasn't premature.

"You'll be sitting next to me at the meeting with the President on Friday morning. I want you to keep an eye on the operation, okay? Meanwhile, I'd like you to go and see the Chief of Employee Relations. Her name is Minnie. She'll need you to do some paperwork so that she can issue you a paycheck."

Julia told Ivan he had the rank of Under Secretary now, so he didn't have to take any crap from anybody except her.

"Have you met your administrative assistant?"

"No. Not yet."

"Well, go and check that out as well. You'll like her. And after the meeting with POTUS, I'd like you to take the weekend off."

As he left, he asked Julia's assistant to direct him to the location of his office.

"It's just up the hall, second door on the right," she said, with a bright smile.

Ivan opened the door of the large corner office, taking a moment to look around. He detected the influence of the same interior decorator that had done the offices of the chief administrators at Harvard University. The furniture was elegant and conservative. Leather, polished wood and expensive trappings predominated, giving the room a sober, weighty appearance. Ivan wasn't sure he was old enough to balance out the antiques in his new office. He put his envelope on the desk, and looked into the drawers. He noticed a button built into the desk, so he pushed it.

"Yes, Dr. Welland?" a voice inquired.

Ivan asked the voice to step into his office. He hadn't used the intercom speaker button, but his special assistant, anticipating his lack of familiarity with the communication system, entered the room anyway. Ivan was impressed with her good common sense. She introduced herself as Betty Brocklyn, and they shook hands.

"Most people call me Brooklyn," she told Ivan. "That's because they don't know any better. I'm actually from the Bronx."

"Pleased to meet you, Brooklyn. I'm Ivan."

"Sorry, but here you're *Dr. Welland,*" she corrected him.

"But I don't have a doctorate yet."

"You're a doctor, ABT," she insisted.

"True, but All But Thesis doesn't hold much water with me."

"You're too hard on yourself, Dr. Welland."

Betty Brocklyn graduated from the Bronx High School of Science, and then received her BSc in mathematics from Hunter College. She had been at the State Department for ten years, so she knew her way around. Ivan decided that her nickname, *Brooklyn*, was somehow very appropriate for her personality. She was fast-talking, fast-moving, and her eyes shone with quick intelligence.

"May I call you *Brooklyn,* too?"

"Be my guest."

She told Ivan her grandfather had escaped from Russia just one step ahead of the Cossacks. When he arrived at Ellis Island he couldn't speak a word of English, so when the immigration officer asked him his name, he kept telling him where he wanted to go instead. The immigration guy knew his name couldn't be *Brooklyn*, so he wrote *Brocklyn*. He became Ben Brocklyn from Brooklyn for the rest of his life. But the Cossacks didn't get him or the Nazis either, so it was worth the kidding he had to endure.

"Old Grandpa Ben was the last of his line," Brooklyn said with a sigh. "Looking back on it all now, that was pretty important for me, too. My dad moved us to the Bronx to avoid the issue, so as soon as I got here they started calling me Brooklyn anyway. Go figure."

Ivan liked his new assistant. She was short, dark, and feisty. He guessed she was about seven years older than he was.

"Where do you keep top-secret documents, Brooklyn?"

"I have a secure file cabinet on the wall in my office."

"Do you know where the Employee Relations office is?"

Brooklyn gave him the directions—short, specific, and clearly expressed.

"Minnie's smart," she added. "You'll like her."

Before he left she handed him a special secure phone and told him to have it with him twenty-four/seven.

"Thank you very much. But I won't be calling you at all hours, don't worry."

"Oh, I'm not worried. The phone is so *I* can call *you* anytime and anywhere. Just remember, Brooklyn is watching you."

"I'll try to remember."

"Oh, and by the way, since you'll be at the White House tomorrow and off for the weekend, I'll see you on Monday."

Ivan nodded. He wondered how Brooklyn knew he was off for the weekend when he had just been told himself.

Minnie had delayed going home just so she could do the paperwork and put the new Under Secretary on the payroll. She went over his entire pay package with him, and told him about his health and retirement benefits. She had him sign loyalty statements, tax deduction forms, and beneficiary assignments for insurance policies. At the end of her spiel, Ivan told her that he guessed he was a bona fide bureaucrat now.

"Yup," she said. "No different from the rest of us."

He traced his way in reverse back to his office. He picked up his attaché case, put the papers Minnie had given him inside, picked up the envelope that he had left on his desk, and headed out. He got a cab and told the driver to take him to the Marriott.

When it came to eating alone, Ivan was a creature of habit. He really didn't care what he ate. He was capable of skipping meals entirely, if he was busy. He liked a fine meal if he could share it with Marina, but if he was by himself he was content to call room service and eat while he watched the news on TV.

He decided to call Marina while he waited for his dinner to arrive. She seemed very chipper and told him that they would be together tomorrow, so she was getting happy again.

"I met my new assistant today. Her name is Brooklyn."

"Yes, and my name is Moscow," said Marina. "You may not introduce her to Bernard, or I send Russian Mafia."

Just then the waiter rapped on the door.

"Good night, Spunky. I miss you. See you tomorrow."

Ivan flipped on the TV and watched a report of how more good men were being ambushed and killed in the Middle East. He thought to himself that the next day would be the beginning of the end for terrorism.

CHAPTER THIRTY-ONE

Ivan, dressed in a freshly pressed suit and wearing a starched white shirt with his best tie, was seated next to Julia at the huge conference table used by the Cabinet for its meetings. He sat back in his chair so that he wouldn't obstruct Julia's view of the other conferees. The ambience was austere and the mood somber as the gathering awaited the guest of honor.

Suddenly everyone present arose as the door opened and the President, his Security Advisor, and his Chief of Staff made their entrances. The President took his customary seat, flanked by his advisors. The table was so large that those on the same side as the President saw only his profile.

"You may be seated," he said.

While everyone was getting comfortable and POTUS was arranging his papers in front of him, Ivan studied the man. Seeing him on TV and being ten feet away from him in the flesh were two different things. In his second term now, the President was comfortable in his role.

"Who initiated the plan that I have here?" he asked.

Julia rose to her feet and said, "It's a cooperative effort, but the man responsible for breaking the code, uncovering the covert council of caliphs, and suggesting the operation is this young man sitting on my right, Dr. Ivan Welland of Harvard University, whom many of you have already met."

"So *you* put together the team of experts who deciphered the code of the terrorist leaders, did you? Julia, you always were a lulu," the President said.

"Yes, Mr. President," she replied.

As he waited to hear what the most powerful man in the country, and probably the world, had to say to him, Ivan took comfort in the fact that he was the protégé of a good and trusted friend of the President.

"Welland, what are you a doctor *of?*" POTUS asked.

"Russian Language and Literature, Mr. President."

"I see. So I may assume that you know nothing about Middle Eastern politics, military tactics, and Islam?"

"No sir, Mr. President," Ivan answered.

"No sir, you do, or no sir, you don't?"

There was some sniggering to be heard around the table.

"I believe I know quite a bit about those areas, sir," Ivan said matter-of-factly.

"How do you know this if you specialize in Russian?"

"I read a lot, Mr. President."

Some of the military men laughed outright.

"What have you read on these topics?"

Ivan knew he was being baited, but he liked the game.

"I've read the Koran several times in two languages, done a critical comparison and discussed it with a noted Arab scholar. I've read the Sunnahs, the Hadith in nine volumes, the Ijma consensus of Muslim scholars, and I've studied the Qiyas, or new case law, rendered by Sharia judges. I've also read some volumes of criticism and various studies in comparative religion."

"You may rest your case, Dr. Welland," the President smiled. "This plan of yours is written almost as if it were a play to be mounted on the stage. Why is that?"

"I'm a professor of literature, sir, so I plotted it like a play. Hence the name *Operation Playwright.*"

"Well, the whole thing read better than a pot-boiler."

Thank you, sir, I think," said Ivan.

"Do you believe it'll work?" the President asked him.

"I do, sir. The advantage of knowing when and where to attack has always been in the court of the terrorists, and it has cost us dearly. In this plan *we* have those advantages, and

I for one, think we should sock it to them very hard," Ivan answered.

"Audacity, more audacity, always audacity, isn't that what Napoleon said?"

"It's what Napoleon *did*, but it's actually what Danton said. I hate to put a damper on things, but Napoleon was defeated and exiled, and Danton was guillotined."

They all had a hearty laugh.

"Thank you, professor. You're a lulu, too. I guess it takes one to know one." He looked at Julia and smiled.

The levity had warmed things up, and the discussion proceeded to some questions that the President had about various phases of the plan. Eventually the Commander-in-Chief gave *Operation Playwright* the green light, and everyone clapped as the President left the room.

The plan was duty-specific, so all those present had tasks that needed doing. The room emptied quickly, as purposeful senior officers and officials went about their business. Ivan followed Julia out of the cabinet room, and they headed for her car.

As they drove toward the State Department building, Julia complimented Ivan on his presentation.

"POTUS liked you, I could tell," Julia said.

"I'm glad," Ivan said. "I liked him, too."

"Your job of coordinating the efforts of very powerful egos won't be an easy one, you know. You might as well get some rest while you can. You have the weekend off, because until the operation is implemented there'll be nothing to coordinate. So have a good time with Marina. I've placed a driver at your disposal to take you to the airport to pick her up."

"That's very thoughtful of you, Julia. Thank you."

"How do you like your office, and your assistant?"

"The accommodations are very comfortable. I like my assistant, too. *Brooklyn*, they call her. Do you know her?"

"I was the one who assigned Brooklyn to you."

"Well, then, my compliments to central casting. But I've never had an assistant, so I hope I'll know how best to employ her. I don't want to waste her time."

"Don't worry. You may be a virgin boss, but Brooklyn is an experienced assistant. She'll know what to do."

"Does she have a level of security clearance that allows me to share the details of *Operation Playwright* with her?"

"She has sufficient clearance to be your assistant, which means you can work with her in complete confidence."

"This is good, ya?" Ivan said.

"This is like Marina, ya?" Julia smiled.

"You notice everything, ya?"

When they pulled up at the basement garage entrance to the State Department building, the door sprang open and a security guard helped Julia get out of the limo. Ivan unfolded his body and alighted from the car, following her into the cavernous entranceway. They were escorted to the elevator that took them up to their floor, and then they headed off in opposite directions to their respective offices.

Ivan found Brooklyn at her desk in the room adjoining his office. He greeted her, and noticing that she seemed very busy, he asked her what she was doing. She told him she was writing up a few tips about protocol to help him in his new job.

"I'll be finished with your *Don't Do or Say* list in a minute. I'll bring it to you as soon as I'm through. Your instructions and the *Do* list will be ready for you on Monday morning."

Ivan, who had been a lone ranger all his life, wondered what a *Don't* list in a huge bureaucracy would entail. He sat down at his desk and resolved to go over *Operation Playwright* with Brooklyn as soon as she came in. In preparation for this, he removed the huge sheaf of papers from the large envelope and placed them on the desk.

Brooklyn soon appeared with a two-page list of things not to do. It contained such advice as, "Never use first names in public, always use titles, e.g. *Congressman, Senator, Mr. Justice, Mr. Ambassador, Madame Secretary, Doctor,* and so forth."

"You should memorize this list before Monday. I don't want to have to break in a new boss again on Tuesday."

Ivan looked at the list for ten seconds, told her he had committed it to memory, and was there anything else before he gave her an assignment? Brooklyn was from New York, so she was skeptical about everything and doubted that Ivan had given her list the attention necessary to memorize the whole thing so quickly. Ivan looked at her, handed her the list, and recited it verbatim. He hoped this would cure any tendencies she had to disbelieve what he told her. Brooklyn had worked for older, slower men in her career at State, and had generally been smarter than her bosses. This time she could tell things were going to be different.

Ivan handed her the *Operation Playwright* folder. He told her she should read it but not remove it from the office.

"Our job is to coordinate this operation," he told her. "We are to make sure the responsible people are doing their job well and in a timely fashion. I need you to maintain a diary on a daily basis of the actions taken and those remaining to be done. There should be a book for each of the groups, and a page for each day. If you're comfortable with computers you can set it up on yours, but file it with a password so no one can use the program except us, *just us,* you and me. When you finish reading this document you'll understand better what we have to do, and how important this work is. The operation was approved by POTUS today, so it will be all right to begin tracking on Monday, since nothing can be done before then. As a result, I'm on my way to the airport to meet someone, so I'll see you first thing Monday."

He began packing up his attaché case and was about to head for the door when Brooklyn stepped back into his office and told him there was a call for him on line one.

"It's the Secretary for you, Dr. Welland," she said.

"Hello Julia, what can I do for you?"

He purposely called her by her first name so Brooklyn would not be too cocky about giving him instructions.

"Ivan, I'm glad I caught you before you left for the airport. I've just had a call from the President. He wanted to invite you and Marina to dinner tomorrow night, but I was able to get him to wait till Sunday. Apparently he thinks you are some kind of budding luminary. Oh, and I'm invited too, so I'll have my driver pick you two up and we'll go over there together."

"What next?" Ivan thought to himself as he went looking for the car and driver that was to take him to the airport.

Little Washington, Virginia

Ivan was waiting for Marina at the arrivals gate. She could see him because he was so much taller than the other people who were waiting to meet folks on her flight. He could not see her quite so easily, as she was in the middle of a throng coming down the ramp toward the exit. When she got to him he kissed her and grabbed her luggage.

"Julia sent me to get you in one of her cars. The driver is waiting for us outside by the curb."

When they left the building the observant driver caught sight of them at once and pulled the limo up to the curb. He took the baggage and stowed it in the trunk, while Ivan and Marina climbed into the back seat. The black limousine moved slowly into a long line of traffic and headed out of the airport.

Ivan was so busy talking to Marina that he didn't notice that the driver was going in the wrong direction. After about half an hour, however, he saw that the landscape was unfamiliar. He leaned forward and asked the driver why he was heading away from the city.

"I'm following the Secretary's instructions, sir."

"Be patient darling," Marina said. "You're not being kidnapped."

Ivan stared at her. "What do *you* know about this?"

Marina smiled her best Mona Lisa smile.

After about forty-five minutes the limo rolled to a stop in front of a picturesque little inn hidden deep in the country-side. A uniformed employee opened the car door and welcomed them to the *Inn at Little Washington*. As they got out of the limo another uniformed man removed their luggage, placed it on a cart and rolled it into the Inn. Marina took Ivan's arm and walked him into the small room that served as a lobby.

"We've been expecting you, doctor," said the clerk at the registration desk. "Welcome to the Inn at Little Washington. I trust you had a pleasant drive?"

"We have nice drive, thank you," Marina replied.

A hotel employee picked up their baggage and asked them to follow him. Ivan was perplexed, but he obediently walked along behind Marina, presuming that she would eventually tell him what they were doing there.

Ivan's first impression was that it was a caparisoned warren. They went up a spiral stairway with landings both left and right. He assumed they had reached the uppermost floor of the inn, and he was almost correct. The employee opened a private door off the last and smallest landing and showed them into a sitting room that Ivan would have entered in a contest for fancy living quarters to compete with the caliphs' digs. A door off the sitting room led to a roof terrace with a view of the town and the Virginia horse country beyond. An elegant bathroom, with a bidet for Marina at last, was located just off the stairs that led up to the bedroom. The bed was located on a balcony which looked down on the living room. The concierge gave Ivan the key, and refused to take a tip when he left.

When they were alone, Ivan's dumbfounded expression reassured Marina that this was a total surprise to him. She sat him down in a comfortable chair, and then she got down on one knee.

"Ivan Welland, here is what I like to say to you. By joyfully giving in to the temptations of sex, we have now discovered that mutual attraction is strong and permanent. We know that it is result of love, and not cause of it. You believed that love was strong enough to build life together. So you proposed marriage, and I accepted. You made me happy woman."

"And you…" Ivan began, but Marina shushed him.

"No, you cannot talk. I am busy. I am on knee, ya?"

"Yes, indeed you are."

"Tempest of events that have attacked us since we come to America has prevented the normal wedding planning. Recently you tell me you like us to be married sooner rather than later. I am not familiar with American cultural etiquette, and I do not know if is proper to propose back to man who has already proposed marriage to me, but I do it anyway. On bended knee I tell you, Ivan Welland, that I love you and I am asking you to marry me, if you still like. But this is last chance to escape."

Ivan laughed and drew her onto his lap. "I don't want to escape from you, Marina. I'll never want to escape from you. I want us to be together always."

"Then you will get wish. We have wedding tomorrow."

"What? *Tomorrow?* Where?"

"Inn at Little Washington does many weddings," Marina explained. "One employee is minister and he performs ceremony here in this room where we sit right now."

"And you arranged all of this? From Cambridge?"

"You are too busy to think about wedding, so I do it."

Ivan was impressed and grateful. No wonder he had dubbed her Spunky. She had been in the country only a month and had already arranged a wedding.

Marina bounced off his lap, grabbed his hands, and pulled him out of the chair.

"We must go to Town Hall to get marriage license, or all my plans are put in ruins."

Marina towed him down to the concierge's desk to get directions to the Town Hall. Fortunately it was only a couple of short blocks away from the Inn. The friendly clerks at the Town Hall processed the paper work rapidly, and a few minutes later they were gripping the precious license and laughing with joy.

Marina pointed out the plaque that described how George Washington, before he became the President of the United States, had done the surveying work on the land, and how the environs of Washington, Virginia were laid out according to his survey.

"Wait a minute," said Ivan, stopping dead in his tracks. "How do you know all this? Have you been here before? How did you know about Little Washington?"

"I am like George Washington myself. I cannot tell lie," said Marina, beaming at him. "Julia told me everything."

"You scheming, plotting women!" he exclaimed. "You spunky, delicious creature, you! I can see I'm not going to be bored for one minute with you in my life!"

Marina led Ivan across the street to the gift shop. It was a charming shop, with none of the touristy merchandise usually sold in such places. They were browsing around when it suddenly occurred to Ivan to ask Marina about the wedding rings. She rummaged around in her purse and withdrew a small envelope and handed it to him. Inside were two wedding rings.

"See," said Marina excitedly, "they match engagement ring you give me, and they match each other, too. I saw name of jewelry store on box you give me with engagement ring inside. So I buy wedding rings in same store."

"You clever little vixen," said Ivan. "I should put you on my team at the White House. You don't miss a trick!"

"I am already on your team. Forever."

"Well, I'm the luckiest man in the world."

Marina tried Ivan's ring on him, and it fit perfectly.

As they browsed through the jewelry and clothing section of the gift shop, Ivan asked Marina if she saw anything she would like to wear when she met the President. Marina had learned by this time in their relationship that Ivan never bluffed. She also knew that he liked to inject a little humor into serious situations whenever he could. She suspected that he was leading her into one of those ambiguous moments, when he hid the truth with humor just to play cat and mouse. She turned to face him and raised one eyebrow to indicate that she was both questioning his meaning and showing disdain for his attempt to play with her.

"When do I meet President of United States?"

"On Sunday, when we have dinner at the White House."

"Why do you kid with me?" she asked, a little piqued.

"I'm not kidding you at all."

"Who else will be there, then?"

"Just Julia, and the first lady, as far as I know."

Marina was thoughtful for a few seconds.

"What is occasion for invitation?" she asked.

"I think it has to do with a wedding celebration."

This time Marina raised her left eyebrow; the doubtful one.

"How does President know about wedding?"

"He knows everything. That's his job."

"Tell me truth!" said Marina, raising her voice a little.

"Okay, okay." He knew when he had gone far enough. "He wanted Julia and me to meet with him on Saturday night to discuss the work I've been doing, but she knew I couldn't go because of the wedding. She tried to beg off, but he insisted that she cancel all her engagements. You know how it is. Presidents are sort of used to having their own way. So she had no choice but to tell him about our wedding."

"Ivan, you are so full of, how you say in English?"

"Baloney?" Ivan suggested.

"Yes, bologna. You cannot even pronounce it."

"Maybe not. But even the President wouldn't want us to spend our wedding night with him."

"Is true," Marina said, somewhat subdued. "What shall I wear for dinner with President? I brought nothing."

"You can just wear a dressy blouse and your undulating skirt, which should be enough to bring the President to his knees and the government to a halt."

"I report you to your mother if you don't get serious."

"Oh no, not that! I'll be good, I promise!"

"Speaking of your mom, shouldn't we call her to explain why we get married now, and why she is not invited to wedding? Otherwise she might think you are ashamed of me, or that I may be pregnant and must get married quickly in hunting rifle wedding."

"You're absolutely right," Ivan agreed. "I'll explain what we're up against here, and she'll understand. Both my parents will understand. Besides, it's not uncommon for people to elope these days. Nobody can afford a big wedding anymore. My mom may sound disappointed, but underneath it all she'll be grateful not to have to help with the endless arrangements that would have been involved, especially in a wedding out of state."

They left the gift shop and returned to their suite at the Inn. On the way, Marina told Ivan about the wonderful dinner they were going to have in just an hour's time.

"Okay, here goes," said Ivan. "I'm going to call my parents now. But you'll have to wait till tomorrow to call yours, because it's the middle of the night in Moscow."

"I already call them," Marina said, with a big smile.

"*What?*"

"I call them from Cambridge this morning."

"So all that business about going down on bended knee, and giving me a chance to opt out was just… *bologna*?"

Marina shrugged good-naturedly. "Now you know. Do you want to change mind about plan to marry me?"

"I'll let you know," he said, with a superior air. Then he picked up the phone and called his parents' house. He got his mom on the line, and he explained everything to her. She asked if she could speak to Marina, as it would help her to know her new daughter-in-law. Ivan gave her the phone and left to go wash up before dinner so the women in his life could talk about him without being overheard.

When he returned, Marina told him that she had had a very nice conversation with his mother.

"I feel better now that I speak with new mom," she said. "Now I know I cannot blame your faults on her. You will have to bear responsibility for your conduct all by yourself, and not try to rub it onto your parents."

"I knew I should never have given you the phone," Ivan said. "Now my goose is cooked."

"Yes," Marina said. "And your bologna, too."

Ivan was looking forward to having the meal that Marina had told him would be the *pièce de résistance* of his entire eating life. Since neither of them had done a lot of gourmet dining during the usual course of their lives, they weren't sure that their palates were discerning enough to do justice to the meal they were anticipating. Ivan, particularly, always had guilt problems when confronted by high living. He felt he didn't deserve to be treated in a special way. He didn't know if it was the influence of his Calvinistic upbringing, or the democratic desire in his heart that all human beings should have equal opportunities. All he knew is that he felt awkward when he was treated regally.

Eating from the fatted calf at the Inn definitely made him uncomfortable. However, once he got into the spirit of the place he no longer felt that he should be executed like a condemned man after eating his last meal. Actually, as he and Marina talked to the extremely knowledgeable waiter about the items on the menu, he came to realize that the chef was concerned about providing his guests with the best quality organic and locally-grown ingredients prepared with amazing care, and served by attentive, food-savvy servers. Chef Patrick was not being creative in his cooking just to dazzle his clients with a taste experience equivalent to rococo interior designs. Sometimes his creations simply let the natural flavors of fresh food speak for themselves. In other dishes he blended spices, herbs, or accompanying food items in such a way as to build the flavors of each into a symbiotic combination that exceeded the powers of the individual ingredients, creating a palate-tingling new taste sensation. Everything that Marina and Ivan ate that night was an experience they would long remember.

Inside the suite again, Ivan collapsed into an easy chair. Marina came to him and climbed onto his lap. He was so large that it made her feel small and safe when he put his arms around her. They kissed, but Ivan made it more friendly than husbandly. She took his hand and put it on her breast. He removed it.

"What is wrong?" Marina asked him.

"I don't want us to make love tonight," he told her.

Marina sat up. "Did I say something? Are you angry?"

"Not at all. Of course I'm not angry."

"Then why…?"

He was wearing his serious expression, and faced with the obligation to explain, he became thoughtful and quiet.

"I don't know exactly how to say this," he began. "And I hope you'll bear with me as I try to tell you how I feel right now. Basically, what I'm trying to say is that I've come to believe that sex has been given to us as a very precious gift. But it's a gift in the same way that the gift of a piano is recognizably significant in and of itself. Yet if we're going to use the gift properly, we have to learn how to play it so it will make beautiful music. Does this make any sense to you, so far?"

"I think so. But go on."

"We have to find room for our piano and we have to make time to practice, too. We'll increase our repertoire and we'll get great pleasure from it, but we must never forget that it's a *gift*. So as a symbol of our gratitude, and in recognition of the giver of all good gifts, I'm going to forego using it again until after our wedding, because this gift was meant to be a wedding present."

Ivan looked at Marina to see if she agreed.

"Someday," she said, "we play great music together. We practice faithfully until we can play requiem to God, to thank him for piano."

"That's right," said Ivan, holding Marina against his heart.

They both knew that the sacrifice of not being reunited until after the wedding ceremony was a small, symbolic one in comparison to the generosity of the gift they had been given. And so it was that the young lovers wore night clothes for the first time in their lives together as they climbed into their elegant bed in the loft of the bridal suite at the Inn at Little Washington.

CHAPTER THIRTY-TWO

When Ivan opened his eyes it took him a few moments to move from the dreamy visions of sleep into the posh reality of their suite at the Inn. His one true reality slept next to him with her arm and hand resting on his shoulder. As was so often the case, Ivan could not move without waking Marina. He consoled himself with the thought that it gave him time to think before tackling the problems of the day.

His problems, however, had become those of the years ahead, and not just those of the moment. Here he was on his wedding day, lying in bed thinking about men he had never met, men half a world away who were slated to die prematurely. If these men, these *caliphs* as he chose to call them, knew of their enemy they would immediately order a fatwa calling for his death.

Ivan had long ago considered the ethics of the situation, and like Harry Truman at Hiroshima, he had decided that the action was necessary to prevent even more bloodshed. He believed that Truman's decision to drop the atomic bomb was correct because it was an act against an enemy with whom the U.S. was at war. He also believed that the caliphs' use of terrorism, assassination, kidnapping, and murder in a covert, undeclared war was equally deserving of the extreme punishment that was about to be meted out to them. The question of whether the caliphs should be killed or brought to trial had been settled in Ivan's mind. If they were brought to trial by infidels, the Muslims would refuse to recognize the decisions of any court held outside Islam and the Sharia legal system. But if the caliphs were turned over to Sharia judges, it would result in their being revered, not reviled.

Ivan knew the tangled web of historical and religious perfidy of the past that some Muslims refuse to let go of to this day. He recognized that the rulership of European kingdoms and the papacy had similarly unsavory origins, but he believed it was buried in the past now, and the modern citizens of those countries had moved on to more honorable, democratic methods of distributing power. Perhaps the removal of the insidious terror network controlled by the caliphs would give Islam a chance to reform itself. Ivan hoped this would be the case.

Marina began to stir. She stretched and smiled at him.

"We have had our personal, physical time of *glasnost*," Ivan said, "but today we take our oath to perpetuate it."

They dressed quickly and went down to the restaurant for breakfast. They enjoyed a mélange of perfect fruit, along with some whole milk yogurt, buttered toast, and hot coffee. Just then a man approached them and introduced himself as the minister who would be marrying them that day. Ivan invited him to join them for coffee. He offered them a copy of the marriage ceremony, and asked if it suited them. Ivan joked that he would like the ceremony to be given in Russian so Marina couldn't say she didn't understand the "obey" part, but she surprised them both by saying that she didn't object to the "obey" word at all.

"Why I would not like to obey man I love?" she said. "Ivan is not like master who gives orders to dog. If bear comes into house, is good that someone is in command."

The minister turned to Ivan for his comments. Ivan had attended some weddings where personal statements were included in the liturgy, but he was not so inclined. He thought more attention should be paid to keeping the traditional vows, and less to making them flexible or personal. With this settled, Ivan asked about witnesses.

"That's been taken care of," the minister told them.

Ivan assumed that the inn provided people to serve as witnesses at tiny weddings such as theirs. The time was set for three o'clock that afternoon. The matter of flowers and photographs was also settled. They were both glad that the preparations were in good hands.

They decided to go for a walk through the surrounding countryside. As they strolled along hand in hand through the rolling hills of Virginia, Marina was impressed by the rich farmland, grazing cattle, white-fenced horse paddocks, and the nostalgic feelings that walking in this environment evoked in her. She enjoyed a sense of completeness now that she and Ivan were getting married. In America, freedom shouted its presence from the heart of its rocks and soil. It was as if the temperate climate coaxed the land to perform great deeds of fertility in order to accentuate the spirit of the freedom of its inhabitants.

Life was good in America. Marina had felt great respect for the vast land in her native Russia, but the largesse of liberty in America had given her citizens proof that the Star Spangled Banner still waved in rows of corn and grain. Ivan put his arm around Marina as they walked along.

"Is sad," Marina said, "that other nations cannot make their societies to operate as efficiently and peacefully as in America. I wish the envy and hatred of nations toward United States and its wealth can be redirected instead to more positive ways to bring hope to their own citizens."

Marina was beginning to understand Ivan better now that she had seen the land of his birth. She hoped that a world full of snarling, envious fanatics would not bring down America the Beautiful. She knew that men like Ivan would do their best to defend this land that had given them so much.

"Look! Ships!" she exclaimed suddenly.

"Ships? Where?" said Ivan, looking in every direction. For a split second he wondered if there was a canal cutting through the fields, like the one he'd seen in the Netherlands once long ago.

"Over there! See? Beautiful white ships."

"Oh, *sheep!*" said Ivan, smiling.

"That's what I said."

They leaned on the fence and watched the sheep as they turned their backs and trotted nervously away.

They were glad they had two bathrooms in their suite so they could each clean up and dress for the ceremony at the same time. Marina had bought a dressy white suit in Boston that she felt would be appropriate. Ivan would wear his only suit, which eliminated the element of choice. They were glad that they weren't having a big, complicated wedding with families from two different worlds. It would be much easier to tackle the family communication issues separately, one family at a time, as the opportunity arose.

Ivan was ready about ten minutes early and was waiting for Marina to come down, when he heard a knock on the door. When he opened it he found Julia standing there, with Montcalf just behind her.

"Don't be so surprised, Ivan," said Julia, nonchalantly. "You need witnesses, don't you?"

Julia said she'd go up and see how Marina was getting on. She ran up the stairs and disappeared into the powder room.

Montcalf was the perfect picture of self-importance, with undeniable wedding witness capability. Instead of being sulky or jealous, he was cheery and bright. Something had changed Montcalf for the better. Ivan was glad he was going to be a good sport about things. He could have resented Ivan's swift rise in the State Department's hierarchy, but he didn't seem to mind. He could have been cranky, though without reason, about Ivan marrying his lady friend. Maybe Ivan had been too hard on him. Perhaps *he* had been the one who was jealous and unreasonable, after all.

Just then some waiters arrived with champagne on ice, wine flutes, a bouquet of flowers for the bride, and several gift-wrapped boxes. In short order a local photographer appeared, followed by the minister carrying a black Bible. The sitting room was suddenly abuzz with people. Ivan and Simeon were the only ones not doing anything.

"They also serve who only sit around doing nothing," said Ivan, looking apologetically at Montcalf.

"Doth God exact day-labor, light denied?"

Ivan was impressed that Montcalf could quote from Milton. A moment later Julia came down from the loft and announced that the bride was arriving. She turned and handed the floral bouquet to Marina as she entered the room. Ivan was conscious of a deep feeling of gratitude toward Julia. Knowing how busy she was with matters of state, he appreciated her humility in coming here to act as a lady-in-waiting for her newfound friend.

In an instant they had formed ranks in front of the minister. Ivan looked at Marina with love and pride. He believed he understood how Adam must have felt when God presented him with Eve. Soon he was answering the "do you take this woman" question, hearing himself say "I do" as if in a dream. Then it was over, with hugs, congratulations and kisses all around. They signed the marriage certificate, then the minister and the photographer retired from the room.

Ivan poured champagne into the four flutes, distributed them around, and toasted his bride with another quote from Milton. He thought it would be a suitable one for Marina, but he also wanted to see if Montcalf's knowledge of Milton extended to "Paradise Lost." Looking at Marina he recited one of the passages he loved most:

Our state cannot be severed; we are one,
One flesh; to lose thee were to lose myself.

Turning to Julia and Montcalf, Ivan said, "And to you I have a quote from Yeats."

Think where man's glory most begins and ends,
And say my glory was I had such friends.

The foursome sat down, sipped champagne, and chatted amiably. There was some discussion about having dinner together, but Julia told them it was impossible for her to stay much longer. Simeon complimented Ivan for choosing Adam's passionate speech to Eve in "Paradise Lost" for his toast to his most deserving bride. Ivan thought Montcalf was better educated than he had originally thought, and he was glad to have a worthy quote challenger. Ivan was devoted to the acquisition of knowledge, but even more devoted to the intelligent use of it.

After Julia and Simeon left, Marina opened their gifts. Simeon's was a useful and imaginative one—"his and her" book supporters that would hold books open while they were reading and eating at the same time. He couldn't have guessed that Ivan read so quickly that he could never use such a present because it would impede his rate of page turning. His gift was nevertheless much appreciated and totally appropriate for two young professors. Julia gave them an exquisitely carved wooden box that she had found on one of her trips to Malaysia. Inside was a personally written card from Chef Patrick, saying that Julia had paid the expenses. The generosity of Julia's gift brought tears to their eyes.

They were glad they had nearly starved themselves all day, because the wedding feast was a true work of culinary art. Ivan asked if he could take the menu home as a souvenir so they would always remember what they had eaten at their private wedding banquet. He told Marina that they might be served some delicious meals at various moments in their lifetime, but he was sure none would be better or more memorable than the one on their wedding day at the Inn at Little Washington.

After dessert, the photos taken during the ceremony were delivered to their table. They had a great deal of fun looking at them, since they realized they had never, up to that moment, taken or seen a snapshot of themselves together.

They were also glad that they would now be able to send photos to their parents. After enjoying an amaretto liqueur, they made their way up the stairs to their suite.

Both Marina and Ivan were silently and internally grappling with the nature of the expected wedding night performance. They wanted their first time together as a married couple to be special, but it was a bit difficult when they already knew each other so well in that way. The argument for abstinence until marriage was coming through loud and clear, but they had had a choice and they had made their choice, and truthfully they were not sorry. Perhaps it was too late to wish for abstinence, but they were certainly in time for fidelity. They tried to understand why, if they had no regrets, they were having this strange time of discomfort about marital sex. The sudden shyness, coming after all the obstacles had been removed, was peculiar.

"Maybe the wedding raised our expectations," Ivan said, "so what was always a very natural, earthy desire before, now has to be elevated to an even higher level. And neither of us knows how to make it any better."

Marina thought he was probably right about that.

"I often thank God because he sent you to me," she told him. "What was wonderful before is now permanently wonderful. When I give myself to you now, there will be new sense of security and commitment. This is good, ya?"

"This is very good," Ivan smiled.

Once they understood that nothing out of the ordinary was expected of them, they proceeded without pressure. The frank discussion had liberated them, and Ivan moved to the couch next to Marina and put his arm around her. They kissed, and he slid his hand inside her suit jacket so he could feel her breast comfortably nestled in her bra. They were both relieved to feel the return of the natural stirrings of desire that they had always had for each other. It was not particularly comfortable on the sofa, but Ivan thought he should take time to enjoy the moment.

"Your breasts are exactly the right size and shape to complement the rest of your body," he told her. "I consider myself the most fortunate man on earth, because now I'm married to you."

He told her how, when he had undressed her for the first time in the hotel in Chechnya, he had been overcome with the secret beauty she revealed. He always knew she had a trim little figure, but when he exposed it fully to his view, he told her, he nearly was overwhelmed by its perfection. He continued to explain that he had to marry her if only so that he could look at her once in a while, and also so no one else could ever see her naked.

Marina's kisses were now becoming more passionate. His words built her confidence and aroused her. His hand had fallen to her knee and was slowly moving along her leg. She shivered from his breath in her ear, his words on her mind, and the excitement of his hand's progress.

They slipped under the sheets and into each other's arms, holding each other, touching and exploring, feeling the call to fulfill nature's demand. They were both overjoyed to be together again, and relieved that the earlier awkwardness had disappeared.

Now they were well and truly husband and wife.

Washington D.C.

CHAPTER THIRTY-THREE

A fter enjoying an early breakfast in their suite, Marina and Ivan spread out the wedding photos on the table and wrote letters to their new in-laws to accompany the photos. They also wrote thank-you letters to Julia and Simeon for their presents, and for standing up for them at the wedding.

It was soon time to pack, dress for dinner, and drive back to the capital. Since the President and the First Lady knew that Ivan and Marina had just been married, Marina felt comfortable wearing her white suit again. Ivan decided he should have a different tie, so he ducked across to the gift shop to buy one. While he was there he saw a bright blue blouse that he thought would look nice on Marina, so he bought that, too. On his way past the concierge's desk he delivered the four letters they had written. He mentioned they were having dinner at the White House, and that he would like a corsage for Marina to wear. The concierge told him it would be delivered within the hour.

When Ivan returned to the suite, Marina was getting dressed.

"Please don't wear Julia's choice of undergarments," he said, teasingly. "I don't want to think about how you look under your suit while I'm talking to the President."

Julia's limo was scheduled to pick up the honeymooners at the inn at five o'clock. They were supposed to return to

Washington, pick up Julia, and then the three of them would proceed to the White House.

The corsage arrived with the bellboy who came up for their baggage. Ivan pinned it to the lapel of Marina's suit. She had put the new blouse on under her jacket. It looked great on her, as it picked up the blue in her eyes. Just then the phone rang, and they were informed that the limo had arrived.

As they went down the steps they couldn't help remarking what a special time they had had at the inn. In a way, it had been almost too much for them. Their minds normally worked on a much simpler level when it came to domestic issues such as eating and dressing, but they knew it would be very hard to find a more appropriate place to create a unique memory of this most important day in their lives.

With the luggage loaded aboard and the honeymooners ensconced in the back seat, the limo took off for Washington D.C. Marina seemed calm, considering their destination, while Ivan was struggling not to appear nervous. He had already been to the White House several times on business, but this was a small private dinner with the President of the United States. Marina, who had never been inside the Kremlin in her entire life, not to mention having dinner with Putin, was living the American dream after being in the country for only one month. None of her colleagues in the History Department at Moscow University would believe what had happened to her in America. For that matter few, if any, in the Russian Department at Harvard would have had the opportunity to dine with the President.

They held hands, but they didn't speak much during the drive to Julia's house. When they got there the driver told them to go right in, as Julia was waiting for them. The Secretary of State was a professional at making people feel comfortable—generally they were heads of state and their wives, or high-level diplomats. Julia wanted to be sure that

Ivan and Marina were relaxed and in the right frame of mind to have dinner with the man she so often called *POTUS.*

She was glad to see that they were not visibly jumpy or dressed inappropriately. Julia didn't think it was likely that they would make any gross errors in protocol or manners. She went over a few points with them, most of which emphasized the need to be themselves. She felt they were an outstanding couple just as they were, and she didn't want them to act in any way that wasn't normal for them. She was sure Ivan had been invited to dinner because the President was interested in him and wanted to get to know him and his wife.

"Just be honest, candid, concise, and calm. Act normally, and have a good time. The President is tired of being pandered to and lionized all the time. A little humor, if it's not forced, will also be appreciated by the man with the most serious job in the world. That's about it. Let's go. We can't be late."

They piled into the back of the limo and were driven to the White House, where they were checked in against the guest list. The Secretary of State was well known to the security officers, so they were allowed to proceed to the residence door of the White House, where they arrived precisely on time. They were admitted by a houseman and led into a sitting room. History leapt out at them from every wall; there probably wasn't a stick of furniture that didn't have a story attached to it, or a carpet that didn't hold the footprints of the great figures of recent history.

Suddenly all heads turned toward the door. The President and his wife came in, arm in arm.

The President greeted Julia with a hug. Then he turned to Marina and Ivan and welcomed them to the house of the people. He introduced them by name to his wife, and everyone shook hands. The President's wife offered to take them on a quick tour of the White House. The President suggested that the women go, as he wanted to speak with Ivan privately for a few minutes.

"May I get you a drink, Dr. Welland?" he asked Ivan.

"Sure, I'd like a beer, thank you Mr. President."

"Have a seat here."

"With pleasure."

The President pointed to a chair, and sat down in the one next to it. A waiter entered the room and took their drink orders.

"Let's talk about this plan of yours, Ivan. How did you ever come up with it, anyway?"

Ivan realized that the President was just trying to get the conversation started, so he gave him a shortened version of the various experiences in Chechnya that led up to his discovery of the code. He hoped the President hadn't heard it all before.

"It was just common sense," Ivan explained. "It seemed obvious to me that all these jihadist terrorist attacks were carefully coordinated. They had to be encouraged, or at least tolerated, by the average, ordinary Muslim on the street. Furthermore, as politically incorrect as it may seem, the fundamentalist wing of Islam is the inspiration and the supporter of the terrorists."

"There's nothing politically incorrect about that statement," said the President. "It's true, that's all."

"Well, Islam in its present state is something of an anachronism. Islam is basically flawed because it tries to portray time as unchanging and unchangeable, instead of seeing it as a continuum—as a constant flow. For Americans, time marches on. But for Islam, it stands still. We say that imperfect human beings were given a spark of the divine that enables us to freely progress towards a return to our eternal Eden-like home with God. We're free to choose the route by which we travel, but we're expected to recognize that we can't make the trip alone, or without guidance. Islam deals in what it believes to be absolutes— the absolute immutability of the Koran, the total surrender of free will, and the legalistic belief that people earn their way to heaven through their obedience to the laws of the Koran."

Just then the waiter arrived with their drinks. He served the President first, and then he poured Ivan's beer and left the room.

"How do these absolutist ideas affect us, in your view?" the President asked.

"We could deal with the Islamist fundamentalists if their doctrine included unconditional tolerance for the views of other peoples, but of course, that's clearly a contradiction in terms. We cannot submit to a doctrine that removes our own freedom of choice. We're in the position of a child confronting a bully. We can avoid him and hope he grows out of his belligerent attitude, or we can stand up to him. Our policy, under your leadership, has been fair and measured, but unfortunately our bully has not grown up yet. What is needed is an Islamic Reformation, similar to the Protestant Reformation, and there are some indications that such a movement is out there in nascent form. Our Reformation took hundreds of years and led mankind through the turbulence of religious strife. It's sad that Islam must go through its own Reformation now, for they've learned little or nothing from the Christian experience. But whatever the cost, Islam must be reformed. We can only hope that they accomplish this mission quickly, but we must be prepared to wait them out no matter how long it takes."

"And your plan, how exactly does that fit in?" asked the President.

"If it works, it buys us some time, perhaps as much as a generation. We've seen the rate of progress that liberty and democracy can make once it gets started. The burst bubble of communism in Russia and in Eastern Europe is a prime example of how quickly an ideology can go bankrupt. Once begun, who knows how fast Islam can reform? It has taken very little time for the terrorists to adapt to new weapons and communications technologies. But if we manage to inflict a massive blow to fundamentalist Islam, perhaps we might be able to persuade the Muslim nations to accept the counsel of democratic nations and reject the council of caliphs. As you've already pointed out, freedom and democracy, once experienced, are never forgotten. And everything is a work in progress, isn't it?"

"What do you see as the biggest risk in your plan?"

"Our failure to sell it to the leaders of the Muslim nations. As I mentioned, the average citizens in these countries are at least nominally in favor of anything that harms infidels. They will support atrocities done by Muslim believers to non-believers, out of religious fervor and pride. The average Muslim has nothing to lose that is more valuable to him than his acceptance among his peers. If they support unpopular Western ideas, or are half-hearted about their loyalty to Islam, they face ostracism and possibly death at the hands of their neighbors. As a result, they can't be interested in our kindness lest they be regarded as weak, or traitors to Islam. So the leaders are our only hope. These individuals have tasted the good life. They've seen that coexistence is only possible through negotiated, long-term business arrangements and political compromises. But the Arab leaders don't want to give up their wealth and power. They know from experience that their only rivals come from the ranks of the Muslim clergy."

"So what do you see us doing about that?"

"Our plan provides them a way to separate Mosque from State. They need this plan even more than we do. It's the catalyst that can secure their power, and keep them out of the greedy, power-hungry hands of the fanatical fundamentalist clerics. Unfortunately they appear to be weak and self-interested, and they will not take any action that may be seen as being in opposition to Islam's world program of religious cleansing that has been percolating since the time of the

Prophet. Right now their numbers are over a billion, and growing faster than any other religion.

"Why do you think their numbers are growing so fast?"

"Fear is a great motivator. People are rightly afraid of being beheaded if they resist conversion to Islam. In the same way, there's only one thing that could motivate the leaders of the Islamic world to help us clean out the jihadist terrorists among them, and that is the fear of their own annihilation. We can't clean up the extremists in their countries. They have to do it themselves. We can help, but the main thrust has to come from the rulers of these countries that are permitting terrorism to thrive in the midst of their populations."

"So you suggest that we motivate these temporal rulers by pointing out to them the danger that they will be annihilated by fundamentalist clerics in their own lands."

"That's right. As I see it, the only way to help them to help themselves is to paint a realistic picture of the certain destruction that awaits them if the terrorists acquire atomic weaponry. They know that we won't allow that, however. If these madmen use a nuclear device, they know that we'll rain down destruction on them on an unprecedented scale, starting with their palaces. They must be made to believe that the acquisition has occurred, and that Al Qaeda is planning the atomic attack now. That's why I say the most important part of the plan is to sell this very small distortion of the truth to the governments of the Muslim nations. If we don't succeed in this, we'll only be giving the beehive another poke."

"I wonder why, with all the employees we have in the various branches of government services, I was never presented with any plan of the scope and foresight of this one."

"I couldn't answer that question, sir, but if the plan fails for any reason I'm pretty sure I'll be spending the rest of my career teaching Russian in a high school located in the last remaining Russian ethnic community in Alaska."

The President chuckled. "Consider yourself lucky. If this were a Muslim country we could have your head."

"If this were a Muslim country, Mr. President, you'd have had it already."

"I don't have very many big thinkers on my staff, Dr. Welland, and none that can also handle the details as well as you do. I hope to have many more policy discussions with you in the very near future." He took Ivan by the elbow and led him out of the room.

They caught up to the women in the China Room, where the First Lady was holding forth about Dolly Madison's dinner service. The room was lined with shelves of plates displayed on edge behind glass doors. To anyone interested in antiques, porcelain, or historical dinnerware, the room was a museum of fascinating articles.

"I think it's time for us to report to the mess hall," said the President.

"Sometimes the position of Commander-in-Chief goes to his head and the military jargon takes over his speech," the First Lady smiled. "There are times when I need to have a translator of military acronyms on hand, just so I can understand what my husband is talking about."

They all laughed as they followed her out of the China Room and down the hall.

The dining room was elegant in an understated way—with dark furniture, white linens, and red and white wine in crystal glasses. Heavy, ornate silverware of a pattern Ivan had never seen before flanked the elegant white china trimmed in royal blue.

FLOTUS asked the waiter to begin serving dinner.

Ivan looked at Marina to see if he could detect any signs of her being awed by the surroundings. He was glad to see how relaxed she was among the world's most powerful people. The three women seemed more like girlfriends than acquaintances.

Marina had an innate ability to make people comfortable in her presence. Her talent with people seemed to Ivan to come from her ability to project strength of character that extended from deep inside her, covering her every thought and deed. She was the kind of person who would always tell the truth, but in the kindest possible way. It was an unusual ability that enabled both women and men to like her at once. Women liked her because she did not use overt sexuality in her dress or demeanor to attract men, especially *their* men, and she had no trace of intellectual snobbery in her conversation, despite her academic credentials. Men liked her because she was attractive, vital, and intelligent, but without posing any challenge to their male hegemony. She didn't strike men as a competitor, or as a loyalist in the cause of women's liberation. She was in all circumstances natural, and men found that refreshing. Her marriage would now remove, at least to some extent, the underlying sexual tension that so often exists between males and an unattached female.

Now seated at a large table, but one meant to accommodate exactly five diners, Ivan thought this room had to be the family dining room used by the President and his wife and three children. It certainly was not the room used for official dinners of state. Ivan liked the idea that this was a family dining room. When he lived at home as a boy, most of the issues of the day were discussed over a table just this size. Although he imagined the items up for consideration were of greater significance at this table, it was a comfortable setting for discourse.

Marina was seated next to the President of the United States, looking so radiant that Ivan felt proud to have her as his wife. The two older women were looking wise and handsome. Life had treated them well, and Ivan thought they knew how fortunate they'd been. They seemed truly grateful when the President gave a short grace before the first course was served.

The First Lady announced that the soup was mock turtle. The head waiter dipped the steaming clear soup into the bowls of the diners, and then came around again with some hard rolls.

The President asked if anyone knew what mock turtle soup was. Ivan volunteered that it was simulated green turtle soup.

"What's the *mock* part, then?" the President asked.

"As with all simulated things," said Ivan, "we don't always want to know what the substitutions are. But since you asked, Mr. President, the original recipes from the eighteenth century called for boiled calves heads, with wine and spices added."

"Now how would you know that?" The President asked.

"Well, the Mock Turtle is a character in *Alice in Wonderland*. Lewis Carroll has him explaining the origin of the word *tortoise* by saying, *we call him Tortoise because he taught us*," said Ivan. "When my sister and I first read *Alice* I looked up the meaning of mock turtle soup, and that was how the tortoise taught us. Ogden Nash also has something to say about turtles, but he doesn't mock them. He compliments the turtle when he says,

> *The turtle lives 'twixt plated decks*
> *which practically conceal its sex.*
> *I think it clever of the turtle*
> *in such a fix to be so fertile.*"

There was a ripple of polite laughter around the table.

The next course was a fresh Boston Bib lettuce salad with pears and pecans, topped with raspberry vinaigrette dressing. The fortunate five began to pick delicately at the greens.

Ivan, who feared that he had taken too many liberties with his little disquisition on turtles and tortoises, leaned over to the President and said softly, "I hope, sir, that you don't see me as one who is *still in his salad days and green in judgment.*"

"I'm not so sure that judgment has anything to do with age," the President replied. "I'm sixty years old, and I still feel wet behind the ears. Most people think that being elected to the highest office in the land automatically means you're endowed with wisdom and good judgment. To be elected, though, you only need to be popular with your party and with the voters. But to serve effectively you must be intelligent, wise, decisive, and have good character. Unfortunately, popularity and effectiveness are not often found in the same individual. I suppose there should be a Presidential Aptitude Test for candidates for the office. Until then, the country will have to make do with me. People think the office makes the man, but in my experience it isn't always true. When we devise such a test, I hope you'll see fit to take it, Ivan. May I call you Ivan?"

"Of course, Mr. President," Ivan said quickly. "And I'd be honored to take your aptitude test."

The head waiter collected the salad plates. A minute later he returned, bearing a silver tray with a filleted side of salmon on it. The fish appeared to be broiled to perfection, showing just a trace of char from the broiler. Covering the fish was a layer of finely sliced smoked Nova Scotia salmon. The waiter placed the knife on the fish and moved it until each guest nodded to indicate the size of the slice desired, then he scooped the slice and placed it deftly on the plate. Less senior waiters followed him with plates of rice pilaf and vegetables.

"The Head Chef has just retired," said the First Lady, "and now, for the first time in history, a woman has been promoted to the position. The new chef is every bit as determined to keep my husband alive as is the Chief of Security. She insists that all the latest dietary innovations and discoveries be part of his living in residence here at the

White House. This perfectly delicious salmon is probably here mainly because of the Omega-3 oils it contains, and only secondarily because it tastes good."

The President turned to Marina. "Do you intend to be *Mrs. Welland*, or will you keep your maiden name?" he inquired.

"I like to be *Mrs. Welland* in every way, but not name. I have published under maiden name, and I am known in Russia by *Kortikuova*. I like to keep academic continuity, so I use original name on publications and while teaching. But I am flattered if you call me Marina, Mr. President."

"Very well, Marina. Have you any idea how the sturgeon are faring in these days of polluted waters and over-fishing?"

"I think they make good progress with farming sturgeon, just like Americans with salmon. Value of this fish is so great that we must not allow it to become extinct. Therefore, even if motives are poor, prognosis for sturgeon repopulation is good."

"How many wild sturgeon will be eaten as compared to the number of sturgeon that are cultivated or genetically modified?" Julia wanted to know.

"I think more farmed sturgeon than wild fish," Marina said.

The Baked Alaska was now ready to be served. With the main course cleared away, the head waiter ferried the flaming, meringue-covered ice-cream mound to the sideboard, where he cut it into five portions and served it to the diners.

"As a student of history, Marina," said the President, "what do you regard as the most important question of our time?"

"Well, if we get through this fanatical terrorist period without nuclear catastrophe, and if we deal with global warming before we reach tipping point, I think most important question is over-population in China and India. There are more babies born in these two countries every year than entire number of people living in United States, Canada, Australia, and New Zealand, all put together with each other."

"I'm terrible at mental arithmetic," said the First Lady, "but that sounds like a huge number to me."

"In India, population will be bigger than China's by 2020."

"Have you any suggestions about what can be done to solve this problem?" the President asked.

"I am only historian," Marina said, apologetically. "We write about everything in hindsight, after politicians do their actions. We do not make policy for China or India, so I don't know what can be done, but I think is good to ask Ivan to work on problem."

"That is just what I had in mind to do," said Julia, "after he finishes his present assignment."

"Would anyone like a liqueur?" the President asked.

Julia opted for a cognac, and the President joined her. The others preferred not to have any more alcohol, feeling that the champagne before, and the red wine with dinner were sufficient. The President suggested that they move to the sitting room to have their coffee in comfort. The change in venue brought a change in the topic of conversation.

"What do you think is the root cause of the problems in the Middle East?" the President asked, turning to Ivan.

"Well, on the surface it would seem to be the proximity of Palestine and Israel," Ivan answered. "They've been sibling rivals ever since the time of Isaac and his half-brother Ishmael. And now, with the formation of Israel as the Jewish homeland, the situation, as we all know, has gotten much worse."

"And what do you think lies below the surface, then?"

"Below the surface is good old human nature. Jealousy and greed, for starters. The Israelis have turned their patch of desert into a garden, and the Palestinians want it for them-selves. But why stop there? Why not just take over the whole world, in the name of Muhammad? Religion has a powerful sway over people, and the fanatical imams are using its power to further their own goals and ambitions. That's where human nature rears its ugly head again, I'm afraid."

"And the solution?" said the President.

"It's too complicated for an immediate solution, sir. But we'd be well-advised not to underestimate the determination of the enemy. The last thing we should do is try to appease him. We already learned that lesson with Hitler. It would also be advisable for us to learn to pull together as a country. It would be tragic if we were brought down by something as simple as the old *divide-and-conquer* gambit. And we can't weaken or lose our resolve, either. We just have to soldier on, and show some leadership and spirit. That's a lesson we learned from Rome."

"I appreciate your observations," said the President, rising to his feet. "But they get me up at five o'clock on the good mornings, earlier on the bad ones. Ivan and Marina, it has been a pleasure to entertain you in your house. The First Lady and I have greatly enjoyed meeting you, and we would like you to accept this little wedding gift with our congratulations and best wishes for a long and happy life together."

"Thank you very much. You're very kind."

Everyone stood up and began to file out of the room. Ivan was the last to go out the door, and the President softly said to him, "Make your plan work, son. You're a pisser, you know."

"Yes sir, Mr. President."

CHAPTER THIRTY-FOUR

Julia left Ivan and Marina at the Marriott Hotel, then continued the drive to her house in Georgetown. The newlyweds went up to their hotel suite, chatting the whole time about their evening at the White House. Marina told Ivan that she thought the President liked him especially because he behaved naturally around him.

"Is difficult to be President," she commented. "Ordinary man must walk into White House one day and suddenly he is treated with awe and self-conscious respect by everyone. On one hand he is used to being alpha bull, and on other hand he needs clever people to talk with him. But you were very natural with him. Anyhow, Julia will tell me honestly how we did in our first exposure to big time."

"The President struck me as being a very humble and straightforward sort of man," Ivan agreed. "He seemed genuinely interested in my opinions about the important issues, even though he's quite a bit older and much more experienced than I am."

"He was very diplomatic too," Marina added. "He even wanted *me* to give him opinions, too. I do not think Putin is like this. He does not listen to political suggestions coming from mere woman."

"I'm sure Putin would have *put in* his two cents' worth, however, no matter who had been at the dinner table."

The morning saw the couple engaged in a typically choreographed ballet, each hurriedly getting ready for the day that lay ahead. Bathing, shaving, dressing, eating, all became the steps of the dance of duty.

Leaving the suite together, they went to the lobby and asked the doorman to call the cabs that would take them away from each other—Marina to the airport, and Ivan to his appointment with Tim Morrison, the Director of the CIA. Their kiss goodbye was bittersweet, but they also looked forward to getting on with the work that would occupy them until they were together again. They would think about each other often, but they would not let this interfere with the performance of their duties.

Ivan's cab dropped him off in front of the CIA building. He passed through security and was routed to the Director's office. Tim Morrison was a tall, gray-haired, distinguished man of about sixty, with a noteworthy career in government service. There was a touch of severity in his manner, along with a guarded facial expression which was often hidden by his hand. He spoke quickly and confidently, with a certain bold conviction. His ability to keep a secret was legendary in Washington. Ivan wondered if he could also share information, or was he only able to hoard it?

Ivan also noticed a certain element of collegiality in the Director's attitude towards him. He was willing to give the Director the respect his position deserved, but he was glad that Tim was reciprocating. Ivan, after all, was a neophyte in Washington and his position was newly created, all of which could have made the Director of the prestigious CIA adopt a superior manner. Ivan had heard occasional rumors, when he was a student, that the "Agency" was recruiting bright young people from around the campus. He guessed that Tim had encountered his share of smart-Alec kids over the years, and he didn't want to be seen as one of them.

As far as Tim Morrison was concerned, he was pleased that something concrete and positive was going to be done at last about the creeping problem of jihadist terrorism, but he decided to suspend judgment of Ivan's abilities until he had worked closely with him for a while. He had formed a good impression of him during the first general meeting, and he knew Ivan had the support of the President and Secretary of State. Tim had to admit that Ivan's work on the code and the outing of the caliphs was brilliant, but in a long distance race the victory goes to the man with the best kick at the finish. He would withhold final judgment of Ivan until *Operation Playwright* played out.

Tim began their discussion by recounting the findings of his operatives in Saudi Arabia. Mecca was a city entirely given over to Islam. The clerics controlled everything, right down to the smallest detail. The secular government in Riyadh kept its hands off Mecca and Medina. The royal family had developed a *laissez-faire* policy toward the Muslim clergy out of fear that the Islamist fundamentalists could turn on them and cause a great deal of trouble, even threatening the continued existence of the monarchy.

"They cover up their apprehensions," said Tim, "with liberal doses of religious tokenism and policies of non-interference with Islamic precepts and rituals. They recognize that with the support of Islam, they are in absolute control. Without the support of Islam's religious leaders they are at great risk of being overthrown. I found your plan exciting because it clearly recognizes the exploitative possibilities of the mixed motives of Mosque and State in the Saudi nation."

Morrison correctly gathered that Ivan's discovery of the caliphs was intuitive. It struck him as precisely the kind of thinking that the great physicists exercised when they discovered missing atomic particles. He couldn't praise Ivan enough for his ability to synthesize all the political and religious elements into one of the few conspiracy theories that actually held water.

"We have, in fact," Tim told Ivan, "what we consider to be hard proof of the existence of your caliphs."

Ivan was relieved to get this news, because using the code to uncover terrorist cells without removing the root of the problem would merely inconvenience the perpetrators. What was needed was a total purge from top to bottom.

"Just deciphering the code doesn't solve the problem," Ivan said. "As soon as they realized their communication system was compromised, they would quickly evolve a new system. Killing the caliphs, but leaving everything else in place, would only send the jihadists in search of other direct descendants of Muhammad to substitute for those who went before. Of course, since every Arab can have up to four wives, most Arabs alive today would be able to trace their ancestry to Muhammad or his son-in-law, Ali."

"That's not good," Morrison frowned. "The caliphs have an inexhaustible supply of replacements, then."

"Pretty much," said Ivan. "The enemy is not like an animal which dies when you cut its head off. It's more like a virus, and it can only be killed by depriving it of food. The violent fundamentalist interpretation of the Koran is the virus's only nourishment. So the best way to solve this dilemma is to expose it to the light. The secret agenda of the caliphs has to be unveiled and their doctrine made public. It must be done in a credible fashion, and the only hope of doing this in a way that would be acceptable to Arabs is to have the plot be revealed by Arabs."

Morrison recounted to Ivan that right after they began the surveillance of the Ka'bah, they noticed that food trays were flowing into it on a nearly constant basis. Electronic testing devices picked up signals that indicated that sophisticated electronic equipment was in steady use, and coming from under the Ka'bah.

"They could house a nuclear bomb factory under there, and it's expanding every year," Tim said. "Over fifteen acres of marble enclose the 8th century Mosque, and there are seven new minarets, each reaching 300 feet in height. It's truly one of the historic wonders of the world. There could be as many as two million people packed in there during Ramadan.

"Two million Muslims, I take it," Ivan said. "Nobody else is allowed near the place, I believe."

"That's right. The area is restricted to Muslims only. It's the safest place in the world for some self-proclaimed caliphs to hang out, and no one would have noticed the construction of their headquarters with the ongoing Mosque building expansions. But killing the caliphs isn't going to be easy. There could be a great many people down there with them. Still, we've done our best to come up with a few strategic options, and we'd like to get your feedback."

"Not a problem," said Ivan. "I'd love to hear about your strategic options."

"The riskiest approach would be to put some disguised Special Forces guys in there with silenced weaponry. There are police, Saudi army personnel, and secret operatives who have guns under their abas. All the suicide seekers are on their side, and there would be mortal danger to our men. The risk that the attack would be laid on our doorstep would be enormous, and whether we succeed or fail, Islam will be enraged with us."

"True," Ivan agreed. "What else?"

"A second line of attack might be to poison everyone down there. This has the advantage of being silent, and would require only one or two operatives to accomplish the mission. There are poison gasses that would do the job if they were blown in through the ventilation system. Another cute suggestion was that we put the poison in their hookahs so that when they smoke their hashish they die. That would be fitting since these people are assassins, and the word derives from the drugged behavior of wild Ishmaeli warriors under the influence of hashish, who were therefore called *hashashins,* or hashish eaters."

"You're kidding! I love it. How ironic!" Ivan exclaimed, delighted with this lesson in word derivation.

"This might be more plausible than it sounds," Tim went on. "It presumes, probably correctly, that the only ones in the living quarters of the caliphs who would be smoking hashish would be the caliphs, not the servants, harem girls, or workers. The old faithful method of poisoning the food or drink, or course, is also a distinct possibility, one that would require few manpower resources. Then you have arson, bombing, flooding, and earthquakes, too. These are other killers that could be considered."

The Director saw that Ivan's expression was incredulous at this last suggestion. Tim felt that a small, clean atomic weapon exploded in just the right place could simulate an earthquake, or provoke a real one. If the entire complex were destroyed, and the government in Riyadh supported the earthquake explanation, the Muslims might consider it the act of an angry Allah.

The last possibility is the wimpy one, though," said Morrison. "We could just out the caliphs, and publish in the world media how we discovered their centralized control of terror all over the world. This scenario assumes that the pressure of world opinion will force Islam to back off the jihadist strategy. Unfortunately the Arab press, never as concerned with truth as with Arabic pride, would probably make heroes out of the caliphs."

Morrison went on to say that he'd lost good operatives over the years in the Middle East, and that the deaths had not always been quick.

"These enemies are no respecters of human life, and they'll kill believers or infidels alike if any of them get in the way."

Ivan thanked him for the summary of the possibilities, adding that he had a couple of questions, mostly about the statistical probabilities for the success of some of the methods.

"Fire away."

"Well, I'd like to know more about the nuclear alternative. I can see how a nuclear device exploding in Mecca could be attributed to the terrorist's acquisition of such weapons. At least it wouldn't look as though we were involved. This would secure the cooperation of the Muslim world leaders, and also back up the American intelligence warning them of just such a happening. But could a novice make a mistake and set off a nuclear explosion?"

"That's always a possibility," said Morrison.

"Is it possible, then, to make an explosion look like an earthquake?"

"It's possible, but I'm not sure that we can provoke a tectonic plate movement and cause an earthquake on demand," Tim admitted. "But we can get the geologists in for a conference."

"Let's do that. How about the day after tomorrow?"

"No problem. I'll arrange it."

"Let's include some military bomb experts in the meeting too," Ivan suggested.

"Good idea."

Ivan's mind was racing ahead, and he had to rein it in. He suddenly remembered a quote from Oliver Wendell Holmes, *Insanity is often the logic of an accurate mind overtaxed.* He could not afford to go nuts just at this moment, so he forced himself to slow down. Holmes also wrote that *knowledge and timber shouldn't be much used till they are seasoned.* Ivan resolved to use Tim's vast experience to balance his youthful innocence in matters of intrigue. He decided to confess this to Tim, and to ask for his assistance. Morrison appreciated Ivan's honesty.

"There's lots of room for feeders around this carcass," he said, "but *we* are the hunters who must bring the animal down."

They shook hands, as though they had signed a pact.

"I've always felt that back-up strategies are necessary," said Ivan, "so maybe we should keep that in mind."

They agreed they'd have only one chance to complete this mission, so it had to be done swiftly and decisively. It was true they could only kill a caliph once, but they wanted to be certain he was dead. Ivan wondered if the two events, the explosion and the poison gas, could be timed to take place simultaneously. Tim promised to look into the possibility, as well as arrange to have Special Forces personnel on stand-by, ostensibly to do rescue work but charged with cleaning up any caliphs or henchmen that survived the blast. The surveillance was to continue, for the more recent the information, the better it was.

They parted, feeling convinced that they both had a good understanding of their challenges and a firm connection with each other.

Ivan's next meeting was with a group of nine information officers from various government agencies. Even though he had the home court advantage of holding the meeting at the State Department, he found it more daunting to talk with these "spin doctors" than with the President himself. He equated the upcoming gathering to a faculty meeting in which everybody was too verbal for his own good. This conclave, however, had responsibilities that went far beyond the parochial.

Ivan would be the ranking person in the room, but he wanted to make sure he retained control from the moment he called the meeting to order. He could not afford to let this conference turn into a chat fest. The entire success of the operation hung on the ability of these people to convince the rulers of a large part of the world that the terrorists had obtained nuclear weapons capability. This lie was more a question of clairvoyance than untruth. In time, perhaps a surprisingly short time, these suicidal maniacs could come into possession of such weapons. If there was ever a good lie, this was it.

Ivan had given a lot of thought to this assembly of people, so when he entered the room he was thoroughly prepared to be in charge.

"Ladies and Gentlemen," he began. "This morning, in this place, one might easily say we are the "chosen people." Our superiors have selected us to create the most important disinformation campaign since World War II, when we convinced the Nazis that we would *not* invade the European continent at Normandy. I remind you that our primary job is to use false information leaks to notify the leaders of all Islamic countries that the terrorists have acquired nuclear weapons. Our secondary objective will be to assure these leaders that America will not retaliate with atomic weapons if they cooperate with us in purging their nations of all terrorist cells. Those are our objectives. Now I want to hear the plans you have made to accomplish our goals."

Ivan thought about the various ideas that had been presented to him. Sometimes he played the devil's advocate, and at other times he simply offered encouragement. He harangued them when their ideas were not sufficiently subtle, warning them that they were dealing with the masters of deceit. They had to be able to lead them to the inescapable conclusion that they themselves had cleverly uncovered the information.

"If we can arrange it so that they ask us if we have any supporting or contradictory evidence, that would be nice," Ivan said. "But if they feel that *they* are bringing this matter to *our* attention, we will have achieved mission success. Our ambassadors will report this kind of inquiry to the Secretary, so we will hear of it in due course. And finally, I want to remind you once again that no leaks or lies are to be traced back to the U.S."

In four hours, the group had amassed seventy usable ways that operatives, informants, or the press could release leaks and rumors in fifteen Islamic countries. Ivan was satisfied that the seeds of worry would be successfully planted, and that the interests of these unelected leaders in perpetuating their own power would be primed and pointed toward real cooperation with the United States in its efforts to clean up terrorism.

After returning to his office, Ivan met with Brooklyn for a few minutes to go over the latest messages and other matters that needed attention, and then he retreated to his private inner office. His plan was to think deeply about his next meeting with Tim Morrison. They would decide on the exact plan to be used to exterminate the caliphs and de-claw the Islamist fundamentalist jihad. He had already made peace with himself over the moral issue, and had decided that taking lives in this case was justified. The saving of other lives would vastly outnumber the taking of these few lives, and he was entirely convinced that no amount of diplomacy or other non-violent tactics would halt the march of these would-be Muslim dynasty builders.

With the issue of moral justification resolved, he was free to concentrate on the practical details. For some days now he had been thinking of using the nuclear option, but he needed some additional technical information in order to cement his plan.

He called Brooklyn on the intercom and instructed her to connect him to General Donohue. Bill Donohue was Army Chief of Staff, and he would know the answers to his questions, or else he would know who could answer them. He also told Brooklyn that he wanted to speak to the Surgeon General as soon as he finished talking to Donohue.

Ivan knew that if he wanted to get anything done in Washington, he would have to start at the top. The plan had presidential approval and urgent status, so he was prepared to appeal to him if any government employees delayed giving him their full cooperation. Fortunately, calling the President never became necessary.

"I'm looking for some specific data about our tactical nuclear weapons," Ivan said, when the Army Chief of Staff came on the line. "Could you kindly send me your most knowledgeable expert in these kinds of weapons?"

"Absolutely," Donahue said. "Colonel James Bloodworth is the man you want."

"Is he there at the Pentagon?" Ivan asked.

"Yes, he is."

"Could you stick him in a car at once, and send him over to the State Department? Have him ask for me."

"I'll do that, Welland," said the General.

"Thank you, General," Ivan replied, and hung up the receiver.

A few minutes later Brooklyn informed Ivan that the Surgeon General was on the line.

"Hello, sir," Ivan said. "I'm working on a project that has top secret clearance requirements, and full presidential urgent status. I need the advice of the country's best expert on the effects of radiation poisoning. I also need similar advice about poisons, particularly airborne ones. It could be the same man, or a different one, but I need this information at once. Can you send them over to the State Department right away?"

"I suppose I could. You say this has presidential urgent approval?" the Surgeon General asked.

"Yes, sir."

"Very well. I'll send Captain Bartholomew and Captain Mandretti. Whom shall they ask for when they get there?"

"Have them ask for Dr. Welland. I'll be waiting for them. Thank you very much for your cooperation. I'm sorry about the short notice."

"That's all right, Welland. Emergencies are what we do around here," said the Surgeon General.

Ivan told Brooklyn to notify the proper person in security that he'd be expecting Colonel Bloodworth and Captains Bartholomew and Mandretti.

"Have them shown into an empty conference room, and notify me as soon as they arrive. Oh, and see if you can find out who's the most knowledgeable geologist at the Atomic Energy Commission. I don't actually know if they have geologists working at the AEC, but if they don't have one on staff, get them to recommend someone who knows about underground nuclear explosions. Then please get him on the phone for me."

Ivan leaned back in his chair, thinking about all the many ramifications of the action he was contemplating.

CHAPTER THIRTY-FIVE

Brooklyn buzzed Ivan to say that she had a Dr. Joshua Mapleton on the phone from the U.S. Geodetic Service.

"Hello, Dr. Mapleton. I'm Ivan Welland, from the State Department."

"Good morning, sir," said the geologist.

"I have a few questions regarding the geology of Saudi Arabia. Are you familiar with the area?"

"Indeed I am, sir. I used to work for ARAMCO, so I'm quite knowledgeable about the area in the context of oil prospecting."

"Tell me, then, Is Saudi Arabia in any way prone to earthquake activity?"

"It is. It's susceptible to both earthquakes and volcanic action."

"When was the last earthquake, do you know?"

"Off the top of my head I can tell you that there was a strong earthquake that measured 6.3 on the Richter scale. It took place in the Gulf of Aqaba, in 1995. I remember that one very well, because I was there then," said Mapleton.

"Was ARAMCO one of the companies that conducted experiments with underground explosions to identify geological structures?"

"Yes, sir."

"Weren't you afraid you'd kick off a quake?"

"We didn't think anything we could do would initiate the large plate tectonic shifts that would be needed to start a quake. In this area the Arabian plate is subducting to the North and moving under the Eurasian plate. The forces needed to provoke this activity are beyond our capacity to calculate."

"Would that be true for nuclear explosions, too?" Ivan asked. "Have you any idea what the AEC discovered when they were conducting underground nuclear weapon tests? Could a nuclear device positioned over a fault line start a quake?"

"Well, there is a lot of seismic data available, but I don't think anyone ever intentionally tried to set off a quake. Even a nuclear bomb doesn't develop enough wallop to create a plate shift. If the plate were about to shift of its own accord, though, I suppose a bomb placed in a critical position might be just enough to get it moving. That is, if the fault line location could be exactly determined, and if we had some way of determining its readiness to shift. Frequent and increasing tremors sometimes telegraph an oncoming earthquake, but there's no blueprint to tell us exactly when, or even if, a quake will occur.

"Can you tell me the location of the most likely fault line in the Arabian Plate?"

"If I had to guess," Mapleton said, "I'd put it in the Red Sea at about the same latitude as Jeddah, in the Suakin Deep."

Ivan thought for a while about the information Mapleton had given him. He didn't think the terrorists were advanced enough to overcome the many problems posed by a difficult location such as the Suakin Deep. On the other hand, he didn't want to sell the Arabs short. He knew, having been in graduate school so recently, that American and Canadian technical and scientific programs were crammed with students from the Middle East and Asia. He believed the higher tuitions charged to foreign students by American universities was a very large source of revenue for them. He didn't want to be paranoid, but he sometimes wondered if Americans weren't educating those who would one day become their executioners. He had always tried to put himself in the place of his adversaries in order to anticipate possible hostile actions. He was running out of questions for the geologist, and his incipient plan was not looking good.

"What would you do in a geology scenario if you were a terrorist newly in possession of a nuclear device?"

Mapleton thought for a few moments. "If I were in that position, I'd try volcanoes instead of earthquakes. If the idea were to multiply the power of a nuclear weapon by yoking it to one of nature's great forces, I'd try putting it in the cork of an active volcano. We know exactly where the volcanoes are, at least the ones on land, and all we'd have to do is provide a hole that the tremendous pressure of the molten lava could burst out of, and you'd get a disaster of immense proportions."

"Has there ever been a volcanic eruption on the Arabian Peninsula?"

"Yes, indeed," Mapleton said. "In 1256 A.D. there was an eruption that lasted for fifty-two days. Can you imagine that? The lava came to within eight kilometers of Medina. The geological formations of the various harrats near Medina, Mecca, and Jeddah are potential targets, but with the political situation today I'd be thinking Mt. St. Helen's or Mauna Loa. All of this is just wild speculation though, isn't it?"

"Indeed. Thank you very much, Dr. Mapleton. You were a big help."

"Glad to have been of service," Mapleton said, as he hung up.

Ivan thought that the information he had received was interesting, but was probably not very useful for his present purposes. Brooklyn came in to announce that the colonel and the two captains had arrived and were waiting for him in the conference room. Ivan rose to his feet, thinking to himself that being the President of the United States was too strong an aphrodisiac for anyone to handle. At the mere mention of the chief executive's name, three senior officers dropped everything they were doing and came to his office on the double.

The three officers rose when Ivan entered the room. After greeting them and introducing himself, he invited them to sit down at the conference table. After the three men had made themselves comfortable and were looking expectantly at Ivan, he told them that they had been summoned at the request of the President to supply information from their various specialties. Since he had been thinking recently about nuclear explosions, he began his questioning with Colonel Bloodworth.

"Colonel, I was wondering if you could kindly give me a rundown on our tactical nuclear weapons arsenal. I'm eager to know things like the effective ranges of each weapon, the dimensions, weight, detonation methods, and the expected radioactive fallout. Are there any clean bombs that leave no radioactive signatures? We've heard of late of the risk of a terrorist showing up with a nuclear weapon in a suitcase. Is this a real threat? Assuming one has such a weapon, how much know-how does it take to use it? I'm guessing that the Army has provided such a briefing to the House Armed Services Committee. Maybe if we could start with that, we could save time and possible redundancy. I'll call my assistant to work with you on developing the information I need. She can get you access to a computer terminal if you need it."

He called Brooklyn on his cell phone and asked her to come to the conference room. When she got there he quickly told her what he wanted from the colonel. He asked her to take Colonel Bloodworth to her office and to call him when they had finished preparing the report. Ivan was glad to have the two captains from the Surgeon General's office separated from the colonel for security reasons. There was no need for the officers to waste time on weapons issues. These two were medical doctors whose research had led them to become experts in the fields of radiation poisoning and airborne poisonous gasses.

"Which of you is the radiation specialist?" Ivan asked, after Brooklyn had ushered the colonel out of the room.

"I am," said Captain Mandretti, a dark, heavily bearded, medium-sized man.

"Stop me if I'm wrong, but as I understand it, victims in a nuclear explosion die in the following three ways; they are blown to pieces by the blast, they are burnt by the heat, or they die later from complications caused by radioactive exposure."

"That's essentially correct," said the medical officer.

"I need to know everything I can about the lethal effects of atomic or nuclear blasts, and the level of radiation burns they deliver. I'm particularly interested in understanding the ranges of distances and dosages that assure death, not life. Is there a graph, for example, that delineates the 100% effective kill rates of nuclear weapons using heat generation, distance from the blast, size of the explosion, and other pertinent data? I need something that will enable us to model the expected effects of a nuclear device exploded by a terrorist. I remember seeing charts showing the effects of a one, five, or ten mega-ton bomb. Can we reduce the scale to the size of a suitcase bomb?"

"I think that could be done," Mandretti said, "but it'll be more a question of mathematics, rather than evidence-based information."

"Okay, but keep it on the conservative side. If you claim that people can't survive a blast from closer than fifty feet, make sure the explosion leaves no one alive at forty feet," Ivan said. "The numbers you give me could be taken as gospel, and used in life and death situations, so be accurate. I need to have this data in three hours or less. May I count on you to get back to me by then?"

"Yes, sir, I think I can get it together in three hours," said Mandretti. "But I know I can accomplish my mission faster from my own office, if I may. I'll come back as soon as I assemble the information, if that's all right with you."

"That's fine," said Ivan, dismissing him with a nod of the head.

Now alone with Captain Bartholomew, Ivan focused on poison gasses.

"I need information about which gas is most deadly under various conditions. Do you have a list or a chart indicating the properties, handling methods, availability, lethality, antidote if any, and dispersal rates of the range of deadly poison gasses with which you are familiar? Is there such a summary that I could have in the next three hours?"

Bartholomew's glasses partially hid his sad, pale blue eyes. His wispy blond hair was receding, and he used his approaching baldness as an excuse not to bother getting haircuts. He was nervously tapping the table, but only with the pads of his fingers, so he made no noise.

"Sounds to me like you want the poison gas crib sheet."

"Good! Can you give it to me in three hours or less?"

"I could make one up for you, yes. We keep a folder for each gas. It says what it consists of, where it's made, and who makes it. It also keeps a chronological record of every known usage and the results of each exposure. I believe I can summarize them, organize them on a spread sheet, and get them to you within your time constraint."

"Good man," Ivan said. "I'll see you later, then."

Ivan left the conference room and headed back to his office, where he found Brooklyn and the colonel working away at the computer. He did not disturb them, but went directly to his private office and sat down behind the big desk. It didn't matter how large the desk—once Ivan sat behind it, the desk immediately looked smaller. Ivan wished it were the same with his present project. The more he thought about removing the cancer from Islam, the less confident he was that his surgery would prove successful. But this was no time for doubts, so he forced himself to let logic conquer his apprehension. If he were a surgeon facing a large tumor, he thought, he would expose the field, excise the mass, seal up the wound, and aid the healing process. It was simple—the caliphs were an invisible, cancerous malignancy that had to be removed if Islam was to be healthy again. Once the lethal carcinoma was excised, the healing could begin with some hope of recovery.

That was the situation as seen from the patient's side. In this case the surgeon had to be anonymous and the procedure kept secret, but that was not so unusual in emergency traumas. If the patient (Islam) did not die during the surgery, or afterwards in intensive care, Ivan hoped that the State Department could play the role of physiatrist and assist with the patient's rehabilitation. He made a mental note to speak to Julia about what would be done to heal Islam after *Operation Playwright* moved it from B.C. (beyond caliphs) to A.D. (altruistic dialectics).

Ivan also had to find the time to digest the technical information that would soon be supplied by Colonel Blood-worth, and Captains Mandretti and Bartholomew. He was prepared to work all night if necessary to piece together a detailed plan to present to Director Morrison of the CIA in their morning meeting.

The colonel was the first of the three men to be ready with his material. Ivan wondered if he was a colonel because he was faster, or if he was faster because he had Brooklyn to help him, or maybe it was because he was right there outside Ivan's office. The captains still had some time before their deadline, but Ivan decided to get a head start by working on the weapons survey while he waited for the other data.

Most of the nuclear weapons listed were too powerful for Ivan's purposes and could be rejected at once. Others were too dirty, and would leave a radioactive fall-out that might last for centuries. Stealth was important, too. The device had to be small enough to smuggle in, powerful enough to do the job, and it must leave no fingerprints allowing it to be traced to the U.S. He had to be sure the device he chose was already manufactured and in stock. He had several questions for Colonel Bloodworth that were not answered on the list he had provided. He wanted to know if the explosion could be shaped, or in effect if it could be aimed or pointed in a pre-chosen direction. He also needed to know how these devices were detonated. Could they be detonated remotely? He needed to know the distances of the kill perimeter, too. Did Bloodworth have the ability to calculate how close to the target the device must be located in order to be successful? These questions and many others occupied Ivan and the colonel for an hour.

When he felt he had the information he needed, he dismissed the officer. After the colonel had gone, Brooklyn stepped into Ivan's office and put a brown paper bag on the corner of his desk. She knew he hadn't eaten anything all day, so she had taken the initiative to send out for some food. Ivan opened the bag and found a large sandwich, an apple, and a Coke inside. He thanked her for being so considerate.

He realized how hungry he was when he took the first bite. It was a London broil sandwich made on a very nice, foot long French baguette, with a side of cold slaw. As Ivan munched on his sandwich he read the information the colonel had provided. It became evident to him that one particular weapon had all the necessary attributes. Although it was not small enough to fit in a suitcase, it would fit inside a crate containing an air conditioning system. Ivan assigned Brooklyn the task of finding out which U.S. air conditioning manufacturers had sold equipment to Saudi buyers in Mecca. He asked her to obtain a phony export invoice for a model that came in a case large enough to contain the weapon. He was quite sure that the caliphs had air conditioning in their underground lair, so he decided to deliver the bomb device concealed in a crate containing this type of equipment.

Ivan continued munching and musing. Mapleton had put a halt to his idea of using the bomb to trigger an earthquake.

Who was most likely to get the blame for an explosion in Mecca? Ivan suspected there were three likely candidates—the U.S., al Qaeda terrorists, or Shiites. The Americans would be the least likely to launch an attack of this sort on the holiest city in Islam because it would set off a worldwide jihad of revenge and dry up all oil shipments from OPEC.

Ivan hoped the improbability of U.S. involvement in such a scandalously planned operation would shift the blame to al Qaeda, or to Shiites looking for some sort of retribution from Iraq. Rumors had been circulating for a number of years that the terrorists had gotten hold of nuclear materials, along with specific know-how from Pakistani scientists. Iran was suspected of building an arsenal of nuclear weapons in spite of the world's efforts to make them give up the production of weapons-grade uranium.

Ivan's disinformation scheme, if it worked, would make the explosion seem like an accident that was caused by the ignorance of inexperienced terrorists handling fissionable substances and weapons of mass destruction. That would be ideal, as it would play into the fears of the royal households in the Arab world. Under no circumstances, however, could the United States be linked to the event in Mecca. But plans and intentions do not always work out the way the planners intend. Was it worth the risk?

We have had over sixty years of nuclear détente, Ivan thought. Perhaps the world needs a fresh reminder, and what better place for it to be delivered? If we could send this message and remove the head of the terrorist snake simultaneously, would it not be well worth it? If the lesson could be learned, rather than taught, as it would be if the terrorists were believed to be the ones who accidentally blew up their own secret headquarters, wouldn't that be a tremendous education for those badly in need of it? Ivan continued thinking in this vein until Brooklyn announced that the captains had returned.

Ivan decided that he would see them separately. He asked Brooklyn to send Captain Mandretti in to see him first, but to entertain Captain Bartholomew until it was his turn.

"What are you a doctor of?" Ivan asked him.

"My doctorate is in statistics, sir, but my specialty has slowly evolved into calculating and predicting morbidity and casualty rates for diseases, catastrophes, and epidemiological events, and this includes exposure to radioactivity."

"A sort of numbers man for the Surgeon General," Ivan remarked.

"Right, you might say that."

"Good, that's just the kind of information we need. I see you've got some papers in your hand. Are those for me?"

"Yes, sir, they are. If you wouldn't mind reading them to see if they answer your questions, I can wait outside until you are finished, and I'll come back in if you need additional data."

Ivan told the captain to stay put. He took the report and read the ten pages in about the same time it would have taken most people to merely turn the pages. The captain, believing that Ivan had only scanned the report, felt miffed that he had given his work such short shrift.

"You seem displeased about something," Ivan observed.

"No, sir," the captain replied, looking nervously at him.

"I'm impressed with your report," Ivan said. "Especially the paragraph on nuclear radiation morbidity."

He quoted the paragraph in its entirety to assure the captain that he had read the report carefully. Then he began asking him a series of questions that were thoughtful, and reflected knowledge of the subject material that could only have come from a person who had totally comprehended the report.

The captain, now mollified, deduced from Ivan's questions that he was trying to envision the results of a nuclear weapon being discharged in a subway or a tunnel. Ivan did not disabuse him of this idea because everything having to do with *Operation Playwright* was on a need-to-know basis, and this captain had no need to know anything.

"Tell me, Captain, would bodies be identifiable under ground at about 500 meters or so from ground zero?"

Ivan's question convinced Captain Mandretti that Homeland Security was worried about another London, only nuclear this time. Ivan, on the other hand, was hoping that the CIA operative in Mecca could get DNA samples from the corpses, but the captain told him that there was no hope of this.

"Any bodies that were so close to the explosion would be vaporized," said Mandretti, "and any that lay further away would be burnt beyond recognition."

At the end of their discussion the captain left the office with a totally different opinion of Ivan's abilities than he had entertained on his arrival. He looked heavenward as he passed the other captain on his way out, but Captain Bartholomew didn't know how to interpret the gesture.

When Captain Bartholomew was seated in Ivan's office, he reached into his attaché case and pulled out a sheaf of papers. He passed them over to Ivan, and asked if they were suitable for his purposes. Essentially the report was a list of all the known poisonous gasses in order of most, to least lethal. Included in the material was the required number of parts per million of each gas needed to provide fatal doses when released into graduated volumes of ordinary air. Ivan paid particular attention to the release mechanisms, and was pleased to note that most gasses came in canisters whose valves could be opened remotely. Thus whoever planted the device would be able to make his escape.

"Which one of the nerve gasses did Saddam Hussein use on the Kurds in Iraq?" Ivan wanted to know.

After listening carefully to the captain's answer, Ivan followed up with questions relating to how long it would take to disperse a lethal amount of any of the top five deadly gasses if released in a subway or underground tunnel. Which countries would be likely to have a supply of weapons grade poison gas canisters in spite of there being a United Nations ban on all such poison? Ivan was full of questions for the captain, but finally he decided that he had garnered enough information, and he dismissed the officer with a formal statement of thanks.

Now he felt properly prepared for his meeting in the morning with Tim Morrison, the Director of the CIA.

CHAPTER THIRTY-SIX

After a hearty meal, a quick call to Marina, and a good night's sleep, Ivan was on top of his game when he arrived at Tim Morrison's office at the CIA headquarters. He was taken immediately to a conference room adjacent to the Director's office, and seated at a table with four senior agency men and one woman. Tim introduced Ivan to the other conferees, and then proceeded to chair what he called the Operations Committee. The others were the department heads of the sections of the agency that would be in charge of actually pulling off the attack on the caliphs in their underground palace in Mecca. Ivan had thought that he and Tim would be discussing exactly how and when the attack would be launched, but evidently the Director had skipped over the discussion stage and had moved to the action portion of the plan. Ivan suspected that Morrison's decision was calculated to convince his staff that he was in charge of this mission, and that Ivan was only a liaison man from the State Department.

Ivan hadn't expected to be in charge of the plan, but since he had uncovered the code and the existence of the caliphs, and had received presidential approval for his *Operation Playwright* and *The Council of Caliphs* on which it was based, he felt it wasn't completely unreasonable of him to conclude that he was being bypassed at this meeting. It certainly justified his original fears that the military and the intelligence communities would focus on doing the job at hand, but might not care enough about the ensuing diplomatic consequences.

Ivan was not really concerned about the politics of the situation. He didn't need to be given the credit personally, but as the representative of the State Department he had to make certain that the potential for diplomatic blunders was minimized. He realized that he most likely would have to assert himself at some point in the meeting, and he hoped reason would outweigh clout when push came to shove.

He decided to wait for the proper moment to intervene. At this juncture, for all he knew, they might be going to proceed exactly as he envisioned. Unfortunately his instincts were warning him of an upcoming power struggle.

Tim Morrison had his game face on, and his lieutenants recognized it. He dimmed the lights and rolled a screen down from the wall at one end of the room. A drawing of what was purported to be the layout of the underground headquarters of the caliphs was flashed up on the screen.

Ivan looked at it dumbfounded. Unless one of the caliphs was on the CIA payroll, he thought, he could not imagine how the sketch could possibly be accurate. The computer-aided simulation superimposed the mosque, the Ka'bah, and the various other buildings over the sketch, so that the actual and the imagined were joined as though there could be no other way.

Ivan couldn't help wondering how they could be so sure of the layout since it was, after all, underground. He could see that these people were used to working with high altitude photos, so he decided to wait a bit before injecting his two cents' worth. It was possible that the CIA had thought of everything. He would wait and see.

Director Morrison had chosen the poison gas option, just as Saddam's Iraqi henchman, Chemical Ali, had done when attempting to "ethnically cleanse" the Kurds.

"Supplies of nerve gas might have been cached in Iraq," Morrison observed, "and it would then appear that the Sunni Iraqis were responsible for the attack. The motive for the attack would be to prevent descendants of Caliph Ali from ascending the throne of a new theocracy. The murder of Ali, and the subsequent slaughter of his son Hussein, the beloved grandson of the Prophet Muhammad, is still the sore spot that divides Islam."

Ivan waited to hear the rest of the plan, but there wasn't any more. He couldn't believe that Morrison had missed the most important parts of his careful presentation of *Operation Playwright*. This was not to be just another case of multiple murders, followed by a series of ambushes of terrorist cells. This was a plan that would give Islam time to reform, and by exposing and removing its unholy jihadists, it would have a reason to reform itself into a peace-loving faith. Ivan's plan was not supposed to be only a means to rid the world of a few violent, hate-filled men and their supporters. The needed results were change, and a stable environment in which to encourage religious reform.

Ivan was astonished by the obvious lack of subtlety in the Intelligence Agency's plan to assassinate the caliphs. How stupid did Morrison think the Arabs were? Ivan's views were diametrically opposed to those just voiced by the Director. Although he despised the jihadists' motives and methods, he had great respect for them as an enemy.

"These were the people who used our own airplanes as weapons against us on 9/11," Ivan thought to himself. "These leaders directed cells all over the world that have succeeded in creating the most terror for the least cost. Men like these have much more experience with murder than we do. They even know how to twist their religion to inspire large numbers of people to martyr themselves, and that is no small feat.

Would any of the men in this room be equally sure of their cause? What had happened to Morrison between his first meeting with Ivan and today's meeting? He had seemed to comprehend the plan perfectly, but now he was lame. It was almost as if someone had gotten to him. What motive could the influence-peddler have had? Was the Director reacting to orders from above? Was there bribery of some sort involved? Ivan had been sure that he and Morrison had had a good understanding at their first private meeting, so this change in attitude had to have some cause. Until he could determine why Morrison had decided not to consult with him, Ivan had to change the direction of this meeting. But how?

At that moment Ivan could only think of one tactic, and that was to delay the operation. He believed he had absorbed enough technical information about poison gasses to raise a sufficient number of practical questions, which until they were answered, would force the holdup of the CIA version of *Operation Playwright*.

During a brief pause in the meeting Ivan stood up, using his height as a weapon of status, and began asking questions about the selection of Chemical Ali's choice of nerve gas as the intended poison. He explained the chemical composition of the gas, adding that later chemical developments indicated the use of one or two other possible choices, both preferable to Ali's more primitive gas.

Ivan was not a chemist, but he had taken enough courses to be comfortable with the science. He made his case as though he were in perfect synchronization with the CIA plan, but just thought a little more research should be done on the choice of gas.

"After all," he concluded, "we all want to be sure that the targeted caliphs are eliminated, or our mission will fail."

When it became obvious to everyone that Ivan was not going to give up on his quest for more information, and no one had the technical knowledge to silence him, the meeting was scheduled to reconvene the following day, at which time experts would help them decide on the best nerve agent.

One day was not a very long time to find out who was pulling the strings at the CIA. Ivan's mind was racing. As soon as he left the "Company" headquarters, he found his driver and headed back to the State Department. He whipped out the secure cell phone that Brooklyn had given him at their first encounter.

"Brooklyn, please call Captain Bartholomew and tell him I want him to attend a meeting with me at the CIA in the morning. Get Bartholomew Top Secret Clearance, and do whatever it takes to make sure he gets it before the meeting. Also, would you please call the Secretary's office and see if my scheduled meeting with Julia can be extended beyond the ten minutes I requested. I'm on my way to the office now, but you can start on these items right away. And please get me any background information you can find on Mitch Richmond, the Deputy Director of the CIA.

After he hung up he sat at his desk thinking long and hard about the possible culprits who might have influenced Morrison. The list of people who could be opposed to *Operation Playwright* was lengthy, altogether too lengthy, and it had to be reduced. The only thing Ivan knew for certain, although he had no proof, was that Richmond had looked daggers at Morrison when Ivan had begun with his technical questions. As Ivan interpreted it, Richmond was pissed at Morrison for not knowing that an Under Secretary of State knew enough chemistry to delay the operation. Why did Richmond care so much? And how did he dare to show such displeasure to his superior? Whatever was going on, Ivan was quite certain that Richmond was bound to be involved somehow. His instincts were working overtime, and the only similar feelings that Ivan could remember were those concerning Imam Mansur. He resolved to find out if he was entitled to carry concealed weapons.

When Ivan got back to his office he found Brooklyn on the phone, heavily engaged in a conversation. He slowly lowered himself into his chair and continued thinking. He was going to need allies, but whom could he trust? For all he knew he had been chosen to be the fall guy. Some powerful interests might want the operation to fail and the blame to be

laid at Ivan's door. He was, after all, the new guy on the
block who had risen too rapidly in Washington's hierarchy.

He mulled over the list of those he could trust, and found
it to be painfully short. Marina for sure, Julia and Brooklyn
almost certainly, the President most probably, but the rest of
them were not above suspicion until they proved themselves.
Who might be powerful enough to influence the policies at
the CIA? He called Brooklyn into his office.

She handed him a two-page bio of Mitch Richmond. Ivan
quickly read it, noting that the Deputy Director had a degree
in petroleum engineering, and had worked for eight years
with ARAMCO in Saudi Arabia where he had moved swiftly
up the ladder to a management position. Then his career,
which had been flourishing with the international oil giant,
took a sudden turn, after which he went to work for the CIA.
Richmond had been with the Agency for thirteen years, the
last two as Deputy Director. He had worked his way up
through the section devoted to Middle Eastern affairs, and
was considered to be an expert in Arab relations, oil politics,
and other matters concerning Islam. The résumé was brief
and factual, but contained nothing about the man himself.

Then a small piece of yellow paper caught Ivan's eye.
Attached to the résumé was a short FYI note from Brooklyn
to the effect that Richmond had gotten Morrison's daughter,
a student in international relations at Georgetown, an intern-
ship with ARAMCO in Saudi Arabia, and she was there at
the present moment. Ivan felt that this might explain why
Morrison was kowtowing to Richmond.

"Brooklyn," he said, turning to his assistant. "Do you
think you could get me a psychological profile on Mitch
Richmond, and also some peer reviews and job evaluation
reports?"

"I'll pull a few strings and see if I can manage to pry the
information out of the Human Resources files. But I can't
promise anything. The CIA doesn't like giving out this type
of information about its employees."

"Can you obtain a pistol for me?" he asked her.

She didn't show any surprise at this request. Ivan liked it that she was never taken aback by anything he asked of her, but he did wonder what she might be thinking.

"On rare occasions," she told him, "State Department officials are issued weapons for self-protection. Is this a situation like that?"

"It is," he replied.

"Then I'll see to it," she promised.

"I need it before I leave here tonight," Ivan said. "And I'd prefer it if you had one, too. Can you use a gun?"

This time Brooklyn raised an eyebrow and said, "My grandfather's experiences in life made us all paranoid, so we were trained to shoot. He saw to that."

"Good, then you can show me how to shoot, too," Ivan declared. "Now, may I ask you if you got me an extended appointment with the Secretary?"

"Yes, that's been arranged," she replied.

"Brooklyn, I'd like to ask you, completely off the record, if you think it's possible that the CIA has been penetrated by private or foreign entities."

She looked at Ivan meaningfully and said, "I do, sir, and other government agencies as well."

"What do you base your suspicions on?" asked Ivan.

"Contradictions, mostly."

"Can you explain the things you see as contradictions?"

"Well, our government's policies and its actions are so often opposed to one another that I simply can't make myself believe that it's accidental. We say one thing, but do another. Our motives sound pure, but too often we compromise them to achieve immediate objectives. We proclaim freedom, democracy, and the rule of constitutional law, but the rats are chewing around the edges of our country. The world sees the dichotomy between the purity of our ideals and the greedy compromises we create in order to justify and continue our policies. But unfortunately I've seen so many contradictions, over such a long a period of time that I'm convinced our ideals are being intentionally subverted. Our system has been weakened and our leaders hamstrung by political correctness and a simple lack of spine. Anyway, that's the way I see it. Off the record, of course."

"I'm pleased to know that at least one other American sees things the way I do. I picture it all as a greatly expanded international pastime much like baseball, only without a commissioner. We have the American League that includes Canada, and then there's the CAFTA league, the European League, the Arab League, the Asian and African Leagues, and they're all playing ball together. Each league is trying its best to be popular with its own fans and make profits. Every twenty-five years or so we have a lethal World Series, and the American League was lucky enough to come out of the first two Series relatively unscathed, but we may not always be so fortunate. It's a strange sport, where having the home field is a disadvantage. I could continue the sports analogy forever, and it would apply very well. But you're not exactly a Brooklyn dodger, so I'm sure you get the idea."

Brooklyn was bent on returning her boss to the matters at hand, so he could draw the necessary conclusions.

"What do you intend to do about this conspiracy of the status quo?" she asked him.

"I haven't worked it out yet. My first objective was to make sure you'd be on my side. Can I count on your total support?"

In spite of her worldly-wise attitude and her down-to-earth views based on her personal experience, Brooklyn was prepared to sustain her idealistic, activist boss.

"I have one request before I give you my unconditional support," she replied. "I need your assurance that I can have ongoing input into any actions that you might undertake."

"I agree your advice will always be sought and heard," Ivan said with a smile, "but not invariably taken. You can include in this agreement a clause allowing you to withdraw your support with thirty days' notice."

"I just want to clarify that a situation requiring me to carry a gun also calls for me to have a clear idea of exactly what it is I might be defending myself from."

"Okay, we understand each other. So carry on with your work, and see if you can protect me from interruptions until it's time to keep my appointment with the Secretary."

"I'll protect you from the din and clangor of regular office work, but since I'm not yet armed, you're on your own if Hezbollah shows up."

Ivan sat back in his chair, put his feet up on the desk, closed his eyes, and began to think. Who was there in the government who wasn't totally cynical, self-interested, and power-hungry? Not many, he supposed, but the exceptions might be those who already had mastery over their domain. Were there any moral reasons to choose between a power-seizing dictator and a conniving, ambitious, elected power-seeker? A president of the United States must know that his administration will be held up to the light of history. He can enter the pantheon of presidents with Washington, Jefferson, Lincoln, and Roosevelt, or he can be given only a mention in the pages of history. Do men in the office really consider how they will be regarded in the future? Or do they just go about their business and face death with as little pretension to a deserved legacy as the rest of us?

Ivan was willing to bet that a man who had reached the pinnacle of national eminence would wish to be remembered in heroic terms, and not as just another historical also-ran. The number one issue that required a solution was the question of Islamist terrorism. Any American president who could solve that one would rise to the top. The operation against the caliphs offered the present office holder an excellent chance to defeat terror as a serious weapon and bring peace to a weary world, as well as to at least another generation of its peoples. The more he thought about it the more essential it became that the President be involved in his latest version of *Operation Playwright,* one that would simultaneously remove the caliphs and expose the traitors who were busy selling America's principles for a mess of petroleum profits.

The time for his meeting with Julia was fast approaching. He hoped his opinion of her was justified, because he needed her support to get to the President. If she was skeptical of his plan, or worse, if she was involved in the secret scheme to keep oil prices high by supporting limited terrorist activities, then his plan was destined to abject failure, and so was his career. He would have to devise a test to determine what her stance really was. It would have to be subtle enough so that Julia wouldn't recognize it as probing her ethical center. He decided to ask her for her opinion of Mitch Richmond, the Deputy Director, who was playing Iago to Tim Morrison's Othello. If it turned out that she was protective of Richmond, he would have reason to doubt her non-involvement. He had nothing to lose. He was sure Richmond already hated him.

If Julia turned out to be above suspicion, he'd be very happy to share his new plan with her, and if she agreed, he'd take it to the President. On a personal level he knew that Marina was fond of Julia, and he would not like to be the instrument that severed that relationship. And, of course, Julia was his boss, so he owed her the respect and fidelity due her from a subordinate. He silently prayed that Julia would prove to be that unusual public servant who truly served the public, instead of using the position she'd been given to enhance her own image while feasting at the public trough.

"I'm on my way to the Secretary's office," Ivan said to Brooklyn as he passed her desk. "Say a prayer for me."

"I wish you well," she replied, as he left the office. He waved at her without turning around.

"How are you today, Dr. Welland?" said Julia's cheerful assistant.

"I'm fine, thank you." Ivan replied. "I'm here to see the Secretary, but I'm sure you know that."

"The Secretary is on schedule today, so you may go in."

"Good afternoon, Ivan," Julia said, from behind her large desk. "Have a seat and tell me what's on your mind."

Ivan sat down and got straight to the point. "What do you know about Mitch Richmond, the Deputy Director of the CIA?"

"You mean Mr. Murder?"

"Mr. Murder?"

"I'm told that he's in charge of the dirty tricks department of that illustrious agency," said Julia, cynically.

So far so good, Ivan thought. Julia's opinion of Mitch Richmond was definitely derogatory, but did she think him a traitor? Ivan decided to risk going a little farther.

"Richmond seems to have sidetracked the Director into blunting the operation against the caliphs. Their plan of attack downplays its importance and perverts its intentions. Did they discuss it with you before going ahead?"

Julia's face expressed more displeasure than she normally showed. It was obvious to Ivan that she had had no part in Richmond's plan. He was pleased to have at least some of his faith in democratic governance restored. Now he could tell Julia about his suspicions, and his plan to counter the treachery at the CIA.

"Please go on, Ivan. I want to hear more about this."

"I suspect there are elements that would like to control America's Middle East policies for their own devious reasons. I believe they've penetrated the CIA, and I think they're trying to confuse our leaders by releasing false intelligence designed to influence the U.S. government to take actions that suit their insidious purposes. We've seen how easy it was for these people to manufacture misleading evidence concerning Iraq's possession of weapons of mass destruction in order to support the war against the Saddam regime. Now I believe they want *Operation Playwright* to fail. If they achieve this, they'll be able to demonstrate publicly to the Arab world that America is a false friend, only interested in their oil, and supportive of lethal plots against their leaders. In other words, to extend and solidify the suspicions they already hold."

"To what end?" Julia asked.

"They want to make sure that power and money stays in the hands of those who already have it. If the current state of world insecurity can be continued, or better yet, heightened, then the unparalleled profits from petroleum will flow unimpeded into the bottomless coffers of those with the coffers."

"Wait a minute, Ivan. Slow down," Julia said, holding up her hand. "Explain to me how you've come to these startling conclusions."

"It's simple free market economics. If the supply is restricted, shortages will occur and the prices will skyrocket. Unprecedented revenues have enriched the international oil companies, the OPEC nations, and also those individuals connected to those entities. So it's clearly to their advantage to have things continue just as they are so they can become wealthier still. I believe these countries and individuals have conspired together to purchase the cooperation of those in positions of power, who might otherwise have offered opposition to things as they are."

Ivan hesitated a moment to see if Julia was following him.

"We saw evidence," he continued, "of the corruption that can exist in the oil world when an investigation of the Oil for Food Program in Iraq turned up the billions of dollars that Saddam Hussein fraudulently bled off the U.N. program designed to feed the poor citizens of his nation. This is not the only occurrence of joint corporate and governmental conspiracy. There have been many others through the years, but no scandal, no matter how clever, can be as effective as manipulating the market so that oil prices rise to unheard-of levels. That's the situation today, and we need to know whether the U. S. is in on the scheme, or wants to clean up the mess."

Julia sat back in her chair as though slapped in the face. "Are you saying that this government has been knowingly turning a blind eye to the largest corruption scandal in the history of the world?" she asked.

"In the case of most people, not knowingly, but in the case of some, absolutely," Ivan replied. "It feels to me as if I have been working here for many years, but I've actually only been in my present job for a week. And yet here I am reporting crimes involving high-level people in government and industry. If I can uncover graft of this immensity in such a short time, isn't it likely that this situation is pervasive?"

"What is your take on Richmond?" Julia asked him.

"I think he's up to his eyeballs in Arab collusions. He's a petroleum engineer, and he worked for ARAMCO before he joined the CIA. My guess is that he made contacts while he was in Saudi Arabia, and kept up with them as he climbed the ladder at the CIA. I'll bet he's dug up some dirt on Morrison and is forcing him to play along with his game. If he doesn't have a huge pile of money stashed away somewhere in the world, I'll eat my hat."

"What do you think we should do about it?" Julia asked him.

"The first thing we've got to do is to see the President. If we get him behind us we can still turn things around, but without his total support we can do nothing. I must warn you that there is the smallest chance that the President is in on this. In which case we should probably make sure our wills are up to date because Mr. Murder and his boys are not going to let us walk away unscathed. The stakes are so high that I'll have to just leave it up to you. Do we tell the President? You know him. Can we trust him?"

"I've known him for a very long time and I trust him completely. I wouldn't have agreed to serve in his cabinet if

I had had any doubts about his character or the purity of his motives."

"Last chance," Ivan said. "Do you trust him with your life? If we go to him with this and he's involved in it, or if he doesn't believe us, you and I could be dead in a very short time."

Julia picked up the phone and instructed her assistant to connect her with the President. Her lack of hesitation told Ivan all he needed to know.

CHAPTER THIRTY-SEVEN

The President sat back in his chair and scowled at the Secretary of State. He hated to be summoned on the spur of the moment, without notice. He always felt unprepared in situations like that, and he knew there could be consequences to being caught off guard.

"So then tell me, Julia, what's so urgent that you and Dr. Welland have to see me right away?" he asked.

"If it's all right with you, sir, I'll let Ivan tell you."

"Go ahead, Welland," the President said.

Ivan launched into a detailed description of the conspiracy he had uncovered. As he did so he observed the President's facial expression, hoping not to read his own death sentence in it, but all he could see was mounting anger. Ivan took it as a good sign, as long as the anger was not directed at him. When he finished recounting his suspicions, the President grew silent for a minute.

"If what you say is indeed true," he said finally, "next to Benedict Arnold, Richmond is the second worst traitor in our history."

"No, sir, I believe Richmond is worse," Ivan remarked.

"That could be the case." He observed Ivan thoughtfully. "Knowing you as I do, I suppose you have a plan to put this mess right."

"Yes, sir," Ivan said sheepishly.

"Well then, let's have it."

"I'm sorry I can't give it to you in writing, sir, but I only discovered the treachery this afternoon. So if it's all right with you, I'll tell you verbally."

"Go ahead, Welland," said the President, impatiently.

"My plan calls for the immediate arrest of Richmond. He must be cut off from communicating with anyone. He should be questioned by the best inquisitor we've got on hand, then if we can break him we'll be able to get some invaluable information. Whether he confesses or not, my plan is not altered."

"Go on," said the President.

"Simultaneously with Richmond's arrest, you must get Morrison's daughter out of Saudi Arabia and bring her home. Richmond has been using the girl as an ostensible hostage to get Morrison's compliance. The Secretary of State can handle that for you."

"I'll be happy to help in any way I can," said Julia.

"Perhaps Julia could notify the King, through diplomatic channels, and tell him that the girl's father is very ill and that we would be grateful if she could be sent home at once. Simultaneously with these first two acts, you must haul Morrison in and tell him that you'll let him resign without disgrace if he'll testify against Richmond, and then act as a figurehead CIA Director to help us clean out any scoundrels that have been working with Richmond. I think Morrison will be grateful to you for rescuing his daughter, and he will probably cooperate fully with us. Step four is to put a lid on *Operation Playwright.*

"That would be a damn shame, Welland. That plan of yours was a thing of beauty," said the President.

"Thank you, sir, but we're not giving up the plan. We're just going to begin *Operation Act II* instead. You'll order the CIA to stand down, but we'll mobilize the Special Forces to pick up the ball. The CIA was planning to use poison nerve gas to kill the caliphs, but I wasn't in favor of that approach. Fortunately for us, Richmond never let me get a word in edgewise about my preferred method."

"Which one is that?" asked the President.

"I recommend that we use a low yield neutron bomb similar to the ones that we considered using in the Vietcong tunnels during the Vietnam war. There are thousands of these tactical weapons out there. The Russians have Atomic Demolition Munitions, or ADMs. The Israelis and the French have them, we have our REBs, and so on. My plan has always been to scare the rulers of the Islamic nations into thinking that the terrorists in their midst have acquired nuclear weapons. What would scare them more than a small nuclear explosion caused by inexperienced handling of such weaponry? It would certainly verify the rumors about the terrorists having obtained them, and it would stampede the rulers into cooperating with us to get rid of the jihadists. We'll fix it so that the source of the weapon can never be identified. The bomb itself will be inside some large air-conditioning machinery that our Special Forces men will deliver. Then they'll detonate the bomb remotely from a safe distance."

"Then what happens?" the President asked.

"During all the confusion that takes place immediately after the explosion, the Special Forces will reenter the underground headquarters of the caliphs to verify the results. At that time they'll steal any pertinent documents, take a casualty count, and if possible get DNA samples of the dead caliphs. As soon as we have an exact date and time for *Act II* to begin, my code guys will contact the terrorists in cells around the world and order them to attack. They'll use the code I've broken, of course. But we will have alerted all the anti-terrorist security forces everywhere, and they will be waiting in ambush to arrest or kill these murderers."

"Isn't this part of the original plan?" asked the President.

"Yes. This phase is unchanged, and it's underway right now. Meanwhile you'll have the FBI clean up the graft and corruption in our own government. When all this is done, the Secretary of State can put the world back together again in the diplomatic sense. And that's about all there is to my plan, except for the presidential seal of approval."

"Richmond and his henchmen may have compromised the operation," the President said, "but the idea of ordering them to stand down is a stroke of genius."

"Thank you, sir. I hope it all works out."

The President approved *Operation Act II,* and authorized Ivan to contact the appropriate armed forces officers and launch the operation as soon as possible. On his end he would have the Attorney General arrest Richmond at once, and he would have the Director of the CIA on the carpet within the hour. They would need to be in frequent touch, so the President asked Ivan to give him daily progress reports. In order to facilitate these discussions the President would leave instructions with his staff to patch Ivan through to him whenever he called. For the time being everything seemed to have been covered, so the meeting was adjourned. The President was already on the phone to the Attorney General as Ivan and Julia left the Oval Office.

In the car on the way back to the State Department, Julia and Ivan discussed their meeting with POTUS. Julia believed that the surest way to make the Islamic leaders believe they were at risk of being violently overthrown by their own radical elements was to have a nuclear weapon explode accidentally in Mecca. She stressed the word "accidentally," and reminded Ivan of the dire effects that would ensue should the United States be found to be involved in this plot. Ivan told her that the disinformation program had already been started, and that hints, tips, and evidence pointing to the al Qaeda terrorism group were already worming their way into the consciousness of the Arab leaders.

"By the time the shaped neutron charge is set off under the Ka'bah, these leaders will be certain it's the work of their own fundamentalist Muslims, and we'll heap coals on their deserving heads. The Special Forces Unit selected to do this job would be totally aware of the consequences if they failed in their mission."

Julia had perfect confidence in Ivan. By the time they were back in their offices, she was feeling sanguine about *Operation Act II.*

Ivan asked Brooklyn to get the Chairman of the Joint Chiefs on the phone as soon as possible. He soon heard the General's voice on the other end.

"General, this is Ivan Welland. I've just been with the President, and he has instructed me to coordinate *Operation Playwright* with certain amendments that require that the name be changed now to *Operation Act II.* He wants the placement of the weapon to be done by members of the Special Forces, and not by the CIA as originally planned. It's the President's wish that you and I meet at once to plan the details of this operation. I suggest that you round up your Senior Special Forces Staff, especially those with experience in Middle Eastern operations. If you'll be kind enough to tell me when and where we can meet together, I'll make it my business to be there."

The General, with a lifetime of experience behind him, was nonplussed. He would have to double check on the priority that POTUS put on this mission later, but for now he would round up his best people and meet with Ivan in an hour at the Pentagon.

"One hour. The situation room in the Pentagon. I'll be there," said the General, with the brevity of a battlefield commander.

Ivan thought how those poor devils in the Army made their reputations by being men of action, so they couldn't help coming off as tough and cursory in their relations with civilians. Recent efforts by the staff colleges to make senior officers more diplomatic had met with only moderate success, but Ivan didn't care. He was every bit as driven for results as the military men, but less macho about it.

"Brooklyn, please order me a car to take me to the Pentagon in a few minutes," he said to her when he got back to his office. "And by the way, were you able to get me the item I requested?"

She silently handed him a heavy, bulgy, sealed Kraft envelope. Without waiting for him to ask, she showed him a pistol tucked into her purse.

"Good. Now, please get the President on the line."

In a minute POTUS answered the phone.

"Ivan? I was about to call you to tell you that Richmond must have gotten wind that we were on to him, because we can't locate him anywhere."

"That doesn't surprise me. I'm sure you had an APB put out for him, but being Deputy Director of the CIA puts him in a position to know how to disappear when necessary. Did you get Morrison, and did he know where Richmond might have gone?"

"We got Morrison, and I've spoken to him. He's pissing in his pants, but cooperating. He'll do anything to get his daughter out of Saudi Arabia alive. He didn't know where Richmond was, but he seemed afraid of him. Do you think Richmond has compromised our plans for the caliphs?"

"No, sir, at least not yet. Being washed up at the CIA means the end of his usefulness as an agent for the Saudis. This is his last chance for a big score. He'll want to sell this information for a very high price. My guess is he's going to try to make one last big deal – a killing, so to speak. He's probably had a getaway plan for years, for just such an occasion as this. I only met the man twice, but he came across as being very proud and arrogant. He knows he's been making fools of the CIA for years. He thinks he's smarter than everyone else in the government. The only hope of catching this guy, who visualizes himself as some sort of super spy, is if he allows his pride to trip him up. His character flaw could be his downfall."

"That would be convenient," said the President. "So what kind of error do you think he'll commit?"

"I believe he may attempt to kill me, sir."

After a brief silence, the President said, "Why you?"

"Well, sir, I can only guess, but I had the feeling that he hated me on sight. I think it was the old green-eyed monster. He saw me as a young squirt, a rising Harvard smart-ass who was wet behind the ears. He'd like to bring me down if he can. It also may seem to him that I'm responsible for his current plight. If this is true, he might try to kill me to put a flourish on his last act as an intelligence bigwig. This would be a most undesirable event from my point of view, so I was wondering if you could assign two of your secret servicemen to look out for me during the next couple of days."

"Leave it to me. I don't want this traitor knocking off my favorite Harvard smart-ass."

"Thank you, sir. I'm glad we see eye-to-eye on this. Would you have the T men go to my office at the State Department and stay there with my assistant, Brooklyn, until I get back from my meeting with the Special Forces commander at the Pentagon?"

"Your assistant's name is *Brooklyn*?"

"Yes, sir, Mr. President. Well, not exactly, her real name is Brocklyn, but people at State have been calling her Brooklyn for years, even though she was born in the Bronx. I suppose they could have called her *Bronxlyn*, but somehow Brooklyn stuck. Whatever they call her, she's nothing short of terrific at her job."

"I'm glad someone around here is good at his job."

"We should hand everything over to the women, sir. Except your job and mine."

"You're a pisser Welland, but you're the only one who treats me like a normal person. Ever since I was elected, people defer to me so much you'd think I'd had an apotheosis, instead of only a nine-vote electoral majority."

"That must be an occupational hazard, Mr. President."

Ivan told Brooklyn to stay put and be on the lookout for two secret servicemen that the President was sending over to protect them from any irate Deputy Directors of the CIA who might be in the neighborhood.

"I'm on my way to the Pentagon," he said, "and I'll be back as soon as I can. You stay here with the bodyguards."

As he put on his jacket and adjusted his tie, he tried to decide if he should take along the package with the gun in it. He picked up his laptop in its case, and in the last instant before leaving his office he quickly grabbed the bulky package and kept on going, remembering how useful in a similar situation Kahnsultan's gun had been. Brooklyn was relieved that the secret servicemen would be there soon. From what she knew of Ivan, carrying a gun for him was not just a precaution, it meant that war had been declared.

Ivan was comforted that the driver assigned to take him to the Pentagon had driven him once before when he was with Julia. That meant he had security clearance to transport government officials at the highest levels. But the same could also be said of Richmond, who, as Deputy Director of the CIA, was cleared all the way to the top.

It was six o'clock, and most of the government employees had already left their desks and gone home, so traffic was light. Dixon, whose name appeared on the tag pinned to his chauffeur's jacket, made good time. Ivan had surreptitiously removed the pistol from the envelope – a 45-caliber monster that looked like the ones carried by the Marines who guarded the White House – and had hidden it in the well of the arm rest in the back seat. He couldn't fit the lid back in place because the gun took up too much space, but he was able to close it enough so that the weapon wasn't visible.

Ivan knew he would be scanned through a metal detector at the Pentagon, so there was no question of carrying the gun on his person. Dixon, an African American man of considerable girth, opened the door for him when they arrived. He smiled, showing beautiful white teeth below his moustache.

"I'll be waiting in the driver's lounge for you, sir, until you're ready to leave again," Dixon said.

The Pentagon maintained a room just outside the building where chauffeurs could wait for their passengers to complete their business. In the lounge they could have a cup of coffee, read the paper, and chat with other drivers, and it saved the security staff at the Pentagon from having to check their IDs. When someone was ready to be picked up, the intercom would notify the driver to bring the car around to the entrance. While Dixon settled into a seat in the lounge, Ivan, with his visitor's badge clipped to his lapel, was shown to the Chief's conference room by a young Marine.

The room was empty when Ivan entered, so he took his computer from its case and placed it on the table. In just a moment the Chairman of the Joint Chiefs of the Armed Forces of the United States plowed into the room, with another general and two colonels in his wake. Chest ribbons were rife, but words were sparse.

"Sit here please, Mr. Welland," said the man who was second in command of all the armed might of the U.S.

Whether born to command or trained for it, the General was nevertheless in charge. He directed Ivan to describe what it was the President wanted his forces to do. The colonels had not been at the planning meetings when they were called *Operation Playwright* so Ivan had to explain everything again, but this time he told them the amended plans called for Special Forces to take over the critical portions of the plan now to be called *Operation Act II*.

"In the new scenario," Ivan said, "several Arabic-speaking men dressed in the local style will deliver a commercial air-conditioning unit to be placed beneath the Ka'bah in Mecca. Ostensibly this A/C unit would be used to cool and filter the air in the secret quarters of the caliphs beneath the holy building, but in reality it will contain a small neutron bomb capable of killing all the people in the tunnel when it's detonated."

Ivan went on to explain how it was that these caliphs directed the bloody terror attacks mounted by jihadist hard-liners all over the world. He also made it patently clear that the mission would not be successful unless the explosion were made to seem like an accident caused by inept handling of a nuclear device by inexperienced Islamist terrorists. The origin of the weapon could be attributed to any of the possible sources of such weaponry, as long as it was not the United States.

"So," he concluded, leaning back in his chair, "do you think this mission can be pulled off, and can the Special Forces do it? If there are any foreseeable problems here, now's the time to talk about them."

The officers agreed that it was entirely possible. The two Colonels who were operations commanders seemed quite intrigued.

"Who thought up this scheme?" asked the Colonel on the left side of the table.

"It was my idea," Ivan replied.

"So who are we going to pin this on?" asked the General. "The nuclear weapons limitation treaties don't yet include tactical weapons, so one of these weapons could come from any country that stock-piles them. There are thousands of tactical nuclear weapons in the world today."

"You're absolutely right, sir," Ivan agreed. "But as I mentioned before, I'd say the ideal scapegoat would be an Islamist terrorist, someone inexperienced and inept, who accidentally sets off the bomb."

"Because who else would be running around down there in the tunnel, anyway?" said the second Colonel. "The guy would at least have to be a fellow Muslim, whatever his politics are."

"Okay, let's get on with it then," the General said. "What Islamic country is this inept Muslim going to be from?"

"The fundamentalists in the sub-continent of India are known to have leaked some stolen fissionable materials and weapons into the black market, so Pakistan is a likely source from which a rich buyer could have acquired a weapon for al Qaeda agents," said the second Colonel.

"Maybe," said the first Colonel. "But Iran's recent posturing and muscle flexing in regard to nuclear materials and weapons make them a tempting target for blame."

"Welland? What do you say?" said the General.

"The Colonels have both made excellent suggestions," Ivan said, diplomatically.

"So which country do you choose?" the General asked.

"If the device has been traced to Iran," Ivan continued, unflustered, "it might serve several purposes that would be helpful to future U.S. nuclear policy. First of all, no one would believe that Iran had nothing to do with building such devices, and the pressure of world opinion on Iran's recent excursions into power-building using a nuclear capability platform would come conveniently into play. Secondly, Iran is the largest Shiite-based Islamic nation, and the one most interested in the rule of a theocracy run by the caliphate. Funding and support for these caliphs operating right under the noses of the Sunnis may well have come from these supporters of Ali and the Ayatollahs, and if discovered by al Qaeda, it could have provoked a first strike by Sunni terrorists to avoid a Shiite takeover of Islam. This kind of Muslim rivalry would focus Islamic hatreds internally, leaving the rest of the world with many fewer problems."

The General finally got the group to reach consensus. They would let the signs point to Iran as the manufacturer of the device, and to Hezbollah as the group guilty of mishandling the weapon and causing the explosion. Then the Arabs could fight it out among themselves to determine who was responsible for the explosion and what their motives might have been.

Next, the meeting moved to a discussion of the details of how the deadly air conditioner could be taken to the site. It could be delivered in an ARAMCO truck which could either be a stolen vehicle or a truck painted to look like a delivery van.

"Mission-sensitive details could be discussed in a later planning session," the Special Forces General decided.

"That's fine by me," said Ivan, "as long as I'm kept up to date on all the details decided upon by the Army strategists. You'll have to keep in touch with me on a daily basis so the other elements of the operation such as disinformation, de-coding and diplomacy can be worked into the picture."

"No problem there," said one of the colonels.

"Good. So approximately how long do you think it will it take to mount *Operation Act II*?"

"If given top priority," said the General, "the attack could be carried out in a week's time."

"This operation has the President's blessing," Ivan reminded them. "He's waiting to be informed of the final details before we proceed with the mission."

Ivan saw that the officers understood the importance of the mission—both the risks and the rewards. He never felt the CIA understood the operation in the way the Military did. The CIA tended to over-complicate everything. It was as though the mission were too simple to be important enough to challenge the masters of deceit at the CIA. Ivan knew that the genius of the plan was in its simplicity, but he also knew that for ordinary men problem-solving meant conquering complexities. For extraordinary men, however, solving puzzles involved doing it with artistry and panache, and that usually required a simple, straightforward, unique solution.

CHAPTER THIRTY-EIGHT

Ivan left the meeting feeling encouraged. He believed the operation against the caliphs was back on track. He silently prayed that the Arabic-speaking men chosen to be Special Forces operatives were trustworthy and loyal. If he encountered traitors among the elite military forces, as existed in the CIA, he would be forced to despair for his beloved America. It sickened him to think that highly-placed and deeply-trusted government employees could be wooed into seditious betrayals by promises of big payoffs in U.S. dollars from those who would destroy the government that guarantees and underwrites the very funds they use to sell out their honor and their comrades. Ivan mused about how similar these traitors were to the supporters of the Confederacy who had piled up millions of confederate dollars and then found them to be worthless because the South lost the War between the States. In the same way, the turncoats at the CIA would be paid in the funds issued by the country that would end up being the newest third world nation if their treachery succeeded.

"How temporal and foolish these conspirators are!" said Ivan to himself as he wended his way back to the car that had brought him to the Pentagon.

As he was thinking about these issues, he was suddenly jolted back to his senses when a different driver stepped out of the car to open the door for him.

"Where's my own driver?" Ivan asked. "Where's Dixon?"

"Dixon has had a personal emergency, sir," the new driver said. "I was sent to relieve him so he could go home."

There was no sense in pursuing the matter with this driver. If he was lying, as Ivan felt almost sure he was, he would get no truthful answers. He could refuse to get into the car, but then he would never know who had sent this driver. He wouldn't be any safer, anyway, because the men who were brazen and clever enough to switch drivers could also find other means to get rid of him, if that was their intention.

Ivan looked at the back seat to see if the armrest was still slightly open. It was. He put his attaché case on the ground in front of the unsuspecting driver who was holding the door open for him. It seemed to the driver that Ivan was expecting him to hand the case in to him after he got into the car. When the driver bent down to pick up the attaché case, Ivan reached into the back seat, flipped up the armrest, removed the weapon, and turned back to face the driver who now had the attaché case in his hand and the 45 between his eyes.

"Slowly put the attaché case on the ground and raise your hands," Ivan said coolly, without raising his voice. "Now, turn your back to me, and keep your arms up."

Ivan poked the pistol into the spine of the fake driver so there would be no doubt that he meant business and would shoot him if necessary. He marched the faux chauffeur to the entrance door. The Marine on guard there, seeing what had happened, drew his weapon. He pushed a silent alarm button to summon additional assistance.

Ivan wasn't absolutely sure whether the Marine would be on his side or the driver's side should the man try to escape. The Marine, however, had been trained to observe carefully those who entered the building and he had not forgotten Ivan. It was he who had processed Ivan through the metal detection station, so he was satisfied to side with him until help arrived and the situation could be resolved. In short order three additional Marines arrived on the run.

"I don't believe this driver is a legitimate replacement for Dixon. My guess is you'll find Dixon or his body somewhere nearby."

He asked the Marines to search the driver and the car for a weapon of any kind. They hauled the man through the metal detection station, which immediately set off the alarm. At first they didn't see what had activated the blinking light and its buzzer. Then, on closer inspection, they found a pistol in an ankle holster, and a garrote wire in the jacket pocket of his chauffeur uniform. When they emptied his other pockets, they found valid CIA identification.

"This man must be held for questioning," said Ivan. "He must not be released under any circumstances. Is that clear?"

"Yes, sir," said one of the guards.

The Marines tossed him into the brig, pending further orders. A Marine captain arrived to take charge and to see what the fuss was about. Ivan explained the situation to him and asked him to call General Black, the Chairman of the Joint Chiefs, then turn the phone over to him. The captain did as Ivan asked, and when the General was on the line he gave the phone to Ivan. Ivan explained the situation to him in detail.

"I'd like you to call the President, sir," Ivan said. "He'll tell you how to proceed with the prisoner's questioning. The President is personally in charge of the undercover investigation that's currently underway."

Just then two of the Marines ran up to Ivan.

"We found Dixon in one of the toilet stalls in the driver's washroom," said the first Marine, somewhat out of breath.

"He seemed to be asleep," said the second Marine, "but we couldn't wake him."

"We think he's been drugged," said the first.

"Have you requested medical assistance?" Ivan asked.

"Yes, sir," said the second. "The medics are on the way."

Ivan related this latest news to the General, who was still on the line and could overhear the commotion.

"In view of the developments at the Pentagon," Ivan said to the General, "I'm concerned that some chicanery aimed at me or my assistant might be in progress. I'm going to drive myself back to my office, but I'd like you to ask the President for the names of the T-Men that he dispatched to the State Department. I don't want any more killers with phony identification showing up around here unannounced."

"Give me your cell number," said the General. "I'll call you back with the names as soon as I've spoken with the President."

Ivan turned to leave, then turned around to thank the Marines for their assistance. He left the Pentagon reception hallway, got into the State Department vehicle, and headed back to his office. When he was about halfway to his office he received a call from General Black.

"The Marines were right. Dixon was heavily sedated, but he'll be okay. They'll put him in sickbay for the night and question him in the morning when he wakes up."

"I'm glad we'll be able to question him. It would have been a bit harder if he'd been dead," Ivan said.

"Maybe that's what was intended. We'll find out after the medics examine him."

"Did you get the names of the two secret service agents?"

Their names are Tyman and Wentworth. They're on their way to the State Department right now. What's going on here, anyway?"

"The attempted kidnapping was a plot against me and was directly related to the cancellation of *Operation Playwright*. Nothing that happened had anything to do with *Operation Act II*. In fact, no one at the CIA knows about the new operation, nor should they be told."

Ivan and the General agreed to meet the next day to discuss the progress of the new operation. Then Ivan got Brooklyn on the phone.

"Have the two agents from the Secret Service shown up over there?" he asked her.

"Yes, they're here with me right now, and they're waiting for you to arrive."

"Do you know their names?"

"No, I don't."

Brooklyn, who ordinarily spoke like a machine gun, was being uncharacteristically taciturn. She had also hesitated long enough in answering Ivan's questions to arouse his suspicions.

"Just tell them I'll be there soon."

"All right," said Brooklyn, and hung up abruptly.

Ivan had no time to ponder. He did what he always did when things had to be done—he went to the man in charge. In this case, of course, it was a woman.

"Julia, please listen to me carefully. I believe that two of Richmond's CIA agents are in my office right now, holding my assistant captive. Please alert the Marines, who also serve as the building's security personnel. Two secret serviceman named Tyman and Wentworth have been dispatched by the President to serve as bodyguards for Brooklyn and me, but my guess is the bad guys arrived first. So please tell the Marines to close the building and stop anyone from entering or leaving. Tell them to wait for me to get there, and tell them Tyman and Wentworth are on the way."

"I'm on it," said Julia.

Ivan jumped out of the car and approached the group of people that had assembled along with Julia in front of the building where Brooklyn was likely being held captive in her office.

"Madame Secretary," Ivan said, "with your permission I can take tactical command of this rescue operation now."

For the first time Julia was seeing another side of Ivan, the one that came forward in times of crisis.

"Carry on," she said.

Ivan spoke to the Marine captain. "Please deploy your men with automatic weapons outside the windows of my office. Post two at each window, and have them show their weapons. Tell them not to use them unless it's absolutely necessary. I want to take these men alive so they can be questioned. The rest of you follow me. You two in civvies, what are your names?"

"I'm Tyman, and this is Wentworth."

"Okay, you come with me."

"I think I can get the hostage-takers to surrender," Ivan told the Marine captain as they moved out. "I'd like to do this without any shots being fired. I believe I can talk them down."

Ivan had the captain position his men around the office door, guns at the ready. He asked the two legitimate secret service men if they were prepared to take the two turncoat CIA agents into custody. He suggested they stand ready to transport them for questioning to the same location where the bogus driver was being held.

Tyman got on his cell phone and made arrangements with his headquarters to be prepared for this eventuality. When Ivan was satisfied that everyone was in position, he made a call on his cell phone.

"This is Under Secretary Welland's office," Brooklyn answered.

"Brooklyn, may I speak to one of the two men who are holding you prisoner, please?" Ivan said, clearly and calmly.

Brooklyn gave an audible gasp and passed the phone to the larger of the two CIA agents. "It's Dr. Welland, and he'd like to speak to you."

"Yes/?," said the man gruffly.

Ivan suspected that these men were mercenaries. No doubt they'd kill for money, but if they knew they were surrounded they wouldn't choose to die like suicide bombers on a mission for Allah. Ivan reasoned that these men were American traitors motivated by greed; probably they had been accumulating illegal gains for years against the time when they could retire as pashas in some foreign country. Men like that don't intentionally go out in a blaze of glory. Ivan was sure they would rather take their chances with the liberal American justice system than fight a losing gun battle against overwhelming odds.

"Your operation is a bust," Ivan told him. "Deputy Director Richmond is exposed and on the lam. The deal at the Pentagon has been blown. I'm offering you a chance to surrender and live. Think about it. When you go to trial you can claim you were just following Richmond's orders. You might even trade information for a suspended sentence. But if even one shot is fired inside my office you two are going to die. Now put your weapons down on the desk in front of my assistant, pass this phone back to her, and raise your hands. We'll come in quietly, take you into custody, and no one will get hurt."

Ivan waited until he heard Brooklyn's voice say, "Hello sir, I'm here."

"Good." Ivan spoke quietly, almost hypnotically. "Are they putting their guns on the desk in front of you?"

"Yes," Brooklyn answered.

"Are they standing still with their hands up?" Ivan asked.

"Yes," she said.

"Good. Tell them we're coming in and we have weapons, but we won't point them at them."

Through the phone receiver Ivan could hear Brooklyn telling the men what he had said.

"Can we come in now, without the risk of gunfire?"

"Yes," Brooklyn said firmly.

"All right gentlemen," said Ivan to the men in the hall outside his office. "This is the State Department, and we're going to conduct ourselves with decorum. I'll enter the office first, because it's my office. You will follow behind me. Do not point your weapons at the culprits, but keep them at the ready. They've agreed to surrender to my assistant, and she tells me they're standing with their hands up waiting for you to take them into custody. Please search them for concealed weapons and then help Tyman and Wentworth get them transferred into safekeeping. Ready? Let's go."

Ivan opened the door and walked in. The Secret Service men and the Marines took the conspirators into custody and marched them out of the office. The van arrived at the entrance and the prisoners were loaded into the back. Ivan called Julia to advise her that her department was intact and operational once again, and none the worse for the wear.

"Good for you, Ivan!" she said, when she heard his voice. "How on earth did you work it so there was no violence?"

"At the State Department, negotiated settlements are the preferred method of conflict resolution," he chuckled.

When Ivan and Brooklyn were alone, he told her he was proud of the way she had warned him about the two men being in the office. Brooklyn thought it was amazing that he had understood her unspoken warning.

"The excitement might not be over yet," Ivan warned her. "Richmond might very well try to take a shot at us. He hates me for canceling *Operation Playwright*. I'm sure he'd have been paid good money for ratting us out. I don't think his pride will allow him to run away without getting even with the man who exposed him as a counterspy. Richmond needs a grand victory of some sort so he can quit a winner. I think his pride will make him want to micro-manage one last assassination—my own. Killing you, Brooklyn, would only be collateral damage as far as he's concerned. I'm sure this is personal and not business, because his henchmen didn't search our files. They want to get us personally."

"I think you're right about that," Brooklyn agreed.

"If they had searched our documents, they might have found information about *Operation Act II*. That would have been an even bigger coup for Richmond. As it is, his greatest potential achievement in the world of espionage will be sacrificed for an act of personal revenge. Our next challenge is to make sure we're not killed to satisfy his perverted need for vengeance."

Ivan would have loved to have a quiet evening alone in which to read a book and have a phone chat with Marina, but staying alive would have to take precedence. He forced himself to think like Richmond. If he could anticipate what this dangerous man was likely to do, he could be prepared to defend himself. Ivan was largely ignorant of the man's previous strategies, so he was thrown back on intuition to help him guess the malevolent tactics he would use to satisfy his desire for mental supremacy over his opponents.

Ivan was content to be regarded as a fool by Richmond. To be held in low regard by an egotist gives one the opportunity to surprise the swaggerer in mid swagger. Richmond would no doubt have prearranged his escape, and likely that would entail meeting some schedule or other.

"If I can delay Richmond's act of revenge long enough to interfere with his departure plan," Ivan said to Brooklyn, "I may be able to put sufficient pressure on him to force him to hurry, and that way I can lure him into making a mistake. You're still in serious danger. It's possible that Richmond might try to kill you as a way of getting at me."

Brooklyn, as usual, had an excellent grasp of the whole situation.

"See if you can dig up some information about the recent operations in which Richmond has been active, Brooklyn, if you would. Under time pressure perhaps he might fall back on some tactic that has worked for him in the past."

Brooklyn went straight to work to try to find out what Richmond's previous MOs had been, but she knew that getting information out of the CIA was next to impossible. While she was absorbed in that project Ivan returned to his own problem, which was to predict and counter Richmond's plan for his demise.

One of Ivan's concerns was that he didn't know how much manpower Richmond had under his control. Richmond had supervision of the CIA purse strings, so he could have taken very good care of those who were close to him. Ivan assumed the FBI investigators would delve into the financial affairs of employees who were subordinate to the Deputy

Director. When Richmond's detection eventually became common knowledge, those connected with him would expect to be scrutinized. Some would flee the country, and some would bluff it out, but not very many would remain loyal to the exposed criminal who could no longer pay them for favors. Ivan reasoned that most of these rats would desert the ship. Loyalty is a rare quality in those who sell out their country, so why would they be loyal to Richmond?

Ivan guessed that Richmond already knew about the failures of his men at the Pentagon and State Department. By this time he would be thinking that the only way to get the job done was to do it himself. His ego would demand face-to-face satisfaction. Ivan was beginning to feel quite certain that Richmond would show up in the flesh, and soon. He might be disguised, but he was sure Richmond would want to be there in person when he doled out Ivan's punishment for toppling him from the world's largest and most well-known intelligence agency.

Motives of revenge, like haste, contribute to failure. A third negative that was on Ivan's side was Mitch Richmond's overweening pride in his own intelligence. He believed that he was the most brilliant operative in the spy business, and he would not be deposed easily, or so he thought. Ivan had learned during his flirtation with theoretical mathematics that many people were smarter than he was. That piece of news had been rather hard for him to digest, but once he had acknowledged it, he was better off. Evidently Richmond had not yet had that experience, or worse, had not accepted the truth of it. This was a blind spot for Richmond, and one that must inevitably lead to his undoing.

On Richmond's side of the ledger was his experience in matters of arranged deaths. His nickname, *Mr. Murder*, did not inspire much hope in the potential victim. Like terrorists, Richmond had the element of surprise on his side. Ivan could not know when or how he would be attacked—he only that sooner or later he would be. Another advantage that Mitch

Richmond shared with terrorists was his complete lack of conscience. Ivan had always pondered the questions of good and evil in the hearts of both friends and enemies. It was unacceptable, of course, to be on the receiving end of the broken Sixth Commandment, but he still struggled with his own ability to pass favorable judgment on the murder of the caliphs in Mecca.

Ivan conducted a mental simulation of Mitch Richmond's possible plans for revenge. The most likely scenario for his own murder had to include Richmond taking action very soon. Richmond's original plan was to kidnap him so he could conduct his execution on his own turf and at his own timing. The arrest of the chauffeur and the men at Ivan's office in the State Department must have been frustrating to a man like Mr. Murder.

Exercising the timeless tenacity of his Muslim employers was not an option in this case. If he was going to make his escape and also deal with Welland, Richmond would now have to act fast and ruthlessly. Ivan had removed the home field advantage, but the element of surprise remained with the assassin. Likewise, Ivan would not have time to go on the offensive and locate Mitch Richmond's hiding-place, which, although it must be nearby, could not be found in the amount of time available. No, Ivan thought, there was no choice. He had to play the black pieces in this match.

In the game of life-and-death chess, a stalemate is a victory. Ivan decided he would settle for a draw because it was not only his life that was at stake, it was Brooklyn's as well. He hoped that Richmond would be caught before he escaped the country, for he knew that this man, who thought of himself as the master of international cloak-and-dagger operations, would have prepared a foolproof exit strategy. Ivan resolved to keep Brooklyn and himself out of harm's way until Richmond had either been caught or had managed to flee. Ivan knew all too well that the impressive electronic assets of the CIA, combined with an unknown number of double agents that might still be working for Richmond, presented a formidable challenge to a targeted man trying to stay alive.

Ivan remembered with considerable discomfort a quote by Herodotus who said, *Until he is dead, do not yet call a man happy, but only lucky.* *

---

* Many people believe incorrectly that these are the words of Greek historian Herodotus (484?-425? B.C.) but he was actually referring to an observation made by Greek statesman Solon (638-c558 B.C.) (Footnote by historian and scholar Marina Kortikuova)

CHAPTER THIRTY-NINE

Ivan had two problems that needed immediate solutions. The first concerned whether Richmond had told the caliphs that their code had been broken. He thought long and hard about what the traitor would do with this information. Finally he decided that Richmond had not yet told anyone about this secret to which he had become privy as Deputy Director of the CIA.

Ivan based this conclusion on his knowledge of Mitch Richmond's character, and on the fact that his (Ivan's) deciphering group, headed by David Feingold, had not reported suspicious code message activity. The information that the caliphs' code had been cracked was worth a fortune to Richmond. He would most certainly want to sell this intelligence to his malevolent benefactors, but because his personality required praise to fuel itself, he would likely want to be there in person to make the deal and receive the accolades.

Since Mitch Richmond knew that *Operation Playwright* had been cancelled, he would believe there was no particular urgency to tell his Islamist patrons about the code, and would therefore wait till he could amaze them with the information in person, and not inconsequentially increase the value of this intelligence.

If this line of reasoning was correct, Ivan concluded that Richmond would be heading to Mecca. If this city was his first destination, it would be helpful if the agents now trying to apprehend Richmond were aware of it. Ivan decided to call POTUS to inform him of his suspicions.

The second problem was simpler—where could he and Brooklyn safely hole up until Richmond had been caught? When he decided to call the President to take care of his first problem, he never dreamed that he would also be solving his second.

Ivan asked Brooklyn to place the call to the President. When they were connected, Ivan recounted his narrow escapes and his theories about Richmond's probable next moves.

"Tell me, sir," said Ivan, "when the arrested men were questioned, did we get any information about the scope of the corruption at the Intelligence Agency?"

"I've turned the matter over to the Attorney General, who in turn has galvanized his Justice Department into action. The investigative arm of the Justice Department is the FBI, and they're the ones actually doing the digging."

"I hope Richmond's dirty tricks haven't affected that vaunted agency as well as the CIA."

"One can only hope."

"While we're on the phone, sir, I've another question."

"Fire away."

"I'm looking for a safe place to live till Mitch Richmond is caught."

"I've been thinking about that, too, Welland. I'm prepared to have you come and live at the White House until the affair with the caliphs is concluded."

The President had a selfish motivation as well. He had recognized in Ivan the extremely rare quality of complete trustworthiness, and he wanted him close to him to render intelligent advice untainted by political self-seeking.

"Thank you very much for the invitation, sir, but I feel I should decline your generous offer because I have to find a safe place for my assistant, too."

"I'll arrange for accommodations for Brooklyn, as well," said the Commander-in-Chief.

"I still have one more condition."

"How would it be if I changed my invitation to an order?" snapped POTUS. He was not used to having civil servants put conditions on their service.

"I serve at the pleasure of the President," Ivan replied calmly. "In that context, may I change my condition to a small request?"

"That would be much better."

"Very good, sir, then I stand corrected. May I respectfully request that you have a bodyguard assigned to my wife, Marina, in Cambridge? It occurs to me that she could be in serious danger too, since the hostile party could get to me through her."

"I'll do that, Welland. Anything else?"

"No, sir, and thank you very much," Ivan said. "Then if it's all right with you, Brooklyn and I will move into the White House tonight."

"Agreed, but now *I* have a condition. I want you to come to my eight o'clock staff meeting so I can introduce you around."

"Certainly," Ivan said. "I'll be on tap for the meeting."

The President, harried as he almost always was, had hung up without a hint about what he wanted Ivan to do for him. To Ivan's way of thinking POTUS was sometimes curt, but he knew that the job of President was an all-consuming task, so he was willing to forgive slights as long as the decisions made were the right ones. As far as Welland could tell, this President's decisions were intelligent and upright in the moral sense, and he would follow him until such time as his executive actions left the rails, if they ever did. Welland preferred the President to be right in his actions and in his grasp of the international situation, than to be a master of literature and etiquette, even if his own ego was slightly bruised now and then.

The system of government checks and balances toned down the potential damage of glaring philosophical errors, but there was much room for haziness in the application of policies. The U.S. generally preferred not to interfere with the internal affairs of other nations, but in fact the opposite occurred with surprising regularity. Removing the caliphs was an example of how the U.S. was willing to do international surgery overseas in order to preserve the life of the principles of freedom and democracy. America is always touting the idea of having transparency in government, but the secret removal of the caliphs was a far cry from transparency. On the other hand, the rule of terror by a group of secret religious fanatics whose egotistic nationalistic goal is to conquer the world for Islam is hardly transparent either. In the end what justified the projected action against the caliphs and other clerics, in Ivan's mind, was not transparency at all. A transparent evil was still evil, after all. A hidden good was much to be preferred.

In the end it came down to a question of image. Ivan believed that the Old Testament vision of man having been made in the image of God was correct. Ivan, being a thoughtful man, did not understand image to mean strictly a visual interpretation. To a greater extent, according to Ivan's view, people fashion their God after their own way of thinking. If some men think that God is a fearsome authoritarian who wants us governed by tribal rules of blood succession and blind adherence to the immutable legalism of a system bypassed by time, then right-thinking people must reject this vision of the world. Ivan thought that human beings had a long way to go before their thoughts conformed to God's, and therefore to his image also. He agreed with Emerson when he said, *We think our civilization near its meridian, but we are yet only at the cock-crowing and the morning star. In our barbarous society the influence of character is in its infancy* "Politics," *Essays*, Second Series (1844).

Ivan called Brooklyn to his office and asked her to sit down.

"I'll get right to the point, Brooklyn," he said. "Your life is in jeopardy because of your association with me. So we'll both be living at the White House till the operation in Mecca is over, and Richmond and his men are apprehended, and the depth of the corruption at the CIA is exposed."

Brooklyn's eyes were wide with surprise. "The White House? They're asking *me* to go live in the *White House?*"

Ivan smiled. "Although that's not the only safe place for us, it's probably the best place, so I've been seconded to the President's staff for a while. This means that you will be temporarily transferred, too."

"What should I do at this point?"

"Prepare a list of things to take along with you as if you were going on a trip. When you finish that, I'll arrange to have you escorted home by the Secret Service to pick up your things, and then you'll be transported to the White House."

"Do I at least have time to make myself something to eat at home?"

"No, Brooklyn. There's no time for that. I'm sure the White House staff can give you a light supper. Please tell the kitchen staff I'll be coming too. I'll try to get there at about the same time as you do. That way we can eat together and save the staff the trouble of serving us separately. Okay?"

"Wow! We're going to be living in the best billet in the whole country!"

After Brooklyn left the office, Ivan began thinking about what he would say to Marina when he called her. It had only been a day since he had spoken with her, but it seemed like much longer to him. The hardest part of all was that he couldn't tell her everything that had happened in the interim. He didn't want to worry her, and he didn't want to sort out what might be classified information and what would be permissible to discuss. He decided to try to keep the ball in Marina's court, and ask her about her day and her work, and stay away from the subject of his recent experiences. He would, of course, have to tell her that he would be staying at the White House over the weekend. He had decided, too, that it would be out of the question for her come to Washington that weekend, when Richmond was still on the loose and there was so much to do to prepare for the attack on the Ka'bah. He hoped she would understand.

They had agreed to cope with the temporary situation that had given them only one weekend as man and wife, but neither of them had expected to miss the other so deeply. Their relationship had been honed to a fine point of reciprocity, and it was difficult for them to pick it up Friday nights and let go of it on Monday mornings. But to miss one of their precious weekends together was going to be hard to bear. Even though their careers were interesting to them, and even though they fully understood that the separations were temporary and the eventual rewards would be worth all the sacrifices, they both yearned for each other more than they had ever imagined.

Ivan picked up the phone and called the woman he loved. He couldn't wait to tell her all about his new living arrangements.

"White House?" Marina repeated, hardly believing her ears. "You are moving to *White House?*"

"Yes, but not for long. I have to be there till we finish the project I'm working on. But you know I can't tell you any more than that. Please try to understand. We're extremely busy, and the work is unbelievably important. That's all I can say."

He changed the subject as quickly as possible, so that he wouldn't be questioned too closely about the reason he had been invited to stay at the White House when the Marriott was so close by. They spoke of many things, but carefully avoided saying anything at all that would make the longing worse. Ivan told Marina he would be thinking of her all the time.

"Is okay, darling," said Marina. "We see each other next weekend. I wait with impatience. I miss you so much!"

Everything was settled, so Ivan packed up a few papers from his desk, put them in his briefcase, and headed out of his office, intending to drive Dixon's car to the White House. On the way out he met Tyman and Wentworth waiting for him in the hall, as they were still detailed to protect him.

"I'll be moving to the White House for a while," Ivan told them, "so you guys will probably be folded back into the security system over at Treasury."

When they got to the car, Tyman slid into the driver's seat and Wentworth opened the rear door for Ivan. At the White House Ivan checked his gun with the security guards and passed into the foyer, where he was greeted by a cheerful, middle-aged woman with a ruddy complexion.

"Good afternoon, Mr. Welland. I'm the Chief House-keeper. Please follow me. You've been assigned the Lincoln bedroom."

"Is Miss Brocklyn here yet?" Ivan inquired.

"Yes, sir. She will be joining you for dinner in fifteen minutes."

The housekeeper led Ivan to his room. "Perhaps you'd like a few minutes to freshen up before dinner," she said. "The meal will be served in the informal dining room at the foot of the stairs, to the right."

"Thank you."

He examined the room that in recent times had become famous when the Democrats had been accused of more or less renting it out to wealthy, status-hungry supporters in exchange for heavy campaign contributions. Ivan, who usually remembered everything he read, had forgotten what connection the room had to Lincoln. He disliked anything having to do with ego-tripping and status-seeking so much that he believed his memory had rejected the information on purpose. He would have to ask the housekeeper if the room had been named after Lincoln because it was his room, or if it was merely named in honor of President Lincoln. He hoped that Lincoln hadn't died in the bed that he would soon be sleeping in.

Brooklyn and Ivan were glad for each other's company as they ate their supper together in the informal White House dining room. Eating and sleeping in the White House was awe-inspiring for these relatively junior civil servants.

"When I'm free to tell my parents about this, they'll be too flabbergasted to speak," she said to Ivan. "But don't worry, of course I won't say anything till we're back to our normal lives."

"It's hard to believe our lives were ever normal, isn't it?"

In his mind, Ivan traced the progress of his skyrocketing career back to his first meeting with Simeon Montcalf. It was that annoying little man who had provided the impetus for him to attain lift-off. There was something about him that transcended his ordinary appearance and slightly pompous demeanor. Ivan hated to have to admit it, but in his own way Montcalf was the most effective civil servant he had met so far. He might not be an expert in anything himself, but he always recognized excellence when he saw it. He wondered if that was an aptitude that could be developed. There was something almost mystical about it. Perhaps he *was* God's Personnel Manager for the North American Division of His celestial enterprises. Ivan would have liked him much better if he hadn't been oiling his way around Marina all the time. He wondered if he had been in touch with her in Cambridge. During their phone conversation she hadn't said anything to him about Montcalf, but then she knew the subject annoyed him so she might have avoided talking about him.

As he slid into Lincoln's bed, he tried to put aside his silly jealousy. He wondered if any men taller than Lincoln had ever slept in this bed. He guessed that his assignment to the Lincoln Room was based on the thoughtful housekeeper's idea that he needed a commodious bed of at least eight feet in length.

* * *

The President was a ball of fire, a real morning person, raring to get on with the business of the day. Ivan was a morning person too, but he was less overt about it. Brooklyn wasn't usually very peppy at seven in the morning, but she was holding her own in a conversation with the First Lady.

The President launched into a description of what he wanted Ivan to do for him. It consisted of two main parts. The first was to continue to be involved in the caliph affair in the capacity of an active coordinator. The second was sort of a job within a job.

"Now, here's what I want you to do," said the President. "In your capacity as Caliph Operations Coordinator, I want you to enter into the planning mode with the CIA to formulate a scheme for the removal of the secret caliphs and the demise of their terrorist organization. At the same time, I want you to judge the loyalty and competency of those assigned to the project by the Director. One of the benefits of these new planning sessions is that we can now convince any wannabe traitors that might still be operating at the CIA that attack plans have been discontinued until they can be restructured, while at the same time we keep it a secret that an attack plan is still in the works. Even if Richmond reaches his destination in Mecca, he certainly won't be expecting a direct attack in the short term. I've made myself as clear as mud, right?"

"No problem, sir," said Ivan. "I understand what you want me to do. Actually, I have been working on developing a loyalty detector that will function the same way as a metal detector."

"All right, Ivan, enough of that nonsense, the President smiled. "Still, I would have thought that by this time there'd be some sort of psychological computer profiling system that could pick out those whose loyalties were too flexible. As you can imagine, it worries me that someone like Richmond could climb the executive ladder at the CIA for years and never be suspected of high treason. That has to stop, and I'd like you to do whatever you can to help stop it."

Unfortunately for Ivan, the President was serious about cleaning up the CIA. Ivan's view was that the system was flawed from the outset. He believed that the very nature of American democracy—which allowed for dissent, but naively assumed dissent would never turn to deceit—could not be corrected without major restructuring.

"I can provide the CIA with some ideas and some red herrings to keep them occupied until *Operation Act II* is concluded," Ivan said, "but I don't feel that I'm the man to revamp the Agency. The State Department is a better venue for me. I hope that you'll see fit to find someone more experienced than I am to do the job at the Agency. If we focus on seeing that the caliphs are removed, the urgency will be reduced and the person you appoint to be the new Director can go about the business of house cleaning in a more orderly fashion. Excuse me for presuming that you will be replacing Tim Morrison, but the Richmond affair is bound to bring him down anyway, if it ever goes public."

"I've already decided to accept Morrison's resignation, and to look for a replacement as quickly as possible," the President declared. "I've left his departure date open, and I offered him a soft landing in exchange for helping us clean up the Richmond mess. There's no doubt that the intelligence buck stops at the Director's desk, so I can't tolerate ineptitude or naiveté in that office. Now, if the operation in Mecca isn't successful, the fault can be laid at the feet of the CIA and portrayed as a unilateral action on the part of the Agency. Hence Morrison's resignation will be tied to the failure, and the embarrassment caused by it will be placed on his doorstep. He won't want to suffer the embarrassment of a failure of this magnitude, so his level of cooperation with us as we clean up the Agency will be high. My staff advises me that this can be made to be seen by the nation as a triumph of overt diplomacy over secret, behind-the-scenes plotting on the part of intelligence operatives acting outside of their charter."

Ivan was not surprised to learn that the present leader of the Western world was perfectly happy to put Machiavelli's conniving principles of behavior into practice. He was sure the President's strategy of divorcing himself from Morrison would also exonerate him if the attempt on the lives of the caliphs failed.

After breakfast Ivan and Brooklyn were assigned to an office in the West Wing. Brooklyn sat down at her desk and began to sort herself out in her new work environment.

Meanwhile Ivan hurried off to the staff meeting, where the President introduced him to the people around the table. After the introductions were made, he launched into the affairs of the upcoming day. Ivan observed the members of the staff closely, as each made their contributions to the planning session. He felt he was a different sort of person than the others. They were all smart, but their intelligence was of a contemporary sort. He imagined how Plato would feel if he attended a MENSA meeting. Although there was no dearth of intelligence in the room, Ivan suspected there might still be a shortage of wisdom and perspective in this group of presidential advisors. Bismarck's observation that *Politics is the art of the possible* was to Ivan's mind too down-to-earth, and lacked the spiritual dimension that was so often the corollary of true greatness. Democracy sprouted healthy plants, but they still needed to have a sun to turn toward. The best Ivan could say about the staff meeting was that it was going to be a cloudy day, and if that was the case in Washington, he hated to think of what black holes of planning existed in the other capitals of the world.

At the conclusion of the meeting, Ivan returned to the sanctity of his temporary office in the West Wing. He was determined to stay out of politics as much as possible. He decided to stick with the planning and coordinating functions that Julia had hired him to do for the State Department. In his role as coordinator of the operation against the caliphs, he could put his two cents' worth in without having to play political games. He wasn't cynical enough or self-promoting enough to succeed as a politician. His intellect and his intuition about people were both very good, and therefore he was a considerable asset to a President, but he didn't believe that he could ever be President himself. His analytical ability enabled him to recognize the motivations of plotters. His good character enabled him to serve without compromising his own integrity. Because he was honest and not seeking to supplant his superiors, he was the ideal counselor to elected officials in high places, or as an advisor to influential political appointees. His talents, as it happened, had not been overlooked by either the President or the Secretary of State.

CHAPTER FORTY

Ivan's next days were totally involved with planning, coordinating, and visualizing the details of *Operation Act II*. He went from meeting to meeting, trying to make sure that no detail had been overlooked. Eventually a provisional time and date was set for putting the plan in motion. The strike would take place shortly after Muslim evening prayers on the last day of Ramadan. Evening meals would have been served, the caliphs' concubines would have arrived, and the atmosphere would be relaxed and comfortable, as another day out of the *Arabian Nights* came to an end.

It was agreed that Ivan should present the final arrangements to the President for his approval. A meeting was scheduled to be held in the Situation Room, and all those concerned with *Operation Act II* would signify assent and approval of the details that had most recently been worked out. The CIA was not invited.

When the venue of a meeting is the Situation Room in the White House and the attendees include the President, the Secretaries of State and Defense, the Chairman of the Joint Chiefs of Staff, and several generals, admirals, and their civilian peers, it is not easy for the youngest person in the room to feel himself worthy to lead the session. But that is exactly what the President had asked Ivan to do.

With a metal pointer in hand, he began by describing why the contemplated action was necessary. He said how much he wished that a diplomatic solution could have been found to the problem of Islamist terrorism. Having tried and failed for many years to negotiate a peaceful settlement with the Wahabist Muslims, the State Department was now in favor of a direct surgical strike to remove the deadly blight of terror that these caliphs had unleashed on the world. Ivan went on to review the developments that had made this time especially propitious for a military solution. First of all, there was the urgency created by the possible acquisition of a thermo-nuclear device by the terrorists. Secondly, the discovery and deciphering of the code hidden in the Koran, the unearthing of the caliphs' headquarters in Mecca, and the exposure of the double agent Richmond at the CIA—all these events made inaction impossible.

Ivan continued his presentation by explaining in detail how the mission was to be accomplished. He apologized if some of his instructions were a repeat of previous meetings, but he wanted to make absolutely sure that everyone present was on the same page. He laid out the entire plan, citing what would be done, how it would be done, and who would do it. When all that remained to be agreed upon was the precise day of the strike, he passed the pointer to General Black.

Black outlined the Army's reasons for wanting the operation to take place in the evening. There was some discussion about the day of the week that should be chosen, but in the end it was decided that *Operation Act II* should go forward on the coming Monday at 18:00 hours Mecca time, the final day of Ramadan. That schedule suited Ivan very well, as reports from the Middle East would start coming in at around noon on Monday. They would have the weekend to work out any last minute details before staging this real-life drama.

The President thanked everyone, and wished them God-speed. As the members of the inner circle left the room, several of them gave Ivan a pat on the back to signify that he had done a good job. Ivan prayed silently that they would still feel the same way after the operation.

As Julia passed by, she stopped for a moment to have a word with Ivan.

"The President told me he has filed you and Brooklyn away in the White House for safekeeping," she whispered. "He also mentioned that he arranged for bodyguards to keep an eye on Marina in Cambridge 24/7. I think that's a great idea. I hope we get Mitch Richmond soon. What a miserable wretch."

Ivan and Brooklyn worked for the rest of the day in the office, with a quick time-out for lunch. They both tried their various sources to see how the search for Richmond was progressing. In spite of all their efforts, they learned nothing that could be thought of as encouraging. Richmond seemed to have made a clean getaway—there was no trace of him anywhere.

Ivan was tempted to be angry about it. Why could all the resources of the greatest nation in the world not find one man? That was the trouble with the search for Bin Laden. That hunt had lasted for many years before it was finally successful. Ivan also felt that the U.S. had just gotten lucky when the troops found Saddam Hussein. Would finding Richmond be just a matter of luck, too? Ivan was not one to put his faith in luck, but he was even less inclined to put Marina's welfare into the hands of fate.

Marina's bodyguard in Cambridge had reported no suspicious activities. The men that had been arrested in Ivan's office had stuck to the story that they were just acting on the orders of their boss, Deputy Director Richmond of the CIA. No amount of careful interrogating had been able to shake the similar story of the replacement driver that Ivan had turned over to the Marines at the Pentagon. Apparently these men had turned out to be real employees of the CIA. These agents had not detected anything unusual in their tasks. To them, it was just business as usual.

If murder, violence, subterfuge, betrayal, and just plain evil were accepted as commonplace functions of a U.S.

government agency, how surprising was it, then, that foreign governments behaved in like fashion? Ivan wondered if men capable of the same malignity as those they opposed would ever even try to control the seemingly unlimited evil in the world.

He began to feel depressed. Were all the serious choices in life a question of picking the lesser evil?

Ivan was eager to find Richmond and also to monitor the progress of *Operation Act II*. He walked from the residence area of the White House to his temporary office area in the West Wing. Brooklyn was hard at work. She handed him his messages and continued what she was doing. Ivan had no idea what that was, but he trusted her enough to be willing to wait until she told him. Among the things that Ivan liked about his assistant were that she was never idle, never lazy, and never needed to be directed in her work. A few words of problem definition from Ivan were all she needed. He would just discuss a project, go about his business, and try not to interfere with the ensuing Herculean effort that Brooklyn applied to her work.

Brooklyn's commitment to her country and her job were legendary, but those with whom she came in contact who were less engaged by their government jobs disliked and feared her. Over time, mediocre government employees usually assumed that Brooklyn was being driven to her frantic work pace by mean, ambitious bosses. Her colleagues found it hard to imagine that anyone would voluntarily work that hard, and as a result her bosses' reputations as slave drivers grew to mythic proportions.

Ivan just shook his head, considering himself fortunate indeed to have such an able assistant. He thought about how he had unleashed law enforcement, the military, and the executive forces of government to bring them to bear on the world's problems. Now he had to stand back and wait to see if his prescribed treatments were indeed the correct ones. His favorite passage from the Psalms was, *Be still and know that I am God*, which translated into his present situation as, *be quiet and think about the big picture*.

Ivan sat quietly at his desk and pondered. Brooklyn knew by intuition that he needed time to himself. When he went into one of his trances she was especially diligent to protect him from interruptions while he ruminated about the complexities at hand.

The question of Richmond was particularly vexing. This guy could be anywhere, Ivan thought. But there was so much Arabic in his past connections that Ivan was willing to bet he would go to Saudi Arabia. He had been tied into intelligence operations for so long that he certainly would have prepared an exit strategy long ago.

Ivan had two thoughts about how a crafty double agent might plan his disappearance. The first was that Richmond would have set up an identity so that in an emergency he could disappear and slip into the waiting shell of that false personage. He would have thought of every possible detail, prepared all the documents, and arranged financial and passport affairs so that he could travel offshore using his other identity or identities.

The second idea was that Richmond would know that hiding in plain sight was the best way to disappear off the radar screens. The people working in the intelligence field would be aware of these tactics, but unfortunately most of those types worked for the CIA, and using their services to search for their ex-boss had to be excluded on the grounds that they might have been in collusion with Richmond in selling out the Agency. Ivan would have to turn elsewhere for help in the hunt for Richmond.

It was Sunday morning, and Ivan was just leaving the office of the Director of the FBI. The purpose of his visit had been to find out what progress was being made in the hunt for Richmond and also to learn how deeply the CIA had been compromised. It had been a bit more than a decade since Richmond had brought his pro-Arab skullduggery into the Agency. How many intelligence agents were privy to his idiosyncratic style of patriotism? With unlimited oil dollar financing, probably amounting to more than the entire budget of the CIA, Richmond had been able to corrupt the Agency. What if all the intelligence information about the Middle East had been vetted by Mitch Richmond before it reached the policy-making levels of government? Had U.S. foreign policy been compromised by false information supplied by a paid-off staff of traitors?

Ivan had not been very satisfied with the meeting. The Director, like all FBI agents, had been trained as a lawyer. Ivan could not immediately tell if his interrogative approach to their discussion was a cover-up for his lack of personal knowledge or just a mannerism born of being an investigator most of his life. For fifteen minutes Ivan rendered his autobiography in answer to the Director's probing, but when he had tried to reverse the tables to obtain some information about *him*, he was rebuffed in such a way as to make him feel that he was the only one who was ignorant of the great man's accomplishments.

Ivan knew in very general terms that the Director had overcome multiple hardships. He came from a poor family, graduated from a small, undistinguished college, and then obtained his law degree by attending evening classes in New York while he worked as a cop by day. After graduating at the top of his class in law school, he was accepted by the FBI training school in Quantico. He had risen through the ranks, working on some of the most important cases in the country. He had become the agent in charge of the New York City office of the FBI. His reputation was above reproach, and he was regarded as tough, thorough, and protective of his beloved Bureau. Ivan knew all that, and admirable as it was, it didn't tell him much about the man's ability to fence with the caliphs.

Ivan wondered if just being a tough cop from New York was enough preparation for dealing with the evil fanatics who were attempting to conquer the entire modern world, just as they had vanquished large parts of the ancient world so many times before. Could the man from the school of hard knocks compete with the devious caliphs who were brainwashing hordes of feckless young men whose dreams were to become martyrs for their cause?

By demonizing the West, the caliphs had managed to unify thousands of these disaffected youths all over the world, and there was going to be hell to pay. Successfully fighting neighborhood crime, though praiseworthy, still fell short of the experience needed to win the worldwide war for the souls of men.

Ivan was disappointed once again by the deplorable quality of leadership in the men running the government in Washington. Parker was droning on about how the FBI had thrown a blanket over the country from under which Mitch Richmond could not possibly escape. Ivan's money was on Richmond. He believed that Richmond was long gone. He knew that even the servant in the house of the wise knows more than the leader of the ignorant.

Richmond was working for the most diabolic villains in the world. They had kept themselves secret for centuries. It was foolishness to think he had learned nothing from his exposure to the caliphs. What Ivan didn't know, and now feared he would never learn, at least from Parker's FBI, was how many incipient Richmonds were left behind at the CIA.

It seemed to Ivan that Parker was using the mess at the CIA as a comparative foil to demonstrate the lofty virtues of the Bureau. Parker did not want to sort things out at the Intelligence Agency. He was more interested in seeing if his turf could be expanded while the CIA was in a vulnerable position.

Ivan was disappointed. Was no one capable of seeing the big picture without putting himself in the foreground? So many times the interests of the Arabs were in concert with those of special interest groups in the United States. Each time the price of oil went up it also benefited the sellers, refiners, and distributors. Why had so little effort been expended to find out if there were illegal linkages between the oil interests in the Gulf and those in America?

Political trouble is the fuel that sustains high oil prices and enriches the sheikhs and the oil companies. Islam is the yeast that keeps the fermentation process bubbling. As long as there is fermentation in the Middle East, the profits roll into the coffers of the oil magnates on both sides of the Atlantic.

The cost of the conflict between Islam and the West was staggering. The cost to the average Arab of having billions of dollars in profits skimmed off for the personal use of their leaders is only exceeded by the costs incurred by Americans to defend against Islamist terrorism. If Ivan had only one contribution to make while he was with the government, it would be to focus politics on ideas, facts, and principles, and not on profits, special interest groups, and greed.

Ivan did not believe that the Bureau would ever catch Richmond. He could see that the Director would never openly share information with him, so Ivan just thanked the man for his time and left. To expect that an agency working for the Justice Department, a domestically-oriented legal organization, could sift the world and locate an international spymaster was the height of optimism. It seemed to him that the FBI had been chosen to conduct this investigation for the very reason that it was unlikely to succeed. He wondered if the President had made this choice on his own, or if he had been advised by a self-interested party. And if so, who might that be?

As he returned to his interim office in the West Wing, Ivan permitted his mind to do a bit of *what iffing*. What if the fabulous wealth of oil rich Islam had been brought to bear on senior administration officials, and as a result the President had been given some very bad advice? Ivan was feeling good about the fact that since *Operation Playwright* had been scrubbed he had told no one that a successor mission was planned except the Secretary of State, the Joint Chiefs, the President, and those who would actually carry out the raid. He felt he could trust these individuals, but what if he were wrong?

He decided to clear his calendar so he could be in the Situation Room when *Act II* began, which, if everything went according to plan, would be in one hour. He called David Feingold to see if there had been any changes in the coded messages coming from Mecca.

"Nope. No changes," said David. "We're all set to go. All we have to do is press the *send* button. Is this call about turning us loose? Because if you're wondering about us, I can assure you we're ready to go. All you have to do is give us the word."

"Just hold on a little bit longer. I'll let you know when it's time."

When Ivan entered the Situation Room, there was a hushed buzz among those present. The great majority of the observers were military personnel of the highest rank. The expected presence of the President, the Vice President, the Secretary of Defense and the Secretary of State gave the meeting austerity and a sense of purpose.

The buzz stopped instantly and everyone stood to attention when the President entered the room and took his seat. In his role as Commander-in-Chief, he ordered them to be at ease. Everyone knew this was an event that required absolute secrecy. Nobody had missed the significance of exploding a neutron weapon in a foreign land, and especially in the hallowed site of the Muslim heartland. Even though the U.S. would feign innocence, the world would still suspect American involvement. No one in the room was unaware of the risks involved. The critical moment came when the Chairman of the Joint Chiefs announced to the august gathering that all systems were go and awaiting the President's order to proceed.

The President stood tall, paused a moment to achieve full effect, and then said, "Send the order to proceed."

PART THREE

Mecca, Saudi Arabia

CHAPTER FORTY-ONE

Slowly, in the dark of night, the silhouette of a U.S. submarine surfaced in the Red Sea. The crew stealthily launched a motorized, inflatable boat, loaded with equipment. A team of six black-clad Navy Seals clambered aboard, and the small boat pulled away from the larger vessel. The submarine gradually sank back down into the water, leaving no trace of its outline in the murky seascape.

The Seals pointed their skiff to the east and headed toward the island-dotted shores of Saudi Arabia. The specially insulated motor was almost silent. The young men had been trained not to communicate verbally with one another when on the water, as voices carry very clearly over large distances. One of the Seals held a satellite navigation instrument as they homed in on their pre-selected location—a deserted, dune-spotted spit of land on the mainland that lay only a hundred yards from the north-south coastal road. The seaward islands overlapped, hiding the chosen landing site from vantage points at sea.

As their boat approached land the Seals, operating in silent running mode, heard the voices of what appeared to be some fishermen coming from nearby. The voices were magnified by the water, so that they seemed closer than they really were. So much so, in fact, that the Seals were actually able to make out some of the conversation.

It soon became clear that they were not fishermen at all, but arms smugglers using a fishing boat as cover. The men were heading west, taking their contraband cargo to Sudan, on the opposite side of the Red Sea.

It was obvious that the gun-runners were not aware of the presence of the Seals. Their jovial conversation indicated to the Seal's team leader, Lieutenant Mercer, that they were engaged in a routine ferrying trip and had made the crossing many times before. They were relaxed and unsuspecting.

Lieutenant Mercer would have loved to sink their boat with its deadly cargo, but he and his men had to concentrate on their own mission. The two vessels passed each other in the dark, as each pursued its separate goal.

Silently and without speaking a word, the Seals pulled their boat up onto the shore behind the dune that separated them from the road. They removed their gear and weapons, and covered the boat with a camouflaged, sand-colored tarp. Then they made their way to the road, looking for a truck that had been left for them by an embassy employee in Riyadh. The truck was to be painted in Aramco colors, but it was to have no actual markings or signage to indicate that it was, in fact, a truck belonging to the national oil company of Arabia.

The Seals moved quietly down the road in search of the truck they would drive to their next stop. The men longed to chat with one another along the way and compare notes about their various observations, but there was absolutely no question of their indulging in any sort of spoken communication yet. Attracting attention or arousing suspicion could quickly put an end to their important mission and result in their immediate deaths.

After they had located the vehicle they approached it stealthily, only to find two thieves in the process of stealing it. Two of the Seals quickly stripped off their black coveralls, revealing that they were wearing Saudi army uniforms underneath. Carrying their automatic weapons at the ready, the two men walked along the road speaking casually in Arabic, as though they were doing a routine patrol. The thieves heard them coming and hurriedly disappeared into the bushes.

The two Seals stood guard over the truck in case the thieves returned. When the coast was clear, they signaled to the remaining Seals to board the vehicle. Four of the men scrambled into the back of the truck where they couldn't be seen. They, too, removed their coveralls in favor of the Saudi uniforms they wore underneath. Lieutenant Mercer and Chief Petty Officer Pugni put on traditional Arab robes over their Saudi military officers' regalia and got into the cab of the truck.

Mercer pulled the ignition key out of his aba and started the engine. Pugni pounded on the bulkhead three times with his fist and received three similar signals, indicating that the team in the back was ready to go. All the gear, clothing, and ammo had been put in the horizontal portable locker where they had transported their equipment and had been safely clamped to the bulkhead with load bars. The team was sitting on the floor of the truck with their weapons on their laps.

Mercer put the truck in gear and snapped on the head-lights. Several sets of eyes reflected the truck's beams. The lieutenant threw the truck into first gear, made a hard left turn into the road, and headed south toward Mecca. In the rear view mirror he saw several Arabs shaking their rifles at the truck as it left them behind in the dust.

"We've only been in the country for five minutes and already we've met smugglers and thieves," Mercer said to the Chief. "I don't think this part of the country will attract many tourists."

Pugni laughed. "We could have been in two firefights by this time. We might have had to scrub the mission, or we could have been dead, too. Who knows? My mom used to love saying that man proposes but God disposes. She said it in Italian, though."

"Well, you better sit back and pray that God disposes that we get to survive this mission," Mercer said.

"We've got a long ride ahead of us," Pugni remarked.

"Yeah, well there's no rush. We don't want to get to Mecca while they're all saying their evening prayers."

"Why's that?"

"The square would be full of Muslims celebrating the last day of Ramadan. We don't want to get tangled up with a whole crowd of people. That's the last thing we want."

"You're right. After the square clears out they'll all go home and make whoopee with their women, right?"

"Something like that, I guess."

"Well, I sure could do with a little whoopee."

"Quit your griping, Pugni. We've got work to do."

The strategic plan called for the Ka'bah square to be as empty as possible. But in spite of their good planning they had already encountered two unscheduled surprises—the gun runners and the truck thieves. Mercer and Pugni hoped there would be no more unforeseen occurrences for the balance of the mission. But come what might, these particular Seals had been especially chosen for their skill in dealing with the unexpected.

The truck proceeded along the bumpy road to the city of Jeddah. When it finally arrived at its destination, it pulled up next to a nondescript black car that was parked on a quiet street near the bus station. Mercer and Pugni scanned the street and found it deserted. The Chief switched places with the Lieutenant and became the driver. They banged on the bulkhead. The four Seals jumped out of the truck and got into the black car, then the two vehicles took off in tandem toward the city of Mecca.

CHAPTER FORTY-TWO

At precisely 19:00 hours the five-ton truck resembling an ARAMCO vehicle pulled into the Ka'bah Square in Mecca and rumbled up to the giant mosque, pausing by the large delivery door which received all the construction materials used in the ongoing building projects. Lieutenant Mercer, dressed in the traditional Arab aba and red and white headdress, got out of the truck and went inside the mosque, carrying some delivery documents.

Chief Petty Officer Pugni, also dressed the same way as his passenger, backed the truck up to the receiving door. In a few minutes it swung up on its hinges and Mercer could be seen opening the back door of the truck. The driver got out from behind the wheel and walked to the back of the truck to help him unload. Everyone, including some Arabs on the loading dock, moved around nonchalantly. There was some friendly chitchat in Arabic between the delivery personnel and the receivers on the dock.

After a short while a forklift appeared from inside the building and drove into the truck box. It reappeared with its long tines placed under a large pallet that contained a piece of machinery covered in canvas. The forklift backed out of the truck slowly, the operator looking over his shoulder as he carefully moved his heavy load into the building.

The documentation that had accompanied the delivery of the machine specifically dictated that the air-conditioning unit be put inside the entrance to the tunnel under the Ka'bah. The driver and the man who would help him unload the equipment walked alongside the forklift as it laboriously made its way into a wide tunnel that led down to an elegant, iron-strapped wooden door.

The forklift operator brought his vehicle to a halt outside the service entrance, climbed down from his seat, and knocked on the door. A minute later a large sliding peephole opened, revealing the face of an Arab servant who looked over the scene before opening the entryway. He accepted the documents from the truck driver, and was about to sign for the delivery when he stopped and looked at Mercer.

"I have no instructions that an air-conditioning unit was to be expected. I must ask someone if this equipment has been sent to the right place."

"I work for ARAMCO," said Mercer in Arabic, "and my boss received a call from the imam requesting that as a favor to the work of Allah, we deliver this air-conditioning unit to the Ka'bah tunnel entrance at no charge. I've still got a lot of work to do this evening, so why don't we just leave this unit here in the entranceway. The installers are coming in the morning to connect it. If there are any questions about where it goes you chaps can straighten it out then, okay?"

The doorkeeper thought for a minute, then agreed that it would do no harm if it remained in the lobby entrance until morning. He didn't want to disturb the higher-ups over such a small matter, so he signed the receipt, opened the door, and allowed the forklift to place the equipment on the floor off to one side.

The two-man delivery team uncovered the machinery in order to take the tarpaulin away with them. The driver explained that the cover belonged to ARAMCO and had been lent to cover the air-conditioner crate in which it had been shipped from the U.S. The receiver looked at the equipment, saw that it was brand new, and decided that if such an expensive piece of equipment had not been ordered, no delivery man in Saudi Arabia would simply leave it there and go away.

The two men folded the tarp and laid it on the forklift, and then stood on the tines as the forklift operator lifted them a foot off the ground, turned the machine around, and headed back up the ramp with his passengers standing one on each prong. In back they could hear the great door slam shut behind them.

The forklift operator stopped at the receiving door to let his passengers off with the folded tarp, which they casually placed on the truck floor. Then the delivery men closed the truck box doors and nonchalantly climbed into the cab. They drove away slowly and as quietly as possible, out of respect for the holiest place in Islam.

There were only a few people visible in the huge square. It was just after evening prayer time on the last day of Ramadan, and it was also dinnertime for most Arabs.

When they were a block away from the square, they pulled the truck over next to the black car. The four Seals in Saudi army uniforms got out of the car and clambered into the back of the truck. The truck turned around and headed back toward the square, stopping on the periphery.

Mercer opened a large cardboard box that was on the seat between Pugni and himself, and they slipped out of their abas. Mercer removed gas masks, breathing tanks, gloves and head-to-toe plastic body coverings from the box and they put them on, slinging automatic weapons of late vintage around their necks.

He knocked three times on the bulkhead wall that divided the cab and the truck box. He received three knocks in return. Inside the truck, the four men put on similar protective gear that they removed from the equipment box located against the headboard. The men in the cab looked at each other and gave a thumbs-up.

Mercer reached into the truck's ashtray and pulled out a small device resembling a TV remote with a small aerial. He pointed it in the direction of the Ka'bah, depressed a red button and waited.

In a second or two a deep rumbling sound similar to an earthquake erupted from the bowels of the earth beneath them. Pugni slapped the truck into gear and drove quickly toward the receiving door of the Ka'bah. He backed up to the loading dock and knocked four times on the bulkhead. Mercer jumped out and ran to open the truck doors.

The four men in Saudi uniforms were now covered from head to toe, as was the Lieutenant. One Seal was delegated to stand guard at the receiving door to block any Arabs who might come to investigate the underground commotion.

Mercer and Pugni had been inside before, so they knew the way. They entered the receiving door next to the loading door. The receiving door was always open so that truck drivers could go in to announce their arrival and clear paper work.

There was no sign of anyone moving inside the truck entranceway. The five men trotted down the ramp to the big door. It was locked from the inside. The leader pounded on the door. No one came. One of the men placed charges of plastic explosives on the hinges of the big door. The five men retreated from the door, staying close to the ground. From this distance they then detonated the shaped charge that blew the big door off its hinges.

The five Seals ran to the caliph's quarters. They searched every room as they came to them. No survivors were found. The neutron weapon had functioned perfectly. Nothing had been destroyed. The only sign of an attack were the bent door hinges, some contorted pipes on the air conditioner, and the corpses. In the deepest part of the underground head-quarters they found three apartments and a large electronics room containing the latest available equipment.

The electronics center might have been affected adversely by the neutron burst, but the Special Forces Seal team didn't want to take a chance that the equipment could be used again, so they planted a time-delayed explosive device, collected the loose papers and notebooks in a large plastic bag, and shut the heavy metal door that was designed to keep enemies out. This kept the plastic explosive blast inside the room, thereby protecting the Ka'bah that was on the street level just above.

One of the members of the Seal assault team ran into each apartment and located three corpses of caliphs and a fourth unidentified man who seemed to be a visitor. He obtained a sample of each one's DNA and secured the samples in a special kit he was carrying around his waist for the purpose. These men had been trained to absorb visual impressions quickly so that they could repeat the details when they were debriefed back in Washington. It had been four minutes since they had entered the underground headquarters. It was time to go.

They ran up the ramp and out the door. They had been tempted to peel off the protective gear before leaving the building, but fortunately they had not done so, for when they got out the door, they found their colleague shouting at the imam, his mullahs and some servants, telling them that there had been a terrorist nuclear explosion and they should under no circumstances go down that ramp. The man in the officer's uniform told the imam that he had to take his men to be scrubbed down for radioactive contamination immediately. He also told the imam that he had radioed the Army, and they would be arriving soon. He, in fact, had not put out any such call.

He ordered the five plastic-shrouded men to board the truck, and it took off rapidly across the square. The Special Forces men quickly shed their protective gear in the back of the truck. When they arrived back at the car they felt and heard a muffled thud, which was the time-delayed explosion they had planted in the electronic equipment room.

Four of the men got into the car, and the lieutenant climbed back into the passenger seat in the truck. All the men wore Saudi Army uniforms, and those who weren't driving carried weapons on their laps.

The car, followed by the truck, took the road west toward the Red Sea. At Jeddah, about 45 miles from Mecca, they would find the road that went north toward Medina. Ten miles further along the coastal road the two vehicles pulled off and headed to the water's edge. They approached the small archipelago of low, uninhabited islands named Ra's Hadjibah, where they had hidden their boat the previous night. They left the truck by the side of the road.

"Now the thieves can steal it if they like," Mercer said to himself. He was certain that they could make the vehicle disappear better than anybody. But before abandoning it he made sure his companions removed every trace of any gear that could connect the vehicle with the incident in Mecca.

They stripped off their Saudi uniforms and put them in the box with the air bottles, protective clothing, and the other weapons and equipment that they had brought with them. They removed the load bars that were keeping the box in place, and two of the Seals carried the box to the rubber boat that the other Seals had meanwhile uncovered. Four men carried the boat to the water's edge, and the other two set the box athwartships, resting it on the gunnels. They pulled the rubber boat deeper into the water and jumped in one after the other. They paddled out until they were half a mile offshore, then the Squad Leader started the engine.

They skimmed around the sand islands, heading on a westerly course further out into the Red Sea. The Chief held his portable GPS in one hand, and steered the boat toward their rendezvous. At precisely ten o'clock a submarine surfaced, picked the party up, and submerged again. Inside the sub Lieutenant Mercer told the Communications Officer to send a coded message to the Admiral in the Situation Room at the White House: *Scene One of Act II well received by the audience.*

When their work was finished, the Seals enjoyed a beer in the ward room. They were glad for the chance to be speaking English now with the crew. For the past two days they had been moving silently, adhering to pre-arranged hand signals, performing a mission they had rehearsed many times. They toasted their success, and agreed it was a perfect Navy Seal operation.

Washington D.C.

Back in the Situation Room, the brass had not yet received word from the Seals. They had been given some intelligence reports about an explosion in Mecca that had registered on military seismic equipment, so they were pretty sure the neutron bomb had been set off. Two smaller detonations, however, had occurred within minutes of the first big one. It was not yet clear what had caused these smaller explosions, so the matter was being busily discussed by those who were waiting for the final news about the Seals' mission. Then suddenly the message was received that *Act II, Scene I* had been a success.

Jubilant, spontaneous cheering erupted in the Situation Room. When the din subsided, Ivan addressed the august group and requested permission to begin *Scene II*. This phase of the operation was to send the coded orders for terrorists to attack in those places in the world where Islamist jihadist cells operated. Pre-warned international forces were waiting for the opportunity to kill or capture the terrorists. They had decapitated the snake, and now they would clean up the body.

The President, feeling full of confidence now that *Scene I* had been a success, gave the executive order to begin *Scene II*. Ivan put in a call to David Feingold.

"All right David, the President has given the order to start *Scene II*, so push the button, and let's get rid of terrorism. What do you say?"

"I say let's get on with it."

"Keep in touch, and I'll do the same."

The Situation Room was now in a proactive mode. Hundreds of small battles were going to be fought, and the prosecution and coordination of these mini-wars at the operations level would be carried out in the Pentagon with the command and control function being handled in the Situation Room.

Ivan figured that he would be incredibly busy for the next two weeks. The fanatics would be coaxed out of their hiding places first in Iraq and Afghanistan, where American military forces would deal with them, and then in other countries, many of them as yet unaware of the presence of the cell groups. But the appropriate national security forces would intercept and handle the terrorists wherever they were found. They might not get them all, but terrorism would receive a massive blow. The State Department was going to be occupied as well, issuing carefully-worded denials, and pledging to help arrest the perpetrators.

Now that the die had been cast, the most desired result of Ivan's plan was that the Muslim rulers of the Islamic states should see the attack in Mecca as a sort of godsend. Cleaning out the only potential threats to their hegemony must be made to appear to be a good thing from their perspective. The explanation of choice for interpreting the explosion in Mecca was that it had come about as a result of a newly-acquired tactical atomic weapon being accidentally detonated by Jihadist terrorists. No information to the contrary need ever leak out of Mecca, where the Arab press was totally under the control of the House of Saud. Who else but fearless Arab patriots would have the steely nerves necessary to put their headquarters under the Ka'bah? The royal house eliminates a threat to its existence without having to disrespect or arrest any Muslim citizens.

An incident such as this should certainly signify to the people that governing was for Muslim politicians, but not the clerics. There was no doubt that the clerics were behind the violence. How else could these impassioned but untrained nuclear-age warriors exist literally right under the Ka'bah without full cooperation from the fundamentalist clergy? Ivan wholeheartedly believed it was too audacious a con for the masters of historical deceit to resist. In one gloriously inspired stroke, Allah had delivered the solution to their hegemony problems caused by the obstinate fundamentalist clerics competing for temporal power to go along with their already overbearing spiritual influence. This would end the clamoring for a caliphate, and return comity to the citizenry.

He would spend the next few weeks monitoring every communication between the Muslim governments and the U.S. State Department. The Arabs would blame whomever they wished for the massacre in Mecca, but it was Ivan's job to make them wish to blame fundamentalist Islam. This was the third and final scene of *Act II* that Ivan had envisioned when he first pitched the operation to the President. The Arab leaders had to conclude that the explosion in Mecca was related to Islamist extremism, or the play would not have a happy ending, and the epilogue he had written for the President would ring false and make the production a failure.

The Situation Room was a happy place, and most of the participants were in a self-congratulatory mood. The staffers that remained would monitor events and notify their bosses if any important developments occurred before the next meeting. The Seal team would be arriving in Washington the next day for debriefing, and Ivan wanted to be there. Until then, there was probably going to be a temporary lull. Ivan wanted to use this time to get a few things done. He sidled over to Julia before she followed the President out of the Situation Room.

"Madame Secretary, may I have a few minutes of your time?"

"Of course, Ivan," Julia said. "But before you start talking to me about whatever it is, I would just like to thank you personally for your creative work on this operation. I realize that most of this mission came about as a result of your work. It's too bad that due to its secret nature the nation will never know about it, nor will the people ever be able to express their gratitude to you. However, that doesn't prevent me from saying thank you. You're a model of the very best of American heroism. You're humble, you avoid any efforts to seek fame, you do what's right even when it's difficult and distasteful, and you dispense justice without malice. You're an admirable man, Ivan. I'm proud to have you in my department, and I want you to know that you are esteemed even though you don't seek celebrity. No, let me correct myself—you're esteemed *because* you don't seek celebrity. Now, what was it you wanted to speak to me about?"

"Thank you for the kind words," Ivan said. "Although you may not think me so kind after you've heard what I have to say. I don't need to remind you that until the President's investigative panel has completed its work on the CIA, we won't know to what extent the remnants of Richmond's influence remains. We must be certain that no leaks about our part in the Mecca affair ever occur. In order to guarantee our control of this information, I'd like to read all direct communications between our government and the Islamic nations before they are sent out."

"I see," Julia said. "Unfortunately, Ivan, I'm afraid that would impinge too strongly upon my jurisdiction. I can assure you that I will stay on top of America's diplomatic interests in the Middle East. In the meantime, you may continue to coordinate the efforts of the military to remove the terrorist cells. If you wish to ensure your input into our diplomacy concerning the Middle East, write a short position paper that summarizes the five or ten most important factors that you feel are most likely to influence the region in the vacuum left by the departure of the caliphs. When you have done that, we can construct a policy that will help bring this region back into the sphere of political modernity."

Ivan realized that Julia had cut him down to size. It was gently done, but it was a reproof nevertheless. When he thought about it, Ivan understood that he had overstepped his bounds. It was fatuous of him to think he could control the entire diplomatic correspondence between twenty some odd Islamic countries and the State Department of the United States. The way that Julia had handled his foolish request indicated that she understood how he worked. She might have observed that he preferred to do things himself. She might also have suspected that his desire to do it all himself came from an innate confidence that he could do it better than other people, and therefore he didn't trust them to do the job correctly. Was his nature so transparent that Julia could read him like a book? Actually he approved of the project she had assigned to him. It was a much better use of his skills, and as he thought about it, he came to like it more and more. He was about to say something, but Julia just looked him in the eye, smiled, winked, and walked away as though she had read his mind.

Ivan returned to his office. He spent the remainder of the day searching the Arab media for a report about the explosion in Mecca. There was no mention of the incident by the Arab press or any other international press. Sometimes he wished he could turn off the spigot of media information as completely as the Arab leaders did.

Ivan could imagine the consternation that was taking place in Riyadh as the Royal leaders tried to deal with the challenges posed by the affair in Mecca. He was counting on them to choose the reaction that was most likely to benefit the tenure of the 6,000 members of the royal family. He was certain they would choose to offload the terrorists from the retinue of Islamist dissenters they were always tolerating so as not to provoke a revolution. If Ivan spotted a report of the Mecca explosion in the newspapers or on the television, he would know what the rulers were thinking because no items got into the newspapers that were not approved by the Princes of Saud. He didn't think they could ignore the affair, because too many people had seen and heard the commotion.

There were deaths to be accounted for, and blame must be assigned to a credible source other than the government.

The recent rumors that the terrorists had acquired a nuclear weapon provided a wonderful opportunity for the governing family to pin responsibility for the blast on the extremist Islamist fighters and their clerical inciters. The site of the explosion was in itself a fortuitous thing for the royals, as they could emphasize the gall of the jihadists in choosing to operate in the heart of Islam, in the holy of holies, where they would surely be safe from foreign foes.

Ivan wished that he could write in Arabic so that he could publish the definitive article affixing the blame on the violent fundamentalists, and praising Allah and the royal family for their policies that elevated Islam and the peaceful faithful to new heights of prosperity.

CHAPTER FORTY-THREE

After a lonely night in the Lincoln room, Ivan was looking forward to the debriefing session with the heroic Navy Seals. Anticipation was in the air in the Situation Room as one by one the members of the august assembly reconvened. The President entered last of all, and everyone in the room stood at attention until he told them to be seated. The six-man special operations team of Navy Seals in their dress uniforms was seated at a table in the front of the room. Off to the side, at another table, were three senior operations officers from the Special Forces—an Army colonel, a Marine colonel and a Navy captain. These officers were to conduct the debriefing. Everyone else in the room was there out of curiosity, and because they ranked high enough to be invited.

The Chairman of the Joint Chiefs called the meeting to order. He outlined the purpose of the gathering, reminding everyone present that the procedures followed would be in accordance with the usual debriefing protocols, which meant that the three operations officers at the table in the front of the room would ask all the initial questions. At the end of the regular briefing there would be time for questions from others in the room.

The six men to be questioned looked uncomfortable in their dress uniforms as they awaited the start of the inquiry. They would have preferred to go on another mission rather than sit around discussing the past with senior officers, and especially with the President in attendance. Mercer, the lieutenant, had been the team leader, and he knew he was the one who would have to answer for any shortcomings that the brass felt had occurred. He had been number one in his graduating class at Annapolis. To be one of the 1,200 accepted annually by the Naval Academy out of the 50,000 applicants was a distinction in and of itself, but to be first academically was not so much an honor as a burden for Mercer. The stress of his achievement came immediately after graduation when he chose to enter the Navy Seals instead of pursuing a more traditional naval career path, as advised by his more conventional instructors.

Lieutenant Robert Mercer didn't choose the Seals because he was a masochist, or because he was a gung-ho warrior type of man. His choice of the Navy Seals came about as a thoughtful rejection of the other alternatives. He shied away from becoming a pilot because he didn't like flying. He rejected the idea of becoming a fleet officer because he felt that aside from aircraft carriers and submarines, the tin can Navy was finished in modern warfare. The things he liked most about the Navy were the command structure, the history, and the effects of sea power on world politics; in other words, the people side of the military. Mercer preferred not to wait long periods between assignments, and he wanted to lead men as soon as possible. He wanted to command a small group of men right away, rather than wait years to command large contingents of sailors.

In the four years that he had been in the Seals he had gained notice among his senior officers for his abilities to plan and lead tactical missions, and he had been promoted as a result. His selection to head up the caliph mission was not a difficult one for his superiors. He had attended and excelled at every school from bombs and weapons, Psy/Ops, Arabic language, electronics, and further officer's training classes. He had been on missions in Afghanistan and Iraq, and was now a Seal commander in line for promotion. He had hand-picked his team, and its success was primarily due to his competence as an officer. He was the natural choice to be the spokesman for the team.

The Navy captain, because he was from the same branch of service as the Seal team, had been chosen to lead the debriefing. He asked Lt. Mercer to describe the mission in his own words from beginning to end. By way of a prologue, Mercer began by complimenting the ingenious designer of the mission. He told the group that he had never participated in any action that was so well thought out, right down to the least detail. He claimed that he was not just sucking up, because he had no idea who had originated the idea or why it was referred to as *Act II.*

Ivan was a bit red-faced when Mercer praised the anonymous planner, because most of the people in attendance knew he had been 90% responsible for the operation. As Mercer described how they had landed on the beach in the dark, hidden their boat, and moved inland to Mecca in the car and truck that had been left for their use, Ivan's mind was formulating the questions he thought might not be asked by others. Mercer continued his expert narrative of the mission in a capable military fashion. He explained that each team member had an area of specialized training, such as photography, computers, medical technologies, and the like. Ivan appreciated the man's no-nonsense way of presenting the unfolding of his play.

Mercer's understated description of his team's waltz with the devil in the bowels of the Ka'bah had the stamp of the true hero about it. Like any great cast of dancers, Mercer's troupe had the benefit of having a creative choreographer, and so the performers made the work look easy. Ivan knew it had not been as easy as this modern day hero made it seem. Ivan's literary background searched for a heroic rendition that would sound more like Beowulf than the military code. He would not get it in this theater, but in Ivan's mind the saga of this officer and his men was worthy of a much more flamboyant leading man than Mercer's practicality would allow him to be.

During the question period the Army colonel took the microphone and introduced himself. Then he turned to Mercer and thanked him for his presentation and for the successful mission that he had led in Mecca.

"I have one question," said the colonel. "You were not under direct orders to destroy the communications room, so why did you set the plastic explosive and detonate it?"

This was one of Ivan's questions, too. He was concerned that two explosions could not be made to look like an accident.

"I admit that it was a spontaneous command decision," said Mercer, "and I accept total responsibility for it. My men were only following my orders. The logic behind my decision was that the room contained the heart of the terrorist communication systems, and it was too important a target to pass up. I felt that if the Arabs asked any questions about the second explosion, a case could be made that the terrorists had a pre-timed scuttling device that was set off automatically by the neutron explosion. What's more," he continued, "we had already gathered up whatever hard copies of information were in the room prior to the explosion. We took photos of the room, and removed the hard drives from the computers."

Mercer produced a large duffel bag full of papers, drives, photos and notebooks, and asked that intelligence experts analyze the material. The bag was turned over to the Chief of Naval Intelligence.

The next questions dealt with the bodies that the Seal team discovered after the first explosion.

"How many corpses did you find?" asked the Marine Colonel.

"I counted twenty-one bodies, sir," said the Chief Petty Officer, who had been trained as a medic after becoming a Navy Seal.

"How were you able to tell which of the bodies could be identified as belonging to the caliphs?" the Marine Colonel wanted to know.

"We found three separate apartments down there," said the NCO. "They were furnished like something out of the Arabian Nights—lots of pillows and silk fabrics everywhere. Inside two of the apartments we found bearded Arab males about forty years of age. In the third apartment we found one bearded Arab man about fifty years of age, and one clean shaven man that appeared to be a Westerner in a Brooks Brothers suit.

"Well, exactly how did you conclude that three of these men were the caliphs?" the colonel asked.

"The clothing, the jewelry on the bodies, the luxurious harem feel of the place, and the absence of this level of opulence in the other rooms. This convinced us that these three were the caliphs. There were no other living quarters, so we concluded that the other people worked there, but didn't live there."

"What were the lab samples you collected down there?"

"DNA samples," said the Chief. "I was ordered to take samples, and I was given a kit to keep the samples straight."

"What were the DNA samples for?" the colonel asked.

"I wondered about that myself, sir."

"Is there someone in this room who was responsible for the planning of this mission who can answer that question?" the Colonel asked, looking around the room.

Ivan stood up and said, "The idea could be described as forward-looking forensics. The caliphs claim to be direct descendents of Muhammad, but obviously we'll never have a control sample of Muhammad's DNA, so no one will ever be able to substantiate their claims that way. But we thought if we had enough DNA from enough would-be caliphs, we might be able to see some correlations. Anyway, we had this once-in-a-lifetime opportunity to collect the DNA sequences of these claimants, so we took it. We intend to bank the sequences and hold them for future use. None of us knows what the science of the future will develop, but I felt it was better to have them than not to have them."

"Thank you, Dr. Welland," the colonel said.

He directed his next question to the Chief. "What did you make of the fourth man, the one in Western dress?"

"We don't know exactly what he was doing there. He had no I.D., so we have no way of knowing who he was. Only Muslims are allowed in Mecca, so this man must have had a special dispensation from the caliphs to be there."

"Were there any other physical anomalies that you noticed, Lieutenant?"

"Well, sir, I noticed that one of the caliphs had two recent bullet wounds in his chest. He seemed to be the one in charge. The head caliph, I guess you would say, sir. He was slumped over on a very ornate sort of throne. Or at least, it looked like a throne."

As soon as Ivan heard him say that, he began to think that the man in question might be Imam Mansur. If so, he would be relieved to know he was not a killer, after all. He made a note to remind himself to examine the photos closely when they came around.

At this point the Navy captain took over the questioning from the Marine Colonel. He directed some technical questions at Lieutenant Mercer about the sub's performance, the landing craft's suitability, and how it was that his team had not had to fire a single shot during the entire mission.

"It was due to the impeccable timing and planning of the operation," said Mercer. "It was the most important mission I have ever been on, and yet it was just like a walk-through rehearsal. We were in a square that holds two million Muslims making their hadj during Ramadan, but at the time of the attack there were only a handful of people there. That was because the attack took place on the last day of fasting for Ramadan, right after evening prayer time for Muslims. It's the traditional feast of *Eid ul Fitr* that ends the month of fasting. I'm sure there were no Arabs in all of Mecca who weren't feeding their faces at that time. That's what I mean by excellent timing. I'd like to buy the guy who planned this operation a drink."

Julia smiled at Lieutenant Mercer. "Although various people contributed to the plan," she said, "I think we can all agree that Dr. Welland should be the recipient of that drink offer. He was the one who discovered the existence of the caliphs, broke their code, and planned their demise, which you and your team executed with such professionalism."

The President thanked everyone for their efforts. He praised the Seals for their heroism, for a job well done, and their service to their country. Then he adjourned the meeting.

Lieutenant Mercer approached Ivan and said, "Well, how about that drink now? I really meant what I said."

Ivan accepted the offer gladly. He was sincere in his high regard for these men, who had walked into the mouth of the lion and returned alive to tell the tale. Although Richmond's henchmen might still be gunning for him, he couldn't visualize being unsafe in the company of the Navy Seals. Nevertheless, he took his pistol with him when they left the White House.

The seven men settled into the comfortable leather chairs in the remotest corner of the bar on Pennsylvania Avenue. Ivan felt a strong kinship with them. He had been spending most of his time of late working with people considerably older than he was, and he was very pleased to be among peers. He was especially glad to be accepted by them as an equal. The male camaraderie shared with these brave men was a tonic for him after his depressing bouts with Imam Mansur, Inspector Leshenko, and Mitch Richmond, the Deputy Director of the CIA.

When they had had a sufficiency of beer, the Navy Seals walked Ivan back to the White House. They had been awarded leave time, and were on their way to their various hometowns. Ivan was going back to work, and sadly his wife would not be there to greet him. As he shook hands with each of the team members, Ivan thought he could feel the warmth of comradeship in each sturdy hand that he grasped. He would especially miss Lieutenant Mercer, who was called "the Admiral" by his men. It was easy to understand why, as Ivan was sure this fearless, intelligent, and patriotic young Navy Seal would one day, in fact, be an admiral in his own right.

CHAPTER FORTY-FOUR

Back in his temporary office, Ivan knew he could not rest on his laurels. The most important thing at that time was for him to monitor carefully the mopping-up operations against the terrorist cells all over the world. He must also keep his eye on the leaders of the Islamic nations to see how they were going to react to the affair in Mecca. If the leaders, and their lackeys in the Arab press, took an active part in rounding up the extremists and withdrawing the sub-rosa toleration they had shown them for years, then, and only then, could the war on terrorism be won.

There was ample evidence to convince the world that Islamist fanatics were highly organized. The broken code, the electronic messaging, the caliphs' headquarters in Mecca, and the statistical correlation between the messages and the attacks, were sufficient to convince any fair-minded person that there was a centrally-controlled terrorist organization at work in the world whose intention was to install a new Islamic caliphate. The evidence was irrefutable, and more corroboration was on the way.

Scene II called for the release of a huge number of coded messages ordering terrorist cells to attack targets that the security and military forces had pre-selected as the sites for effective ambushes. When the Navy Seals confirmed that the attack on the caliphs had begun, Ivan's team of code busters sent the false messages to incite the cells. According to prior arrangements they also notified the governments of the countries harboring terrorists within their borders that the attacks were coming.

Preparations that had been stealthily made for weeks in advance of the raid on the caliph headquarters were now put into action. Information disseminated by the U.S. State Department had alerted the internal security forces of the world to the presence of the perpetrators of violence in their countries. Far Eastern nations, whose version of Islam had strayed too far from the original Arab version to suit the caliphs, were not exempt from receiving the wrath of Allah at the hands of local jihadists. So battles were fought with groups of terrorists in such far-flung places as Indonesia, Malaysia, the Philippines, and Australia. Weapons were seized, and many extremists were apprehended and taken into custody. In the more traditional terrorist regions the fighting was even more widespread. Thousands were killed, and many tens of thousands of terrorists were arrested in Afghanistan, Pakistan, Saudi Arabia, the Emirates, North Africa, and Iraq.

The countries that had more or less supported the Islamist Jihad were spotlighted because of the absence of violence in those nations. Since the security forces in these countries were in league with the terrorists, Syria, Iran, and Yemen did nothing to oppose the merchants of death, and so they proved beyond doubt their guilty participation in the cause of the caliphs. They became rogue states, politically martyred for their lost cause.

Sleeper cell members, whose Western hosts had generously and innocently allowed them to immigrate from Muslim nations, gleefully responded to the false coded messages that Ivan's team transmitted to them, and walked right into the ambushes set by security forces. Countries like France, Germany, and Spain were amazed at the number of participants that were rounded up. The early warnings had served to assure that the government forces would succeed in capturing nearly all the secret fighters that had made a home among the "infidels" in order to do them harm. Weapons caches of enormous proportions were uncovered, many of which had been hidden in mosques to avoid discovery.

There was a tremendous backlash against jihadist Islam as more and more terrorist cells were dislodged from under the very noses of neighbors and supposed friends. In countries having a free press, articles showed how the Wahabist interpretation of the Muslim religion was involved in fomenting enmity between so-called infidel faiths and cultures. The evidence was too great to be challenged. Moderate Islam would need many years to repair the damage done by the fanatical elements of their faith. The Muslim world had been forced to take an emetic.

Conspiracy confessions were rife. It was as if everyone in the world had taken a dose of truth serum, and only in swallowing it could health be restored to the population. It was impossible even for the most devout Muslim nations to contain the details of the round-ups of terrorists in their midst. The Saudis never mentioned the raid on the caliph headquarters, but they did actively weed out the extremists, not because they were evil, but because they rivaled the power of the royal house. Ivan had been correct in his analysis of the motives of the leadership. He suspected that they kept the lid on the true story of the caliphs in their subterranean Mecca so that no one would ever know how vulnerable the country was to commando attack, but perhaps even more so because the caliphate plot was centered in the very heart of Islam.

One morning, shortly after the raid on the caliphs, Ivan was in his office when he received a call from the Admiral in charge of Naval Intelligence.

"I'm coming to the White House to show the President various pieces of evidence collected by the Seals when they were in Mecca," he told Ivan. "He asked me to call you and request your presence at the meeting."

When Ivan was shown into the Oval Office, he found Julia already there with the President. A moment later the Admiral arrived. After the usual introductions he opened his briefcase and removed a handful of photos of the caliph's headquarters, taken by the Navy Seals just after the neutron device exploded.

The photos were passed around, and eventually landed in Ivan's hands. He peered closely at them. There, slumped over on what was undeniably some sort of a seat of honor, was Imam Mansur. This was the man that Lieutenant Mercer had identified as the caliph with the recent bullet wounds in his chest. Ivan was glad to know that he had not personally sent him to be with his seventy virgins in paradise. The man in the suit was clearly Mitch Richmond, the missing Deputy Director of the CIA. No one else recognized him from the photo until Ivan pointed him out.

"What was he doing there?" the President asked.

"Chances are he was asking for asylum," Ivan said. "But he might have been selling information, too. Our Seal team probably arrived at exactly the right moment."

"What information do you suppose he was offering?"

"At that particular moment, I would guess he was trying to negotiate an attractive reward for himself, in return for telling the caliphs that their code had been deciphered."

"Well, Dr. Welland, I hope this means that you can move out of my house now," the President smiled.

On his way out of the Oval Office, Ivan collared Julia in the hall, and asked for permission to go to Cambridge for a few days. He assured her he could monitor all events through his assistant, Brooklyn. The military would handle the remaining skirmishes with the terrorists as outlined in the final scene of *Act II.* Julia was monitoring the political reactions, and could consult with him anytime she wished.

"I can write a position paper just as easily in Cambridge as I can in Washington," he added.

Julia agreed. "Of course you can go to Cambridge, Ivan. That's the least I can do for you after all your good work."

"Marina and I are coming back here over the weekend to look at some apartments."

"I'm glad to hear it. I'll look forward to seeing Marina again. Please tell her I'll call her in a day or two to arrange something for the four of us to do on Saturday night."

Ivan was so excited about the idea of joining Marina that he almost missed Julia's reference to the number "four."

"Who is the fourth wise man going to be for Saturday night?" he asked her.

"I thought you knew," said Julia, beaming.

"Knew? Knew what?"

"I have a new man in my life."

Just then Simeon Montcalf came around the corner.

"Oh, there you are my dear lady," he said to Julia. "I've been looking all over for you. I've made reservations for us in a delightfully small, intimate restaurant. The chef has prepared a special luncheon for us."

"How thoughtful of you, Simeon."

Montcalf offered his arm to Julia, then turned to Ivan.

"Hello, Welland. Congratulations, dear boy. I understand you've done marvelously. I'm sure the world is now going to be a better place, at least for the time being, thanks to your efforts and to those of your team."

Ivan stared at the couple, at a loss for words. Julia looked happier and younger than ever on the arm of her new man, and Montcalf looked, well, like a new man himself.

"I had quite a long conversation this morning with Kahnsultan," Montcalf continued. "I'm quite sure I wouldn't be breaking a confidence if I told you that he has found himself a lady friend."

"Kahnsultan? A lady friend?"

"Yes. You young people always seem to be surprised at that sort of news. Anyway, he says you know her, and that you would approve of his choice."

"I know her? Me?"

"Yes, you and Marina both. Kahnsultan told me he decided to go to Tolstoi-Yurt and make her acquaintance because of the many interesting things you said about her incisive intelligence and excellent character."

"Are you talking about Sawdah Dudaeva?"

"Yes, I am," Montcalf said with a big smile. "She's the widow of the courageous Chechen separatist leader."

"Yes, and she's also the mother of Akhmad, the student who was murdered. He was one of Marina's best students. We attended his funeral together in Tolstoi-Yurt, and that's how we met Sawdah. Please tell Kahnsultan when you speak to him next time that I most heartily approve of his choice, and we wish them all the happiness they deserve. Also tell him that I'd love to host him and Sawdah at a celebratory dinner any time that life provides us with the opportunity."

"You seem cheered by this news," Montcalf observed.

"I am. Aside from being dear friends, these two people represent for me the only hope for a lasting solution to the Chechen situation. In fact, in my opinion, they are exactly the kind of Muslims who could provide the world with a solution to Islamist terrorism."

"Those are strong words," said Montcalf.

"I mean it. They've suffered terribly, but they've turned their grief into hope instead of hatred. They represent the spirit that must reform the violent elements in Islam. This Muslim couple is full of grace, and wisdom, and generosity of spirit. I would even go so far as to say that the future of Islam depends on the leadership of people like them."

"Maybe you should write me a position paper on your ideas on this subject, too," Julia said. "But right now you should go home to your wife. Don't keep her waiting."

"Please thank your beautiful wife for all the memorable times we shared together," said Montcalf. "We had the most edifying conversations while you were doing algorithms."

"Let him go home now, Simeon," said Julia. "We'll have plenty of time to talk when we get together for dinner on Saturday. Oh, and Ivan, don't forget to tell Brooklyn that Richmond is dead so she can go home now, too."

"Come Julia dear," said Montcalf, taking her delicately by the elbow. He turned and winked at Ivan as he escorted her down the hall.

When Ivan got back to his temporary quarters in the West Wing, he told Brooklyn the news about Richmond.

"He's dead?" said Brooklyn. "Damn, I guess that means I'll have to go back to eating my own cooking."

"Please take care of moving us back to our office in the State Department building while I'm gone. If you have time, you can monitor the clean-up of the terrorist cells for me and keep an eye on the political situation in the Middle East. I'm going home to Cambridge for a few days to write a position paper on the Middle East for the Secretary. You can call me any time."

"Have a good rest. Nobody deserves it more than you."

Just then the phone rang, and Brooklyn picked it up.

"One minute, sir. I'll see if he's in his office." She put the caller on hold. "It's a Mr. Bagwell," she said. "He didn't say what it was about. Do you want to take it?"

"Sure, I'll take it!" He put the phone to his ear. "Good to hear from you, Bagwell. How are you doing?"

"I'm just dandy, thanks for asking. Listen, I'm calling to congratulate you for the opening night of the, uh, play you wrote. My connections tell me this was mainly your show, although Mercer and the other actors were slick, too. You seem to be getting the hang of things in D.C., with or without my help."

"Things always go better with your help."

"Thank you, Ivan. You know you can always count on me if you need me. By the way, I heard you tied the knot recently, so I called to congratulate you for that, too."

"I appreciate that, Bagwell."

"Anyhow, your play is going to make it a whole lot easier for us oil men to do business, and we're grateful for that. I hope a lot of people read it and learn something from it. You've got cojones, son, marching right in like that and cleaning out all those hornets' nests. They should make your play into a movie, if you want my opinion. It would be a shoe-in for an Oscar. Anyway, I just wanted to touch base with you. Congratulations again, and please tell Marina to expect a wedding present from big bad uncle Bagwell. I'll be in touch."

"Thanks, Bagwell. It was good to hear from you."

Ivan couldn't help wondering how Bagwell had found out he had anything to do with the operation in Mecca, and how he knew its code name had something to do with a play. He decided to check this out with Julia the next time he saw her.

Cambridge, Massachusetts

Ivan couldn't wait to see Marina. He didn't call ahead so he could surprise her. He still had clothes in Cambridge, so he just grabbed his laptop and ran out of the office.

During his flight to Boston he thought about the academic projects that awaited him. He had to write his PhD thesis. He had to help Marina with her book. There was also a pile of reading he wanted to tackle. There was work he had to do for the Secretary of State. But the only thing he wanted right then was to be with his wife.

He was standing on the doorstep, fumbling with his keys when he heard Marina cry out in climactic fashion, like a tournament golfer who birdies the last hole to win.

"Yes, yes, *yes!*"

He burst into the apartment, not knowing what to expect. Marina was in the bathroom. She had just come back from her job at the university, and was changing into her casual clothes. Midway into the procedure she had decided to give herself a pregnancy test. She had left the bathroom door open, since she was alone. She was holding the test strip in her hand and looking at it when Ivan came running in.

"Ivan, what are you doing here?"

"I came home to be with you. What's going on? Why were you shouting?"

"Oh, I am so happy! Look, is positive!" She held up the test strip for him to see. "If test is accurate, it means you are going to be father," she cried, jumping into his arms and wrapping her legs around him.

"Me! A father!"

"I am so glad you came home right now when you did it! It is so wonderful news. I cannot believe you are here with me at just this minute!"

"What do you think we should name our child?" Ivan asked her, lowering her to the floor. "What should we call him if he's a boy?"

"We call him *Simeon.*"

"What? No! Not *Simeon!*"

Marina laughed. "All right, *Lincoln,* then. Lincoln is good name for boy. After all, we both admire President Lincoln."

"*Lincoln Welland.* I like it. We could call him *Link* for short. And if it's a girl?"

"If she is girl, I like to call her *Julia.*"

"*Julia.* That's a great idea. By the way, that reminds me. It appears that Julia is in love. Or at least she seems to be."

"I know," said Marina.

"What? You know? How can you possibly know? You hardly ever see her!"

"This is true. But I have spent great deal of time with gentleman who loves her."

"Montcalf told you already?"

"It makes very long time that he loves her, but he was worried to love boss. Is not good etiquette. Is very hard to be in love with impossible dream."

"Is that what the two of you talked about when you were together?"

"We talked about many things, but never about cabbages and kings. We talked mainly about Julia."

"You never told me this! Why didn't you say anything to me about it?"

"It was Simeon's secret, so I told nobody. You had secrets too, when you were working on breaking code of council of caliphs. You kept secret for President of United States of America, and I kept secret for God's Personnel Manager."

"You're something, you know that?"

"But regime changes soon. We will have new elections, and Julia will get new work. Now they can love each other without breaking protocol. Is good, ya?"

"Is mighty good," said Ivan, smiling.

"Since I show America that I can keep important secret, maybe they let me become citizen."

"That's wonderful, Hon. I'm so glad you're pleased to be here in the United States. I was worried that I was away too much, and that you might be unhappy."

"Why you call me Hun? I am not Hun. I am Slav, as you know very well."

"Sorry, Slav," Ivan said. He kneeled down in front of his bride and gently kissed her beautiful, fruitful belly.

WHEN CAPTAIN NIKO CONSTANTINE (able seaman and womanizer of note) is selected to command the largest cruise ship in the world, he looks forward to enjoying the most challenging, exciting journey of his life. But what he doesn't know is that a group of jihadist terrorists is plotting to turn the luxury liner's maiden voyage into a trip to hell.

Once again Aidan de Vries has written a riveting story about Ivan Welland, the hero of *Council of Caliphs,* who is suddenly called upon to save the carefree passengers from certain death. This time, right out of the blue, he and his team of brave collaborators are given some assistance from an unprecedented quarter.

AIDAN DE VRIES was born in New York. He worked for a time with the FBI, and later started a business of his own as an executive recruiter. This is his second novel.

Available on Amazon and on erserandpond.com

The Peacemaker
Aidan de Vries

AFTER A METEORIC RISE in the government, Harvard PhD Ivan Welland us appointed Secretary of Defense by the newly-elected President. By understanding that defense is not possible until peace is secured, he evolves a plan whereby, with the help of his faithful team and some remarkable supporters, he is able to thwart the many enemies of global harmony and offer the President a brilliant new program to make peace and true defense a welcome reality for all.

This is the third thriller in the series about Ivan Welland's adventurous life as he dedicates himself to returning the U.S. to the original principles of the Founding Fathers.

Available on Amazon and on erserandpond.com

WHEN IVAN WELLAND DISCOVERS that the freedom of the press provision of the Bill of Rights is about to be exploited by an international media conglomerate, he is forced to come to terms with what may be some basic flaws in our democratic system. His investigative team delves into the world of international mergers and acquisitions, and discovers that the people in control of words and graphics can be at least as worrisome to the Department of Defense as terrorists armed with guns and bombs. Is the media obligated to report the truth, or does the First Amendment protect a reporter's right to twist the facts? Is America only a reflection of the hidden agendas of various interested parties?

In this fourth political thriller by Aidan de Vries, hero Ivan Welland is cast into a dangerous void where appearance and reality become blurred. The reader is challenged, along with Dr. Welland, to re-examine the meaning and perception of truth, and how it should be presented to the public.

Available on Amazon and on erserandpond.com

WHEN THE NEW PRESIDENT TAKES OFFICE, Dr. Ivan Welland's term as Secretary of Defense is over. He agrees to chair the Foundation for Democracy Research, with a mandate to design a presidential election system that will better serve America. Welland soon learns about secret machinations that take place without the knowledge of the voters, and that have huge consequences for Americans. His efforts to restore democracy, amend the Constitution, and force the corrupt and treasonous President to return to the principles of the founding fathers becomes a deadly adventure that takes the reader into the realm of murderous power mongers, FBI investigations, and federal prosecutions by the U.S. Attorney General. This thought-provoking cautionary tale is the fifth political thriller by Aidan de Vries. It may be prescient in its reflection of possible future events, and is sure to challenge every reader's idea of what democracy should be.

Available on Amazon and on erserandpond.com

IN RESPONSE TO THE ECONOMIC CRISIS in the United States, Dr. Ivan Welland decides to take on the challenge of curing the ills that have caused the problems. He leads his non-profit Foundation for Democracy Research into a study of the alphabet soup of regulatory agencies responsible for the economy. We learn about the functions and failings of the SEC, Fed, FDIC, IRS, BIS, OMB, and the network of complexities under which our economy barely survives.

Along the way we discover a plot to defraud the United States Treasury of TARP funds intended to save a bank from insolvency. The reader is led into the center of a corruption scheme which, if successful, would turn out to be the largest known embezzlement in history.

This is the sixth cautionary thriller by Aidan de Vries. It takes us where we need to go to understand the risks that threaten the economic pillars of our democratic system.

Available on Amazon and on erserandpond.com

www.ingramcontent.com/pod-product-compliance
Lightning Source LLC
Chambersburg PA
CBHW061301170626
46817CB00001B/1